DAISY

A NOVEL

LIBBY STERNBERG

Copyright 2025 by Libby Malin Sternberg. All rights reserved.

The characters and events portrayed in this book are not real, or, if real, used fictitiously. Any similarity to real persons, living or dead, is purely coincidental and not intended by the author.

Cover Design: Jaycee DeLorenzo, Sweet 'N Spicy Designs
Interior Design: TracyCopesCreative.com

978-1-61088-587-4 (HC)
978-1-61088-588-1 (PB)
978-1-61088-589-8 (ebook)
978-1-61088-590-4 (PDF)
978-1-61088-591-1 (audio)

Published by Bancroft Press
"Books that Enlighten"
(818) 275-3061
4527 Glenwood Avenue
La Crescenta, CA 91214
www.bancroftpress.com

Printed in the United States of America

To Truman, Penny, Mina, and Winnie

Stow the costumes, the golden hats,
The silver capes and purple plumes.
Mute your clever tunes.
Cease your acrobatic displays,
Your awful jousts and warring ways.
I want one thing, lover, one thing alone:
Tenderness.

Pamela D'Invilliers

CHAPTER ONE

Nick made a lot of money off my story. I penned the first words, and we exchanged more through letters after it was all over—a sort of game we played that helped us massage away the hurt of that wild summer and its consequences. We compared memories, filling in what each of us didn't know or had forgotten. So if you've read his version of this tale, you'll find differences in mine, some small and some significant.

You see, he'd been helping me overcome some difficulties after the tumult, and we started a long conversation by writing all about it. Then, before I knew it, the whole thing was published, first in magazines, and then as a book. He had my name on the story, too, but he was the one who received all the fame and most of the money, and eventually my name disappeared altogether from the tale, blasted away as if written in sand. So this is my chance to right that wrong, to tell it solely from my point of view, and to get credit for the telling.

The afternoon my cousin Nick Carraway came by our East Egg house, I felt as if I could fly on the gauzy breezes inhaling and exhaling our long white curtains through open doors, and I kept glancing out the window for some pure dove to invite me on a journey across the Sound.

Nick intruded on this dream as he strode into the hall trying so hard to look confident. He had this way of hesitating, sometimes in speech, sometimes in gait, just the tiniest of moments as he teetered on the edge of choosing between doing what he wanted to do or doing what he thought others expected of him.

DAISY

I'd invited him after learning he lived in the less fashionable West Egg area just across Long Island Sound from us. It had been ages since I'd seen him last, and I was in need of good company. I thought of Nick that way—a good man who could see to the core of a matter. As for chosen profession, he was in bonds then, learning the trade.

Poor, dear Nick. He had tried so hard to measure up to my husband, Tom, when in reality he was Tom's superior merely by existing.

A warm wind blew wildly that day, making the curtains dance in the vast parlor that fronted the Sound and my hair a fluttering halo. I thought we were in for one of those exciting storms that sometimes rushed up the coast, whipping the house with rain and making Tom worry about trees falling and the boat going out and never coming back.

When those storms hit, I wished I could be on the boat, sailing smoothly between huge waves and torrential rain, untouched by either but finding the calm, true course in the center away from everything, and especially from Tom.

No tempests arrived, though. And Nick was ushered in by Tom, dressed in riding pants and looking like some East Indian company leader about to punish an errant dark-skinned servant.

Jordan, who was staying with us at the time, caught a glimpse of him first and immediately turned her head up and away, a habit of hers when meeting a man for the first time. Makes them nervous, she had confided to me. She also stayed quiet as a cat, another strategy of hers for causing a man to feel ill at ease, wondering if he'd inadvertently offended and then setting him on a course of talking too much, as if trying to find the precise thing that would make up for the deficiencies Jordan clearly saw in him with her silence. I could see that concern flicker across Nick's face.

Of course, she knew I had designs on setting them up together, so she was playing a role, one I'd assigned to her and she had accepted. I had the parts written in my head already, and I immediately stepped into the scene, smiling and offering a greeting. I provided some light banter about the longest day of the year – don't you always wait for it and miss it – something I'd charmed new guests with several times already, and they all thought it so original and somehow bright.

"Nick! I've missed you! Come give me a kiss and make Tom jealous!"

He did as instructed, and I could see him eyeing Jordan, so I laughed and introduced them.

"Nick Carraway, dearest cousin. Jordan Baker, dearest friend," I said, nodding to them both.

"The golfer," he said with that hesitant timidity again.

"The scandalous one, yes," Jordan said, finally bestowing on him her sweetest smile that made him think, I'm sure, they shared a secret. That was another skill of hers, making men feel they knew something only the two of them acknowledged.

Drinks and small talk followed—chatter as light as the afternoon air—and soon I floated above it all, borne on the wings of a good white wine as we went into dinner and drank and laughed some more. Tom presided at one end of the table like a grand pasha.

When Myrtle called—yes, I knew it was her—I cringed, and the bruise on my finger, where Tom had squeezed my hand so tightly he'd nearly broken a bone, began to throb.

I'd known about Myrtle Wilson for some time. I'd picked up the phone one day at the same time Tom did when she was purring at him to come visit.

DAISY

I even knew she was married and lived above a garage—a garage, for God's sake. Did it make him feel as if he was doing something dangerous by cavorting with a woman of such low status?

I sometimes contemplated writing an anonymous letter to her husband alerting him to her infidelity.

Though it angered me that Tom carried on like this, I was still curious about how he had met the woman. On a trip into town, stopping by the garage? How louche!

I imagined her wearing stained dresses and sagging stockings, with a face too fleshy to be attractive.

I winced again when I heard his hushed tone, but part of me was amused by Tom, trying so hard to keep from embarrassing himself in front of our guests. Having a mistress suited him. Having it revealed in front of his wife's guests did not.

When he didn't return to the table quickly, Jordan grimaced and said, "You'd think she'd have the good taste not to call during the dinner hour."

Nick quickly turned his head to her. "Who?"

But Jordan didn't answer. And I wasn't about to mention Myrtle's name and explain who she was because I'd feel compelled to do it in a clever, amusing way to make my guests comfortable. Neither Tom nor the Wilson woman deserved such admirable treatment.

As his conversation dragged on, I had the impish desire to add to his suffering, so I wandered inside, pretending to be surprised he was still on the phone.

"Darling, if it's business, it can wait," I said. "We have guests."

His face reddened, and I made the mistake of smiling, too direct an acknowledgment of the game he was playing. Red turned to purple fury, and he slammed down the phone and came over to me. He pulled me to him, crushing me, his hand behind my neck as he forced a whiskey-flavored kiss on my lips, pushing so strong and hard I felt I couldn't breathe.

"Make them go away," he whispered, still holding on to my hair. It hurt.

I murmured something conciliatory so he would let go. But as he walked away and then poured himself another drink, I knew I would do no such thing. They'd stay until the stars crept into the black void. They'd stay until Thomas Buchanan, he of the white man's swagger, was too tired to do anything but sleep after they'd all left, or, in Jordan's case, gone up to bed.

I think it was at that moment that a dream began to drift into my heart and mind just like that light breeze. At first, it was merely a shadow, joined by a vague outline, and not painting a full picture yet.

I remember that summer as one glorious day after another, most of them sunny and hot, but out there on our water-bordered piece of land, you could always escape into the shade and wait for ocean winds to cool your brow.

On one fine morning, I was the only one in the house other than the servants. Even little Pammy was off on a walk with her nanny and would nap soon after their return. Tom went into town, probably to see that wretched Wilson woman, and he'd taken poor Nick with him. I heard him make the arrangements over the phone. Jordan, too, left the roost, to practice, she said, at a nearby course. She came and went as she pleased, sometimes staying with other friends in town or closer to courses where she played.

DAISY

I didn't often have time alone like this, with no one to tend to, no directions to give to the cook, no questions to answer about Pamela, no querulous husband to avoid, so it took me a few minutes to think of how to spend those precious hours before life intruded on my peace.

The day was once again warm, but I hungered for entertainment. I wished I could scurry into town myself to go to the cinema. We'd not been often, but I loved losing myself in those flickering stories.

I changed into linen sailor pants and a blue-striped top, grabbed my straw hat, and set out on a walk of my own. I followed an almost invisible path along the water's edge where I could enjoy the cooler salt air and see across the Sound to a mansion where nightly parties lit up the sky.

I paused at a promontory and gazed toward the jut of land where the mansion stood, somewhat hidden by towering pines and shorter maples. Nick, in his remembrances, seems to think I knew then who lived there, but I didn't. It never occurred to me to ask because one didn't envy things in our circle; we created envy, so why should I be curious about parties at the mansion across the Sound?

Still, the house intrigued me. It shouted gaiety, abandon, and unfiltered joy. With a sigh, I realized I hadn't felt those things since I was a girl on the cusp of womanhood, when summer meant effervescent happiness, filled only with potential for unbounded pleasure.

The wind shoved at the brim of my hat, and I removed it as I sat on the grass, hands around my knees, staring. I wanted something, I didn't quite know what, and I felt rather girlish.

I knew I'd been a lucky child. My doting parents would have given me the world if I'd wanted it. As it happened, I had never lacked for comforts or extravagances. Mother decorated my room in whites and golds, and

Father treated me like a princess. My debutante ball took place one exquisite spring evening on the country club grounds, with nearly two hundred in attendance. I wore a dress of the purest white silk embroidered with gold thread ordered from Paris.

I'd never wanted for beaux that summer. A parade of them sought me out at every social event I attended, and I went to many.

I didn't realize it then, but my mother had taken an egalitarian approach to my socializing. She allowed me to be courted by both wealthy heirs and lowly soldiers. With war imminent, she declared that one never knew who would be the best match. By that I took it she meant who would survive and who would flourish was out of our hands, and planning was a fool's task. I think she worried there'd simply be fewer men to choose from.

That said, she was happy when I abandoned all others and chose Tom, one of our class, maybe even above us in wealth and social status.

Truth be told, I chose him because I became deathly afraid of everything that year, and he offered a safe harbor. Afraid not just of the war, the reports of which I read with horror, but of loss more personal.

Father ultimately fell ill, was pale and distant, sometimes sitting alone in his study for hours on end. He would forget things and appear confused and distracted, so it was no surprise when Mother telegrammed to beckon me home shortly after I'd married, because Father had suffered a grievous accident.

He'd collapsed, she told me, not looking me in the eye, after tripping on the steps. He broke his neck and died instantly.

Of a woman she knew who'd just lost her husband, Mother had once observed that it was good she had married—even though it hadn't always been an agreeable marriage—and now that she was free of her husband,

DAISY

she could perhaps have a good life. Mother had been married to a good man, though, and they'd been happy, as far as I could tell. I think she intended that message for me, since rumors had already started about Tom's wandering eye.

Tom, I later learned, helped Mother considerably after she was forced to sell our beautiful sprawling home above the river, the one with my white-and-gold bedroom, and move to a more modest abode with just a cook and day maid. Family finances had apparently dwindled, unbeknownst to her, and that had contributed to my father's decline.

Movement at the mansion across the Sound again caught my eye. A man of indeterminate age and coloring strode to his dock, where a new two-masted cutter rhythmically kissed its moorings. The man unslipped the knots and jumped onboard with the agility of a ballet dancer. Then he hoisted the sail in smooth, muscled motions, one arm over the other, until, with a startling flap, the wind caught before he was ready. With a quick shake of his head, he corrected the error in judgment and guided the boat away from the pier's gentle waves. Warming with blush, I noticed he looked my way, and his gaze was so long and intense that I swore he was staring only at me and nothing else.

For one breathless moment, I wondered if he would sail over to me, and I shivered, both tempted and repulsed by that possibility. Ultimately, good sense won out, and I started to rise, but just as I unfurled myself, he let the wind pull him on a northerly course, and was soon gliding over the pulsing waves with a grace and speed I envied.

It was then I realized I wanted to be invited to a party at the house across the way. I wanted to get uproariously drunk and dance until dawn.

I wanted to sail, as he was doing now, with nothing holding me back and only the wind ahead. I wanted to feel young again.

"Teach me how to sail," I implored Tom a few mornings later. He hadn't returned the night before, and looked hollow-eyed and in pain at this breakfast. "When we moved here, you promised you would."

He grimaced, but I knew his aching, whiskey-soaked head would make him pliable, and sure enough, he muttered a short, "All right."

"Wonderful!" I continued. "The cutter is so beautiful. It's a shame to not use it more, and I love how graceful it looks with the sheets up."

"It's a sloop," he corrected, as I knew he would. "And those are sails, Daisy, not sheets. Good god, don't you know even that?"

Of course I knew. I knew more than he did. I was an excellent swimmer and diver and longed to be on the water, but I was laying the groundwork for my request to be fulfilled, and I knew if he thought me an absolute dunderhead, he'd have to school me. Tom enjoyed feeling intellectually superior. It was one of his few pleasures these days. Like many young men, something had been cut off in him after the war. He hadn't served, and as the years went on, I think he regretted it. So many others had had their manhood tested while his had been spent on polo fields and in smoke-filled clubs.

"That's why I count on good instruction," I cooed. "If you're too busy, I'm sure we can find someone."

"No, no. I'll do it. Let's go out this afternoon."

DAISY

He looked up and squinted as the maid entered the room. "Get me some bicarb, would you? I thought I'd asked already."

Before she skittered away, I asked for more coffee, which I knew she'd entered the room to serve, so I made Tom wait while she filled my cup.

The rest of our miserable meal was spent in silence.

True to his word, Tom met me at the dock at three that afternoon, the hottest time of day, and on this day, the breezes off the Sound were strangely calm. It felt as if we were holding our breath before imminent disaster arrived.

I had known it would be a difficult lesson. I'd prepared myself to be patient, to jolly him when he was snappish, to follow instructions, and to keep my mouth shut when I disagreed. I'd learned to do all that early in our marriage.

It didn't take long for me to lose my resolve, though. He'd supplied all the names of things, and explained how to tack, and how to choose the right sails, and with delight, I realized I instinctually knew how to go with the feel of the boat and not the science of sailing.

At one point, when we were dead in the water waiting for some errant wind to fill the sails, I pointed at other boats skimming by and said, "Why don't we do what they're doing?" I had seen Tom surreptitiously glancing at them, evaluating what they were doing right that we were doing wrong, so I knew this thought had also crossed his mind.

"Because I'm trying to teach you how to keep the damn boat from sinking!" He muttered a curse and mopped sweat from his brow before fixing the sails to the positions on those other sloops. Soon, we were gliding as smoothly as they were.

"No one likes a pushy woman, you know," he said after straightening out our course.

I bit my tongue to keep from pointing out he had done what I'd suggested. Men didn't like women who were right. I'd learned that early in our marriage, too. During a similar discussion a week or so ago, Tom had excessively squeezed my hand, bruising my finger. I was being too aggressive, he thought, by suggesting after dinner that maybe the white man wasn't in danger of being oppressed.

Though the first lesson was a bit nerve-wracking, it didn't dim my joy for sailing, and following that afternoon, we sailed together just three more times before I felt confident piloting the *Virginia Marie*, named after his mother, on my own. I sailed when Tom went into town, so he wouldn't know.

I sailed around the Sound, never venturing out into the wider sea, though once I was caught in a strong southerly wind and had to fight mightily to get back to our safe harbor. That incident both scared and thrilled me. So, after that, I set small challenges for myself, deliberately going out in gusty blows, even once when rain threatened. Little by little, fear gave way to confidence, and these small escapes made me feel my carefree youth returning. Even Nick, on one of his regular dinner visits, commented on how happy I was looking.

Yes, I found happiness on those afternoon excursions. I found both hard work and time to think. I loved sailing back toward our safe harbor.

DAISY

I loved looking up at the promontory I walked on and wondering how it would feel to dive from there into the sea. Another challenge I set for myself, perhaps on a blistering day when the water would cool my skin.

The movement of the boat made me feel as if I were moving through time, and as I bounced over each wave, a resolution hammered its way into my soul, lit by a vague dream that had started to form earlier.

Tom had to go. And so did that Wilson woman.

CHAPTER TWO

Shortly after my reunion with Nick, he betrayed me. I know he doesn't think of it that way, but what else can you call it when your cousin accompanies your husband to meet his mistress?

When Tom wandered like this—because this was now a pattern—I took a condescending attitude. Boys will be boys. It wasn't the first time a husband had strayed.

But lately, it bothered me because I began to worry that one day he'd fix on some woman who'd become more than a passing fancy. He had obligations, to me and to Pamela, and I would protect us both… if I could figure out how.

So, while he and Nick were partying in New York with Myrtle and her seedy friends and relatives, I drove myself in Tom's coupe, swathed in the softest white scarf, to meet Jordan to see a show. She was in town that day, staying with other friends as she got ready to head upstate for another tournament to play.

My attempts at matching her with Nick had met with only limited success. Or at least, no success they told me about. I knew she talked to him and had seen him for lunch in town, but little else. When I asked how things were going with him, she simply shrugged and said, "He's nice. I have fun," which told me nothing and everything. I determined to find out more during this excursion.

I loved the city. To me, it felt as if things were always happening there.

DAISY

I decided to make it my own personal holiday. I booked a room at The Plaza, met Jordan for dinner, and off we went into the sparkling dusk to some musical revue I remember little about, except lots of dancing and colorful costumes and enough comedy that my face hurt from laughing when it was over.

The city night was filled with light, from cars, marquees, streetlamps, and the symmetrical rectangles of windows, where a thousand eyes peered at us from above. Those artificial stars would have to do. The real ones dimmed amidst all that light, as if allowing these pretend-cousins their chance to shine.

Though the weather wasn't oppressive yet, the theater was warm, and once the show started, the two huge fans on either side of the stage were cut off so we could all hear the players.

The hall became a sauna, and I regretted wearing my blue jersey dress, for it clung to me like syrup, despite fanning myself with my program for the entire performance.

"I think I lost several pounds in there," Jordan said as we made our way past the crowd into the cooler air outside the theater after the show. "I'd forgotten why I never go to the theater in summer."

"Oh, it was divine," I gushed, still happy from the laughter, fun, and sheer brightness of it all. Sometimes, I felt like a squire's wife out in East Egg, leading a quiet life while others enjoyed "the season" in town. After the first exciting honeymoon days, I'd frequently felt that way. Tom seemed to prefer us both at home. Or me, at least.

"We need a cold drink," Jordan said, stepping forward to hail a taxi.

"Do you know a place?"

She looked at me as if I were a child on her first outing into the big city.

"I know just the place," she said as a cab pulled up to the curb.

Once inside, she gave the driver the address of a speakeasy—some new place on Bedford Street she'd heard was good.

At our destination, she paid the driver. And then we were making our way into the smoky interior, crammed with people, a jazz group playing in the corner, more excitement and fun, overlaying a sense of Prohibition naughtiness. We were disobedient children, up to impish fun.

"Here!" Jordan announced as she grabbed a table two lonely hearts had just vacated.

"What if they're coming back?" I said as we slid slowly into the chairs.

"Well, they aren't. Not when someone's at their table!" she shouted over the hubbub.

Soon we had ordered and downed iced gin cocktails and laughed at how we each felt like limp rags.

"Or wet dogs," Jordan said, pushing a strand of hair from my face. I couldn't bring myself to look in my compact. I must have been quite a sight—dress clinging to me in the wrong places, damp hair plastered on my head.

"Woof, woof!" I countered.

"It doesn't really matter here," Jordan observed, as she lit a cigarette. "They must have imported this fog direct from London, and I'm sure we look like gauzy nymphs, all a blur, like in French paintings."

I lit a cigarette, too, and we enjoyed the music along with the sense that we were doing something mischievous and decadent. "What'll I do when you are far away?" some nasal-voiced singer bleated out.

"How is Nick?" I asked, keeping my promise to myself to find out more about their romance.

DAISY

Her mouth quirked into a lopsided grin. "He's fine. But you probably know more than I do. He's your cousin."

"Aren't you still seeing each other?" I prodded.

She paused after our second round of drinks came and took a drag from her cigarette. "We see each other," she said. "But he has someone else."

My eyes widened. Timid Nick a double-timer? Oh, no. Had he followed my husband's example? I felt sick.

Seeing my distress, Jordan went on. "Not someone he's seeing. It's a girl he left behind, out in California somewhere. She must have thought they'd marry. I don't like worrying if she'll show up bent on avenging their true love."

At that, I smiled. I knew, from talking to Nick before he came to dinner, that he had broken off with a girl out west. He must have told Jordan the story, too, which made me wonder just how over the girl he was. Jordan was no fool, so I didn't blame her for being cautious.

"Has he invited you to tea?" she asked.

"No, why? Was he supposed to?"

She shrugged. "He mentioned to me that he wanted you to see his place."

After that brief exchange, the gin began to lift the heat and vexation off me. I had just about worked up my courage to go powder my nose and see what damage the hot theater had wrought when a familiar figure walked by—a broad-shouldered, long-faced man, not a hair out of place, in a tan, unwrinkled flannel suit. At first, I couldn't believe who it was, and I stared at him at length until Jordan inquired if he was a gangster or someone on a Wanted poster.

"Edouard?" I said as he strode toward the bar. He turned. Yes, it was him, and my heart gave a little leap, even as my hand fluttered to my sweat-dampened hair.

He looked at me as if he didn't recognize me, at which point I wished I'd made that trip to powder my nose earlier. When I'd known him, I was always well-dressed and well-coiffed and felt like the loveliest woman alive.

He, of course, was stunning; his blue eyes fixed on me as the corners of his sensual lips rose in an amused smile. At last, recognition seemed to dawn and he came over to our table.

"Cherie, is it you?" He leaned down and kissed me on both cheeks, and then I introduced him to Jordan.

"This is Edouard Janvier," I said. "He flies airplanes. Tom and I met him in Paris last year when we did the Tour."

Another man Tom felt inferior to, Edouard had been an aviator during the war and went on to start an airplane company. We'd met at a tea at some Frenchwoman's apartment, an acquaintance of Tom's family or something. It was a rococo flat with lots of cake frosting decorations on the ceiling and walls, and it felt so silly and formal when just outside the city were charred fields, lonely graveyards, and utter destruction.

I'd been horrified when Tom and I had taken a drive through the countryside. Tom, by contrast, had seemed unmoved, or at least stone-faced with resentment, muttering "What a waste" when I knew he secretly wished he'd been part of it, now that it was safely over.

Edouard had been there. If he had great charm, he also exuded great sorrow, and his eyes held a sadness that no smile could hide.

He had charmed me with his broken English and formal manners, and his refusal to joke about those battlefield horrors. He'd scolded Tom for

DAISY

making light of something related to the war with a quick question: *Avec quel regiment avez-vous servi?*

He told me he was impoverished royalty, that his father or father's father had been a duke or maybe an earl, or perhaps they had just been peasants, but he never knew because he was raised by nuns after being orphaned. It had been a sweet and sad story, and I knew parts of it were an exaggeration, but his war record was not. We encountered several people who spoke of him with awe when I mentioned meeting him. Later, we danced at someone else's house, on the veranda, a waltz, and at the end of it, he kissed me, pulling me to him as if he couldn't resist me, his strong warrior hand on my back, his chest against mine, his wine-scented breath on my face.

I could have been his lover. He sent notes and flowers, and when Tom flitted off to ride horses with some old chums, I had the time and opportunity to take Edouard to my bed. But after a sunlit afternoon of drinks and strolling, holding hands, and sipping orange-flavored liqueur at an outdoor café, I ultimately kissed him goodbye. I was still devoted to my marriage then.

"Let me introduce you to my wife," he now said, and before us stood a stunning brunette, with dark eyes and dark wavy hair she'd pinned at her nape to appear as if she had a bob. From every man in the room, she drew admiring looks. She wore a dark maroon dress that, with her hair and eyes, made her smooth porcelain skin all the more luminous. She was easily the most beautiful woman in the room.

"Patrice, this is…I'm sorry, but I have forgotten your married name." He smiled more broadly, but I recognized the lie, and a deep disappointment draped over me. He'd forgotten my entire name, not just the Buchanan part. My face warmed anew, and I knew I now sported a red glow that probably added a feverish glaze to my swamp-rat look.

"Daisy Buchanan," I said to the two of them. "Edouard and I met in Paris last year."

Patrice nodded, smiled, and said something to him in French. Though I couldn't quite catch it, I knew enough of the language to make out her question: Was I one of his "romances?" She said it in a light and breezy way, as if amused and unthreatened by his past, and he responded with a vigorous, "*Mais non, non,*" that humiliated me afresh.

"So nice to see you again," he said to me. "You look well."

I looked anything but, and his easy lies made me wonder how many of them I'd accepted as truth a year earlier, not just the fantastic stories of his childhood but his claims of devotion to me.

"And you," I said. "Don't let us keep you. It's a madhouse here." I waved him off, as if dismissing him, and this restored a little of my dignity, to be able to push him away. Again. I swallowed my disappointment.

Excusing himself to go to the bar, he put his arm lightly on his wife's back to usher her safely through the crowd. As they stood waiting for their drinks, she leaned her head onto his shoulder. He glanced at her with a loving smile before kissing her thick hair. The gesture made me feel jealous.

"Tell all," Jordan said, catching my gaze. "Leave nothing out."

"He was a friend. That's all."

She barked out a laugh.

"If I'd wanted more, it could have been more, but I didn't." I nodded my head as I said this to emphasize I had been the one rejecting him.

DAISY

She opened her mouth to comment but tactfully closed it before uttering a word. I could have provided the words myself. *He certainly didn't look like he'd wanted it to be more. Why, he barely remembered you.*

After that, I did make that trip to powder my nose, and was relieved to see I didn't look as bad as I thought. After a quick splash of water on my face, some powder, a comb through my hair, and a straightening of my dress, I felt my old self again, pretty and confident, and strode back into the room, ready to make every woman envious.

It was too late, however. Edouard and his bride had left.

When I sat down again, Jordan leaned forward. "You shouldn't hold yourself back, dear…if you want to take a lover, that is. Men do it all the time."

She knew about Tom and never seemed as upset about his affairs as I was. She accepted his behavior as the way of the world.

"I don't think I could," I said. "It takes up so much of one's time."

She laughed again. "Too much time or too much…courage?"

I frowned with irritation. I was a bold girl, always one to take risks and show both beaux and belles alike that I could swim farther, dive deeper, drive faster than anyone else.

"Not courage," I countered. "The opposite. I think it takes more bravery to make a go of things."

Jordan shook her head. "To what end? So you can both feel equally miserable?"

"Jordan!" I sat back. "Is that what you think marriage is?"

She didn't hesitate. "To some… and for no good reason, if you ask me." She leaned forward. "Keep your heart open to love, Daisy. I know you miss it."

The music got louder, and our conversation ceased. It was just as well. Her words made me uncomfortable. Did she think I was a coward for not following Tom's example? Did she think him a good example to follow? Was I the fool and Tom the wise one?

We stayed only a half hour longer, when I begged off, complaining of a headache.

Like a prophecy, it came true. My head was pounding by the time I crawled into bed after a soothing bath, downing a glass of bicarb and reading the latest copy of Vanity Fair.

In the morning, I awoke refreshed but troubled, and I ate breakfast alone in my room trying to figure out what vexed me so.

It wasn't that Edouard had married.

It wasn't even that he'd married such a beautiful girl.

It was that I had not occupied as great a place in his memory as he occupied in mine.

I stood and paced to the window, cigarette in hand. Perhaps all my memories of infatuated suitors were similarly false. In my fairy tale youth, perhaps I'd just imagined being more popular than I had actually been, and I began perusing my past for evidence that I'd not been fooled by a conspiracy of friends in order to mock me behind my back.

Once, at a country club dance, one of the girls' fathers came over to me with a box of long-stemmed roses. I smiled and said, "For me?" as I reached out for the gift.

"Oh, just one. They're for all the girls," he said. Somewhat surprised, I flushed with embarrassment, made a joke of it, and took one rose.

Now I wondered if I'd thought of my beaux that way—as a carton of roses just for me when that wasn't the case at all.

DAISY

No, no, no. I shook my head, remembering: the many dance partners, the constant stream of callers, the men who tried to impress me with their athletic prowess, their daring, their looks, their money.

That hadn't been a dream.

Even Edouard's attentions hadn't been a fabrication. Perhaps he was a gigolo. Perhaps he'd forsake his wife at some point. But when he'd paid attention to me, he had been my gigolo, and I became the one to forsake him.

This soothed me, and I moved on to the other thought that troubled me—Jordan's suggestion that I needn't be as faithful as I thought married couples should be.

You must not think I was a paragon of virtue. No, it was more that I loathed self-righteousness. I particularly despised religious leaders urging temperance in the most intemperate of tones. I despised hypocrisy, and that's what bothered me about Jordan's idea.

If I thought Tom was wrong for his adultery, how could I then turn around and engage in the same behavior without being a hypocrite?

Maybe that was all that was holding me back, though. It wasn't that I clung to some unrealistic ideal of a perfect marriage, one where each spouse was as passionately in love years after the wedding as they were on the day itself. But I did cling to some small romantic notions, such as keeping one's promise to stay true. I suppose I thought if you managed that single accomplishment, maybe the bigger romantic picture would become real, that the original passion would return, and you could once again revel in the warm, sweet days of first love.

I balled my fists as I thought about this, feeling once again as if I were a naïve fool. Tom would likely never return to faithfulness now that he knew he could sin with impunity. Ever since he had first strayed, I'd wondered if I should divorce him, take Pamela with me, and go far away… maybe even find another man who would stay true.

Marriage to the right man had been what had given me meaning in life. It had been the goal of every girl I knew. Once I attained it, though, any sense of greater purpose evaporated, and I felt adrift, constantly looking for things that would replace that original aim. Motherhood had briefly filled the space, but mothering was such an ongoing constant in my life it hardly felt like a goal. It was too easy. I needed something to strive for, something difficult. Maybe I had made fidelity that "something difficult."

Jordan's suggestion, however, was that I just accept marital affairs as part of marriage, that instead of waiting for Tom to change his ways, I should change mine.

What kind of life would that be? Could I be happy then?

I'd pondered these questions before, and had no answers, just as I had none now, so I finished packing up and left.

After a morning spent shopping, I then drove back home, enjoying the solitude in the car, the sense that I was in charge.

When I arrived, Tom was still away, but the maid told me that Mr. Carraway had called.

"Did he leave a message?" I asked, handing her my bag, gloves, and hat.

"No, ma'am. He said he would try again if he hadn't heard back from you."

With a puzzled frown, I started up the stairs, then stopped and called down to her.

"Tell Cook that Pamela and I will have dinner in my room tonight. Just something light. If Mr. Buchanan returns, tell him we're not feeling well."

DAISY

Tom didn't return that night, but Nick did call again, just an hour after I'd changed and unpacked. After some breezy chatter about the show I'd seen in town, he got to his point.

"I'd like to invite you to tea," he said. "To show you my place. You would like to see it, wouldn't you?"

"It's my life's goal," I teased. So here was Nick's tea invitation, the one Jordan had mentioned. I wondered if they were conspiring behind my back.

"Wonderful! I'd hoped it was," he responded.

"You realize, though, you mustn't disappoint me. I expect nothing less than service as if I were Queen. I've always wanted to be a queen. Or at least a princess."

"You are, though, most definitely. The Queen of East Egg," he said. Then, after a pause, "But don't bring your king. Just you."

"What king?" I replied. "This monarchy has but one ruler, and it is I, a woman!"

He laughed, and I went on: "Why not bring Tom? You're not going to kidnap me and ship me to some savage country, are you?"

"Oh, dear, you've discovered my plan." But after another pause, he said, "I just thought it might be nice to…to see you alone. We are family after all."

It seemed odd, but I liked a mystery. Besides, after my encounter with Edouard, my spirits needed lifting, and maybe a gossipy afternoon with Nick would be just the ticket.

"Name the day and hour, and I'll have my carriage at the ready," I said.

CHAPTER THREE

Nick tricked me.

Later, I found out Jordan had been in on the ruse, that she'd reached out to Nick to set all this up, this crazy romantic scheme. She knew of it the night she and I had drinks together, when she talked of infidelity as if it were part of the marriage vows.

The clues presented themselves immediately. As I walked up to his door, the scent of flowers was so overpowering that I wondered if he'd spilled some particularly poorly chosen cologne before my arrival. Rain seemed to amplify the smell, or maybe it was the umbrella acting as some sort of megaphone for rich perfumes.

Working out the details for this "tea," I had suggested another day, but Nick had insisted on this one. When I pressed him for a reason, he replied with vagueness, mentioning something about perhaps getting a closer look at his neighbor's manse, where all the festivities regularly occurred—he knew I was curious—and how this day was the best for his schedule because he was a working man, after all.

He'd repeated that I should come alone.

I'd begun to think he had some family issue he needed to discuss in private, and I imagined spending a pleasant hour sipping tea and eating sandwiches, hearing about some decrepit uncle or imprisoned third cousin, and we'd decide whether we should help him out or let him rot.

I even started looking forward to it. Before I married, I often had gossipy afternoons with girl friends, and I thought I'd come away from this

DAISY

encounter with some interesting dinner talk to amuse Tom with, stories of Nick's work, or maybe even a war tale or two.

Now, as I walked toward the door, I had an odd sensation that something was off, something I hadn't imagined or couldn't even imagine. Perhaps this was the kind of fairy tale about ogres and monsters rather than princes and granted wishes. I became afraid, wondering if I should have sent the chauffeur away so soon. The quick patter of raindrops. The overpowering scent of flowers. My footsteps softly clicking on the stone path. The door ajar.

"Daisy, come in, come in," Nick said nervously in the shadows. He disappeared as he opened the door more fully, revealing another man, standing with his hands clenching and unclenching by his side, nervous as a pony about to start its first trot around the track.

I couldn't see his face, just the fine cut of an expensive white flannel suit with wide lapels, cuffed pants, crisp silver shirt, which seemed to shine like a beacon in the dim interior.

I approached, unsure of this surprise, now wondering how well I really knew my cousin and if his work had taken him into dark alleyways and evil intentions, if my joke about kidnapping had cut too close to the truth. I couldn't seem to stop, though. As I neared the house, just ten feet away now, the man's features came into focus.

I inhaled sharply and, on the cusp of leaving, halted, but how could I leave? Not now, not when I saw before me a relic of my past. Him.

Rain beat against my umbrella. I stood still, unable to move forward or back. This man…

This man who almost caused me to abort my wedding to Tom with a letter that scorched my soul.

This man...

As suddenly as it started, the rain stopped. It left a strange silence punctuated only by the thrum of water through a roof gutter and a brave chirp from a faraway bird.

I couldn't move. I couldn't even blink.

"Daisy?" He said it so softly that for a moment I wondered if he'd really spoken at all or if I had imagined the running water somehow pulsing out my name. "Why—why are you alone?" he asked as if he'd rehearsed it.

I felt a giggle rise in my throat. The first thing he'd said to me when we first met. The giggle would have turned into a sob if I didn't act, so I moved forward.

As if in a slow procession, I propelled myself through the door, hypnotized, wanting to ask this ghost so many questions about what had happened to him.

Jay Gatsby.

I'd not known him by that name before he went to war. I'd known him as one of my sweetest and most ardent suitors, the one I might have married had the war not carried him away and Father's change in mood had not sent me into a paralyzing spiral of fear.

He'd been one of those who'd stolen kisses from me, sometimes even on our front porch on warm evenings as golden as those here on the Sound. He'd been the one who'd charmed me—and Mother—with his talk of moving up in the world, of making something of himself.

The eagerness that had shone in his eyes—my, it took one's breath away. You believed everything he said, and his desire for me wasn't the same kind other boys bestowed on me—a combination of lust and awe and envy and pure greed that I'd come to accept as expected.

DAISY

His was pure, a simple, driving longing to have what he wanted, and what he wanted was beauty and love and tenderness.

The same as me.

For a while, he had seemed like the only man in the world, and I his Eve. For a while…

"Oh…oh…" was all I could muster, and there was the same sweet hesitation from him, not borne of timidity but of affection. He wouldn't make a move without my approval.

It was as if we had spent our lives waiting for this moment. I hadn't realized I'd been waiting, but now I knew why I'd been so desperately unhappy. It was him. I had been aching for him.

For several long seconds, we just stood across from each other and stared, me on the threshold, him by the settee, surrounded by a dozen funerals' worth of flowers, tea sandwiches and pastries on a polished silver tray wilting in the greenhouse atmosphere.

At some point, Nick must have taken my dripping umbrella and excused himself because all I knew was that I was suddenly alone with a man I'd been deeply in love with years ago.

"Daisy," he breathed out, and I closed my eyes and remembered him whispering my name, as if it were a supplication to the heavens, and all he asked for was my favor. "Daisy."

Truth be told, I never liked my name. The daisy is not a distinguished flower, and though it's associated with a bright youthful sunniness I hoped I embodied, I wished I had been called something more romantic, less quotidian. Lenore, perhaps, or even Elizabeth or Beatrice, a name one could envision men fighting for.

But when Jay Gatsby said it, Daisy sounded like the only name on earth worth having, and I could imagine a ballroom full of women looking up and envying the girl announced with that moniker.

"Daisy."

As if in a dream, I walked over to him and was about to let him embrace me—I saw his hands begin to move up and out—when lamplight caught my wedding ring, and a dancing glimmer of its reflected sparkle flashed a warning. I was married.

"Jay?" I said and sat in a chair across from the settee, the tea items spread between us like a chaperoning matron. "I didn't realize…"

I didn't realize it had been his house, his parties, his sailboat. I didn't realize he'd become everything I'd wanted before marrying Tom—comfort, security, love, joy, and, yes, even money.

I didn't know whether to laugh or cry, to curse Nick or to thank him for setting up this rendezvous.

For the first time, I felt unsure of myself around a man. In my debutante days, I was always the one to put the fellow at ease. I was the one who enjoyed watching them preen and bow, flatter and twitch. I was never nervous, never at a loss for words.

Yet now I sat mute, a tentative smile on my face as I thought what I should say, if I looked all right, if the breeze had tousled my hair too much, if I'd sufficiently covered a blemish on my cheek with powder, if I'd applied too much rouge.

I was still smarting from my reunion with Edouard, and now I wondered if this, too, would lead to humiliation in some way, if I was being set up for disillusionment.

DAISY

I thought of leaving, but instead I sat like a schoolgirl, legs crossed at my ankles, back straight as a board, hands demurely in my lap, and I nodded and listened. Or tried to listen. Jay was telling me of the war, how hard it had been, how he'd lost good friends, how he'd come out of it with two goals in mind—never to waste a day, and to live the life he wanted, no matter how difficult it was to attain.

"Daisy?"

He had asked me a question, and I'd not heard it. Instead, I was lost in that question that plagues so many after a certain time: *What if?*

"Yes?" I asked and smiled, drifting back to an earlier time.

Jay in his brown uniform, looking as if it were a size too big, his right cheek raw from a close shave, his straw-colored hair, as always, in need of a brush, or the stroke of my hand over a boyish cowlick that would never stay down.

Jay laughing at some silly thing I'd said, sipping lemonade on my porch, the sun angling across the land as if aiming right for us, turning us both golden with its rays.

Jay taking me in his arms the night before he was to ship out and telling me he'd always be true, and would I wait for him? Yes, he knew I would. He knew I would wait.

"Are you happy?" he asked simply, his brows coming together. He knew that was a hard question to put to someone.

"Very happy, thank you." I said it simply and quickly, just as I would have, had I been meeting with any old acquaintance. "Tom and I have a daughter, a beautiful little girl, and he bought this house—the one across the bay—when business brought him to New York more and more, and it's so lovely being here, so many things to do, especially in the city, and I absolutely love where we are, close to everything but far enough away to breathe, and…and… and I'm very happy, so happy…"

I bowed my head, bit my lip, and could not stop the tear that fell onto my gloved hands. The lie had torn me open.

He saw, and in an instant was by my side, kneeling before me, holding my hands.

"Oh, Daisy. Has it been hard on you?"

I couldn't speak. I just nodded, and then he folded me into his arms. I had forgotten how muscular they were, and I cursed the gods for splitting us apart because of war. He dabbed at my eyes with a handkerchief of the softest silk, and we stayed there, though it must have become frightfully uncomfortable for him on the floor beside me. Yet, I knew that if we moved, it would only be even closer toward each other, and that had to be a conscious decision, not a hastily made choice when I was emotionally fraught.

At long last, a clock chimed, serving as the cue for us to part, so he stood, quick and careful, and pointed to the tea.

"Here, let me get you some," he said, acting the servant as he poured me a cup. "Wish we had something stronger."

He handed me the tea with a steady hand, though mine shook enough to make the cup rattle in the saucer, a beautiful china set I couldn't imagine Nick owning. I usually took a dot of sugar in my tea, but I couldn't bring myself to reach for it, too afraid I would spill my serving and embarrass myself even further.

The tea was the right choice, however, and after a few calming sips, I regained my composure enough to engage in real conversation.

"This is a good time to run into you," I now said, affecting the light, teasing tone of my younger days. "I'm at a point where I need to get out

DAISY

more. With the move, we've not done much socializing except for family. Nick, you know, is my cousin. So it will be good to get to know more people. We have the most beautiful house—not as large as yours, of course—but a perfect setting for entertaining."

"I do a fair amount of that," he said, and I detected in his voice an eagerness blended with amusement. The very attitude I'd always had when entertaining suitors.

"So I've heard."

"Then you'll have to come to one of my parties. I throw one almost every night. Everyone comes. Show people, judges, stockbrokers, even a classical pianist or two."

"Sounds lovely."

"I enjoy the parade of them. I enjoy learning things I didn't know." Now he was back to his old self, the striving joyfulness that attracted me. The vast openness that assumed you'd not judge him for being ignorant as long as he strove to learn more.

After that, our conversation flowed with ease. I even managed to nibble at one of the watercress sandwiches, while he downed several, plus cucumber toast and petit fours galore.

We talked about people we had known, and I was distressed to hear of even more war deaths than I'd previously been aware of. We talked of my father's passing, my mother's worsened circumstances—I made sure to credit Tom for helping her financially—and my new love of sailing.

"We'll have to go out together. I've got a fine big boat," he said.

"I know. I saw you." Warming, I looked down. I shouldn't have let him know.

"Well then, it's decided." And with a clap of his hands, like a boy who'd just opened a present, he said, "Tomorrow at one? I could sail over to get you."

"No, no. I…" I was about to refuse, but I thought of the boat, the water, the sense of freedom it gave me, and I realized that this was what I wanted right now, more than a party, more, in fact, than anything else. "I'll come to you. I'll sail to Nick's little dock and see him, then walk over."

The perfect excuse, one of many I was to make in the coming weeks.

Then Nick reappeared and Jay suggested we look at his house. Of course I wanted to see it. I wanted to know how he lived.

The rain stopped, and Nick said he didn't need to come with us, but I insisted because I didn't want to be alone in Jay's big place with only Jay. I was afraid. Of myself.

Room after room of Versailles-like splendor, a library full of books no one could read in a lifetime, artworks I recognized as belonging in a museum. His suite was the most wonderful of all, not something big and grand, but lovely little rooms, and a gold hairbrush on his dresser so attractive I couldn't resist running it through my own coiffure.

He seemed extravagantly pleased that I was pleased, and it touched me and saddened me all at once. It seemed he had stored all of this up for me, as if it were a huge gift he'd waited five years to present.

He opened his closet to reveal shelves of neatly folded colorful shirts and began to laugh and throw them onto the floor. I laughed, too, and picked one up, and then I cried because it was so beautiful. He so much needed me to say it was beautiful, and I felt, when presented with this great, awful gift of enduring love, I didn't know if I was worthy of it.

DAISY

I felt inadequate, as if I couldn't muster enough gratitude for this stunning display. As if I couldn't sufficiently demonstrate how happy I was for him, and for us that we'd found each other again. I ached with inadequacy.

When we finally walked out into the steaming sunlight, I felt wilted and old, as if seeing myself from a time far in the future, looking back at what I could have had. Here was that romantic ideal I'd held in my heart, a love who had stayed true.

I should have waited for him.

INTERLUDE
1917

I didn't want to go. The dance was a big patriotic event put together by Louisville mothers to honor the boys about to go "over there," but I hated pretending.

I thought it a foolish war, and even more foolish to celebrate it with a dance. Though I was only a young girl with no understanding of the world, I did comprehend one simple fact—that this particular war wouldn't be over until one side had let enough men sacrifice themselves on the altar of Mars. Somehow, I knew that adding American soldiers to that pile would tip the odds in our side's favor but at the cost of thousands of lives. That's how I saw it: a huge pile of soldiers, and whichever side had the bigger pile won, because they wouldn't run out before everything was all over.

It seemed like such a waste, and I will admit that back then, part of my anger and disgust was very personal. I knew the number of eligible men would diminish, meaning I'd have fewer choices.

I was courted by many. Dozens of beaux sought me out at dances and teas, croquet parties, polo matches, and strolls along the Ohio River where some stole kisses. Others were too timorous to even hold my hand.

So far, though, only a few men interested me enough to trigger daydreams of walking down the aisle with them. One was Rupert Templeton, a tall, lanky redhead with a penchant for reciting poetry. His poor eyesight

DAISY

was keeping him out of combat, but he still signed up to do some cartography and other desk-bound jobs. I liked his bookishness and dreaminess.

A more amorous beau was a man named Andrew Cash, and despite his last name, he was a poor New York soldier whose family owned a bakery. It wasn't his poverty that made me think twice, though. It was that he was a Catholic. My parents would never tolerate that match, and I spent many hours wondering if that was why I found him attractive—he was forbidden fruit, and I always felt delightfully rebellious whenever I saw him.

Neither of these men, nor the parade of others who tried to win me over, had me swooning the way some of my friends did over their beaux. Malvern Haskell, one of my best friends at the time, talked only of her fiancé, Dewitt. And Helen Beaufort canceled all long-made plans to go out with her beau, Theodore Clarkson. I'd long ago stopped counting on her as a friend.

So I was angry at everyone—at my girlfriends for abandoning me for their gentlemen, at the war for simultaneously placing so many men within reach to tease me when fate might snatch them away in an instant, and at my own heart for never lighting up with anything but mild interest. I wondered if there was something wrong with me.

"Daisy, dear, are you getting ready?" My mother knocked lightly at my bedroom door and I rose from the bed where I'd been looking through a fashion magazine. Still in my robe, I opened the door.

"I'm not feeling well," I said. "I want to stay home."

She immediately held her fingers to my brow. "You're not warm. Your color is good, and you took a drive with your friends earlier, didn't you?"

Yes, I had. My mother knew me too well. I turned and went back to my bed, sinking into its soft surface, hands in my lap.

"I don't want to go. I think the whole thing is silly, and I don't want to be part of it."

Mother walked over to me and sat beside me.

"Yes, it is silly, and I know it is hard to take part in something one doesn't believe in. But these boys are leaving soon, and it will do them good to see some pretty girls before they head out. Think of it as doing them a favor," she said softly. That musical voice of hers went up and down ever so slightly, making you want to listen to her forever.

"You can wear your pink chiffon," she went on when I didn't respond, "and stay just an hour, just long enough to smile and talk for a bit. You can say you're needed at home and must leave early. Your father can pick you up at eight."

"Tell a lie?" I asked, giggling.

My mother wrapped an arm around my shoulders and kissed me on the temple.

"It's not a lie. I always need you at home," she said. "You brighten my days." Then she hugged me and kissed me again on the forehead. "Here," she said, standing up, "let me get your dress."

Knowing I had to stay only an hour, I quickly slipped into my pink garment. I favored simple clothes—I still do—with clean lines and no frills. This dress was a recent acquisition, bought at a New York house and altered by a local seamstress. It had a straight neckline and long transparent sleeves in filmy chiffon, an overlay of the same fabric that stopped a foot above the hem of the satin cloth underneath. The original design had a two-inch fringe of black thread at the overlay hem, but I'd had the seamstress remove that and a matching fringe collar, as well as the wide satin belt. Instead, it barely cinched my waist with a gold cord. I wore it

DAISY

with the thinnest gold necklace and a lapis lazuli teardrop pendant. I loved pairing deep hues with lighter ones.

It was warm that night, so I didn't bother with a wrap. Father drove me to the country club in our Model T, as if he were my chauffeur. He loved to drive.

Before getting out, I gave him a peck on the cheek. As he rumbled away, I went up the steps to a wide porch circling the huge building. Already I could hear music from within, a dance tune with flutes and violins.

The place was awash in flags, and the patriotic theme continued to the food tables, where a red berry punch bowl sat in a plate piled with blueberries and white frosted pastries. Red napkins sat next to blue plates and white cups. As I helped myself to the confection, I wondered where they came by it all.

I waved to some friends across the room, and when they came to talk to me, I told them of a fierce headache I was battling. "I doubt I'll stay long," I said.

"But you're so good to show up when you're not feeling well," Candace said, squeezing my arm. She wore one of those fringed dresses so popular at the time, which made me glad I'd had them removed from my own frock.

"You look divine, though," Lilith remarked, squinting at me. She usually wore glasses but had removed them for the occasion. "Are you going to bob your hair?"

We'd all talked about it—getting our hair cut short—and Lilith had pioneered the look in our group. She had thick dark hair, almost black, and the style enhanced her pixie-like features, but I wasn't sure yet if it was for me. I had pinned my wavy locks at my neck, letting a few tendrils free.

"Not yet, Lil. Maybe I'll do it once my soldier goes off to war," I teased.

"What soldier?" Candace asked. "Andrew or Rupert? Or are you seeing someone new?" She always kept track of the boys, as if those of us who had two or more callers were hoarding them somehow.

"Neither. Someone new. I haven't met him yet."

They laughed. "Maybe you'll meet him tonight." Then she added, "I don't think you're ever going to bob your hair, Daisy. I think you just say that to keep us all interested."

Candace could be such a prissy thing, tallying up boys and pointing out our "lines."

"Well, then, I'm successful if you've remembered how many times I say it. You're interested," I countered. "You'll be the first to know when I cut it!"

I excused myself after that and wandered outside, sitting on one of the long wicker couches. I was the only one there enjoying the dusk, listening to the music and laughter, thinking that I could soon go home and stop the pretending. I'd heard they might auction off dances. I cringed at the thought.

"Why are you all alone?" His voice came to me before he appeared because he was climbing the steps to the porch, hidden behind a massive boxwood. At first, I thought he was addressing someone else. It was a rude question, after all, but then he appeared, broad-shouldered in a brown uniform, hair ruffled from the breeze, his hat in his hand, and a huge open smile on his face. His question hadn't been a mark of discourtesy. He was being frank.

"Why are you so late?" I said.

DAISY

"My car broke down," he said. "It's actually not mine exactly. Some of us went in on it so we could get around when we wanted to. It's a bright red touring car, but it doesn't like to start in rainy weather."

"It's not raining," I said, and liked how he just went on unabashedly telling me every detail, as if we'd known each other for ages.

"Oh, yes, I know. It rained yesterday, though, and that seemed to be enough to set her back on her heels. I think she's a woman. Kind of temperamental."

By then, he'd reached the porch and come over to me. Without waiting for an invitation, he sat down next to me, and I was ready to take offense when he immediately scooted away a few inches, as if realizing he had taken a liberty. He leaned forward, holding his hat between his knees.

"Where are your friends?" I asked. "The ones you bought the car with?"

"Oh, I didn't buy it. I fixed it. I'm good at that, so I get to use it pretty much whenever I want. I'm James," he said, holding out a hand. "James Gatz."

"Daisy Faye," I said, shaking his hand. His grip was strong and his hand calloused. I was sure I saw motor oil under his fingernails.

"So, you never answered my question," he went on. "What are you doing out here all alone?"

"I wanted some air," I said, then added, "I don't much care for these events. All the patriotic songs. The flag waving. It's all too much for me." His honesty apparently had brought out my own, and I waited for him to lecture me on how much it meant to the boys and how important the war was, and how we were saving the world, but instead he just nodded.

"I imagine they've told you how you keep our morale up and all, you pretty girls." He turned and gave me a quick smile. "Though it is true that looking at a pretty one like you does something for a man's outlook." His grin broadened. "I like your hair."

I shrieked with laughter, then covered my mouth at such an unladylike outburst. His compliment was so sweet and genuine, although it could have been interpreted as more rudeness, as if my hair were my only attractive feature.

"I mean, I like that you haven't cut it like a bunch of the girls have," he went on.

"I'm going to get it cut, though," I said, making the decision then and there. "For the war effort. Don't they need hair for something?"

"I guess they could use it as sort of a decoy, you know, waving it over the edge of a trench so the Germans think there's a pretty fräulein nearby."

"How wonderful—to think of using one's hair to tempt men to run to their deaths. I'll imagine I am Helen of Troy."

"At least they'd die happy thinking they were running to the likes of you," he said, smiling.

"Where are you from?" I asked.

"West of here. Nowhere you would have heard of. It's not where I'm from, though. It's where I'm going. After the war, that is. I'm going to build things, houses and factories and even castles like this one." He swept his arm around toward the country club, and I suppressed a smile that he'd likened the main building to a castle.

"What about you?" he asked. "What are you aiming to do?"

I cocked my head to one side, ready to give the answer all the girls of my age would give. To marry. To bear children. To run a household. But I stopped and instead said, "I want to be loved. Wildly and extravagantly. Absolutely worshipped and never forgotten."

DAISY

He looked up at me with a bright eagerness, and I knew in that instant he was applying for the job.

We sat and talked there well after the hour my father came by. I saw him sitting in the Ford in the drive at the foot of the steps, reading the newspaper, but Jay—he insisted I call him that even then—continued talking. He didn't talk to me like the other boys who were so eager to make sure you knew how smart and clever they were.

No, Jay asked me about myself. Had I any sisters or brothers? Were my parents alive? Had I lived in Louisville all my life? Did I want to see other places?

No boy who had courted me had wanted to know so much about myself. I didn't even know the answers to many of his questions. They made me think. And by the time I decided to put my father out of his misery and join him in the car, I felt as if Jay were already on the road to adoring me.

"Will you be here next Saturday?" he asked. "It's another dance, but not one of these big war effort shindigs. Just the regular punch and cookies affair."

I smiled. "Yes, yes, I will," I said. "But you might not recognize me. With my bobbed hair."

"Oh, I'd be able to pick you out of a flock of bobbed heads," he said, grinning. "You're the prettiest of them all."

Though I engaged in a dozen other activities the following week, I thought often about that dance. I swam at Lilith's beautiful lake house.

On our bright veranda, I painted a picture of bold red geraniums I'd been working on for some time. I took a dancing lesson with Mademoiselle Larchon. And during everything, I thought of what I would wear and whether I should really cut my hair before the event.

Rupert and Andrew and a few other boys came by to call, but they made me feel restless. So I begged off strolls and outings, claiming a headache. Jay didn't come by. He didn't know where I lived, of course, but it bothered me he hadn't tried to find out.

As I brushed my hair the Thursday before the dance and winced at the knots in my unruly tresses, I finally made a decision. I found a pair of scissors and sheared it off, straight across from my chin all the way around the back. Grabbing a mirror, I looked at what I'd wrought. It was shaggy.

"Mother!" I called, hurrying into the hall.

"Oh, my!" she said, her eyes wide as I entered her bedroom. "We should fix that," was all she said. "I'll summon Mrs. Dale."

In a half hour, the woman arrived. She was a tall, stylish brunette who provided fashion advice and arranged coiffures for many in our social set, usually from her small shop downtown.

She passed no judgment on my hair, just worked away, snipping at my rough ends, then shaving my neck. When she was done, I had a cloud of hair around my face that, like Lilith's bob, showed off my features to advantage.

"I'd been wondering when you would want to do this," Mother said.

"She looks very chic," Mrs. Dale said, putting away her implements. "It suits her. She won't have to do a thing to keep it nice, not like some who must curl it or straighten it. Many regret the choice. I had a girl come in—Bernice is her name, from the other side of town—who did it on a

DAISY

dare. She's the plainest girl, so she needed a full long crown of hair to make her something special." She smiled, though she didn't smile often, and patted my shoulder. "You'd look beautiful in any style, my dear."

I saved a lock of my long hair before Mother had the maid clean up the debris, and placed it in a small beaded box on my dresser.

That Saturday, I wore a jewel-red silk with a dropped waist and lace cap sleeves. I sported the lapis lazuli again and adorned my hair with a white diamond clip.

When I walked in the door of the country club, Jay was already waiting there. He had arrived a good hour early, he told me, to make sure he didn't miss me if I decided not to stay long.

"Look at you, all patriotic," he said, taking my hands in his. "Red, white, and blue."

I smiled. "And with bobbed hair."

"Oh, you did something to your hair?" he asked, and I was about to gently hit his shoulder when he laughed and said, "You look mighty fine, like a real princess. I hope you won't mind being escorted by a man who's yet to earn his own noble rank."

It was my turn to laugh. It was just like Jay to act as if one could earn one's way into nobility. "I don't mind at all. I'll just pretend you're already a prince."

I danced every dance with him, and when he wasn't waltzing me around the floor, we wandered outside along the porch and the paths under heavily scented magnolias.

He kissed me for the first time there, under those plump blossoms, and I knew all at once why my other beaux had left me cold. I hadn't fallen in love with them.

That night, I gave him the beaded box with a lock of my hair in it. A few weeks later, in that magnificent red-colored car he'd bragged about, I gave myself to him, becoming Jay Gatsby's lover.

CHAPTER FOUR

The day after meeting Jay at Nick's, a drenching, cleansing downpour cooled off the earth and sent the Sound into a tempest. It was exhilarating, and part of me wished I had the courage to venture out.

But I didn't. I saw the rain as a directive not to go sailing with Jay, to be careful, which was probably for the best. I didn't even send a note of regret, figuring he'd see the weather and understand.

Still, I could think of little else but him. A calmness descended over me with this glorious secret: I'd found Jay again. Eventually, I pieced together the how and why of it.

Jordan had been to one of Jay's parties, it turned out. He already knew of her connection to me—he had met her once during our Louisville days. She'd told him my cousin lived next door. He had asked her if she could set up a tea for us at Nick's, something for "two old friends who hadn't seen each other in a long time."

But Jordan had known it was more than that. She had seen it in his eyes, in the little trembling in his voice, she said. She had figured out that he'd even moved to West Egg, across from us, precisely so this reunion could eventually come to pass.

So she'd happily talked to Nick about setting up the tea.

Jay occupied all my thoughts after that tea. I had even begged off dinner that night, claiming another headache. In my sitting room alone, I dined on some cold ham and salad, staring out at the water, watching

DAISY

the light bid the day farewell. On my face, a gentle smile appeared, one I couldn't discard.

All these years later. He'd not only remembered me, but longed for me. Even through the war, he had kept a picture of me, he said, in his breast pocket and always looked at it before "going over the top."

Yesterday, he'd pulled out the photograph, an awful thing of me standing rigid and staring at the camera. To this day, he still had it. A tear came to my eye.

Just at a time in my life when I needed to believe in that kind of love, in love at all, he arrived.

He had personally arranged the flowers, the linens, the food, for our little tea. He didn't need to tell me all the details, but he'd extravagantly poured them out. Now I tried hard to remember the precise rose and gold pattern on the cups because it seemed so precious, so tender that he had wanted so earnestly to impress me.

I'd not realized then how assiduously I had been playing a role—that of the sophisticated modern woman— because that's what women did then, after the war, after the plague of the Spanish flu, after death and loss incomprehensible. We all acted on a stage, a comedy with tragic overtones where the jester garners all your sympathy right before his death scene.

I'd been part of that play, trying so hard to grab from the spotlight a sense of life again, of hope, of striving for something better. For meaning.

That's what wanted. Meaning. A reason to be happy and not hurt anymore. I'd not realized how hurt I'd felt, seeing the world I knew disappearing, and seeing the man I married regularly taunting me with words and actions. I covered my pain with a stilted sophistication, as if I was too important to experience sorrow.

I absolutely ached with it, and Jay was like a balm.

Confused, torn between wanting nothing to change and wanting to step into the unknown of this new possibility, I spent the afternoon on the nursery floor, throwing a ball back and forth with Pamela, helping her dress up in my discarded gowns and jewelry, rocking her to sleep for her nap.

Oh, I know I had told Nick I hoped she'd be a little fool, but that was another story meant to startle and then charm, and, as with all stories, it was based on both truth and lies.

The truth was I adored my little girl, and I would do everything in my power to make sure she was no fool, even though I knew the world preferred foolish-seeming women, pliable and empty-headed.

After she was born, Tom had difficulty being with me. My new role as mother must have changed his view of the woman he'd married, and though I regained my svelte figure within several short months, I could tell his attraction to me had waned considerably, and he often had to be drunk to consider lovemaking—with me, that was. He found no such hesitation with other women.

Instead, he treated me either as a fragile goddess he shouldn't provoke or, when liquor peeled off his inhibitions, a woman to punish with a quick and rough bedding.

Although I preferred to keep myself in the former category with Tom, I now wondered, especially after Jordan's urging in this regard, if I could cross the lines that Tom had so easily stepped over, finding warmth and affection elsewhere.

After Pamela's birth, the doctors told me I likely would be unable to bear any more children, so I sometimes wondered if this also accounted

DAISY

for Tom's reticence, knowing he wouldn't be producing any more progeny with me. I dreaded the possibility that he'd foist an unwanted secret son on me some day, born of a mistress I didn't want to know about.

After Pammy fell asleep, the skies calmed, and I pulled on a sweater and walked to the promontory, looking across the Sound to Jay's dock. The boat wasn't there. So he'd gone out despite the rain. With a sigh, I realized I wish I had met him after all. How exciting it would have been for the two of us to battle a storm while sailing his cutter.

Now I'd have to devise a pretext to see him, or hope for an invitation.

I stayed awhile, waiting to see him and his boat return, and at length, I could make out the fine tall shape of his masts and knew he was all right and headed for home. I left before he could see me watching, hurrying around the path and eventually up the walkway to see Tom standing in the door, a note in his hand. I thought he'd been at his club.

"What is it?" I asked, fearing a telegram with bad news.

"Where have you been?" he responded. "Another storm's coming!" He nodded toward the bay, where a thunderhead darkened the horizon.

"I outran it!" I said gaily, unknotting the scarf tied around my hair. "What's that?" I pointed to the envelope in his hand.

"Nothing. An invitation to one of those circuses across the way."

My heart sped up. Jay. I hadn't gone sailing with him, so he'd sent over an invitation. I'd longed for one, and it had appeared, as if by magic.

Tom's attitude, though, seemed to indicate he wasn't about to lower himself to attend.

"Really?" I said, pulling the note from his hands and glancing at the languid script. "What fun! We should go." I tried to sound light, but then I was bold. "Or you can stay here, and I'll report on it for you!"

That tipped him off, and he squinted at me. "I've heard stories of what goes on over there. Not fit for a woman on her own. I'll go, too."

Thus assured of his role as chivalrous protector, he walked back into the house.

The invitation was for two nights from now, and all the next day I chose and discarded dress after dress, wishing I had thought of shopping for something new. And then I realized I did have a new frock, one I'd never worn because Tom had declared it scandalous at dinner with friends in Chicago right before we'd moved.

I found it in the back of my closet and fingered its soft chiffon overlaid with intricate gold embroidery, then quickly donned it.

It *was* scandalous. Pale gauzy chiffon, almost flesh-colored, with a draped neckline that could show hints of real flesh men liked to see. Its embroidery swirled and curved so that it drew attention to breasts and hips before dropping into a cascade of scarf-like layers just below the knees. When I walked, it made me feel like a graceful swan, and I remembered buying it because the gold thread had reminded me of my debutante gown.

I'd had it altered to fit perfectly, thinking Tom would be proud to escort such a unique and tantalizing creature anywhere. Instead, he'd been mildly embarrassed, telling me it made me look as though I wasn't wearing anything at all, and he wasn't going to take a tart to a dinner with important friends.

DAISY

This time, I would wear no jewelry except a gold bracelet I'd had as a girl, and peacock-colored shoes with tiny heels. Tom would probably object, but I'd tell him I was sure I would look as demure as a nun compared to everyone else at that party.

Nick came by that evening for dinner. The three of us dined on the veranda on vichyssoise, sole meunière, and pommes Lyonnaise, a French meal I'd had Cook prepare to make me think of Jay in France keeping my picture in his pocket everywhere he went. We ate in the blue twilight. When I told Nick we'd received an invitation to a Gatsby party, he nodded.

"They're quite the circus," he said.

"Then maybe we should just go to a circus," Tom said sourly.

"Jordan's gone to one," Nick hastily added, as if this would provide the imprimatur Tom needed. "One of Gatsby's parties. I saw her at one last week. She had a perfectly lovely time, she said."

Last week. Was that when they'd hatched their plan to get me to Nick's cottage to see Jay? I noticed Nick said he'd seen her there, not taken her. As I said, their romance never became a romance, although I knew they'd happily make a couple for any event I chose to hold.

"Two bands, performers, two dinner servings, liquor of every kind," Nick went on, waving his fork as he talked. He seemed excited to share stories of the event to boost Tom's enthusiasm. "So many people, you need to be careful not to accidentally open a door or you might walk in on someone *inamorata*."

Tom leaned back, finished with his meal, and lit a cigarette. "This is supposed to make me want to go?" he asked.

"Oh, Tom, I told you it was all right if you didn't want to. I will be your own personal correspondent and give you a full story on the absurdities of the night. Why, I'm already writing the tale in my head."

"I bet you are," Tom mumbled.

As the maid cleared the plates and brought dessert, the phone rang, and I knew, even before the butler came for Tom, that it would be the Wilson woman. I looked at my husband, smiled, and said sweetly, "Go on. You know it's for you. I don't mind, as long as you're keeping business humming. I'll just talk to Nick about bonds. Bonds fascinate me, you know. Utterly fascinate me."

Actually, there was some truth to that. I wanted to probe Nick about how one bought stocks and bonds. Jordan was doing it through Nick, and it sounded exciting and useful.

He nodded, looked down, and left, and my smile immediately dropped. Nick and I ate our dessert in silence while Tom's hushed voice traveled onto the veranda. Occasionally a clear word would drift out, and I became embarrassed that we might overhear something that could humiliate me even more than this awkward silence, both Nick and I knowing my husband was on the phone with his lover.

I finished, got up, and went to the balustrade around the veranda, smoking and staring into the shimmering gloaming. Nick joined me.

"Tom's business going well?" he asked.

I laughed. "Oh, stop. We both know he doesn't do any business, and we both know who is on the phone. That Wilson witch." Then I turned to him. "Is she beautiful, Nick? Even in a…a cheap way?"

DAISY

He grimaced but shook his head. After a pause, he said, looking away from me, "She's not a beauty. She's kind of, well, stout. You have nothing to worry about. Tom loves you. He even roughed her up."

My eyes widened. That Nick had met her was, as I've said, a betrayal. Despite my question, I hadn't expected him to so readily admit it, and for a moment I felt angry that he'd seen her and not immediately insisted they both end their liaisons, or at least come and tell me the whole sordid tale. I also felt betrayed anew by Tom that he had not chosen a beauty, even a cheap one, but instead had settled for someone Nick deemed fat. I didn't think he was lying to me. I think he would have told me the truth. I knew I was pretty. I liked pretty things. I filled our home with them. I thought Tom liked them, too.

"Roughed her up?" I repeated.

Now he did meet my gaze. "Yes. She was saying your name, and Tom didn't want her so much as breathing it. He told her to stop it, but she kept saying it over and over, just to taunt him. Finally, he pulled back and punched her. Well, slapped her is more like it. But it caused an awful ruckus and lots of blood."

Imagining the scene, I bit the inside of my cheek to keep from smiling. Good for Tom, defending his bride. Too bad that defense didn't include fighting off his own bad impulses. I had no illusions about what probably followed his burst of violence.

At least I could be grateful for that, I supposed. Except for the occasional too-tight squeeze, Tom had never laid a finger on me. If he did, I'd leave him for sure.

"Why does he...oh, never mind," I said. I really had no interest in exploring the depths of Tom's melancholia, the reasons he needed to prove over and over what a man he was by building a harem wherever we went. Perhaps I should just let him go on more about the white man's burden. Maybe that would feed his masculine pride.

Nick moved closer and said on a whisper: "You should ask him to stop. I bet he would."

At that, I laughed. Poor, naïve Nick.

"Oh, darling, I'm so glad we've reunited. I need to hear this kind of talk. It reminds me how I used to feel before I became so damned sophisticated."

That was another line I used to charm people, and Nick was appropriately entranced, his eyes shining with sympathy.

This particular line contained more truth than fiction, though. As I moved from girlhood to womanhood, from debutante to wife to mother, I learned the world was cruel, that it injured and killed, that unkindness could be masked by a smile, meanness by good intentions and religious fervor.

We went back to staring out in silence over the darkness, and I became mesmerized by the little green light at the end of our dock, the one Jay told me he looked at, thinking of me.

It shed its glimmer on the ripples of water, and I thought of those ripples making their way across the Sound to him. I wondered at that very moment if he was looking out at that fairy light and seeing me, the true love he had never forgotten. I wanted to measure up to that devotion. I wished I could dive off the promontory and swim to him.

"I think what bothers me most," I said, almost to myself, "is that he can't seem to shake the habit. You know, of seducing women. It seems… dirty in a way that just a long, satisfying affair wouldn't."

"You'd rather he have a lifelong mistress?" Nick asked. I heard the surprise in his voice.

DAISY

I sighed. "I'd rather he choose…" Me? No, I couldn't say it, not now when I was unsure if it mattered. In fact, it didn't matter. What I wanted wasn't for him to choose. It was for me to choose. With a profound sadness, I realized I wanted to choose to go back, to correct my errors, and marrying Tom seemed like one of them. This was a chasm I couldn't afford to peer into, so I shook those thoughts from my head.

"I'd rather he choose some other scandalous behavior." I laughed. "Perhaps acrobatics or fire juggling or maybe even walking on a tightrope over Niagara Falls! Has anyone done that lately? Maybe we should suggest it!"

Nick laughed softly, then said, "You might see some acrobats at Gatsby's party. Jugglers, too."

"Oh, I hope so. Armies of them! That would be wonderful, if they are very tall and swarthy, with thick black moustaches, and march and juggle at the same time."

"To music, of course!" Nick said, joining in.

"Of course! I can hear it. A snake-charming tune where the dancers have to do complicated steps as they stride through the guests, and we all gasp as they try not to set some poor woman's hair on fire, while we're secretly hoping to see such a disaster."

"You're impossible," Nick said, laughing harder now.

"Am I? Why, thank you, Nick. A high compliment coming from you."

As I watched the dock light flicker, I wished I were the most impossible of beings and could be the sparkling green fairy in that lamp, sprinkling magic on everyone around me so I would get what I wanted… after I figured out what that was.

CHAPTER FIVE

To this day, Nick and I argue about what I wore to that party. He remembers it as a costume event, with a country theme, and describes in detail a peasant outfit I supposedly wore that fit me perfectly and made me the most beautiful woman in the crowd.

I remembered wearing my gauzy gold and cream confection, with the peacock blue slippers and a gold bracelet. Yes, I remembered others in costume, but I didn't mind not having dressed for the occasion. I liked swimming against that tide.

Nick and I disagreed over other details of this whole story, as you know by now. He insists Jay had yet to go to war when I married Tom, but Nick wasn't really in my life at the time and relies on now faulty memories of things. Jay, as you know, was a fabulist, but on that memory we agreed. He left for war, and I married Tom.

Jay himself was in tails and patent leather shoes, and when he saw me, he took in his breath and stammered over his words.

"The Buchanans," he managed to bluster as if a footman making an announcement upon our entering.

No one heard, of course. Not in that meleé.

How to describe it? It *was* a circus, but one you wanted to be a part of, not just observe. It beckoned you to enjoy life, to lift a cup, to sing a song, to dance, to laugh. It felt like a sin not to.

Nick's description had been accurate. There were two bands, one playing all the latest popular tunes. On a big parquet dance platform, couples

DAISY

jounced to the animalistic rhythms of the music. Another band, somewhere upstairs, played waltzes and classical fare for those who couldn't bring themselves to admit they enjoyed savage beats.

There was food and drink everywhere, and people doing outrageous things, wanting to outshine each other. Someone jumped into the pool in full dress just as we came out to that area, and as we made our way to a table, I watched a sopping wet woman, laughing hysterically, being pulled out of the pool by both her arms, one man on each side, her dress dangerously close to sliding down to her waist.

I half expected that army of jugglers I had joked with Nick about to pass by at some point.

Though Tom had ostensibly accompanied me to be my protector, he overcame that impulse quickly enough, along with his snobbish disdain, when he saw two attractive women by a bar and recognized them as moving picture stars. Of course, he had to get something to drink, and it took him nearly an hour to return as he engaged in laughing conversation with them.

I didn't care. The whole thing was an emporium of fun and delight, and, like a patron at a museum, I wandered about drinking in each exhibit, pondering if I liked it or not, passing judgment on the artists who made up the tableau.

Sometimes I walked alone, sometimes with Nick, and often with Jay. Never with Tom.

Presently, Tom appeared at my elbow, holding out a glass of champagne. He polished off his in a gulp, then grimaced. "Not a good vintage, nor a good year."

Buoyed by his pronouncement of personal superiority, he then moved on, deciding to be somewhat generous of spirit. "You do have to hand it to him, though. He might have no taste, but he knows how to make money. There is no way he could pay for all this using borrowed cash. A place like this. Parties every night. Why, he's had palm trees brought up from Florida. See them over there by the pool? No one would do something this extravagant unless he's got capital."

Tom himself would never indulge in such ostentatious displays, but he somehow seemed to envy a man who did. Maybe it was the freedom of it, not caring if others thought you were showing off, but Tom stayed rigidly in his class, his one act of rebellion being his tendency to bed inferior women.

But I knew Jay didn't think of all this as rebellion or ostentatious display. To him, it was simply a boyish sharing of his own happiness, at having achieved what he wanted. His display wasn't a finger in the eye of anyone. It was an outpouring of pure joy.

"He's got a good selection of liquor, too," said Tom. "Talked to him 'bout it. A good deal, he said. Might use his man," Tom added. This after he had just criticized the champagne.

We all moved to a table together and sat down—Nick, me, Tom, and Jordan. Jay was about somewhere, but I didn't see him as Tom babbled on about investments, deals on liquor, and more.

In recent months, Tom had been talking more and more about "deals." He seemed to think he was missing out, just letting his fortune accumulate the old-fashioned way, and he'd become interested in investing, growing his capital. Talking to his father about it, too. I let him go on. It was a better way of feeding his manhood than accumulating mistresses. Or pummeling

DAISY

them. And I picked up information from these brief conversations, especially when Nick was around to offer advice.

"Gatsby was telling me about buying stocks on margin," Tom now announced. "Nick, you learn anything about that in all your midnight-oil burning at the Yale Club library?"

Nick reddened. "If you have the money, sure, buying on margin is a good way to accumulate a lot of stock quickly. It holds some risk…"

Tom clapped him on the shoulder. "Risk for those without money. Maybe I'll talk to you about this some time. I have an idea we're all going to need to fortify our homes, take care of ourselves, as the lower races attempt their ascent to the top."

Before he could go on, a short, balding man in a constable costume nearly tipped over our table as he clumsily tripped and fell into it.

"Say, watch it," Tom said, now rising to his protector role.

Jay caught sight of the problem, and rushed over, putting his arm around the fellow.

"Steady there, old sport." To us, he said, "This is Anthony Delacorte," as if we should know who that was. "Big into imports, exports," he added when he noticed our blank stares.

Anthony took that as an invitation to join us and promptly sat down in the only empty chair at the table. Jay beamed at me with raised eyebrows, standing behind Anthony.

I closed my eyes and gave my head the tiniest of shakes, trying to convey that I couldn't get away from Tom right there.

"Jay here's a great man, y'know. Not just a great frien'. He's got good music, books." Delacorte waved his arm, almost smacking a passing woman in an elaborate peasant frock who didn't seem to notice. "Went to Oggsfur, y'know."

"Oggsfur?" I asked. "What's that?"

Jay looked down and suddenly left us, walking with a sense of taking over the band, as if he had to alert them to some special request.

"It's in London. Or round there," Mr. Delacorte informed us, shouting over the noise. "You haven't heard of it? Most famous college in the world, by golly." He looked at me with suspicion, as if I were teasing him.

"Oh, Oxford," I said, finally understanding. "But Jay couldn't possibly have gone to Oxford." Not if he was making his fortune. Why would he waste time on college, even one like "Oggsfur"?

"Seen a pitt-chur of him there with some of his buddies," the man said. "Go on, ask him. He went to Oggsfur'."

I sighed and looked for Jay in the teeming swirl of humanity. He had disappeared. I had no doubt he'd spun that tale to friends, acquaintances, and business associates, and it saddened me while also igniting a fire of sympathy, a desire to defend him. In that story, he had been trying to impress, or at least fit in with the Toms of the world. Why do that, Jay? You don't need to.

He shouldn't feel the need to try to impress these people, especially people like Tom. Tom had gone to Yale, but I had met enough of his fellow alumni to suspect that their education had been more about making the right kind of friends than the actual pursuit of wisdom or any kind of meaning.

Tom wasn't even listening by now, his gaze scanning the crowd for more suitable people to talk with. Soon, he went to the bar for a refill,

DAISY

and it wasn't long before he was deep in conversation with a pale-skinned redhead in a dress of the same hues as mine.

Anthony Delacorte left our table, too, and Jay returned. This seemed to be a signal for Jordan and Nick to go, as well. They sprang up as Jay sat down, so the two of us were alone in that swirling throng of partyers. There were so many of them, making so much noise with laughter and talking and even singing that it felt as if we were alone. Jay placed his hand over mine and looked into my eyes.

"I've missed you," he said.

"It has been several years," I answered.

"No. I mean since the other day. At Nick's. I've missed you since then. I've counted every second."

"I've missed you, too." This was no lie, and I felt so comfortable here with him that it became even more apparent to me how much I pretended in front of Tom and others. With Jay, I felt relaxed. I became who I really was, even if I didn't quite know who that was.

"Daisy, come over any time you want. Any time. I'll always be waiting for you. Always." He pulled my hand to his lips and kissed it.

There is nothing more intimate than two people in a noisy crowd. We existed in a place all our own, as if we were invisible to the throng around us, as if we were king and queen of this fairyland, and our subjects were cavorting secretly for our pleasure. If Jay had made love to me right there in that moment, I would have believed no one could see us.

Hours later, when Jay was interrupted by a servant asking a liquor supply question, the spell was broken. Nonplussed, Jay grabbed me by the elbow, looked around, and whispered, "Let's go!" He nodded toward Nick's place.

Did I know that, by accepting this invitation, I was crossing a line? Yes, even if I didn't articulate it to my conscience. I burned for Jay. I remembered how he had touched me when we were young. He was my first lover. I'd been no perfect flower on my wedding night.

"Nick!" I cried, spotting him as we meandered toward the front door. "We're going to sit on your steps and talk. Will you mind, darling, sounding the alarm if Tom comes looking for me, though I doubt that'll be any time soon?" I moved to see Tom dancing with one of the moving picture stars now.

"Sure thing."

"Thanks, old sport," Jay said to Nick, and as soon as we were out of the light and into the shadows, he grabbed my hand and we raced like children down the little hill and through the small stand of trees that separated his property from Nick's rented place.

Giggling and breathless, we neared Nick's steps, and I knew, as Jay pulled me into an embrace and a long, deep kiss, that we wouldn't be doing much talking here.

This, I realized was the moment when I discarded the last of my girlish rules. I knew it as soon as we stepped onto Nick's porch and opened his

DAISY

door. There on the threshold, my mind was whispering yes over and over to my heart, and I felt no remorse, no guilt, not even a pinch of indecision.

Jay pulled me into an embrace at the door, and when he felt me respond with equal fervor, he began to kiss my neck, my shoulders, and my hands. I remember—oh, God, I remembered—what it was like to be adored so, to be cherished and treated as something fine and beautiful.

I felt fine and beautiful, the moonlight glinting off the gold thread on my shimmering fairy dress.

Jay lifted me into his arms and took me to the guest bedroom, where, in our eagerness, we stripped each other until we were in the bed. Here was a lover who made me feel as if I was the only woman on earth he could ever have.

Whether inspired by drink, Jordan's talk, or my own musings on fidelity, I no longer had any doubts. I had tolerated Tom's wandering. Now he'd have to tolerate mine. But unlike him, I wouldn't flaunt it, and at least my choice was our equal in wealth if not in status.

From across the way, we heard the muted sounds of the party, music from the pool area and the upstairs salon creating discordant melodies, a pure line of Mozart on strings interrupted by the slide of a trumpet pulsating up the scale to some victorious wail of ecstasy. We heard laughter and the occasional crash, perhaps of a tray or glass. We heard a woman yelling, as clearly as if she were next to us, "Just shut up about it!" And I thought I picked up the splash of the pool—perhaps another woman had imitated the first.

It felt like the best place on earth. In Nick's guest room that night. Just on the very edge of frivolity, it was close enough to enjoy without having to witness its distasteful details, letting its waves lap at our feet, not drowning in its depths. This was what I'd craved, a sweet sample of exuberant life, at a distance, to keep me safe.

I wanted to stay there forever, close to home, yet far enough way, close to those I loved—Pamela, and, yes, Jay—and not cut off from the hubbub of life that could make it so much fun.

After our passion had exhausted itself, he asked softly, "Why didn't you wait for me?"

I was stroking his cheek as he tried to balance on his elbows so as not to crush me with his weight. He was still finely muscular, like a statue of a Greek god. I wondered if he boxed or lifted barbells. I reached up and touched a firm shoulder.

"Oh, Jay," I said. "I thought…I didn't think you'd…"

"Make it home?" he answered and sat up, grabbing and holding my hand, bringing it to his lips again.

His gestures were gentle, not angry, just like his tone, so I nodded in the dim light.

"I was so afraid then. Of so many things."

"Aw, Daisy, you had to know you'd see me again. I would have done anything to get back to you. We all had gals we wanted to return to."

"Not everyone returned," I said.

"You didn't get my letters," he said.

I paused. His letters. I'd received one the night before my wedding to Tom. I didn't want to tell Jay I had read it. That seemed too cruel to both of us, after we'd just found each other again. I wanted to be the woman who *would* have stopped her wedding after reading such a letter, and I didn't want him to know I wasn't.

DAISY

"On the eve of my wedding to Tom," I said on a breath. "One—just one—arrived then. The night before." This was sufficiently vague, I decided, not suggesting I'd read it, only that I had received it.

He leaned back, taking this in, and then pulled me to him. I rested my head on his strong shoulder, and we didn't speak. He kissed me on the head, just as Edouard had done to his wife at the speakeasy, and this, too, felt right, part of the balancing of my world.

I don't know what Jay was thinking, but he seemed to accept my statement as a suitable explanation, even if he had preferred another outcome. At last, he said, "But you never loved him."

So that was the calculation he had been making, the conclusion he'd been finding his way to. Sweet man, he needed to hear I loved him alone. Had he been equally faithful, I wondered? Surely not. Why did men think they had the right to claim uninterrupted devotion from women they would forget in an instant whenever they themselves found a charming substitute? But Jay hadn't forgotten me, I reminded myself. He had built a life around not forgetting me.

"Oh, Jay, I was numb." The night before my wedding and the day of, I was someone else observing all that was happening, a smile on my face, little sparks of joy flashing from time to time, but nothing that started a fire like this one—the one we'd just enjoyed. I'd been a different person then, and I didn't want to talk about that girl with Jay. There was only this Daisy in this moment.

He hugged me tight and kissed the top of my head again, satisfied.

We lay there for quite some time until I heard footsteps rustling through the brush on the border of Jay's property, so we promptly dressed and walked to the front steps, holding hands. We sat down and Jay lit a cigarette for me.

When Nick approached, it looked as if we had been there, just talking, for the past hour.

"Tom's looking for you," Nick said. I saw his eyes gleam in the light spilling from Jay's mansion. "Wants to go home. Sent the chauffeur, who's out front."

I stood, and Jay handed me my wrap, which had fallen onto the steps behind me, gently pressing it around my shoulders. He placed a bold kiss on my cheek, and I leaned into him for a last embrace.

Together, we headed back to Jay's mansion, where Nick and I found Tom and Jordan in the main hall. Jay followed shortly after, as if he'd been somewhere else on the property. Soon we were all scurrying to the car, hastening inside, the cool night air erasing any dark moments from before.

"Don't hesitate to come back anytime!" Jay called to us, but I knew he was speaking only to me.

As we pulled away, I reached out the window to wave. I knew Jay would be standing on the steps watching.

CHAPTER SIX

I did go back. In fact, I went back the very next afternoon. Tom woke up that day hung over, and once recovered from his over-imbibing, drove into the city again, maybe to pursue some of those new deals he was enthused about and maybe to see Myrtle. Likely both.

I didn't care. I really didn't. Not a wisp of vexation blew into my blue-sky happiness. Feeling light and wholesome, I hopped into our Ford and made my way over to Jay's, as if this was the life I was meant to lead, going to a lover who had spent years trying to woo me, even if I'd been unaware of it. We were mending a cloth ripped open by war, stitching it together again, thread by thread, so this, too, felt like something greater than ourselves—greater, even than our own personal happiness.

Despite my joy, there was at first a strange awkwardness to our meeting that afternoon. The maid ushered me in, telling me to wait in a small parlor off the front door. I wasn't convinced she would really fetch Jay, and I walked around the room looking at the *objets d'art* on various shelves, deciding to call out his name if he didn't appear soon and then head home. Was that a Fabergé egg, a Japanese porcelain plate, a Meissen figurine?

In the corner was a plain wooden desk, the kind a schoolboy might use. Bending over it, I saw his initials carved in the corner, barely visible: JG. My hand floated over it, this remnant of a past of which I knew little.

When Jay had entered my life in Louisville, he had no past. He was one of many soldiers billeted nearby, and their uniforms created class equality. Rich and poor were identical. When he came to that dance at the

DAISY

local club, I was blissfully unaware of his social class. I only knew he was smart and kind and honest.

It seems strange to contemplate now how I almost missed this meeting. My feelings about the war had been part personal spite and part prescient foreboding. I thought it all silly and awful and wasteful. To voice those opinions was heresy.

But my mother knew how to gently push me into doing the right thing, whether I had the spirit for it or not, and maybe it really hadn't been so hard for her to nudge me into attendance. I liked parties at the country club. I liked being on my own, seeing who I could flirt with, charm, entrance. I'd felt pretty that night, contrarily so, with my unbobbed hair and lack of much jewelry, with little decoration on my dress, and a scant bit of powder on my face, just enough to keep perspiration from making it shine.

My contrarian mood dimmed my spirits a bit as I tried to decide whether to give in to my inclination to have a good time or hold tight to my resentment at being forced to pretend support for a cause I didn't believe in. Why were men always so eager to show they could kill and die?

Looking back, I see how that contrarianism served me well. It kept me out on the porch, ready for the moment when Jay arrived that night. If I had been inside, dancing, laughing, talking with friends, would he have noticed me or only seen me as one of the crowd of pretty girls?

And my contrary nature had kept me faithful to Tom all these years, even when I'd been tempted—by Edouard and a few others—to stray. No, not faithful to Tom, I decided. Faithful to the idea of the kind of love I'd shared with Jay. Now I had it again.

"Daisy!" Jay walked into the room, heading toward me with long strides. He kissed me immediately, holding my arms and looking at me, as if years had not parted us, as if it were the day after that country club dance, and our future together was settled. "You came!"

"You invited me," I reminded him.

"Yes, yes," he said and put his arm around me, guiding me toward a big sunroom at the back of the house. "I'm so glad you came."

He seemed distracted, though. He looked over my shoulder. Was he expecting someone else?

"This is a bad time for you," I suggested. I didn't want to be humiliated, and I began to feel that once again I had dreamed up an affection that wasn't as deep as I'd first imagined. I was new to this, after all, crossing the line Tom had a habit of hopping over.

"No, not at all," he said as he closed a door to the sunroom behind us. "I just…I don't want staff gossiping. I want you safe." He reopened the door. "I will be right back."

Then I heard him in the hallway telling a servant that everyone was off for the day, with pay. The maid, or whoever it was, protested she had a lot of work left to do, but Jay insisted they all be gone within the quarter hour.

"There," he said, returning. He sat next to me on a cushioned settee. "We're all alone."

And we were. With a thrill, I realized the entire house was now our playroom, and it didn't take us long to make good use of it. No hurried lovemaking on a guest room bed this time. He took my hand and led me slowly to his own bedroom, picked me up, carried me over its threshold, then laid me on crisp laundered sheets and told me he had never stopped loving me. And never would. Our lovemaking was slow and sensual, different from our first hurried sessions when we were young and had to steal moments in discreet places. These were different from Tom's awkward

DAISY

beddings, where I sometimes felt the need to reassure him that he was doing all right.

This coming together was a dance of pure bliss, both of us enjoying each other, with nothing to prove.

We swam in his pool, too, naked and unashamed, and made love like sea creatures finding each other in the depths.

It was the first of many contented afternoons spent together. We danced, we talked, we laughed, we swam, we made love.

Oh, to be forever young! That's how I felt on those serene days. Worries faded, even the future disappeared. Just those moments of joy remained, and it was like revisiting the past, those lovely days of feeling loved unconditionally by the world. Yet my pleasure was now a hundredfold amplified because I now knew just how rare it was to feel this way.

Jay's parties ceased. Once he and I became lovers, he didn't want the house full of strangers, no matter how star-studded the guest list might be. He told me he had sometimes found a stray guest in his home mornings after parties. He wouldn't risk that.

That changed with us. So careful was he with my reputation, that he even changed his staff, hiring men and women Mr. Delacorte recommended to him, who knew, he told me, that their jobs and their lives depended on their discretion.

There would be no town gossip about us, and I was able to drive myself over to Jay's place in the afternoons, often when Tom went riding or into town to make the many deals he now seemed to be fascinated with. I suspected Jay had something to do with those deals, enticing him into one meeting or another with men of finance and industry. Tom would have loved mingling with that crowd, feeling as if he were an agent of business and not an idler whose best years had faded behind him.

Tom had even started using Jay's liquor supplier—an arrangement I wasn't particularly fond of because I feared the bootlegger wouldn't be as discreet as Jay's home staff. So I made a point several nights in a row of reminding him how he'd criticized Jay's champagne, complained of the taste of the gin, and groaned about the sourness of the wine, intimating it must have been cheap liquor labeled to look like top-shelf brands. I suggested to Tom that he might have been taken in by unscrupulous providers who knew he had the cash to throw around. That was enough for Tom. He stopped ordering, even stiffed the supplier on a bill for the last delivery, telling him he wouldn't pay for goods that weren't real. He didn't stop his forays into business, though.

That left Jay and me in the clear, and the summer began in earnest as an idyll drenched in love. I felt as bright as the flickering fairy in the light at the end of our dock. I felt that my line about the longest day of the year being worth remembering, yet often forgotten, was true. The burst of light on that day was a beacon for the rest of the summer. For life itself.

It's odd to think back now and realize that that summer was just a single summer, because it felt at the time as if it lasted a year, a decade, an eon, while the rest of the world raced forward without us.

I was lucky our first few weeks. Tom was often gone when I returned home, and, even when home, disinterested in where I'd been. I always had an excuse at the ready—I'd gone into town to look at clothes for Pamela, I'd taken a drive, I'd played golf with Jordan. I had a veritable book of excuses all ready to offer.

DAISY

Sometimes, on those languorous afternoons, we would sit in his parlor listening to records—beautiful French music, new tunes, Broadway melodies, jazz groups. He'd silently get up to change the record, then come back to repose by my side, giving me a glance of understanding, intimating a strange kind of ennui that was part regret, part hopefulness.

For hours we'd lounge there, smoking and listening, not saying a word, just caressing each other's arms when something particularly sweet would float into the room, immediately communicating that we understood the mood of the musical artist. It was a game, to wordlessly go long periods, to feel utterly understood in the slightest movement, tilt of the head, blink of the eye.

Sometimes, he took me on drives in his ostentatious car, on back roads so no one would see us, even though I enjoyed wearing dark glasses and hideous scarves, cultivating stories of who I was playing that day—a Russian spy, a deposed aristocrat, or a shopkeeper's daughter on a lark. I joked that I might start wearing wigs of different colors.

"Your reputation will be ruined, Jay, but mine will be intact," I said.

To which he replied, "No man's reputation is ruined by being with a beautiful woman."

Some days we went sailing, though I worried during those outings that someone from my house would spot us from our house. Jay always got us quickly out of the Sound, though, and we would sail until our houses disappeared from view, anchor in some quiet cove, and make love in the gently rocking cabin, the boat moving in time with our passion. We were the only beings alive.

It all passed as if a dream, and I felt, for the first time in years, young and hopeful, even if I wasn't sure what I was hoping for. It was how I felt as a girl, that the future held even more happiness, and each day would be like unwrapping a beautiful present selected just for me.

Jay shared that optimism. That's why I'd fallen for him. He had not gone on to build all those things he'd wanted to build, he told me one afternoon, but he'd built other things. Business connections, deals. I knew he dealt in bootlegged liquor, but in those days, that was no sin. If anything, it was virtue of a contrarian sort, the kind I understood well. He had also made considerable investments in stock, he said. I asked him to teach me how to invest, and soon I'd set up my own account through Nick—so I could get in on the party.

If I was careful to have at-the-ready excuses for my afternoon absences, I was careless with my mood. Although I started the summer melancholic and slow, I couldn't keep a smile off my face now, and I practically danced through the house with Pamela whenever we played together.

Tom commented on my change in mood one afternoon after I'd been giggling so hard with Pamela that I collapsed in tears after running races with her in the hall.

Tom stood and stared with narrowed eyes as I laughed uncontrollably on the floor.

"You've changed," he said, and it wasn't clear he thought it was for good or ill.

"I'm...I'm happy here," I offered, and as soon as the words came out of my mouth, I worried I had misspoken. Tom seemed to yank things away from me if he knew I liked them. Though I had not fallen in love with Chicago, I hadn't liked the idea of moving, unless it was back to Louisville. The more I'd argued for a Kentucky destination, the more committed he'd become to our relocation in New York. He had said it was for business,

DAISY

but Tom did no real business that I could see at that point of our lives. He enjoyed pretending he had his finger in this or that, just so he didn't feel left out. That's why Gatsby's connections excited him so. He finally did get to be around the rulers of Wall Street, of commerce, and they treated him like an equal.

When we moved here, I'd heard the rumors. He had gotten us out of Chicago because of a mistress whose brother was a mobster or something comparable. I couldn't keep all of his infidelities straight. Perhaps he thought prolonged absence and physical distance would tamp down her ire at his refusal to leave me for her.

I wondered sometimes how strongly he would feel about that over the years—not leaving me.

"Well, you've worked up poor Pammy," he said, pointing to our daughter, who was out of my arms and jumping up and down for more foot races. "Where's Nanny?"

I stood, dropped my smile, and called for our daughter's minder, who came round the corner and grabbed Pamela by the hand, leading her to the nursery for her afternoon snack.

"You've worked yourself up, too," he said, and I pushed an errant lock from my eyes. "You look feverish. Are you sure you're all right?"

I was more than all right. I was gloriously, exuberantly happy. But obviously, those moods were not permitted in our household, at least not for me.

"I'm perfectly fine, dear. But you look a little peaked," I said, walking toward the stairs.

"Maybe we should have Dr. Prinz come look in on you." he called after me, with narrowed eyes.

So now I knew that Tom preferred me unhappy, or at least melancholic, and I would have to cover my gladness if I didn't want to arouse suspicions. So I began pretending horrible headaches or other odd ailments from time to time. I also set up luncheons with family—Nick—and friends—Jordan and some of her golfing colleagues—where I could loll about as if everything was a bother and I was bored with all the world had to offer. I even talked of taking a cure somewhere, maybe in Europe.

That thought intrigued me. I longed to get away, to leave behind pretense and bask in a happiness I didn't have to hide.

My life became what I'd imagined it would be long ago, filled with happiness and pleasure. Mornings I spent with wifely and motherly tasks. I planned meals with Cook, chose linens, picked place settings. Then I'd spend time with dear Pamela, taking her for walks when Nanny was occupied, reading to her, even teaching her to play some basic notes on the piano. Occasionally, I went on shopping sprees, buying her new clothes, even some jewelry, and treating myself to a new treasure along the way.

And the afternoons were just for me, golden times for a golden girl, sailing, lounging, making love with Jay, worshiped by Jay, adored by Jay.

For once, I was glad Tom had other temptations in his life and often went into the city, or went riding, or otherwise occupied himself. I didn't know if he was still seeing the Wilson woman or some other wench. At that point, I cared so little about him that I didn't even bother to ask Nick.

Nick and Jordan were the only two who knew of my affair with Jay, and though I sensed that Nick didn't approve, he never said anything to me about it other than to comment that Gatsby's new staff didn't seem to keep the lawns as well manicured as before. Jordan, I knew, approved.

DAISY

What you have to understand about Nick is that he could be something of a prude. In his telling of our story, I'm a sexless nymph, and you're lucky if you can conjure up a flesh and blood image of me. I'm an alien creature whose daughter sprang fully formed from my rib at age three, I supposed.

But back then, it would have been shocking to say too much about the intimacies of married life, of lovers' lives. So I can understand how in that first iteration of the tale, Nick pulled the curtain on details most audiences weren't prepared to see.

So I will correct some of those omissions with this: Jay was a wonderful lover, gentle and eager and never going beyond what he sensed I wanted to do, yet still a manly partner with no inhibitions about his own pleasure.

I knew I was living in a dream, a paradise whose snake could soon offer someone an apple too appealing not to eat, tossing us all out into a cold and judgmental universe. I forcefully pushed that knowledge from my mind. I willed the summer to last forever. I willed Tom to leave me alone. I willed Jay to keep loving me.

Finally, as August approached, both the men in my life pulled me from the heights back to the ground, and as I floated down to my perch, I had to decide: Do I stay with Tom, or do I leave with Jay?

CHAPTER SEVEN

Jordan sat across from me at L'Aiglon on Fifty-Fifth Street, puffing on a cigarette as she perused the menu. I had set up this luncheon, suggesting we go shopping in the morning, then have a nice meal. We'd spent an enjoyable hour wandering Fifth Avenue shops but saw nothing except some new hats that suited our fancy. Those were to be delivered the next day, and I felt a sense of accomplishment for finding something to buy when the purpose of this meeting wasn't to acquire things but to seek advice on discarding men. Or at least one man.

We placed our orders for lamb chops and asparagus with Hollandaise sauce, then Jordan sat back, peered at me, and breathed out a plume of smoke.

"Speak," she said, and I smiled.

"I want to leave Tom," I said.

At that, she nodded, and her lack of surprise buoyed me. "Jay wants to move to Europe. He thinks we'll feel more free there."

Again, she nodded, but this time it annoyed me because it felt as if she had known I should do this all along but hadn't bothered to let me in on her secret plan for me. I paused, and she finally spoke. "You don't want to go?"

"Oh, yes, I do. I would love to go. The problem is, Tom wants to go, too."

At that, she chuckled, then stubbed out her cigarette as she leaned into the table. "With you and Jay, I assume."

DAISY

I giggled and gave a fake shudder. "No, thank God. One man is enough." Then I frowned, realizing my problem. One man *was* enough, and, at the moment, I had two.

"So Tom wants to go to Europe—another Tour? Didn't you just get back from one?" she pressed.

I nodded. "Last year. It was lovely. I think Tom felt cheated, though, with everything still being a bit awful after the war. He says things are better now, more cleaned up."

Jordan smirked. "How clever of those French to tidy everything up for him."

I ignored her sarcasm. "I'd love to go. To get away. I wasn't really keen on moving East, you know. Tom had told me we'd move back to Louisville at some point, and then he bought the house in East Egg without even telling me." I didn't go on about the reasons. I was sure Jordan already knew the sordid tale of the mobster's sister. Tom seemed to like playing in that world, and I wondered if the risk of it thrilled him. Maybe he'd mistaken Myrtle for a gangster's moll, and that's what had attracted him to her.

"You never seemed like a New York girl to me," she said, "but I love the city. I might get a permanent place here."

"Oh, but I do love New York. I think I'd prefer being in the city. Sometimes I feel so cut off from everything. Tom didn't consult me before we moved here, and I thought, if we did move, it would be back home."

"Home," she repeated, her mouth twitching up at the corner. I wondered if she considered any place home. "Do go on, though," she continued. "About wanting to get away."

"From Tom," I amended.

"You do that already, though, don't you? Get away from Tom? I thought you were enjoying all that mightily. He's not on to you, is he?"

For Jordan, it was as simple as that. I had a good thing going. Keep it going. If she saw nothing wrong in what Tom did, she would not judge me, either.

I chewed at my lip, wondering if I was the one in the wrong. I wanted only one man, and I didn't want to have him only on the sly.

"I don't want to keep doing this," I said softly. "I'm not like Tom. I can't keep…pretending."

"Are you pretending, though? You have a perfectly sweet life with Tom and Pamela, and an equally exquisite one with Jay. There's no pretense in that, dear."

I frowned. Sometimes Jordan's frankness could be maddening. "I can't be like Tom," I repeated. "I won't."

She accepted that, even if she didn't agree with my rationale. "So you need to choose between them? If that's it, let's draw up some cards, score each man according to value and skills. Where shall we start?" Her voice gained enthusiasm as she talked, and she pulled up her handbag and withdrew from it an old golf card, on the back of which she began to write with a stub of a pencil. "Amorous abilities?" she suggested with a mischievousness lopsided grin.

I smiled. "Oh, Jordan, you are exactly what I need right now. It's a serious problem, but it weighs me down. I need to be lifted up."

"You need a cocktail, and so do I, but that will have to wait." She leaned in again. "Let's do get serious, though. I have no preferences on who you should be with. I see both men's flaws and both men's virtues. Or

DAISY

rather, their values. Tom is good-looking, from a great family, has money. Jay is good-looking, a man of the times, has money. They both love you—"

"Tom?" I interrupted with a cynical laugh.

"You equate fidelity with love. He doesn't. Now, close your eyes and tell me, who do you see yourself with, years from now? Old and withered, gray hair, sagging skin, raspy voice?"

I did as she said, closing my eyes with a smile on my face. "Do I need to sway? Perhaps chant something? Is this like a séance?"

"Yes. But don't be too loud. We are in a public place, and I'm quite hungry and would like to eat before we're kicked out."

Still smiling, I said, "Okay. I see myself with…Jay. No, Tom. No, Jay. No…" I sighed, opened my eyes, and said, "Pamela."

"There's a story," she said. "Tell it." But then our meals arrived. We both paused as the steaming plates were set in front of us.

"Jay never asks about her," I said. "I sometimes think he forgets I have a daughter. He's so eager to have us be who we were years ago, before my marriage, before Pamela."

"Do you talk about her?" she asked after taking a bite of lamb.

"Rarely. I guess I don't because he seems so disinterested, and I don't want to spoil the mood."

"So you don't think his European plan includes her? Is that what you're saying?" She took a drink of water and I took the time to eat, though my appetite wasn't keen.

Avoiding a direct answer, I went on, "Tom, on the other hand, would probably fight tooth and nail to keep her. Not because she means as much to him—though I know he adores her—but because it would be a way of punishing me."

Jordan frowned, dabbing at her mouth with a napkin. "Tom, he's never physically hurt you, has he?"

"Oh, no, no!" I said. "I did hear the most delicious story of him hitting that Wilson witch, though. I have to admit it made me happy. Felt like I was the one throwing the punch."

She put down her fork and stretched her tan arm toward mine, placing her hand on my wrist. "Listen to you," she said seriously. "You like the idea of smacking around his mistress. Is it because you still love him?"

Now it was my turn to frown. "No! I mean, not enough. I just don't like him betraying me."

"You are kind of doing the same thing, though. I'm not judging you, just pointing out the truth. I think it's fine you've been seeing Jay. You're happy again."

"But Tom…" *Started it*, I'd been about to say, to justify my own infidelity. I pushed at the food on my plate, sighed again, and sat back. "I don't know what to do. This summer, it's been like magic. It's reawakened me. I feel part of life again. I want things. I hope for things. I'm ready to…to change."

Jordan cocked her head to one side, holding her fork in midair. "How so?"

"I just know I'm tired of things the way they are, and I'm not going to keep living a life I don't much like." It had been the life I'd aspired to, but as I looked back to my pre-marital days, I realized now that I'd made false assumptions. I assumed that life would take on more meaning once I was married, and then, once I had a child, an even deeper meaning. I married and had a child, and yet meaning remained elusive, and while that wouldn't have bothered me so much just a couple years ago, it began to

DAISY

erode any happiness I did happen to experience. It colored everything. It raised questions: So what? To what end?

"That sounds rather drastic, dear, talking of melancholy when you're something of a pampered princess." She ate for a few moments, then said, "I apologize. I shouldn't make light of it. I know you've been unhappy. Tom can be an absolute boor at times, and Gatsby—well, I think there are a thousand women who'd swoon at the possibility of being the object of his attention. So I do understand, really. I suppose what might help is if you start thinking of technicalities. Not being on the eighteenth hole but plotting how you get to the eighteenth hole, shot by shot."

"Is that what you do?" I asked her.

"Yes. Until I reach the point where a little slip of my toe might help nudge things in the right direction." She smirked again. Jordan had been accused of cheating on the links, but it had never been proven. To that day, I didn't know if she was innocent or not. If guilty, she probably didn't think of it as cheating but just another way to play the game. Then again, she might have enjoyed the thought that some people assumed she had cheated even if she hadn't. It made them fear her.

Nevertheless, Jordan was right. It was time to stop dreaming and start planning. And the first hole would have to be Jay's acceptance of Pamela. I would have to risk spoiling the mood to rid myself of anxiety. It would take courage, something I was beginning to realize I had little of. It had been the reason I'd married Tom. The reason I stayed with him. The reason I hated thinking of sacrificing a scintilla of happiness by forcing Jay to accept me as a mother of a beautiful girl, not just as a lover.

We finished our meals and went to the car: Tom's little coupe, which he'd let me take for our excursion into the city. It had been glorious fun driving it. I was a good driver, just as I was a good sailor.

As I pushed the car into gear and began our journey home, Jordan asked, "Do you still have it? The letter?"

I knew what she was talking about, the crumpled bit of paper Jay had sent me and I received on the eve of my wedding. The one he'd asked about the night we'd made love, at Nick's house when I'd pretended I'd gotten it but not read it.

"Yes," I said, my eyes on the road ahead.

INTERLUDE
1918

On the day Jay shipped out, I was sure I'd see him again. His own self-confidence seemed to block out all doubt and fear. He had been to our house for dinner several times before then, and both my parents took to him, though Mother more than Father. She liked his cheerful ambition, she said. It reminded her of her grandfather, who, unlike my father, who'd inherited money, had made his fortune by owning and buying several stores, and had always been keen on the future, even during troubled times, she told me.

Jay talked about his plans after the war, and he sounded ever more optimistic—he would own a railroad company or maybe an oil field or perhaps a car manufacturer since he knew a good deal about the process.

He seemed so sure of himself that you found yourself focusing on his post-war ideas instead of the battles he faced, as well as accepting as fact that he would return unscathed.

When we said our final farewells the night before he was to leave, he wouldn't let me get teary. He lifted my chin up and said, "I'll write you every week, every day, and I'll keep your picture and lock of hair in my pocket. Don't you worry, Daisy. I'll stay true to my word."

But no letter came a week later, or two weeks after that, or even a month beyond his departure.

DAISY

I ran to the mailbox every day to see what was in it. I received letters from Rupert and Andrew, but nothing from Jay. I wrote him. At least at the beginning.

Lilith heard from her fiancé, and Candace from hers, and then came the devastating news that Helen Beaufort's Theodore died in combat. Shortly after that, word arrived that Dewitt had been grievously injured and might never see again.

The world turned black. I walked to the mailbox timidly, slowly, expecting to receive a letter with bad news from one of Jay's friends. Either that, or I had to face the fact that he had lied to me and didn't love me at all, that his battle duty was an escape from entanglement with me. Both scenarios covered my days with grim dreariness.

You would think from Nick's recounting of our story that we didn't face heartache except of our own making, that we didn't face dramatic losses and awful events that took lives and futures. In his account, he ignored the war years, maybe intentionally, because he, like some men, didn't like to talk about them. Once U.S. involvement produced an armistice, so many wanted just to forget and move on, embracing a wild hedonism to scour out the wounds.

But the war colored everything that happened afterward, in personal lives or general history. The war and the sickness that overlapped its ending had us all reeling. It seemed so pointless, all that suffering. What was gained? If I'd been cynical before about the patriotic fervor that sent men into the mauling war machine, I was even more jaded after. Nothing seemed to matter.

Every day crawled by. Yet every sunrise I wished the days would last longer so that I might receive news—some news, any news.

I worried the army wouldn't know to contact me about Jay, or where. We weren't formally engaged though he'd talked of marriage and it had been understood we'd be together when he returned. He'd given me a small ring, something simple that had belonged to his grandmother, he said, a thin gold band with a tiny pearl. It was too big, so I wore it on a chain around my neck.

I stopped going to dances. I made myself sick with worry. I wrote letters to the army to ask about him, but then tore them up before mailing, disgusted with my pathetic pleading.

Staying away from social events seemed the patriotic thing to do now, so I could hide my sadness behind a mask of responsibility.

My father became distracted by all of it, and retreated to his study early every evening, sometimes even eating dinner alone there, his mood glum.

This went on for months as 1917 dragged into the new year until Mother stood in my bedroom door and ordered me to stop moping.

"You can't do a thing about him," she announced, "and Jeanine March is hosting a party this weekend for her daughter, who's marrying next month. We'll all go. You know her—Claire."

So we went. It was such an unusually cold night that I simply couldn't get warm even though I wore a dark blue long-sleeved serge dress and draped a Russian shawl over my shoulders.

The Marches owned a huge house—much larger than ours—on the outskirts of town. Mrs. March had rearranged their very large parlor for dancing, with furniture pushed up against the walls, and a table set up with refreshments. Claire had forgone a coming-out party due to the war, I'd heard, so her mother must have been making up for it with this big and lavish event. There had to have been close to two hundred people there.

DAISY

I stood in the corner, alone, when Tom came in. Confident, smiling, a girl on his arm, he barely looked at me. Then Mrs. March brought him over after the girl wandered off to talk to some friends.

"This is my cousin's boy from Chicago, Thomas Buchanan," she said. "He's here for the wedding."

When she left us alone, he poured me some punch and proceeded to spike his with some liquor, which he also offered to me. I accepted. I accepted another after that, and soon we were laughing; I hadn't laughed in months! We escaped the chill of that vast parlor, and he drove me in a smart cruiser down to the river, where he became very fresh, and I became very loose.

I missed Jay. I thought he was never coming back. I thought he was gone, like Helen's fiancé, like so many others. I was tired of being despondent. I let Tom take me, on our very first meeting, even though my heart wasn't in it.

Tom not only stayed for the wedding. He lingered in Louisville for weeks after that. He often came around to see me, and I was smart enough to know that it was my willingness to make love to him that probably drove his attraction.

We drank and had sex. That was our relationship. I was happy to lose myself in liquor then, though I stopped short of inebriation. That would come later. Drinking soothed the hurt of losing Jay.

When I asked Tom his plans for returning to Chicago, he said he would go back to see his family and then return to Louisville.

"Oh, what for?" I asked him. "What will bring you back here?"

"To get married," he said. "I'll return to marry."

"Marry?" I asked, surprised he was so bold about double-timing me and his fiancée, whoever she was. "Who will you marry? Do I know her?"

"Why, it's you, you silly little fool." He tapped my nose. "I'll marry you."

I scoffed, even attempted to walk away, but he held on to my hand and said, "Would that be so awful, Daisy? Marrying me? I'm not a bad man, you know."

He was true to his word. He courted me with a ferocity both charming and fearsome. He cheerfully showed up with flowers, chocolates, silk scarves, and jewelry. When he did return to Chicago, he wrote letter after letter, and in my mind they took the place of the ones I didn't get from Jay. The day after I read of a particularly ghastly battle in France, I took off the necklace with his ring and put it away permanently. I felt a fool for thinking he could possibly have survived.

I was convinced he was dead. Maybe at that point, I even wanted that to be the case. I just wanted to know, to be sure, so I could move on.

My mother and father liked Tom; he came from a respectable, well-established family.

"You could do much worse, and you can't wait forever," my mother told me one night. "Tom has spoken to your father."

I did love Tom. Not in the same open-hearted way I'd loved Jay, but more than I'd felt for Rupert or Andrew, and by then I'd heard that Rupert, too, was dead. He, of the poor eyesight and cartography skills, had been in a headquarters building in France when a German mortar hit it.

DAISY

I cried over his death. I wept out all my grief for Jay. The very next day, Tom asked for my hand, and I enthusiastically said yes. Jay would want me to go on with life, I reasoned, and I temporarily put him out of my head.

When Tom proposed, it was at the club after a polo match he had played there, and he gave me a stunning diamond ring circled with emeralds and more diamonds. He'd intended on giving it to me at a romantic dinner later, he said, but his victory on the polo field had him feeling exuberant and ready to conquer the world, starting with me.

I no longer felt fresh and young. I felt a bit used up, and once, even Tom hinted we better be careful about our lovemaking, or people would gossip and my reputation would be ruined.

I had told Jay I wanted to be a princess. I couldn't very well do that without a prince, and Tom was as close to an American one as I would get. His family dated back to the Mayflower, had money by the bushel full, and a name that opened doors from Chicago to New York.

We made plans to marry quickly in the fall. Mother consulted Mrs. Dale, who selected a fine white silk dress with beaded embroidery on its dropped bodice and a filmy floor-length veil held in place by a white rose garland to adorn my head.

Our parlor would be the setting, and Jordan, with whom I'd become good friends the summer before, would be my maid of honor. Flowers were ordered, the menu planned, dinners held to introduce our families to each other. It all happened in a rush— from proposal to vows, a scant six weeks. In those days, fast weddings were as common as long engagements. No one begrudged a couple their happiness.

By this time sickness had crept into our lives. Helen Beaufort came down with the flu and died within a week. Lilith caught it and was bedridden for a month. Barely surviving, she became frail and oddly distant after. Candace too was afflicted, and though she survived, she seemed slower and gentler, no longer capable of the mental lists she had kept before.

Death, it seemed, was everywhere, and if I wasn't reading obituaries of classmates killed in the war, I was hearing stories of civilian friends who had taken to their sick beds.

It didn't matter that the war was ending. Its scythe had cut down everything good in life.

Getting ready for the dinner the night before my nuptials, however, when I'd at last reasoned Jay was gone from my life, maybe from all life, a shock came, delivered by the postman a little before three. I'd awakened from a nap and gone downstairs to get a glass of lemonade before asking the maid to draw my bath.

It was unseasonably warm, even though it was fall, and the light coming through our front door's pebbled glass had an eerie golden-brown hue, as if the sun itself had become an autumn leaf, changing color for the season.

I remember hearing the clock strike the hour as I passed the little table in the foyer, and there, on top of the day's mail, was an envelope of the thinnest paper, with a military return address.

My heart raced. Though I'd long expected bad news about Jay, I faced its reality now. Sure to find a note from a friend telling me of Jay's death, I grabbed the envelope and rushed up the steps again, tears already burning my eyelids as I anticipated grief.

You knew this would happen, I told myself. At least you'll now be sure. You won't wonder any longer. At least that pain will be gone.

Mother was resting, and Father was running an errand. The help was elsewhere in our big house. I was alone.

DAISY

I opened my bedroom door, went to the window seat overlooking the back garden, took a deep breath, and slit the envelope with my fingernail.

Tears came, flowing down my cheeks and spotting my mauve linen dress, as I read:

Dear Daisy,

Darling, can you believe it? I've been writing to you for months now and only just found out you weren't getting a single letter! When you stopped writing, I was sure something awful had happened, but then a nice lady across town from you wrote me back that no Daisy Faye lived at the address I was sending my letters to! She said she'd tried notifying the military, but word never came to me until recently.

I'm pretty sure I have the right address now and you'll write back. I have thought of you every day. It didn't take long to get "over here" after what seemed a year of training and waiting. Now everything is in a hurry and rumors abound that we're going home or facing battle again.

After I left you, I couldn't forget your forlorn face, and nothing on earth would make me happier than to see you again and hold you in my arms, sitting quiet and soft and sweet on the swing of your front porch.

I will be thinking of that time and you, in the days to come. If, God willing, I do come home alive and whole, I know you will still be there, waiting with open arms.

Can you imagine it, dear? Me in uniform with my kit bag walking up the steps to your door? Can you see yourself standing there and jumping up and down a little, the way you would when you got excited about something?

I can.

That's what holds my spirits up, and it's what, I'm sure, will keep me alive, knowing you'll be waiting when I return, just like you promised. Many fellows here don't have a girl back home, and I feel awfully sorry for them. They don't fight the same way as those of us with a girl to get back to. All of you ladies keep us going, and I think of you and kiss your picture every night— the same with that sweet lock of hair that still smells like your perfume— every time it looks like we're headed into battle....

I don't know how long I sat there, rereading his letter, thinking of what was to come—my wedding to Tom.

Jay was alive. He could still be in harm's way. And my fidelity was all it took to keep him alive.

I'd failed him.

At some point, as shadows became longer, as the clock chimed another hour, I bestirred myself. I ran downstairs and found a bottle of bourbon.

I simply couldn't marry Tom. I couldn't do it.

With shaking hands, I poured myself a tumbler. And then another. And another.

I cried some more. The maid came in, looked at me curiously, and said she'd draw my bath. I told her not to bother.

She scurried out of the room, and I heard her calling my mother.

At some point, Jordan arrived, and she looked at the nearly empty bottle of liquor and shook her head.

"Oh, Daisy," she said, and wrapped her arms around me. "Let's get you into a warm bath, shall we?"

Mother was in the room now too—how did she get there? Muddled by booze and grief, I couldn't keep track of time.

She and Jordan practically carried me upstairs, one on either side of me, Mother saying something about nervous brides and obligations, and Jordan whispering that it would be all right.

DAISY

I let them shepherd me. I had no idea what was happening. Jordan said she would telephone to the hotel where Tom's family was staying to let them know we'd be late for the family dinner they'd planned that evening in the hotel restaurant. She went downstairs to place the call.

As I undressed, the doorbell rang. Soon, Jordan appeared in my bedroom, holding a blue velvet box decorated with a gold ribbon. I stood by my bed, naked, paralyzed, Jay's letter crumpled on the floor.

"It's from Tom," she said, and when I didn't move, she pulled at the bow and opened the box. A stunning pearl necklace lay on a satin cloth. Again, when I didn't move, she pulled out a note, and read a sweet message from Tom to go with this gift for his bride.

"I can't do it," I sobbed, now sitting on the bed, my head in my hands. "J-J-Jay's alive. Oh, God, he's still alive!"

Just as my mother came in the room, Jordan saw the letter on the floor and picked it up. She read it silently as my mother fussed.

"Daisy, you'll catch your death of cold! Here, let's get your robe." She brought over a pink silk kimono and pressed it around my shoulders. "Your bath is ready."

She walked me to the bathroom, Jordan following.

"I'll stay with her, Mrs. Faye," she said softly, and closed the door. Like an automaton, I moved forward and slid into the sudsy bath, wanting to sink below its surface and not have to think at all.

"I can't do it," I repeated, not to her, but to the room, to the universe. "If I marry Tom, Jay will die!"

"Oh, Daisy, what nonsense," Jordan said, pulling up a cushioned chair, and placing her hand on my arm. "Look at me."

Turning my head slowly, I peered into her eyes. "You read the letter. He thinks of me. I keep him alive. What will happen when he learns I…" I couldn't finish it.

"Nothing will happen. You don't even know what's happening now. Listen to me, Daisy. You will marry Tom. You will be happy. Jay will be happy, too. He will live or not and it won't have a single thing to do with you. Not a thing."

"But—"

"You can't ruin your life because of one letter. Stay true to your promise to Tom. I know you love him. You told me so."

I had told Jordan that, but I think I did so to convince myself it was true. When I thought Jay was gone for good, I'd consciously moved my affection to Tom.

"Think of that—how you have come to love Tom. Don't toss that aside for one letter. For all you know…"

"Don't say it!" I shouted. "I won't think Jay's dead again. I won't!"

Undaunted, she went on: "Tom adores you."

From the hall, my mother's voice called, "Is everything all right? We need to be going soon."

At that, Jordan picked up a washcloth and started bathing me, as if I were a child, her gentle hands caressing my body as I closed my eyes and tried to gather rational thoughts. None would come.

Eventually, she helped me stand and dried me off, then brushed my hair. Jordan could be very tender underneath her gruff exterior, and she treated me as if I were a fragile invalid, offering cooing encouragement.

She led me back to my room, while my mother, her brow furrowed, stood silently outside in the hall. Then she helped me dress. When she put

DAISY

Tom's pearls around my neck, though, I couldn't bear it, and yanked them free. They scattered to the floor.

Jordan didn't judge. She didn't even cluck her tongue. "He can buy you another one." She stepped back and gazed at me. "There, you look beautiful. We'll tell Tom you've been suffering from a headache, but, Daisy, you will get through this. It's one night and one day, and then…then you can decide what to do. For now, marry Tom. Don't ruin your life."

Somehow I did get through it—the dinner that night, the wedding the next day. Jordan's words—*don't ruin your life*—echoed in my heart and mind every moment. When I was about to falter, she would appear by my elbow and whisper encouragement or ask how I was feeling. For all Tom's family knew, I was suffering from a splitting headache.

I had never felt such a burden before. It was as if, with every step I took up the aisle to wed Tom, I would be firing the shots that would surely kill that loyal soldier, Jay.

My fidelity was the only cost of keeping him alive—my true love, which I so recklessly promised him and then threw to Tom when I was afraid no one decent would be left to take it.

It was the one hard thing I had been asked to do in my easy life so far, the one thing that required courage—wait for Jay. Yet I'd failed in that task. Failed miserably.

Other women waited patiently for their loves to return from war. Why hadn't I been able to do so, too?

This revelation made me sick with self-loathing, and part of me wondered if my punishment was this marriage. I had allowed Tom to buy me, with a promise of safety, security, and peace. The pearls were just a symbol of that price.

Mother and Jordan worked hard to help me recover and be presentable that evening and the next day. At some point, I knew Mother had seen the letter. I think she assumed it stayed in the trash bin, but I'd retrieved it after the dinner party was over, flattened it out, wept some more, kissed my fingers to it, then folded it neatly and shoved it into a far corner of my luggage.

I knew I had to marry Tom. And I felt I was dooming Jay by doing so. I consoled myself by thinking I'd not answer Jay's letter, not tell him of my marriage, and if he should write again—which he did—Mother could send him the news of the wedding. She would know what to say.

So, I married, had the largest and most glamorous reception afterward, then went on a honeymoon, where I forced the past into a box I refused to open. I forced myself to fall in love with Tom.

When we returned to Louisville all tanned and happy for a post-honeymoon visit, my mother took me aside and said she had "taken care of the matter, and that man would not bother me again."

CHAPTER EIGHT

Now I read the letter again in my bathroom, sitting on the gilt vanity chair, door latched, the present and future locked out, only the past intruding.

It still bore the wrinkled marks of the crumpling I'd given it, and a lot of the ink was smeared from bathwater.

This past week, Jay told me what my mother had done to deter him from pursuing me further. She'd sent him clippings of our wedding—it had been written up in major newspapers—and told him, in the sweetest note, he said, that I was married and happy and she'd not given me his pleading letter for fear of upsetting me. My mother, a devout Methodist who never missed church, told an outright lie.

A lie I compounded, of course, by being deliberately vague when Jay asked me if I had received it. So he still believed my mother's story was true, that the letter had "arrived" the night before my wedding, but I'd not seen his heartfelt plea, I'd not deliberately and consciously rejected him. I'm not sure precisely what else he believed. I was too afraid to ask. All he admitted was that he was "mighty disappointed" to hear of my marriage and assumed it was an arranged thing. I didn't disabuse him of that lie.

Why couldn't I be honest with him? With any man? With myself? I wanted to be. I wanted to stay true.

Jordan had cautioned me not to ruin my life when she'd urged me to go through with the wedding to Tom. However, it felt as if I'd done that very thing. I'd ruined it by not waiting for Jay.

DAISY

Pulling myself together, I stood, a resolution forming in my mind. Still holding the crumpled letter, I went back into my bedroom and gazed at my wedding photograph on the dresser by the door. In it, Tom stood straight and proud, his arm looped through mine. I looked pale and ill, but there was more than one reason for that and it was not just Jay's untimely letter or the knowledge he had written many more I'd never received.

My dress was simple and loose for good reason. I had been expecting our first child. Jordan had known, and my mother suspected.

I lost that baby at five months, shortly after our honeymoon, and the doctor told me then I was unlikely to carry a child to term after that.

He was wrong, and when Pamela was conceived, I was filled with joy and fear. Tom's ardor for me had waned considerably by then, so it was only by great luck that his passion burned at the right moment and darling Pammy was the result. I determined to do everything in my power to make sure this child thrived.

I also knew by then that my marriage to Tom was less than perfect. I knew he found pleasure in other women's arms, and I felt like a fool for not realizing this would be my fate, to be the betrayed wife. After all, he'd quickly bedded me. Why would he have any reservations about taking other women he wanted? It was a habit of his.

We had traveled to Europe by then, and he'd had a lover or two while there, I was sure, judging by the smug glances he sent to singers in smoky jazz clubs and a young female reporter we met at a dinner in Paris.

Yet, I stayed true. I decided that I would never give myself so freely again, that Tom was my husband, and I would remain faithful. I embraced it with the zeal of a religious convert. It was a form of revenge: to be what he couldn't be. I knew he was aware of my virtue and resented it.

But I knew he'd resent my infidelity to him even more.

At least I had Pamela. That beautiful creature had come from all this turmoil.

A sob crawled up my throat and almost choked me, and reflexively I felt my hand crumpling the letter once more into a ball. I let out a feral cry and ripped the paper into little pieces, not wanting it to haunt me any longer.

Then I pulled the photograph from its silver frame and consigned it to the same fate, its waxy fragments joining Jay's letter in the trash bin.

The past thus destroyed, I drew my own bath and sank into a field of lavender bubbles, where I stayed until I declined the request to come down to dinner.

Jordan was right. I needed to make a plan. With details, not just vague notions.

Tomorrow afternoon, I'd ring up Nick and this time, I would be the one arranging the rendezvous at his home. For me, him, Jay…and Pamela.

CHAPTER NINE

It was dismal. Not the weather this time, but the atmosphere—the day I'd set up a meeting with Jay at Nick's so he could meet my daughter, maybe even come to love her.

I'd brought a few playthings with me for Pamela to enjoy, but she was in a fussy mood that afternoon. We were meeting during her usual nap time because of when I could get away without Tom knowing what I was doing.

I'd told Tom that Pamela's "Uncle Nick" had proposed a tea party for her, and gushed over how thoughtful it was of my cousin to treat our sweet little princess, and I hope he didn't mind but I'd told Nick I didn't think Tom would be interested in coming. I held my breath until Tom nodded over his morning paper and then went out for the rest of the day.

I dressed Pammy in one of her sweetest dresses, a white smock with embroidered blue rocking horses around the hem and a "Peter Pan" collar and blue bow tie with long ribbons ending in blue beads. I combed her feathery blond hair and secured it with a silver butterfly barrette, though I knew it was unlikely to stay in place for long. She had my fine, wispy hair, which had been an annoyance for my own nanny when I was young.

She was as pretty as could be, and I was proud of her, and when Jay first set eyes on her as we walked up to Nick's cottage, I was pleased to see him grinning in genuine appreciation. At least the afternoon got off to a good start.

DAISY

Even under the best of circumstances, though, having a social event with children underfoot presents a challenge. Children were usually sent away to play after a short appearance among guests. You could then be admired for producing such beautiful offspring without being bothered by the messiness and noise of having them nearby.

Yet here we were, trapped for at least an hour with nowhere for Pamela to go and conversation difficult, as she often interrupted, or I had to see to her.

Jay sat awkwardly on the settee and tried to talk with her.

"You're a pretty little thing," he said, smiling, his hands on his knees. "You look just like your mother."

Pamela responded with silence as she positioned a brightly colored block on top of another, then pouted when they both fell, and wailed when she hit her head on the table's edge as she tried to retrieve the bunch.

After picking her up to soothe her, I placed her in my lap.

"There, there, sweetie. It's nothing. We all fall sometimes." I kissed her head and looked over at Jay. "Actually, she has Tom's eyes," I said.

At that observation, Jay recoiled. It was just the slightest movement, a little crinkling about his eyes and pulling back, but I saw it.

Nick, who was our host, came into the room with a tray of treats—some cookies and small cakes—and a pot of tea. He did not put into use the beautiful rose and gold china of my first meeting here with Jay, but a sturdier white porcelain with no adornment.

"Would you like some, honey?" I asked, and she nodded, still sniffling over her recent hurt.

If I had thought this part of the day would go more smoothly, I was quickly disappointed. Despite my best efforts, Pammy spilled her tea after first almost burning herself on it because it was too hot. This elicited a comment from Jay that she had ruined her pretty dress. At that, she pouted and cried. Then she insisted on having more cakes than I told her she could have, and in the interest of peace, I gave in to her demand.

"You should listen to your mother," Jay announced, as she reached for an iced sweet. "You'll get a stomach ache if you don't."

She popped the cake in her mouth and looked at him as if he were the most foolish man on earth.

After that, she decided to explore Nick's home and toddled off down the hallway. A crash soon followed, and when I ran to fetch her, I saw she had pulled at a towel on the kitchen table, resulting in a pile of cutlery landing on the floor, which she seemed to think were toys meant just for her. Upon returning to the parlor, I scooped her up with some spoons that occupied her for a little while.

By the time the hour was over, I could hardly wait to leave. Jay eventually gave up trying to interact with Pamela and instead ended up treating the appointment as if I were there alone, or rather, just with Nick.

But as he started conversations about stocks, news, music, or his car, Pamela would somehow always manage to grab my attention, and I would have to tend to her, keep her from going out the door, and follow her as she wanted to explore Nick's house again, asking questions.

I was frazzled and eager to leave when I finally picked her up and headed for the door, and I could tell that Jay had enjoyed our get-together as little as I had.

As we said farewell, he started to lean toward me to give me a kiss, but I pulled back and offered my hand, nodding toward Pamela, who would

DAISY

surely report a kiss to Daddy at some point in her garbled-toddler language. He understood but grimaced, and then said he hoped to see me soon.

The only thing that saved the event from being a complete failure was Pamela's farewell. She gave Jay a big grin and waved at him, without prompting. It gave me some hope that we could all enjoy being together sometime soon, after they got to know each other better.

The next afternoon, I did see Jay alone, and we didn't say a word about his session with Pamela. I didn't bring it up, and he acted as if it hadn't even happened. Once again, I lacked courage.

But by avoiding the subject, our hours together were unblemished by discord. I was an expert at pushing away conflict, even if part of me worried it would resurface at some time, that in fact it needed to resurface.

I left that day's rendezvous happy and hopeful, my skin still tingling from his touch, determined to try again to bring him round to loving Pamela as much as he loved me.

You see, as much as Tom liked Pammy to be out of his way, there was no doubt how much he loved her. His eyes lit up whenever he saw her. He seemed proud to have brought into the world such a sweet, beautiful creature.

I had to know Jay would one day feel the same about Pammy, and I approached it like an ordinary task.

Other tasks intruded, however, in the coming days. Specifically, how to stay out of the madhouse.

CHAPTER TEN

As I fell ever more deeply in love with Jay, I decided I needed to work harder to hide my ecstasy from Tom. He always seemed less suspicious if I was unhappy.

So several mornings I faked swooning about, seemingly uninterested in even getting out of bed, and powdering my face to an ashy pale shade.

But I couldn't hide everything I was feeling, and just two days after the tea at Nick's with Pamela and Jay, all the tension of my secret affair, my doubts, and my fears spilled over.

It started with a call from Myrtle. I heard the whole thing. I had picked up the phone just after Tom took the call, and listened in upstairs in my room.

Oh, the cooing from him, the low-class nagging from her, and when he said he might not be able to get away that day, her reply sent an arrow to my heart:

"Oh, Tommy baby, I misses you so much," she said in a simpering baby voice. "And I have some news to tell you. Babykins hasn't been feeling so well lately, and I might need to go to the doctor."

I heard Tom inhale sharply.

I grasped the phone, my fingers turning white from my grip.

"Myrtle, now, you know you have these agues…"

"Oh, it ain't no ague, sweetheart. Aren't you excited? I didn't want to say it on the phone, but you could be a daddy!"

"He was a daddy," I wanted to shout at the insolent bitch.

DAISY

"But you said you didn't go to the doctor yet?" he asked in a desperate voice. "So it might be a false alarm, darling."

An awful sound came over the line, and I realized she was crying.

"T-t-tom," she stuttered. "Don't be so mean to me. Come and see me, please. I don't know what I'll do if you don't come…"

"All right, all right. Let me see what I can do."

I hung up as soon as I heard his click, and I sat on the edge of the bed, seething.

Tears burned my eyes, but I shook my head and willed them away.

His mistress pregnant with his bastard?

Never! No one would threaten my daughter's place in his dynasty such as it was.

I was furious even at the possibility. I was a good mother. It was part of who I was now. I was Daisy Faye Buchanan, mother. Not just a lover. My attempt to get Jay to understand that failed. Now the father of my child was conspiring with another woman to displace that child? Never.

Rising, I paced to the window. I felt imprisoned. Earlier, I had hoped he'd go out for the afternoon. Now I didn't want him to. I wanted him to stay here and suffer, just like me.

I wanted to be the one racing out—over to Jay's, to tell him of this awful occurrence, and to have him reassure me that he would see to Pammy's future.

A soft knock at my door.

"Daisy? Are you awake?" Tom said through the door.

"I'm not feeling well," I said, no longer having to pretend to be upset.

"I'll be going into town. Business meeting. Don't hold dinner."

He sounded so casual, so unconcerned about me. The scoundrel.

Without thinking, I hurried to the door, threw it open, and pummeled my fists on his chest.

He grabbed my wrists and held them still. He cocked his head to one side and peered at me.

"Daisy, what on earth is the matter with you? Are you all right?"

"No, no, I'm not! Where are you going?"

"Just into town. Nothing to concern yourself with," he said, peering at me again as if searching for signs of illness.

"I want to go into town!" I said. I didn't, of course, but I was so damned tired of Tom being able to do whatever the hell he wanted while I had to pretend to be sick, and devise plans to fool him, plan to sneak out, even when he was away. I wanted that same freedom. He could drive off by simply announcing he was doing so. "Let me get a wrap," I said. "We can go together."

I managed to pull away and step back into my room, where I grabbed a bag as if to leave. While I was turned away, he closed the door. And locked it.

"You're not well, dear. You need to stay home. I'll call the doctor for you."

I stomped to the door, jiggling the knob to no avail. Its lock operated with a key on either side. Mine was gone.

Growling, I picked up the nearest object, my bedside lamp, and threw it at the door.

That loud crash provided me such satisfaction that I decided to replicate it. Destroying the things that showcased our wealth made me shiver with delight. I went round the room and smashed every piece of porcelain

DAISY

or china or glass I could find. Expensive figurines, lamps, a Wedgwood hairpin case.

I threw them at the walls, the mirror, which I also cracked, and then tossed shoes and clothes into my bathtub and lit a match to the pile. I wanted to dispose of it all, these signs of indulgence and luxury. Maybe if I literally burned them all, I would be able to walk away from what they offered me.

"Daisy! What's burning? Daisy?!" he yelled at last, and then the door opened, and he entered. He said nothing at first, just looked around, his mouth set in fury, his eyes slit. Then he glanced at the dying flames in the nearby bath and called for the maid.

"Bring buckets of water!" he shouted. By then, my little conflagration had nearly extinguished itself on its own, but soon a maid and the housekeeper rushed in and killed the embers with splashes of water.

At that moment, Nanny walked by with Pammy, now back from an outing. When she saw the scene, she started crying, then wailing and screaming, wanting to know what happened.

"Take her to her room," Tom instructed, waving his hand to indicate Pamela should be pulled away.

"Call Doctor Prinz," Tom told the housekeeper. He gave me a look of utter disgust but still left. My fit did nothing to keep him from going to his mistress. It just meant I couldn't go to my lover.

While unsuccessful in getting Tom to stay home, I did manage to get a syringe of some sort of sedative pumped into me within the hour, and it set me free in an odd way. Dr. Prinz, a middle-aged physician who prided himself on staying up to date with all the latest treatments, informed me that he would speak to my husband about "next steps." That sounded ominous.

Whatever he gave me had me floating over to Jay's through the clouds, and I fell into a dreamy sleep, where I imagined Jay making love to me throughout the night.

I must have been quite vocal during this hallucinatory lovemaking because the next morning, I heard Tom and Dr. Prinz outside my bedroom, after he had checked on me, talking about my "hypersexualized fantasies."

This had an undesirable effect.

Whatever Tom's situation with Myrtle, he must have decided that I was no longer a goddess if I could have such carnal thoughts, and he didn't try to beckon me to his bed. He came to mine three nights in a row.

No matter how many times I told him I wasn't in the mood for anything, he ignored me. I could lie there like a corpse, and that just seemed to fuel his passion.

These sessions left me truly ill and haggard each morning. I couldn't imagine going to Jay's because I felt I'd betrayed him and he would see it in my face, seen I had not been able to fend Tom off.

So now I became miserable. There was no need for pretense.

I didn't care if Myrtle was pregnant. At that point, I wanted Tom to go to her and promise her his undying love, as long as it would keep him away from me.

At last, after five days of imprisonment, I was set free.

Tom went into town and announced he'd not be back until the next day.

DAISY

I bathed. I dressed in one of the new outfits he delivered to replace my burnt ones, and I drove to Jay's.

I'd reclaim myself, even if now the pretense was acting sane, not mad.

"I'll kill him," Jay said in a low, angry voice I'd never heard him use. His fists clenched by my side as we lay in his bed together.

I'd wanted Jay's lovemaking to purify me in some way. His gentle and sweet kisses healed me.

But my bruises remained, and when he asked me how I'd gotten the ones visible on my wrists and arms, I told him simply that Tom had held me down.

"Down for what?" he asked.

I looked away and didn't answer.

He rose from the bed, grabbed a cigarette and robe, and went to the window to look at the Sound, or perhaps at our house across the way.

After smoking for a moment, he said, without looking at me. "You know Tom double-crossed Anthony."

"Anthony?" I sat up and reached for a cigarette for myself.

When he heard me stir, Jay came to the bed and lit the smoke for me.

"Delacorte. The man you met at one of my parties, who helped me get new staff here." He waved his smoke in the direction of the door.

Ah, the gangster.

"How'd he do that? Double cross him, I mean," I asked. I couldn't imagine Tom even knowing how to do such a thing.

"He promised he'd buy a truckload of liquor and then reneged on the deal. Tony told him he had to pay up, but then just as he thought he might have to cut his losses and sell it elsewhere, his driver was arrested and the whole shipment tossed. Somebody must have tipped off the cops. Tony thinks it was Tom, not wanting to pay." Jay blew a plume of smoke into the air. "I calmed him down."

"You did?"

He nodded and sat next to me on the bed, stroking my arm. "Maybe I shouldn't have."

For a long moment, I held my breath. I wondered what gangsters did when they were double-crossed. I wanted to ask, but I didn't want to know. I think I already knew.

So all I did was offer a small nod.

"All right then," Jay said, as if we'd decided something. "I'll tell Tony I was wrong."

I managed to convince Dr. Prinz to tell Tom to leave me alone.

During his next check on me the following morning, I had the chance to talk to him privately. Tom was still out.

I played the demure wife, a woman whose knowledge of worldly things is limited. I looked down bashfully, picking at my robe when I talked, and signaling my embarrassment.

And I told him my husband made me do things I didn't want to do.

DAISY

I broke down crying, and before long, the tears were real, and I was having a very genuine attack of hysteria.

Dr. Prinz was convinced. He wanted to give me another sedative, but I recovered by then and said no; I wanted to regain my strength, to become capable again, especially to be a good mother once more.

Having heard intimate details he didn't want to hear, he stood, red-faced, and told me he would talk to Mr. Buchanan about how much I needed rest. Complete rest.

Tom not only left me alone after that, he went into town more frequently, so this strategy turned out to be doubly beneficial.

By now I was committed to leaving him and no longer had any doubts. I merely had to construct the plan that Jordan had strongly recommended. As I saw it, part of the plan was to ensure Jay's devotion to Pamela and to making sure I'd be able to keep her with me when I left my brute of a husband.

CHAPTER ELEVEN

Throughout that summer, I accumulated cash. I had never thought about it much before—never had to. Tom usually gave me whatever I asked for and more, really: a monthly allotment for odds and ends. Most of our bills were paid by check, by tabs we'd run up at stores and with other services.

So I'd never had to think much about money, about what it cost to live in the world. I went from a household where my father would buy me whatever I wanted to a home where my husband would do the same.

I began arming myself with information, again letting Tom school me on such matters during dinner conversations where I would start by asking why the lower races didn't just live in better neighborhoods instead of the squalor of tenements.

Then I'd be treated to a lecture on those races' natural inferiority, but it would give me the chance to ask specific questions about how much one paid in rent or for a car, gasoline, food, and the like.

I had to be careful, though. After one such dinner, while Tom was replenishing our drinks, Jordan whispered to me on the veranda, "Careful, dear, you don't want to be too obvious."

So I made sure to guide our talk back to the latest Broadway hit, which we all agreed was silly even though none of us had seen it. We did that a lot—talked critically of things we had never experienced. It seemed to bring us joy. It brought Tom even greater joy when he could simultaneously

DAISY

sneer at something while also poking fun at my similar opinions about the same thing.

I'd progressively accumulate this knowledge, and I would often jot random numbers down in my room, only to have difficulty deciphering them later.

When I complained to Jordan about how hard it was to accumulate cash, to even know how much to save, she sat back and laughed.

We were having lobster salad on a perfect summer day, sun glinting off the water while a soft breeze blew the curtains in a gentle dance around the veranda, just the two of us there, a girls' luncheon.

"Frankly, I'm not sure why you're bothering with all this. Gatsby is rich as Croesus. You will be going from one well-feathered nest to another. Why worry about it?"

This was true, but something in me wanted to feel secure on my own. No man would ever be able to lock me in a room again.

"I know," I said, looking out over the Sound, toward Jay's house, something I did more and more often. He was away at the moment, on some kind of business trip upstate. It was the first time we hadn't been in the same locale since beginning our summer affair. Even during my recent confinement, I'd still known he was there across the water, just waiting for me. Now I'd not hear from him until Thursday. It made me fearful.

"These things are complicated," I said at last. "What if Tom tries to ruin me, or ruin Jay? What if everything comes crashing down on us?"

Jordan smiled and pulled out a smoke, which she had trouble lighting in the breeze. When she finally had it going, she took a drag on it, judged it of poor quality, and stubbed it out.

"If everything came crashing down, no budget prowess will help you. We'd all be in the same trouble then. So again, why worry about it?"

I did worry about it, though, especially when I thought of Jordan mentioning the possibility the whole thing could come crashing down on all of us. Anyone who lived through those crazy times knows there was always an air of "eat, drink, and be merry, for tomorrow we die" to them. It started with the end of the war, of course. When that horrible rupture was over and we all regarded the smoking landscapes and the men with ripped faces and brutalized psyches, how could we not feel that you had to grab each day and squeeze the last drop of pleasure out of it whenever you could?

None of us listened to supplications for moderation. Not even Prohibition dampened our desire for more booze. We wanted more of everything—more fun, more music, more dancing, more money.

In fact, if I had to choose one word to describe those years, it would be scandalous.

Clothing was scandalous.

Haircuts were scandalous.

Dances were scandalous.

About the only thing that didn't seem scandalous were actual scandals. Phrases like "Teapot Dome" and "gold digger" flitted through newspaper stories like gnats to be swatted away.

Peggy Hopkins Joyce was on her third marriage—or was it her fourth?—and while old doyennes may have gasped at the actress's shameless

DAISY

couplings with any available rich man, I'm sure many a shop girl thought it wasn't a bad idea.

Boredom was now counted among the seven deadly sins, and the others included prudishness, moderation, false humility, diligence, seriousness, and self-denial.

I had felt I was missing out on life since I married, and now, with Jay, I was in it again.

Jay returned from his business trip early, and as luck would have it, it was the very same day that Tom decided to stay home, forgoing the pleasures of stout "Babykins" Myrtle. I didn't know if she was with child, and I didn't care. If I left Tom, he could have all the bastards he wanted. He could have a whole tribe of them.

As he sat reading the newspaper in the dining room that Wednesday morning, I sat upstairs on my bed, scratching numbers on a piece of paper again, figuring out how much I needed for monthly expenses and how much I had stashed away.

From my reckoning, I had enough cash for four months of living on my own in a modest apartment somewhere. Jordan had told me that costs would be lower everywhere but New York.

I knew she was right about Jay's wealth, and I had no doubt he would spoil me with anything I wanted after we came together permanently, but I still had this nagging sense it was best to plan a life on my own. I knew definitely I wanted to leave Tom. But being with Jay forever? A fog of uncertainty blocked me from seeing that future clearly. I wanted to plan for contingencies.

Perhaps the easiest route was for me to leave Tom, live alone with Pamela for a while, divorce Tom, and then be with Jay. I could handle all that without help, without support from either man that could end up slowing proceedings.

I'd still not talked to Jay at length about Pamela. I just couldn't bring myself to ruin our golden hours with anything that would diminish our happiness.

Pamela was in the sunroom with Nanny when Jay pulled up the drive. I heard the gravel crunch and looked outside, my heart racing as I saw his dashing figure get out of that bold bright car of his.

After quickly running my fingers through my hair and applying a coat of lipstick, I ran down the steps to the door before he could even ring the bell.

"I couldn't wait to see you," he whispered, peering beyond me to make sure we were alone.

"I missed you, too," I said. Then I took a chance and leaned in to kiss him lightly on the cheek.

It was then that Pammy came into the hall. When she saw Jay, she walked forward, grinning. She wasn't a shy child. Like me, she was happy to be around people, and already she had a good memory for those she met.

"Miss'er Gabby," she slurred and then ran toward him, obviously expecting him to pick her up. My heart lifted. She remembered him. Fondly.

Surprisingly, he did pick her up, grinning at me as if to say, "now look at this."

That's when Tom joined us.

"What's this?" he said, taking in our little domestic tableaux, but squinting with confusion and doubt.

DAISY

I reached over and grabbed Pammy, kissing her on the forehead before putting her down and instructing her, "Go find Nanny, dear." She toddled off as Nanny came round the corner of the hall for her.

"Hello, old sport," Jay said, holding his hand out to Tom. "I've been away and was driving back. Before I headed over to West Egg, thought I'd stop by to discuss some good deals with you."

Tom frowned, and at that moment I noticed the tiniest speck of my lipstick on Jay's cheek. Though it was hardly more than a pinprick's diameter, it seemed a flashing red sign to me, and I kept my face away from Tom so he wouldn't notice it was the same shade I was wearing.

"I'm not sure I'm up for that today, old boy," Tom said, emphasizing the last two words, as if mocking Jay. "Come round another time, will you?" It was as if he were dismissing a tradesman.

I still dared not turn completely to face Tom. So I laughed and said, "Tom's out of sorts today. Here, let me see your car." And I walked down the steps toward it. "Tom, would you check on Pamela?" I asked without turning around. After a moment, I heard him retreat into the house.

At his vehicle, I whispered to Jay, "I can come by tomorrow, I think."

"Not today?" he said, his voice filled with longing.

I shook my head. "Tom's moping about for some reason. Maybe Myrtle threw him over."

Jay laughed. "Don't think so. I've heard she's getting a little, well, plumper. He might not like being tied to her and her litter."

My face warmed, and I knew my cheeks were blazing. So she *was* pregnant. How many people knew if Jay did?

Filled with anger, I said, "Wait right here."

I stomped up the steps, opened the door, and called out, "Tom! Jay is taking me for a drive in his car!"

Later, in bed with him, warm from lovemaking, our reunion complete, I watched as Jay rolled on his side and propped his head on his elbow.

"I did come by to talk about a deal," he said seriously. "The one I mentioned, with the associate of Anthony Delacorte's." His gaze probed me for doubt, but I had none that I cared to think about.

I let out a long sigh and stared at the ceiling. "I wish we could just go. Now. You and me. To Europe. To the other side of the world. To somewhere where there isn't a single Tom or Thomas around, where his name is banned for all eternity."

He let out a low chuckle and kissed me.

"All right. Let's." He actually got out of bed, as if he was going to make the arrangements then and there.

He pulled on his trousers and a shirt and was about to reach for the phone, when I said, "Stop!" while laughing at his impulsiveness. "We can't. *I* can't."

After putting the phone down, he turned to me, smile still on his face. "Why not? It's perfect. He won't even realize you're gone until we're far away, and then it will be too late to find us. You don't need anything. I'll buy you a new wardrobe. I'll buy you new everything." He snapped his fingers as if he could make items appear instantly.

DAISY

"Oh, Jay. That's so sweet." I sat up, pulling the sheet to my shoulders. I'd have to go soon. Despite what Jay had said, Tom was probably wondering at that moment why I had been away so long.

Jay came over to me, sat on the bed, and took my hands in his.

"Why not, Daisy? Come with me. Please. Now. We can do it." He kissed me, and in that kiss, I became so lost that I almost agreed to his crazy scheme. But after we separated, I uttered a single name.

"Pamela."

He sighed.

"I can't leave her," I said. Now I was the one reaching for his hand, comforting him. "I was so happy when she went to you today. It made me think…we could be together. All of us."

When I didn't say more, he spoke. "You doubted it? That we could all be together?"

"No, no," I said, shaking my head and knowing he would hear the insincerity. "It's just that I can't leave without Pamela."

"You can send for her."

I shook my head again. "Tom would never allow that. If I run away, he'll use her to punish me. I'd never see her again." Simply articulating that possibility made me shudder.

He stroked my cheek with his knuckles. "You're all I need," he said.

The implication was clear. He needed only me. Why didn't I need only him?

"I won't be your Anna," I said, forcing a firmness into my voice I had trouble mustering. "I won't forsake my child for you." I held my breath in this moment of honesty. This was new for me, to be utterly truthful with a man. It was the first bit of courage I had shown, and for a few seconds, it thrilled me.

His eyes widened, and I wondered if I needed to explain the Tolstoy reference, but then he leaned over and patted my hand and said, "We can have other children, Daisy. Many children. A garden of them." As if it was as easy as putting seeds into the earth and watching them grow.

"No, we can't," I said. "I can't anymore."

He surprised me by expressing no disappointment at all at this. If anything, he seemed happy to hear it. It hadn't shocked me when I'd first been told, but lately, I did find myself wondering if more children would somehow give my life the meaning I continued to crave.

"Oh, darling, that's just fine. More than fine. Really. I want only you. Children? No children? It doesn't matter to me. You're all that matters to me. Since the moment I met you, I knew I wanted you and you alone."

Me alone. There was a day when those words would have exhilarated me, when a lover whispering them would have filled me with light, warmth radiating from the inside.

Tom may never have uttered those words to me, but there had been a time when I knew he had wanted only me and me alone, too. I found out soon enough that once he'd made his conquest, his life seemed to lose meaning, a little more with each passing year. I wondered if this would happen to Jay once he had what he'd been seeking for so long.

But I had Pamela now. There was no me alone. There was me *and* Pamela.

When she was two, shortly after we returned from Europe, she came down with a ghastly fever. For five days, she lay abed, and I thought it was that dreadful infantile paralysis. I thought we'd lose her. Despite Tom's

DAISY

protests, I slept by her bed every night until the fever subsided and the doctor pronounced her recovered.

In those moments at her bedside, I realized I would be broken forever if I lost her. I'd never recover from that.

Now my heart broke anew. I felt the shards course through my veins, cutting every part of my being and entering my very soul. I wondered why I couldn't be honest with a man and have him accept that truth, instead of always needing to pretend, to jolly, to tease, to amuse.

I looked at him, willing him to say he would wait until I could make sure Pamela could be with us. I longed for those words. *Yes, darling, we absolutely must wait until we can have Pamela with us. There is no question we should wait.* But he merely smiled.

This sweet man, this darling man who'd followed me and wanted me and cherished me. Why? Why put in all that effort, devote all that time to this one mission—finding and winning his Daisy again? What had been missing from his life that he wanted me to fill? It was too much to ask of me or anyone, and I knew I'd eventually disappoint him, just as I had disappointed Tom.

With a shiver, I realized Jay was little different than Tom. He wanted a pretty object, a porcelain sculpture to put on his shelf, to look at and admire, to occasionally show off, and, yes, to love. Daisy alone, with no entanglements, no pesky children to change her into a plump matron. Just me.

What would happen when my beauty faded?

With a flash of more painful insight, I realized I was complicit in this. All the things I'd wanted from life I had gotten by playing that porcelain figurine. I'd bent in that same charming way toward men. I had lidded my eyes, bitten my tongue, looked shyly away, come up with clever lines, ceased being in any way intimidating. All so they'd love me. So Jay would love me now that I had lost Tom's love.

"We don't need more children. It can be just the two of us," he said, still smiling.

"Three," I reminded him, crushed he had already forgotten about the importance of my daughter. "The three of us."

"Yes, yes, of course."

With a massive effort, I once more became the porcelain figurine, smiling sweetly at him. "I need to get back. We might not be able to run away today, but we can plan our getaway. It will be the most fun of all, making arrangements for where we'll go, hotels we'll stay in, things we'll do…" I recited the lines as if from a play. I wanted to believe them, but something had changed.

We both dressed—I was very careful not to have a thread out of place—and walked to his car. By the time I got home, Tom had decided to go out, too, apparently, so there was no need for me to worry about an interrogation upon my return.

After I made my way up to my room, I realized I'd never given Jay any indication I wanted the contract with Mr. Delacorte changed, and now a wave of guilt washed over me.

CHAPTER TWELVE

Tom didn't come home that night. I knew he'd gone to see the Wilson woman, so I felt both relieved and angry. I was still feeling bruised by Jay's indifference toward my daughter, his refusal to acknowledge my feelings about her, and now I was confronted with a husband who might have sired another heir, someone who might eventually pose a challenge to my daughter's inheritance. Could neither man be bothered to look out for my child? I was infuriated and confused.

I had little time to make sense of these feelings because they were soon replaced by another emotion: fear. The next morning at breakfast, Tom commented on Jay's visit, and it was clear he had been stewing about it.

"Why does he have to stop by here? It's as if he thinks he's one of us."

I stopped buttering my toast and stared at him. "He came to discuss a deal with you. Weren't you doing deals with him?" I held my breath, hoping that by going on the offensive, I put him on the defensive, and he would stop thinking about why else Jay might have visited our house.

He waved his hand in the air. "Liquor. Everyone does that. Nothing special. And I stopped after a bad shipment." He stared back at me. "Was there something else he wanted?"

Tom was hardly subtle. He enjoyed feeling part of the hustle and bustle of business, of "deals," of buying bootleg liquor. But he always snapped back to his core nature, that of wealthy gentry, disdainful of anyone outside his elite set, especially if they tried too hard to get inside and take what was his.

DAISY

"He did mention wanting to show you his car," I said, staring at him without batting an eye, trying to convey through an exaggerated calm that nothing was amiss. "But you were in a mood, so I did the polite thing and accompanied him for a drive."

He snorted. "The polite thing." After a pause, he said, "If I ever thought he—or any man—was taking advantage of my good graces to make a play for what isn't his, there will be hell to pay."

He went back to reading his newspaper.

I knew who would suffer that hell he promised. Me.

At least I knew where things stood. He suspected something between me and Jay, and, despite Dr. Prinz's warnings, he would most likely want to claim what was his soon if I didn't act. It wouldn't be an act of lovemaking. It would be revenge.

I had to leave. But where would I go and with whom? Just a few days ago, I'd thought it was with Jay. Now I didn't know. My thoughts became a muddle. I couldn't seem to imagine any scenario, any plan. It was as if I was holding my breath, waiting for something to happen that wouldn't require a decision from me.

Once again, I turned to Jordan for advice.

We met for a sail, and she was mightily impressed by my skill on the water.

"My dear, you'll be skippering a pirate schooner in the Caribbean, I suppose. Is that why you've been so interested in how to allocate your funds? Are you planning on securing a chest of gold doubloons to use in your new life?"

"Oh, I'd hoped I'd kept that secret. Did someone tell?" I laughed, the sun and wind restoring my spirits. "Now I'll need a new plan."

Once we anchored in a quiet bay and unwrapped sandwiches provided by Cook, I presented her my dilemma and my fears—that Jay was insufficiently connected to my daughter.

"Jay isn't opposed to having Pamela with us, but he's not enthusiastic," I complained.

"Not opposed—that's good news, isn't it?" she asked as we lolled on the aft section, picnic basket opened, Champagne poured, delights revealed.

"I have no intention of being an Anna Karenina," I bit out.

"I should hope not. What a grisly way to die—run over and chopped to pieces." She balled up her sandwich paper and tossed it into the basket. Leaning back, she closed her eyes and soaked up the sun. "You have to decide, darling. No one can do it for you. Do you want to stay with Tom or go with Jay? I can't tell you what to do. I wouldn't dare. Not now."

She *had* told me what to do, of course, when I'd received Jay's letter on my wedding eve, but that path was clearer. An unmarried pregnant woman did equal a ruined life. Jordan was a realist, and she accepted unchangeable facts, adjusting her attitude to accommodate them. I left out certain facts in my current dilemma.

I didn't tell her how I'd felt the afternoon I spoke to Jay about Pamela.

I didn't tell her about the associate of Anthony Delacorte who might be out to exact some revenge against Tom for his double-cross.

I didn't tell her that I now wondered if I should stay with either man or somehow chart a different course.

I didn't tell her any of these things because they troubled me so much, I could barely think. I had spent my life brushing aside unpleasant thoughts. It was a hard habit to break. Like Tom, I'd retreated to my comfortable position of avoiding any situation that required a show of courage. And

DAISY

that last possibility—charting a different course, all my own—took my breath away and stopped my thoughts. It was as frightening as being spirited away to a place like Mongolia, surrounded by primitives, not knowing their language.

After a while, Jordan closed her eyes as she relaxed against a pillow. "A woman has two choices in life," she said. "She can either marry into money. Or…she can live a terrible life without money."

I thought she was joking and started to politely laugh but, judging by her face, she was completely serious.

She went on: "Men can work for their money, can accumulate great piles of it. Women inherit it or work for it in other ways. Marriage is work."

Still lost in her reverie, she continued her sermon: "There are exceptions, but they are rare, and if you don't marry for money—I prefer to think of it as comfort—you must reconcile yourself to a very modest and possibly shabby life."

After a sigh, she said, "Men make their way in life, with or without a spouse. Women have no lives without a husband."

"Why, Jordan, you have no spouse, and you have a great life!" I protested.

She ignored my comment and at last opened her eyes and looked at me. "There is nothing wrong with choosing comfort, especially when adoring love comes as a bonus."

Was she talking of Jay or Tom? I suspected, deep down, that Tom still loved me. He thought of me, though, as a possession, something to be proud of, to show off. Did Jay think the same?

After a time, I hoisted the sails and directed us toward home, no more certain of what I wanted to do than when we'd left the dock.

Her little speech haunted me, though, as I pondered life without being beholden to Jay or Tom, without always having to be a supplicant of some kind, even in subtle ways. I just didn't know if I could live that shabby, "lonely" life she had talked about.

For a little while, I thought of nothing but enjoying the moment, and once again pushed unpleasant thoughts aside. It felt idyllic.

If I did anything at all to guard against bad outcomes, it was to manage my money. I cashed out of several big stock deals, I withdrew money from bank accounts, I sold jewelry. Yes, I worried about having such a large stash of actual greenbacks in my room, but I figured everything entailed risk, and I would rather have my treasure right there under my nose than a promise of more treasure to come.

As summer approached its last days, it treated us to a preview of fall. Blue skies, moderate temperatures, soft breezes with just the whisper of dying leaves from trees frazzled by the previous heat.

Tom went out of town, back to see his father on some family business. You would never know it from Nick's recounting of our story, but both of us did have surviving parents—he, his father, and me, my mother. I suppose it dimmed the romanticism of his telling, to see us with family still in our lives. Parentage made one real.

With Tom away, I worried about nothing. I rose, I swam—either on our little beach or in our pool. I played with Pammy. I spent afternoons with Jay.

DAISY

It was a mark of my indecision that I never told Jay that Tom was away for a few days. I knew he would use that as a reason to pressure me into leaving at that moment. It was the perfect time to do so. Unsuspecting husband off in Chicago, Pamela and me alone. Jordan was gone, too, and Nick was particularly busy, so I didn't fear someone telling Jay about Tom's extended absence.

I just wanted what I wanted in that moment. Fears pushed aside. Suspicious husband gone. Lover content.

We didn't talk about the future anymore. We made a pact not to, to just live on the island of these moments together, and I devised a penalty for any time either of us used the words "tomorrow" or anything indicating a time beyond this one. The offender would have to rewind a clock to the previous hour, turning back time.

In just a few days, Jay's clocks were all running on different times, but we didn't care. We pretended they represented the times of countries we wanted to visit, so we'd attempt to speak the language of said country when entering that room. This usually devolved into hysterics as Jay had horrible mock accents. His German sounded Romanian, his French sounded Italian, and his Italian sounded like fishmongers in the Bronx.

Sometimes we swam together in his beautiful pool, and became tanned and blushed by the kiss of the sun.

I still had no idea what I wanted to do. Sometimes I thought that I'd just pack up everything, including Pamela, come to Jay's doorstep, and say, "Let's go away now."

Other times, I asked myself why I couldn't just continue as I was. Tom had mistresses and was likely to keep that habit as the years rolled by. Maybe he would have a litter of bastards by the time he was done. My anger over that dissipated as I worked on how to protect myself financially, so that my daughter would not be harmed by heirs showing up at any old moment to make a claim on her inheritance.

With Nick's help, I had already managed to get Tom to agree to let me do my own stock buying with a small budget that I grew quickly. It was supposed to be a game, to see if I could choose good companies and make the money grow faster than Tom's similar investment pile.

I wasn't stupid enough to surpass him by much, though. I knew if I outwitted him by too large a margin, he'd stop the game in a fit of pique, then cut me off from it as well.

So I deferred to more modest selections, letting myself lose money occasionally, sometimes deliberately, sometimes because I wanted to see how a risk played out. But when I sensed some stocks were at a peak, I sold. I deposited the cash, then withdrew most of it. Nick helped me here, too, setting up a bank account for me—something separate from Tom's. Back then, a woman couldn't set up her own banking without a man.

My little stash of cash—in a secret drawer in my dresser—was in danger of spilling beyond its walls. Sometimes, I liked to lock the door and look at it, wondering if it was enough to push Pamela and me beyond just a shabby life and into a more comfortable one.

In fact, I began to dream that she and I would leave, and I'd have time to think, to decide whether to stay with Tom or go with Jay. Away from both of them, perhaps I could think more clearly.

DAISY

Even though I tried to fail occasionally in my investments, I went through one particularly successful week, where I simply couldn't stop making good decisions. It seemed as if I had a sort of Midas touch, unable, even when I tried earnestly, to choose poorly. Unfortunately, this coincided with a time when Tom *was* doing particularly poorly, and, as usual, he didn't like being beaten, especially by his wife.

What was worse, he decided that our stock market game made for good dinner table conversation. Shortly after he returned from his trip to Chicago, we spent a miserable evening hosting Nick while Tom needled me about my luck and suggested I start betting on the horses next.

"You'll have to learn a thing or two about that, though," he said from his end of the table after taking a sip of wine. "It's not as simple as closing one's eyes and pointing to what you want."

"Don't insult Nick, dear," I said, tired of his teasing. "He's the one who does that blindfolded choosing, not me. You have a collection of them, don't you, Nick? Stylish blindfolds imported from Paris?"

Nick, who must have sensed the tension, happily followed my lead. "It's the best method. Written up in all the stocks and bonds articles I've been reading in the Yale Club library. Works between eighty and ninety percent of the time, and only the finest silk blindfolds will do."

Tom wasn't in a mood to be kidded, though. "Then why aren't you using that technique when advising me? I'm beginning to wonder if the two of you are plotting to make a fool out of me."

Nick had had too much to drink, so he injudiciously responded with more joking of his own. "Well, I suppose our plot is working then, isn't it, Daisy?" He smiled at me and winked, but I just gave him a stony stare, and he seemed to realize he'd gone too far, so he added, "Just kidding, Tom. I'll take a look at your portfolio first thing. Maybe we'll get you into some of the things Daisy's taken a shine to."

Instead of calming the waters, his reference to my choices just riled Tom more.

"I'm not taking investment advice from my wife. She can barely keep her household budget. When I married her, did you know she thought one could buy a car for, what was it, dear—five dollars?"

"I'd misread an advertisement," I said softly, my irritation spiking.

"And she buys so many things for Pamela—she bought her a diamond necklace the other day. The little dear will probably lose it if Daisy doesn't first. You lost that one I gave you, didn't you, dear?"

My face warmed. Yes, I had bought Pammy a necklace recently. Knowing its value, I thought it would be another good investment I might sell at some point, one that raised no suspicion. And, no, I hadn't lost my own similar piece of jewelry. I'd sold it and stored the money away. I had wanted to see how one did that—sell off one's jewelry—so I would know how to do it if I needed money. When Tom noticed I didn't wear it anymore, he'd asked about it and I had lied that I'd lost it.

"The chain was always flimsy," I said.

He laughed. "Good thing I manage the money. She and Pamela would be in rags if I didn't."

It was just before dusk, and the light outside was a warm yellow-gold. Tom's gaze turned to the windows and he stared across the Sound.

"I bet she thinks he"—Tom pointed to Jay's place—"has more money than I do. Not a chance. Not even close."

"How vulgar to talk about money at the dinner table," I said. In any event, I'd had enough. I stood. "I want some fresh air. I'm going to take a

DAISY

walk. Please, continue talking about money and how addle-brained I am on my own."

I left the room and hurried to the path that led to the promontory. It wasn't long, though, before I heard footsteps behind me and saw Nick running toward me, holding a wrap, obviously the excuse he'd used to leave the table and come after me.

"Daisy!" he called, handing me the cloth. "He's just a little drunk, that's all. Sorry if I made it worse."

I laughed bitterly. "You'd think he'd be proud of a wife able to do as well as I've been doing. He can't stand for anyone, especially a beautiful woman, to be better than him at something." Maybe that was Myrtle's charm, that she was so inferior to him in intellect and to me in beauty.

"He doesn't seem to mind Jordan being better at golf," he offered weakly.

I laughed again. "He doesn't care about golf."

"He cares about you."

I turned to him. "Then why does he have to destroy the things I love?" I continued walking toward the promontory, stopping when we got there. "Before marrying him, I loved to dance—and not just popular dances, either. I took ballet lessons. I was good at it. I painted. I was good at that, too. Then Tom said the dance lessons took too much time away from Pamela and him, and the painting made a mess the servants had trouble cleaning up."

He didn't say anything, and we just stood there, staring across the Sound to Jay's house, in shadows now except for a couple of lights on an upper floor. I imagined Jay sitting in his suite and reading, maybe glancing my way. How I wanted to be with him. At least with him I could laugh and joke and not worry about hiding my wit or tempering my intellect to suit his ego.

Looking down at the water, I remembered another thing I used to be good at. Diving. I loved the feeling of jumping into the air and hurtling head-first toward the deep end, feeling liberated for those few moments in the air, just myself and the air and the water. Nothing else.

Just then, I saw Tom approaching us. His grim, determined stride suggested he'd yank his silly little wife back to her prison and put her back on the shelf, where he could admire her.

Without thinking, I tore off my wrap and stepped forward; I had wanted to do this for so long. When I'd gone sailing, I'd looked up and calculated the dive on many a trip toward our dock.

"Daisy, no!" Nick cried, too late.

I threw myself into a perfect dive. I knew the water was deep here, and all I thought about was getting away on this perfect summer evening, becoming some kind of sea nymph who could frolic in the waves and eventually land on some perfect foreign shore.

For a few seconds, I felt it—liberation. Glorious, exultant freedom.

CHAPTER THIRTEEN

Later, Nick told me that, after I dove, Tom raced to the promontory, ripped off his tie, and prepared to bolt into the water after me, but he couldn't bring himself to do it. He stood there, trembling with fear, Nick said, until he shouted that they needed to get the boat, and they hurried together to the pier.

By that time, I'd swum a good twenty feet out, but the current was strong, and, despite what my husband thought, I was no fool. Drowning in the Sound while my husband and cousin watched might have given me some pleasure, imagining their terror at the sight, but not enough to rip free of life itself.

I turned toward the pier just as Nick and Tom unmoored the boat and sailed my way. In a few minutes, I pulled myself over the side, dripping wet but feeling wonderful. Strong. Capable. Intelligent.

Unapologetic.

"I used to win prizes for my diving back in school," I said after Nick handed me his jacket. "And I've been wanting to make that dive ever since we moved here."

Tom said nothing, but he gave me a look combining sympathy with disgust, and I knew a visit from Dr. Prinz would likely be on the schedule the following day.

DAISY

Dr. Prinz did come by, but I managed to explain to him what a good athlete I was, how I loved swimming—something Tom could verify—that I had known the depth of the water and wasn't taking a risk when I dove. I even lied and said I'd made the dive before when no one was looking, and it was a wonderful form of exercise—good for both my mental health and physical health.

I don't know if he believed me, and he seemed a little frightened of me. Once he determined I was healthy and not in danger of harming myself, he packed up his bag as quickly as he could and left.

The stock market went back to punishing me as much as rewarding me, so Tom's envy abated. He talked of us moving again, maybe back to Chicago because he said his father seemed to be ailing, and he wanted to be closer to him.

"Chicago is so cold," I said one afternoon when I wished I could go over to Jay's. But Tom was staying in. He was doing that more and more, and I think it was deliberate, to keep a closer eye on me.

"New York is cold, too, at least in the winter." We both sat in the large parlor fronting the Sound, Tom with his latest book on the racial wars yet to come, me with a fashion magazine.

"Then we should head south," I said. "Florida. I've always wanted to see Florida."

He stared at me, and a malevolent sneer lifted up his lips. "Why, that's not a bad idea, dear. Just the two of us. We can leave Pammy with your mother, or Nanny. A second honeymoon."

My heart chilled. Tom's suggestion of leaving Pamela behind was an implicit threat. He was telling me he could direct our daughter away, whether I liked it or not.

I met his stare and said, as lightly as I could, "If we go to Florida, I would be absolutely horrible company without our daughter."

That ended that conversation.

For me, it was time for a final decision, and because Tom stayed close to home, I wasn't able to get over to see Jay for several days, and only then for a short visit, on the pretense of seeing Nick to discuss "family matters" that would bore Tom, I told him.

"We have to get away, darling," Jay told me, holding my hands as we sat in his study.

I'd told him how awful Tom had been to me, about diving, about how I wanted to get my life back somehow, all the things I'd loved to do before marrying.

"I can make it happen in an instant," he said. "You can paint, dance, swim, dive—all of it. I'd buy you a building full of studios, and install a diving board as high as you want for a thousand different pools!"

"I know." I looked down.

"Then let's stop waiting," he pleaded, kissing my hand. "Let's just leave."

"I have to do it when I can be sure I can take Pamela with me." I waited to hear if he'd object and was relieved when he didn't, though I would have preferred he endorse that position with vigor. I always seemed to be testing him on this lately.

"Europe or the South Seas? Which suits you?" he asked, his tone now jaunty. "Or would you rather stay in the States and go somewhere wild? Or we could go to Mexico. I know a great little town there with a villa

DAISY

we could rent. Sunshine and ocean views. Wonderful food. Music. You'll love it."

Again, I waited for him to add, "And Pamela, too. Pamela would not only love the weather, but she'll be brown as a berry by summer's end."

But he never said any such thing. Instead, he walked to the window, stared out, hands in his pockets, and planned our future. When I indicated mild interest in the Mexico plan, he described the villa in more detail. It wasn't as "grand" as "this place," but it had "charm" and lots of rooms, great "fixtures," and even a new garage that would accommodate three cars.

As he went on, I envisioned myself lolling about that mansion, and a great heaviness came over me as I realized I'd be trading one gilded cage for another. One job for another.

In my heart and mind, it was clearly time to leave Tom. What I couldn't quite bring myself to do was decide whether I needed to leave Jay, too. I wept inside at the prospect.

He had given me my old self back. He'd given me the best summer of my life. He'd given me hope and sparked in me little flashes of courage.

"Better hurry on over to Nick's," he said, staring out the window. "Tom's driving up."

There wasn't enough time to scurry over to Nick's. Besides, he wasn't there anyway. My visit to him had been a ruse.

Instead, Jay and I meandered out of his front door together, very casually, and then strolled over to Tom's car in front of Nick's cottage.

"Hello, old sport," Jay said jauntily.

"Nick wasn't here!" I cried, going to Tom. "He must have mixed up the time. Or maybe I did," I added, playing the fool.

"She stopped in to see if he was at my place," Jay said, smiling, and it felt as though we were supplying too many details.

Tom, still sitting in his coupe, looked at the car I'd driven here—a Ford that wasn't nearly as sporty. Thank God I had thought to leave it at Nick's and not at Jay's.

"How convenient," Tom said.

I leaned on his side of his car. "What brings you here?" I kept my tone light and sweet, as if it was the most natural thing in the world to talk to my husband in the presence of my lover, as if I was the most innocent woman in the world.

"Nick called," he said, "and when I said you were supposed to be visiting him, he seemed confused." His gaze flitted between us. "Said he must have forgotten and to offer his apologies."

Good old Nick, thinking quickly.

"I was just about to come back," I said.

"Hop in, darling," Tom now purred. "I'll have someone come retrieve the other car."

"Oh, that's silly, dear. I'll drive it back. I'll follow you," I said, starting to go for the Ford, but he reached out and grabbed my arm.

"No, I actually think it's silly for you to be here alone. Worse than silly, actually. Disrespectful."

His last word hung in the air, and it was clear he was claiming his property—me.

DAISY

Jay took a step forward as if he was going to brawl, but I held up my hand.

"Tom's right. I should be going." I looked at Jay and mentally pleaded with him not to roil the waters. "Thank you for keeping me company while we waited for Nick to show up."

Still, Jay came toward me and opened the passenger door, and I'd barely made myself comfortable before Tom roared us away.

I couldn't get to Jay over the next few days. Tom stayed around the house all the time now. He even insisted on spending time with me. We went sailing one day, swimming the next, and I couldn't shake the feeling that he had figured something out and needed to decide how to deal with it. He was just looking for more clues to solidify his case, like some zealous prosecutor getting ready to go to court.

This made me even more anxious to leave, afraid of what his ultimate plan would be—confrontation? I didn't know what I would say. I practiced denials and confessions that I discarded. No, I had not betrayed him. How could he think that? Or, yes, I had enjoyed time with Jay, but how could he blame me when he himself was not blameless? It all felt weak and thin.

If Tom did accuse me, it wouldn't end well. Admitting his wife was unfaithful would be a blow for him to absorb, and I knew he'd fight back in some way, even physically.

This forced me back to thinking of running away with Jay. He would know how to get us some place safe where Tom couldn't find us. I wasn't confident enough to do that on my own. Not yet, at least.

I felt my daydream of a summer had turned into a nightmare, and I slept fitfully, woke scared, and felt uncertain. All that newfound confidence disappeared.

Now I was committed to retreating to Mexico with Jay, if only to get away from Tom. After that, I didn't know. But it was the first step. I merely had to let Jay know the when and where.

But how could anyone think at all of anything? Summer decided to hurl one last burst of awful heat at us at the end of the month, as if to say "see what happens when you wish me gone—I'll show you."

When you opened the door, all you felt was an oven-like blast and no breeze. There was no sailing now, and no swimming either as the skies promised lightning each afternoon, taunting us before cruelly holding back rain.

The day was all about waiting for the night, knowing that even its darkness would offer sweaty sheets and damp pillows.

I awoke one of those mornings, sighed, and planned to do nothing but look for escapes of the more immediate kind. A swim. A cool bath. Another bath perhaps.

I thought of penning a note to Jay, telling him to let me know when he wanted to leave, but I was too afraid it would be intercepted. I didn't know if I could trust any of our household staff. I kept Pammy near me a lot, so much so that the nanny even complained that it was better for the child if I didn't interfere with her regimen.

Tom was suspicious of me, and I was growing suspicious of everyone else.

I had to get away. I was even at the point where I calculated how much time I would need to pack up our things and get over to Jay's. I thought

DAISY

I could do it all within twenty minutes. Was that enough time to elude Tom's clutches? What if Jay wasn't there when I arrived? Then what?

That night at dinner, Tom pointed out that Gatsby had shut down his parties, and word in town was he'd hired new staff so no one would gossip about a lover he'd taken.

There was a long pause as he looked at me across the table.

Oh, I didn't stir a bit. I didn't blink. I couldn't give him any hint of embarrassment or fear, even though it curdled my stomach.

"Well, it's nice not to have all that tomfoolery going on in our backyard, don't you think, dear?" I said. And please, pass me the roast. "Maybe he's gone out of town."

I desperately wanted to know if Jay was there. I was hoping for information, for Tom to say, oh, no, the man was still over there, he'd seen him. Then I'd know I could drive over in the morning, maybe even tonight.

The next day, however, he did give me some more information about Jay. Or rather, he told me he had decided to invite Jay to lunch, along with Nick and Jordan, to talk over some business opportunities, he said. I sensed another purpose—perhaps an examination of my interaction with Jay, a sleuthing for clues about our relationship, or even some public humiliation of me. The blistering heat pulled good sense and reason from me, and I couldn't think of a way to avoid this encounter. At least I would see Jay, and maybe there would be a private moment when we could plot our departure.

Other than diving into the Sound again and swimming over to Jay's pier, I couldn't conjure up another plan. So I resolved to just get through it, to become the porcelain figure bending toward her rugged cavalier, wait for the heat to end and cool reasoning to return, and then put the final touches on my escape plan.

Yet, like an oracle of old, I sensed it coming—disaster.

CHAPTER FOURTEEN

Jay arrived just before noon the next day, and we all sat on the dim veranda having drinks. Though the curtains were drawn to keep out the sun, sweat coated Tom's face, which I knew made him self-conscious. Nanny brought Pammy in to say hello, and she ran to Jay as if she thought he was some beloved uncle. Nick and Jordan tried too hard to be funny.

I was the perfect housewife and hostess, sweetly attentive to Tom, so if this was some kind of test, some sort of gathering of clues, Tom would find nothing but bright, shining innocence.

I tried, at one point, to head outside alone, hoping Jay would follow so we could talk. I said I thought the sailboat's ropes looked loose and would go check them, but Tom called a servant and had him do it instead. Pointedly, he remarked while looking only at me that he had been instructing our servants to regularly "keep an eye" on the boat. I felt the walls closing in.

We had finished our second round of drinks, and now I thought perhaps we would end the afternoon with a light lunch and goodbyes—maybe goodbyes that would let me talk to Jay at the car alone. Perhaps it would all be over with Tom deciding he was too afraid to ignite a confrontation, when someone—was it Jordan?—suggested driving into the city. It was a quiet afternoon; the drive would at least provide us some cooling air. At least, that was the argument.

I said I was too tired and it was too hot to think of moving even a finger, but somehow this became the plan everyone enthusiastically

DAISY

endorsed, and my misgivings were overruled. Tom in particular thought it a great idea, but he might have thought it was good to punish me this way by forcing me out into the scouring heat when he knew I didn't want to go. I noted this and decided to choose the things I didn't want, knowing he'd push for the opposite.

My mind might have been addled by the heat and drink and apprehension, but I knew how to manage Tom. I wanted it all to be over and I wanted to sink into my bed, sleep, and wait for fall's cooling temperatures to bathe us, and somehow for a path to be lit for me. So far, he had not caused a row, and I suspected this day was some kind of punishment for me that would be followed by stern warnings in private and ever more vigilant servants watching all my moves.

We were soon on the gravel drive, and Tom suggested I take our coupe since he knew I loved to drive, which was true, though not in this burning weather. Using my new strategy, I was about to say that would be delightful, figuring he would then change the plan, when Jay interceded and insisted Tom give Jay's gleaming yellow roadster a go.

Before Tom could object, Jay was in the driver's seat of the coupe with me as passenger, and Tom was behind the wheel of the "circus car," as he dubbed it, with Nick and Jordan in tow.

"Thank you," I said as we took off. "I didn't want to drive."

"I could tell," he said, and smiled at me. "Let's have a few drinks in town and get this over with."

"Yes!" I agreed with passion, though I still wasn't clear what Tom planned for this day. "I couldn't wait to talk to you," I gushed. "I've been a prisoner. It's been awful." At last we could speak freely.

"Oh, darling," he said and grabbed my hand for a quick kiss before shifting gears.

"I think Tom knows," I said. The car stirred up a breeze, but it was a warm one, and it did little to cool our brows.

He nodded. "I hope he does!"

"No, don't say that," I answered. "It's better if he doesn't, or at least doesn't admit it. If we can just keep him in the dark a little longer, it will be for the best." I wanted no confrontations, no fights. I just wanted to safely get away with Pammy. To that, Tom presented the greatest threat. Later, I would deal with my feelings for Jay and what to do about being with him or not.

"How long? To keep him in the dark? Shouldn't we go as soon as possible now?" Jay asked as he smoothly shifted gears again.

"Yes, yes. As soon as possible," I said. "Tonight, he'd be suspicious. Maybe tomorrow. Or the next day. I just need to be sure I can take my daughter with me without Tom knowing."

Finally being able to talk with Jay about these plans calmed me. At last, I was choosing something, at least for the time being. I'd run away with Jay and then decide next steps, if any.

"You'll be patient, won't you, darling?" I needed to find a time when Tom wouldn't be suspicious if I took Pammy somewhere alone. Lately, if I'd even hinted at such an expedition, he'd immediately say he would accompany us.

"I'll try," Jay said.

"I think it might be best at night," I said, "but I don't want Pammy crying and waking up Tom."

DAISY

"Tomorrow night?" he asked. "The sooner, the better. I'm ready. We can fly somewhere. Have you been in an airplane?"

"Yes, but Pammy hasn't."

"She'll love it," he said, his confidence bringing me additional calmness. And the fact that he had thought of her enjoyment buoyed me.

"If we don't make it tomorrow night, the night after," I said.

"I'll wait for you. If it takes a hundred days, I'll wait," he affirmed.

With our vague plan decided on, off we went, into town, past the ash heaps that made me shudder, over the bridge that provided a cooling view, with Tom behind us as if he were a police agent on the tail of an ignominious bootlegger.

Once in the city, we slowed, and those warm winds ended. The heat descended again in full force, wrapping us all in a heavy blanket, unmitigated by the shade cast by skyscrapers. At an intersection, Nick hurried forward to tell us the plan was to head to the Plaza, where we would get a room and cool drinks. We'd wait out the worst of the heat before heading back to the Sound.

Jay looked at me, his eyebrows raised, as if to say, "See, I told you. A few drinks and we'll be done," and we drove to the hotel.

No drink was cool on the tenth floor, however. My god, the heat here was even more oppressive. We opened windows, every single one of them, from the sitting room to the bathroom to the bedroom of the suite, but nothing helped.

I sat on a couch fanning myself with a room service menu while Nick or Tom or Jordan called for ice and whiskey. I was just waiting for the day to be over.

The drinks were delivered, and Jay and Tom both rushed to pay and tip the room service fellow, with Jay winning the honor. Tom stepped back, smiled, and said, "Go ahead, spend your money on my drinks. I'm happy to oblige."

We toasted the end of summer.

And then…it began, everything I had feared. Here I'd thought I had escaped the worst, that all that remained was maybe an hour in this cell of a suite, and we would be back to cooler skies and a cooler home.

Tom began needling Jay, first about his money, then about his education, then about flirting with me. They stood behind the couch, and Tom's sweat dripped on me when he spoke.

I cringed, hoping Jay would stay good-natured since this torturous day was so close to being over. We were so close to our escape—my escape.

He did show restraint. At first.

Jay answered each mocking comment with good cheer, and when it came to me, well, he must have decided honesty was the best strategy.

"Your wife is beautiful and charming, old sport," he said, smiling, the faintest veneer of sweat on his brow. "Who wouldn't want to flirt with her?"

"Gentlemen, that's who," Tom spit out. "Which, it seems, you are not, *old sport*."

Nick attempted a joke from his position by an open window.

"Gentlemen are no longer in style, Tom. I read it in the *Times* just this week, didn't you know? Gigolos and scoundrels are all the rage."

It fell flat.

Then Jay said, seriously, "I'm a gentleman who treats a woman the way she should be treated." He looked at me. "And if she decided she preferred another approach, I'd happily accept the outcome."

DAISY

I thought Tom might swing at Jay then. He loosened his tie and took off his jacket, but Nick interceded, walking over to the two, putting his drink down as if he meant business.

"I can't speak for myself, but we're all gentlemen here," he said, still trying to amuse. "Except for the doorman, perhaps. He looked like a rake to me."

Jordan huffed out her frustration with his efforts and stepped forward from her window perch, as well.

"I officially declare the war over and peace treaties to be signed forthwith," she pronounced, holding up her glass in a toast.

"Hear, hear!" Nick added.

For a moment, this interlude seemed to work, but then Tom beckoned me. "Come here," he said, and when I didn't move, he repeated it, more forcefully. "Come here!"

I felt obliged to respond, if only to keep the truce, knowing resistance would make him bolder. I stood and walked round to him and sighed. I felt like a prisoner being led to execution.

"Tell him you do not like him flirting with you." He grabbed my elbow and turned me to face Jay. "Tell him you want him to stop. Tell. Him."

The room buzzed with silence and heat and a claustrophobic tension.

Somewhere below, a wedding was going on, and the music and cheers reached us on such a still day. How awful, to be married in this heat.

I said nothing. I couldn't think of anything that would make things better, and I had no intention of making them worse. If I did what he said, he'd press for more. If I refused, he'd most likely fight Jay right there in that hideously warm room.

"Oh, Tom," I uttered at last, as if he were a disobedient imp. "Don't be silly. All women love to be flirted with."

That just stirred Jay, though, and he leapt to what he must have thought was my defense. Our defense.

"Tell him the truth, darling," Jay said. "Tell him you want to leave him," he said in a low, serious voice, as if he was tired of pretending this was fun.

Oh, no. I'd figured on Tom's recklessness, not on Jay's. I thought Jay understood; this wasn't the time to provoke Tom. I had told him not to and he'd disregarded my warning. I'd told him to be careful! To be patient!

Who could be patient in this heat? It lit up nerve endings, crackling electricity along every fiber.

But I wouldn't err again, so I remained mute.

Nick, from back in a corner again, said, "Come on, now. Let's stop this. We've all had too much to drink, and the heat's making us crazy. Let's go home." A feeble effort from a feeble man.

"Are you his lover?" Tom blurted out.

Whiskey loosened my tongue. "Lover? Ha! You're concerned about lovers? Do you have one, Tom? A lover? Perhaps a pregnant one? That conniving witch Myrtle Wilson?"

He raised his hand and slapped me, the movement so sudden, the pain so sharp that, none of us registered it for a few seconds and then, I bent over, holding my cheek, crying.

"How dare you, you bastard? How dare you? You're as common as your cheap whore," I spat out as Jay stepped forward, ready to return Tom's blow, but Nick sped into action and pulled Jay back. "Calm down now," he said. "No need for this."

DAISY

Jordan also stepped up. "I think it's time to go," she said, coming over to me, putting her arm around my shoulders. She looked at Tom. "Gentlemen don't hit ladies," she seethed, her voice shaking with fury. She started to lead me toward the door, but Jay objected. Reaching out to me, he pulled me under his protective embrace.

"No, they don't," he said. "Gentlemen fight fair. When they fight at all." That was a blow aimed at Tom's manhood, at his lack of war service, and I waited for more violence.

But between Jordan's judgment and Jay's well-placed verbal blow, Tom seemed confused, unsure what to do next. He clenched and unclenched his hands at his sides.

Emboldened, Jay went on, his grip around my shoulders tighter. "She loves me. She wants to be with me."

When I didn't immediately concur, he looked at me. "You do love me, right?"

Whimpering from my still stinging cheek, I nodded.

"You're going to leave Tom, right?" His voice sounded higher than usual.

"I…I…" I couldn't speak, and the room seemed to spin. I must have swooned, because the next thing I knew, I was lying on the bed in the room next to the parlor and Jay was pressing a cool cloth to my head and whispering something to me. I couldn't focus on it at first, but eventually the words made sense.

"He'll be out of the picture soon. Remember, I've spoken to Anthony. Don't worry. He's not going to do anything while you're around. You don't need to be afraid."

Ah, yes, the gangster. I had pushed that out of my mind and, when nothing bad happened, I figured it never would.

Then Tom came in and pushed Jay away, grabbed the wet cloth, and threw it on the floor.

"We're leaving!" he announced. I recognized that take-charge tone, and I knew I should obey.

"Not if you want to go in one piece," Jay said, barely glancing at him.

Nick stood in the doorway next to Tom. "Let's all go. Come on. All of us."

Jordan brushed past them both and came over to me.

"Yes, let's." She helped me up.

Somehow, I managed to find the strength and wherewithal to stand. With purpose, I shook off her hand and strode to the door, both Nick and Tom stepping out of my way, parting like some sea pulled by an invisible hand. I gathered my hat and bag.

I had one thought in mind at that moment—getting safely home to Pamela. I'd leave Tom within seconds after that if I could make it away, but first I needed to get to her. Tom would never let me be alone with her again, now that he knew of my infidelity.

"I need to go home. To rest. We'll all…see each other tomorrow." I looked at Jay. I tried to convey the thought through my eyes: "Not now, love. Not now."

I don't know if he received the message because Tom came my way and enthusiastically agreed with my plan.

"I'll get you home, dear," he said.

Jay stepped forward to object, but I stopped him. "Let me go now," I said. "I need to get to my daughter."

He understood and stopped.

I said to Tom, "I'll drive. I've had less than you to drink."

DAISY

What you have to understand is that Nick didn't know who was behind the wheel that night. He had assumed it was me because of what I said before leaving, and in his muddled memory, he also seemed to think it was Jay I left with, not Tom, maybe because he was a hopeless romantic and wanted to see us together in the end. We'd driven into the city together, after all. Or maybe it was because Nick was drunk and his grasp of events hazy.

But Tom would never have let me leave that room with Jay. He would have thrown us both out the window before allowing that humiliation. He'd already been bested by Jay in the room. I'm sure Jay's remark about men choosing to fight rang in his ears. He'd been on our bumper practically the whole way to the city, too, probably scared we were going to run off then and there. Why on earth would he acquiesce to my lover driving me home when a short hour before he'd been afraid Jay and I would just drive off somewhere together, lost to him forever?

So it was Tom and me in the car, and, no, it wasn't me behind the wheel.

On the street outside the Plaza, Tom grabbed me, hard and fast around the waist, and I struggled to break free. When I did and managed a few quick strides up the street, he caught up quickly enough, found my hand, and yanked me forward. We were now in front of Jay's bright circus machine.

"Get in!" he shouted, embarrassing me in front of the doorman. "Let him drive my old coupe back." And he laughed, probably thinking of the three of them squeezed into that small seat.

I thought of running again, but the only thing binding me to Tom now was Pammy, and I wouldn't let him reach home first so he could place her somewhere out of my reach. I was stone cold sober at that point and thinking fast. He knew Jay and I were lovers. He feared we would run away together. He would do anything to prevent that, including holding our daughter hostage so I, his prized possession, would return to him.

"Let me drive," I said, but he came round to the passenger side, opened the door, and shoved me down into the car. With a leap that almost caused him to tumble, he jumped into the driver's seat and tried starting the engine. But Jay had one of those newfangled keys needed before the starter button would work, and Tom cursed, obviously remembering. He soon found the key in his pocket.

All I could think of then was my daughter, getting home to her, making sure she was safe and …mine. I started mapping out my plan as Tom drove, not paying attention to his weaving and speeding as dusk settled over the city.

I would sleep in Pamela's room that night, I decided. I'd pack our bags quietly while Tom slept off his drinks. Maybe I would take off in the dead of night while Tom dozed.

Take off to Jay's? He'd be there, waiting for me, I knew, despite our plan to leave the next night.

Would we head for Mexico?

If so, I'd be going from one cage to another. And how safe would that new cage be? Jay knew bad men who could do bad things. I wondered

DAISY

what he would do to me if I ever wanted to leave him, as I was leaving Tom. Would he become as malevolent as Tom was now? He had spent years looking for me already. He could do it again, probably more successfully than Tom.

These thoughts and more tumbled through my mind as the wind blew my hair round my head. I didn't bother securing it with my hat or a scarf. I didn't care. I just wanted to get home. Tom was pressing the vehicle into shudderingly high speeds. I think he wanted to wreck that car, and us in it, and so, as we approached that ash heap section of the drive that I hated so much, I turned to him and said, "Slow down or you'll make me sick."

He glanced at me for a long moment. Too long.

Suddenly, something whacked the car with a loud thump. At first, I thought a tire had blown, but somehow we were still moving, and Tom was swerving so fast that I fell against him.

"For god's sake, Tom!" I cried, now pushing the hair out of my face so I could see. But the lights of the roadster showed only grim roadway ahead. I turned around and saw another car that had just passed us jolting over a big bump of something—perhaps the same obstacle we had encountered, and thought nothing of it.

I thought instead of getting home and safe to my daughter.

CHAPTER FIFTEEN

By now, you know what happened after that awful day, and that horrible drive home. Tom hadn't hit just any obstacle. He'd crashed into his mistress, who had run out into the street fleeing her husband. Flung to the ground, she'd been crushed by a vehicle headed the other way. It was a gruesome death—one I wouldn't wish on an enemy—and I took no pleasure in reading and hearing of it over the next days.

At home that night, I hurried up to Pammy's room, locked the door, and lay down on the small bed reserved for Nanny when the little girl couldn't sleep.

Tom yelled through the door. "Don't think I'll let you go! He's a social climber. He's nothing! He's not like you and me, Daisy! Nothing like us!"

I couldn't resist, got up, and shouted back, "Thank God!"

Then I heard an engine start up and looked out the window. Our poor butler and housekeeper—Tom must have roused them—drove each of our vehicles somewhere away from our house. He was cutting off my means of escape.

There was nothing I could do. I lay down again and tried to sleep.

DAISY

The next morning, I concentrated on just keeping the peace. I'd stay quiet and agreeable, not speaking of the afternoon at the Plaza or even the bruise on my cheek.

But somehow, the papers had gotten hold of the accident before going to press the night before, and Tom, his hands shaking so hard he couldn't hold the pages upright, read that he'd killed his mistress. It was just one paragraph, probably hastily written to make the paper's deadline, merely the who, what, where, and when of Myrtle's death under the headline: "Garage Owner's Wife Killed."

He said nothing. He got up and walked to the windows. He looked out at the Sound. Then he practically ran to the garage.

Although he'd moved our own cars off property, he had yet to return Jay's car, knowing I couldn't start it without the key, so he hurried and made arrangements for it to be driven over to Jay's mansion. He seemed to calm down after that was taken care of, with the murder weapon placed far enough away to keep his hands clean, and his innocence secure.

I had no doubt that, if questioned, he would say he drove his own car home that night and didn't know who drove Jay's. If pressed with conflicting stories, he would probably laugh and admit we were all drunk, and everyone else must have been confused because he had driven the roadster into town, but it's a circus car and one ride in it was enough for him.

I could hear it in my head, those easy lies. Police would believe him. They believed the Toms of the world.

Now, as sunshine streamed through the windows, he came back into the room, hands in his pockets, and walked to the doors.

"We're moving," he announced after a time. "Back to Chicago. I've been making the arrangements, as you know, and I'm speeding them up."

I could sense his fear that the accident would be traced to him, and he'd be held responsible, despite it being Jay's car, delivered to Jay's garage, despite any easy alibis he could conjure up.

So this became part of my plan, to use his fear, and I managed to call Nick later that day, simply instructing him to tell Jay to be patient.

That night, after I fed Pammy, bathed her, and tucked her into bed, we sat in the kitchen and supped on cold chicken and beer. Tom had sent the staff home after taking care of Jay's car, finalizing the arrangements with movers, and securing us a house to rent along the lake in Chicago. I said what we both knew:

"You killed her." I wiped my face with my napkin. "We hit her. You were driving."

He swallowed and stared at me, and for one terrible moment, I feared Tom, that he might decide to get rid of this annoying witness to his crime. He stood and strode out of the room to the parlor, where he grabbed a bottle of whiskey and poured himself a tall glass. I followed and stood by the door.

"It's all right, Tom. I'm your wife. I can't and won't betray you. It's our little secret." As long as he treated me right, as long as he let me do what I wanted, even taking Pammy on an excursion without him.

He poured and downed another drink, then his head dropped to his chest and he let out an animal-like cry, so anguished that I thought he was having some kind of attack.

I didn't go to him, though. I let him ponder his fate alone, and, shaken, I eventually sank into an embroidered chair, still close to the door should I want to flee.

DAISY

He turned and came to me. He knelt in front of me and slurred words of contrition and gratitude.

"I didn't see her. I swear I didn't see her," he cried. "It wasn't my fault. She ran into the road. It was dark. I didn't see her! Oh, Daisy, Daisy. I knew I could count on you."

He wept. He sobbed into my lap like a little boy who longed for his parents' affection after engaging in some particularly devious mischief. He begged my forgiveness. He promised me everything.

In those moments when he was at my feet and I was stroking his hair, I remembered falling in love with him—prizing both his strength and his vulnerability. I'd seen it when we were younger. It had been the same as mine. The same longing for the world to be kind, not cruel, the same yearning for people to understand and accommodate you, not to judge you.

He'd been stuck, just like me, in a time and place, and he, too, was afraid of being less than the best. The best football star. The best polo player. The best son. The best representative of his class and culture.

He tried so hard.

I remembered him on the altar at our wedding, his face freshly scrubbed, his brown eyes shining with confusion.

I remembered my heart about to burst with love for him on our honeymoon, once I had determined that was my fate.

And I remembered our wedding night, when he was tender, sweet, and gentle, treating me as if I were that bit of porcelain that might break.

How could I not soothe him?

So I did, gently shushing him, telling him things would be all right, that we'd go away, and not look back, that everything would be different.

I lied.

Even in these tender moments of remembrance, I knew he couldn't be different. I barely had it within me to change, but somehow I had to find the grit to do so.

I knew he would eventually secure another mistress, and it wouldn't be long before she'd show up with a bastard, and he would be harsher on me now that he had tasted the thrill of roughing me up, as he had Myrtle.

If he had one ability to change, it seemed to be to shed the finer qualities of manhood that his social status had required of him. In these freewheeling years, he was learning he didn't need to abide by any rules, even self-imposed ones.

He had accidentally killed his mistress, a troublesome woman. It wouldn't be long before he lost his remorse and realized how convenient that solution was. I didn't intend to be his next victim.

So I comforted him as best I could, led him to bed, and sneaked back to my own, ever more eager to leave. I was almost ready, but with my leverage over Tom, I could afford to do more. I had some more jewelry I wanted to sell off, and I thought I could do it in at most a day or two, while I finished the details of my plan. I tried ringing up Nick to urge him to tell Jay one more time to be patient, but Nick wasn't home.

In the morning, we awoke to more news. Mr. Wilson had exacted his revenge, finding and killing the owner of the car that had run down his wife.

CHAPTER SIXTEEN

I heard the news from Tom, who reported it coldly over coffee.

"Cook tells me there was a disturbance across the way yesterday. That Wilson fellow tracked down his wife's killer and shot him."

I gripped my coffee cup. I stopped breathing. For an instant, a wild hope emerged, that Wilson had shot a servant. But Jay had sent the servants away.

In that instant, I knew my lover was dead, and I no longer had leverage over Tom.

"Wh-what…" I murmured and then stilled as the news hit home.

I had loved Jay, loved him with all the pure, sweet affection of one's first attachment. To leave him, to betray him, was to betray oneself. And that was why I'd been so tortured all those years until reuniting. I'd thought I had cheated myself, not just Jay, upon marrying Tom. I had given up trying to be good and kind and tender. I'd thought one couldn't be that way and survive.

I wanted to ask for more details but couldn't. I choked on the words. I blinked fast to avoid tears. I stared at Tom, daring him to say more, knowing he would because it would hurt me. How cold he was.

"Just marched in to the house, found him in the pool, and fired his pistol. Good aim, apparently." Tom smirked. "They'll have to drain the pool now, of course."

Of course. I put down my napkin, stood, and walked silently up to my room, where I closed the door and sat on the bed, trembling.

DAISY

Tears came, then sobs that I didn't bother hiding. Let Tom hear. Let him hear how much I loved Jay. I moaned and wailed. I got up and paced. I cursed. I wanted the world to witness my anguish.

Loathsome Tom, giving me the news with such glee. I'm sure he now believed in his heart that Jay had been Myrtle's killer, after all. In a short time, he would erase all doubt and remember it this way, that Jay had run over his mistress. For all I know, Tom might have later told Nick that I was behind the wheel that night, thus triggering his version of the tale.

My heart was again broken, that again the world of sunshine and love and beauty and tenderness had drifted out of reach. The world and life had again disappointed me.

I, like Jay, had lived in a fairyland before the war. Peaceful, hopeful, loving, gentle. Those years, our youthful years, were everything you'd wanted as you stepped into the world. And then…destruction on a level unimaginable. Illness scouring the land as if an avenging angel had come to punish all of us for the folly of the war.

Everything changed after those years of rupture, and he'd spent such a long time searching, searching for me, trying to get it all back. Seduced by Jay's fantasy, I, like him, thought we both could reclaim our pre-war happiness because I wanted the same thing. But I didn't know how to turn back the clock, to go back in time and recapture everything we had lost—that Eden in which we'd grown up.

There was no going back, only moving forward. Jay, of all people, should have known that, he with his aspirations for success, his drive always toward the horizon.

The phone rang. It was Nick. I heard Tom tell him I was indisposed. It rang again. Jordan this time—she'd stayed in the city rather than squeeze into the coupe with Jay and Nick that awful night after the afternoon at the Plaza. Tom gave the same excuse to her. I wasn't feeling well, couldn't come to the phone.

His steely voice told me I had to get away and soon. No more waiting to sell jewelry or finalize plans. Panicked and grief-stricken, I had to find the courage and wits to get out from under his control. With Pammy. No one could make this plan for me. I had to do it myself.

It didn't matter that I couldn't speak to Nick or Jordan. After all, what would I say? Tom was carefully watching me, so I couldn't afford to make him angry. If I did, my future would include a visit or two from Dr. Prinz with his long syringe. Then I'd be lucky to see Pammy when she visited me in an asylum.

My mind and heart were tumbling, my thoughts and feelings a knotted ball I couldn't pull apart. I just put one foot in front of the other that day and during the hours to come. Of Tom's moving plans, I nodded approval. I helped Nanny pack Pamela's things. I boxed up some of my items. All these actions were parallel to my own planning. As my fogged mind cleared, I knew what I had to do and plotted the best time to do it.

Jay's death felt like a constant ache, like a bruise that wouldn't heal. The irony of his loss was that, sometime on the road back home from the city that dreadful night, I'd been coming to the conclusion that I couldn't be with him, not for any length of time, at least. The real reason I'd not immediately fled to his mansion with Pamela was my hesitation at being imprisoned in yet another gilded cell. The real reason I had continued to send messages for him to be patient was that I wasn't sure I would ever show up.

DAISY

Even with those realizations, I never wanted his life snuffed out. Certainly not like this. His life was taken in such a despicable way, killed by a garage owner from that ash heap part of town, and not in some grand heroic way that would have immortalized him in an appropriate fashion.

Now that he was gone, though, I could chart a course free of worrying that he'd come looking for me again. To realize this benefit of his passing only added to my grief.

I'm ashamed to admit it, but eventually, maybe sooner than was seemly, I even felt some relief, knowing I wouldn't have to run away from two men, one of whom had already spent years tracking me down and could possibly do so again.

Nick later reported to me the pathetic gathering at Jay's funeral. Just Nick and a few others. He had attracted hundreds to his parties, and many felt left out if they'd not attended one.

Jay had created a dream life for himself, and it turns out all his friends were imaginary, too.

I couldn't spend too much time thinking of these things, though later I pondered them at length, wondering if I really had been a fairy that summer. Sometimes, I cried at the thought of Jay dying alone, and with so few to mourn him.

At that moment, I had problems I needed to face—Tom. During those days of planning to move, he had a look in his eye that sent shivers down my spine. Cold. Evaluating. Waiting for the moment we were in a new home, with no one around to watch out for me, to protect me from his slowly simmering anger. He would make me pay for my infidelity.

I had to give it one last look before we left, and in the early morning hours two days later, I stole out of my bed, tied a scarf around my neck, and drove to West Egg without Tom's knowledge. He'd felt comfortable enough with my new agreeable nature that the cars were back on our property again. I had presented nothing but the most obedient of temperaments to him, talking of our new home in Chicago, asking how many rooms it had, if I could hire a decorator. He thought I was his old Daisy again, the one who did what was expected of her, the one who was careless and thoughtless in the face of others' misfortunes.

Dawn broke and the light painted Jay's mansion golden, but it stood silent and empty, its master now gone for good, and for a moment it seemed to be rebuking me, mutely asking why I'd not visited earlier, why I hadn't saved its owner. I wondered that, too.

Who would be the next Gatsby, the next man to conjure up a past at Oxford or some other elite school and make a fortune that allowed him to dazzle and charm and have his way with everyone?

As I walked the grounds, I remembered the better side of him, the eager, striving side that approached the world with an openness usually demonstrated only by naïfs. I loved that about him. I wouldn't deny it.

Making my way back to my car, I saw a dark vehicle approach and a man get out, someone I recognized as a Delacorte associate.

With a breezy hello, I introduced myself, using my maiden name, and said I thought I knew him.

DAISY

"It's a shame, real shame what happened to Jay," he said, shaking his head. "A good man. One of the best I ever knew."

"Yes, yes," I said. "I was a friend. I'll…I'll miss him." On that last word, my voice cracked, and I began to cry.

"There, there, Miss," he said. He came over to me and handed me a handkerchief, while I continued to weep.

It was a genuine cry, and I realized it felt good to share this grief with someone, not just in private or in whispered conversations with Nick, because I knew Tom would take offense at any outpouring of sorrow for Jay Gatsby.

The man tried to comfort me, patting me on the back, saying "there, there" over and over.

Finally, I gathered my wits and sniffed, standing straight.

"So much was left hanging after his death," I said. "I don't know what to do."

"Oh, that's right, Miss. That's right. I was hoping to get some counsel myself, about a matter I'm supposed to take care of."

I knew what he was talking about. The matter with Tom.

I paused. I knew I could just leave and say nothing. In those endless seconds, Tom's life and death teetered.

"If Jay wanted something done, I would think he'd want it done. Even post mortem."

I played the part of the fool, the empty-headed woman who leaves business matters to the men.

"Yes, ma'am," he said after some hesitation. "You're probably right."

After a few more moments of empty small talk, we parted ways.

After hurrying home, I found the house to be a jumble of activity, movers lifting and carrying out furniture, servants packing, little Pammy running to and fro with Nanny at her heels. I secured her suitcase and my own, filled with dresses and outfits and makeup and perfume. And money, too. One should always have abundant cash on hand.

I smiled and frowned at all the right moments, playing my role as attentive wife and mother, all the while hurrying as fast as I could, not wanting to be around if Mr. Delacorte's associate decided to fulfill the contract then and there.

Things were a blur, and I was frazzled. It was warm, but the effervescence of the season had long since gone, and we all were stumbling into that season of farewells—fall.

Tom trod out to the car and hoisted a box into the back seat. Turning to me, he smiled and said, "Anything else?"

"Just a few things for the car," I answered and handed him a hatbox and a small piece of luggage for overnight visits stuffed with things I didn't need. It was such an awkward size and shape, it took him some time to secure it. "Stay here while I get them," I said.

I gave him a quick peck on the cheek, feeling his stubble, remembering how his manliness used to thrill me, but he didn't respond. He stayed busy tying down items.

One last glance, and I was off, flitting as fast as that fairy I'd imagined glowing in our dock light.

DAISY

The house reverberated with a quiet hum of activity—thumps of furniture, clicks of doors, murmured voices.

I ran to the nursery. I gathered my two large suitcases, one in each hand, and I told Nanny that Pamela would be in my charge now. I'd thought of stowing our luggage on the boat earlier, but had been afraid some servant would find it, since we would be getting ready to sell the boat soon, and Tom might have instructed some worker to get it in tip-top shape. Quietly, I led my daughter down the back stairs and out to the lawn, where we walked as if it was all part of our moving plan, to the boat.

My nerves jangled with apprehension. I had planned this. I'd known this was my only chance, when movers filled the house, when Tom trusted me to help with directions, even keeping Pammy out of the way. I had to act fast before he wanted something from me or noticed I wasn't to be found.

"Here, darling," I said as we reached the dock. I lifted her onboard the *Victoria Marie*. "We're going on a fun adventure. You love adventures, don't you?"

She smiled and nodded, and I hoisted our bags onto the deck before jumping on myself.

"Go sit quietly and dream of where you'd like me to take you. A fairyland?"

"Oh, yes," she said and clapped her hands.

I expected her to ask if Daddy would come, too. I even had a response ready—*he might, at some point, sweetheart*—to soothe her anxieties until we were safely away and I could deal with that problem later. But she didn't ask, and it thrilled me that she was happy to be with me and me alone.

I pulled on a sailor's cap, tugged on leather gloves, and told her again to sit quietly and not to move anywhere or the sea monsters would find her. I told her we'd be having a great old time and by day's end, we would be in a magical new town with beautiful rooms and wonderful food.

Then, just as I had seen Jay do the day I'd watched him across the Sound without knowing who he was, I hoisted the sail before we were fully under way. But unlike him that day, I was prepared as the wind caught the sheets and puffed their breath of life into them, as the boat tilted and rushed forward. In a flash, I steered us to open water, feeling with every bouncing wave, every giggle from Pamela, a sense of freedom and youth and determination. Just as I had felt diving into the Sound. One, long, glorious exhale of liberation.

I tacked so that we caught every bit of wind, and we raced across the water as if I were in a competition. At last, I felt no fear.

I could see our house and the road as we glided away. Just before it faded from view, I caught sight of the black car of Mr. Delacorte's associate creeping up to the gates.

I would never be anyone's little fool again. I'd not be the golden girl. I'd not be the one treated like an object, or a goddess to be used.

My plan was to make port in Delaware or Maryland by day's end, and then perhaps proceed into the Chesapeake Bay. As confident as I felt sailing, I knew I wasn't up to a long ocean journey, so I hugged the south shore. That night, we would nestle into a sweet old inn, and then I would use some cash to buy train tickets west, somewhere far away, somewhere the sun shone for most of the year. But not before selling the boat, and pocketing that cash for the upcoming trip.

DAISY

As the boat clipped over a large wave late that afternoon, Pammy giggled again, and in her face I saw a reflection of who I used to be—open to the world, confident of everyone's love, and sure that no one would hurt me.

And then I sailed on, in a boat against the current, moving relentlessly toward the future.

EPILOGUE

This is where Nick's recounting ends, but I'm a woman, and so I'll have the last word.

Nick ended our story in a romantic way—the beautiful heroine together again with her original hero, her husband (even if he didn't paint us in the most flattering of tones) after tragedy occurs. Nick was a romantic, and I think, despite his role in bringing Jay and me together, he wanted to believe that I'd make my marriage with Tom work out well, that it could return to some blissful union, strengthened by the drama we'd gone through. So he wrote it that way.

That wasn't to be. I didn't stay with my "hero." He was no hero at all.

For a long time I barely talked to Nick once he wrote our story. After all, he made me a murderer in it, running down "poor" Myrtle Wilson. Of course he made me the villain, the hare-brained, foolish woman, so feckless she's not even aware of the destruction in her wake and careless about it all after she hears what she wrought.

I was no such thing. When his story became a success, Nick refused to tinker with the denouement, and convinced me for a while that if the money helped me, it was best to leave it alone. He published it as a novel, after all, not a work of non-fiction.

Tom's death was the finale in that summer story, though, and he met it in the same way his mistress met hers.

If Mr. Delacorte's "associate" drove up to the house the day I left, he didn't fulfill the contract then, maybe because there were too many people

DAISY

about. All I know is that one day in New York, Tom stepped off a curb or was pushed or tripped, and fell in front of a taxi. So he died as his mistress had, crushed under the wheels of a shiny machine, one he might have even called a "circus car" since it was a bright lavender vehicle, one of the newest of the fleet.

Nick gave me the news. I called him once we'd gotten settled, and asked he not let Tom know where I was, but I needed some help with the very last of the bonds I'd bought through him and not cashed out.

He told me I had no worries about Tom anymore. Tom was dead. I expected to feel less sad than I did, but I wept at the news. He had been my husband, after all, and was Pamela's father. I think I cried longer for him than for Jay. Tom had been more real, our life more substantial, and I cried for what I'd hoped our marriage would be. My time with Jay had been nothing but a dream.

I asked for the details.

"As soon as he realized you were gone, he stopped the move," Nick said. "He didn't figure it out for hours because I guess something went wrong with one of the trucks, and it took a long time to get a new one out to the house."

I could imagine the scene, Tom angry with the movers, supervising the rearrangement of our things once a new truck was brought out, maybe even irritated with me that I wasn't around. I could envision him snapping at servants to go find me.

He called Nick, eventually, demanding to know where I'd headed, but of course, poor Nick didn't know and suggested Tom wait a bit to see if I'd call.

"When he noticed the boat was gone, he was pretty shaken, Daisy, not mad, just quiet. He couldn't believe you'd take Pamela," Nick said, and I wondered if he was deliberately trying to make me feel worse than I did. "He thought maybe you'd taken her out for a short sail to get away from all the mess. Then evening fell, and, well, he knew you weren't coming back. He was worried. I told him to call the police—I didn't know if you'd need help, out in the boat alone—but he didn't want to do that right away."

Of course he wouldn't. Tom might have been shocked I'd left with our daughter, but he wouldn't want to confess to police his wife might have abandoned him, taking his own sloop to do so—it was too embarrassing. So he'd not let anyone know right away that we were gone. He'd want to fix things on his own.

Even if he had headed to the police or coastal forces, they'd not have found our boat. I slipped into our first port in New Jersey and immediately had a new name painted on her stern, something bland, *Calm Waters*. I paid a premium for that quick work but knew it was necessary.

Then Pamela and I had a wonderful day in a fairy palace inn along the shore, with rose-patterned coverlets and china that reminded me of the set Jay had used that first tea we had at Nick's house.

Tom went into the city a few days after I left, Nick said, to hire a private detective to look for me and Pammy. It was there he met his fate, and I don't know if it was at the hands of the Delacorte man or simply bad luck.

I'd not seen the obituary because my life was too filled with deciding my future with Pamela, with arranging for rooms and destinations and travel and all the things I'd relied on men and servants to do for me in the past. I'd not picked up a newspaper for months after leaving Tom.

DAISY

I was settled by the time I got the news, as I said, and after my grief passed, I set about living a new life, one where I alone was responsible for myself and my daughter.

I wrestled with how to make sure Pamela got her father's inheritance, but that would have meant contacting the estate, and Tom's father was still alive. He was an old-fashioned man, and I had no doubt he might try to take over Pammy's upbringing, perhaps sending me to a madhouse to get me out of the way.

So I did nothing to claim what was rightfully mine and Pammy's. I decided I'd wait a while, and when I felt safe, I'd contact the appropriate lawyers.

The party of those crazy years ended, as you know. The big party of the Roaring Twenties burnt out, the lights were flipped off, celebrants went home, it was over. Everyone became more serious.

In the crash of the stock market that came at decade's end, poor Tom would have faired poorly, so his death saved him that humiliation. As it turned out, he'd used a good portion of his family's fortune on stocks bought on margin and other dubious deals, all so he wouldn't feel left out of the big money party going on at the time. His was one of the few old rich families to lose everything. No need for me to claim an inheritance now.

His father, I learned later in a newspaper article, ended up killing himself, just as mine had when a jolt in finances had left him hopeless and ashamed. Yes, I eventually figured that out, that my daddy's trip down the stairs had not occurred at all, and that a rope broke his neck, not a fall.

I suspect Jay would have done all right in the tumult. A lot of his money came from bootlegging, which continued as Prohibition crawled into the early part of the next decade. And then I imagine he would have lit on some other wealth-producing plan. He always, always looked to the future.

Nick lost everything in the crash of '29, too, and headed for Hollywood where he worked as a writer for a while, skills he used when penning our tale.

Jordan married well, someone inured against the economic upheaval. She lived in a lovely apartment overlooking Central Park until she met someone else, an actor without a penny to his name. Then her husband divorced her, and she went back to playing golf, having secured a lovely nest egg from her ex-husband when they ended their marriage. She lives near a golf course in the Hamptons now. I'm not sure if she is still with her actor lover. We exchange letters, but Jordan, like Jay, leaves a lot out of her recounting of her life.

As for me...

I was grateful for Nick's investment advice, but more grateful for my own good sense in cashing out as soon as stocks were high as I sought to protect myself and Pammy. I'd even had the sense to sell all my jewelry before it lost its value. It was a risk of a different kind to have all that money on me, but I managed to keep it safe. We lived modestly enough that we never drew attention to ourselves.

After a short stay in Virginia as I contemplated heading west, I sold the boat, and we eventually made our way back home, to Kentucky, where it was my dream to buy back my family homestead.

That was not to be. Beyond my price when I arrived, it sold to some young upstart who made changes and turned it into a boardinghouse. The most I could do was rent some rooms in it for Pammy and me, and I couldn't bring myself to make that move, even though I did go look at

DAISY

quarters there one day, thinking it might be a good choice for us. But to face the heartbreak of being in my lovely old home, where I'd felt safe and feted and loved, seeing it all chopped up with strangers living in the white-and-gold bedroom I used to occupy—that would have been too much to bear.

Instead, we settled into a very small cottage not far from my mother's own similar dwelling, which I decorated with used furniture and sweet little mementoes, having more fun than when I'd had the money to select expensive silverware. This was all mine, not something bestowed on me by a condescending husband or a sweetly obsessed lover. Never once did it feel "shabby" to me.

Pamela asked a few times that first year where Daddy was, and I told her he'd decided to stay in New York. Eventually she stopped asking, and when she was old enough to understand I said he'd been killed in a horrible motor accident shortly before we were supposed to move. She accepted this explanation, and I gave her some photographs of Tom to cherish, so she knew she'd had a loving father.

It was good to be back near my mama. I told her the whole story of that summer, and then she read it anew when Nick's account was published, both of us shaking our heads at what he'd gotten wrong when I pointed out where our stories diverged. After objections on my part, he agreed to share credit, but that, as I already mentioned, eventually faded, even if the royalties came for a short time at least. It was the least he could do since I'd been the one to inspire him to put pen to paper after I'd sent him my own recollections of the tale.

I made my money last for a considerable time before I had to think of supplementing it, and it did come upon me one panicky night after doing numbers at the kitchen table after Pamela's bedtime that I probably had harbored the illusion I'd find and marry another wealthy man who'd raise me back to my former position in life.

It took just that one night to get over that ridiculous notion, and I was determined the very next day to secure a position somewhere.

In some correspondence with Jordan, she suggested I try looking for work at some country clubs and golf courses. Doing what, I asked. "Dear, you're a pretty face," she wrote. "All you need to do is smile at people and make them feel they're the only ones you care about. It's a talent you've had all your life."

That wasn't much of a duty roster, but I did manage to land a position as a hostess of sorts at a club nearby, greeting people at the door and making sure they knew how to get on the course or find their way to the restaurant on the grounds. It was only a few hours a week—clubs lost a lot of members during those lean years—but it, combined with what was left of my savings, was enough to keep Pammy and me and Mother, who eventually moved in with us, comfortable, and we lived simply and without want for many years. I actually enjoyed the work. I liked meeting people and being nice to them, and they seemed to like me.

Mother passed quietly after contracting pneumonia in the spring of '39, and truth be told, I was glad she didn't live to see horrors visited on Europe again and war come to our very shores.

Pamela turned into a bright young woman, as pretty as I was at that age, with my golden hair and Tom's piercing eyes, a bit taller than I am, and with a fine athletic body and quick, purposeful movements. She always looks as if she has somewhere to go and strides off with the determination of an explorer, even if just to retrieve a notebook from her room.

DAISY

She had a string of beaux in her high school years she didn't take seriously. She was too serious herself, winning honors at school for writing and swimming. I was so proud of her when she graduated and decided she might even want to go to college.

When she enrolled in Vassar, I worried about how I'd pay for it, but Mother had bought a life insurance policy, unbeknownst to me, and after she passed, I used the proceeds to finance Pamela's education, happy she wouldn't have to work her way through.

Then, the war came, and that's where we are now, with men storming the shores of France to reclaim the battlefields Jay had once helped win.

There's plenty of work at last, and I applied and was accepted at an airplane factory. That money let me buy a new car, and that work with all the women around me who'd been a bit beaten down over the years lifted me up. I finally felt my own life had meaning.

They didn't know me as Daisy Buchanan or even Daisy Fay, my maiden name. I chose to be called Lenore at that time, finally giving myself the romantic moniker I'd always wanted.

I thought I'd be lonely for a man's attention, and over the years there had been a few suitors who called on me, treated me to dinner, but all and all, I was content with my single life, especially now as I work in the factory. None of the luxuries I used to have compares with the radio I was able to buy with a bonus for good work or the money I can send to Pamela from my earnings.

I miss her terribly, but rejoice that she is on her own, able to provide for herself. Jordan sometimes sees her in New York when she herself is there, because Pamela occasionally writes for a magazine.

Pamela wrote me she's seeing someone, a soldier named Richard, Richard D'Invilliers or some other ostentatious name, about to go overseas, and she worries about whether he'll be safe, if they should marry before he goes, or if she should wait until he returns.

Thinking of Jay, I started to write to her to wait, that she'd regret not waiting. I tore up that paper and began anew:

Dearest Daughter,

Aunt Jordan says you are doing very well and might be hired as a staff writer soon. You are making your way in the world. I am so proud of you. It's hard for me to advise you on whether you should wait or marry now. Only you know what is best for you and what future you wish to choose. That's the important thing, dear—what you wish to do…

ABOUT *DAISY*

Two novels greatly influenced me as a writer, books I'd first encountered as a girl. One was Charlotte Bronte's *Jane Eyre*, whose sweeping storytelling seduced me from beginning to end. I wished I could tell stories like that.

The other was F. Scott Fitzgerald's *The Great Gatsby*, a shorter and simpler tale, but one whose use of evocative language made me want to be a writer myself. He made you feel as well as understand the story.

It took many years for me to give myself permission to pursue that goal of being a writer, and in the meantime I read virtually all of the Fitzgerald oeuvre and more—his short stories, his novels (including *Trimalchio*, the first draft of *Gatsby*), *The Crack-up*, plus Zelda's book, *Save Me the Waltz*, and numerous biographies of that ill-fated pair.

When I came up with the idea of imagining the Gatsby story from Daisy's point of view, I knew the novel could not be a mere point-by-point retelling of that famous tale. It had to convey something more, something readers either didn't get from the original or felt was missing and would enjoy seeing, a sort of behind-the-scenes look at the story.

This was the approach I used when writing a retelling, *Sloane Hall*, of Bronte's classic. I not only wanted readers to experience that story afresh as if never having read it before. I wanted to expand on Bronte's exploration of characters and themes.

In *Gatsby*, I felt called to develop Daisy's character. The original isn't her story—it's Gatsby's, Nick's, even Tom's. I missed her and wanted to get

DAISY

to know her better. In the original, she is like a sprite, something not real, not flesh and blood, a woman two men coveted but whose physicality is something distant or even symbolic, like that green light at the end of her pier. She is a possession, sought after and jealously guarded.

I wanted to make her real and yet not have her lose the romanticism of the original character, her sweet beauty and grace and desirability.

As I explored her character, I came to ponder how hemmed in women's lives were during that period. I am of a generation that knew only some of that imprisonment. Women couldn't get credit cards when I was young, but in Daisy's time—well, it was virtually impossible for a woman in her position to be anything but the "fool" she wishes her daughter was, and how natural it was for a male author to draw this woman's character as something a little unreal. (This is not a criticism of Fitzgerald. He was a creature of his time, and he always treated his wife with respect on the page, idealizing her, while in real life he protected and supported her financially, no matter how difficult.)

That was my springboard for carving out her figure more fully, and as I wrote, she became a cipher no longer, but a fiercely intelligent woman whose heart was open to the deepest kind of love, if she could only find it.

And, because Fitzgerald always seemed to use Zelda as the inspiration for his heroines, my Daisy is part Zelda, too, incorporating pieces of Zelda's story along the way—her romance with a French aviator, her diving off a high cliff into the Mediterranean while Scott trembled with fear, her desire to dance and paint, and, of course, her madness. All of these are folded into this new Daisy.

I hope fans of the original like getting to know this Daisy and are not disappointed.

There are changes to the original story, some small, some large, that I incorporated to move plot along or to be true to the characterizations I was painting. Lovers of *The Great Gatsby* will surely notice them, but I hope will be swept up in this new tale.

I hope all who read this understand I'm not trying to compete with Fitzgerald's masterpiece. I'm just using it as a springboard to answer questions this devoted fan mulled for many years—such as, what was Daisy thinking? I guess in that sense, it's a love note to the original or maybe a piece of fan fiction. However it is classified, I hope it brings readers pleasure and, perhaps, an incentive to revisit the original.

LS

ACKNOWLEDGMENTS

Every time I publish a book, I thank my family, and for good reason. They not only support my writing habit, they encourage it (and me, of course). Lately, as we've all grown older, I've found myself also consulting my children for advice, a reversal of roles from when they were younger and an "advice chair" sat at the ready in my room. Now they are wise beyond their years, and they, along with my husband, have been excellent sounding boards and counselors through this crazy publishing business and other life events. I can't thank them enough.

I also need to thank my outstanding daughter-in-law, Evelyn, who is a wonderful mother to our grandchildren, and whose own marketing efforts on behalf of her freelance work set a high bar for my feeble similar attempts.

Another thank-you goes out to Deborah Nemeth, who saw this manuscript in its early stages and provided first-class editing services to help me get it where it is today.

I also want to once again thank my writing friend Jerri, hundreds of miles away, but always close in spirit. An excellent published author, she, too, has offered me frank counsel and the much-needed cheering when my spirits were low.

Finally, I owe a debt of gratitude to my publisher, Bruce L. Bortz of Bancroft Press. He has been an unflagging supporter and always interested in my latest projects, no matter what they are. Every author should have such an encouraging editor.

ABOUT THE AUTHOR

Libby Sternberg is an Edgar finalist, a Launchpad Prose Top 50 finalist, and a BookLife quarter finalist twice. She writes historical fiction, women's fiction and more under the names Libby Sternberg and Libby Malin, and one of her romantic comedies was bought for film. Her other retelling of a classic story—a Jane-Eyre reiteration titled Sloane Hall—was one of only 14 books highlighted in the Huffington Post on the 200th anniversary of Charlotte Bronte's birth.

PUBLISHER'S NOTE

One hundred years ago, F. Scott Fitzgerald published *The Great Gatsby*, a novel that captured the glamour, ambition, and illusions of the Jazz Age while exposing the cracks beneath its gilded surface. Over the past century, Gatsby's story has endured as a defining piece of American literature, studied, admired, and continually reinterpreted.

Yet, within this celebrated novel, one character's voice has remained elusive—until now.

With this centennial edition, we present *The Great Gatsby* alongside Libby Sternberg's *Daisy*, a critically acclaimed reimagining of the story from Daisy Buchanan's perspective. For decades, Daisy has been viewed through the lens of Gatsby's longing and Nick Carraway's detached observations. But who was Daisy, truly? What choices shaped her, and how did she see her own life amid the wealth and expectations of her era?

By pairing these two books together, we invite readers to experience Gatsby's world in a new way—first through Fitzgerald's iconic prose and then through Daisy's own lens. We hope this edition will deepen readers' appreciation for both novels, offering a fresh perspective on agency, identity, and the weight of societal expectations—themes that resonate as powerfully today as they did in 1925.

Whether you are revisiting *Gatsby* for the hundredth time or discovering Daisy's story for the first, we are honored to share this literary dialogue with you.

Bruce L. Bortz, *Founder & Publisher* - **Bancroft Press**
February 10, 2025

The Great Gatsby

100TH ANNIVERSARY EDITION

F. SCOTT FITZGERALD

The Great Gatsby
by
F. Scott Fitzgerald

Published 1925

The characters and events portrayed in this book are not real, or, if real, used fictitiously. Any similarity to real persons, living or dead, is purely coincidental and not intended by the author.

Interior Design: TracyCopesCreative.com

Published by Bancroft Press
"Books that Enlighten"
(818) 275-3061
4527 Glenwood Avenue
La Crescenta, CA 91214
www.bancroftpress.com

Printed in the United States of America

Once again to Zelda

TABLE OF CONTENTS

I	205
II	227
III	243
IV	265
V	285
VI	301
VII	317
VIII	351
IX	369

Then wear the gold hat, if that will move her;
If you can bounce high, bounce for her too,
Till she cry "Lover, gold-hatted, high-bouncing lover,
I must have you!"

Thomas Parke d'Invilliers

I

In my younger and more vulnerable years my father gave me some advice that I've been turning over in my mind ever since.

"Whenever you feel like criticizing anyone," he told me, "just remember that all the people in this world haven't had the advantages that you've had."

He didn't say any more, but we've always been unusually communicative in a reserved way, and I understood that he meant a great deal more than that. In consequence, I'm inclined to reserve all judgements, a habit that has opened up many curious natures to me and also made me the victim of not a few veteran bores. The abnormal mind is quick to detect and attach itself to this quality when it appears in a normal person, and so it came about that in college I was unjustly accused of being a politician, because I was privy to the secret griefs of wild, unknown men. Most of the confidences were unsought—frequently I have feigned sleep, preoccupation, or a hostile levity when I realized by some unmistakable sign that an intimate revelation was quivering on the horizon; for the intimate revelations of young men, or at least the terms in which they express them, are usually plagiaristic and marred by obvious suppressions. Reserving judgements is a matter of infinite hope. I am still a little afraid of missing something if I forget that, as my father snobbishly suggested, and I snobbishly repeat, a sense of the fundamental decencies is parcelled out unequally at birth.

And, after boasting this way of my tolerance, I come to the admission that it has a limit. Conduct may be founded on the hard rock or the wet marshes, but after a certain point I don't care what it's founded on. When I came back from the East last autumn I felt that I wanted the world to be in uniform and at a sort of moral attention forever; I wanted no more riotous excursions with privileged glimpses into the human heart. Only Gatsby, the man who gives his name to this book, was exempt from my reaction—Gatsby, who represented everything for which I have an unaffected scorn. If personality is an unbroken series of successful gestures, then there was something gorgeous about him, some heightened sensitivity to the promises of life, as if he were related to one of those intricate machines that register earthquakes ten thousand miles away. This responsiveness had nothing to do with that flabby impressionability which is dignified under the name of the "creative temperament"—it was an extraordinary gift for hope, a romantic readiness such as I have never found in any other person and which it is not likely I shall ever find again. No—Gatsby turned out all right at the end; it is what preyed on Gatsby, what foul dust floated in the wake of his dreams that temporarily closed out my interest in the abortive sorrows and short-winded elations of men.

My family have been prominent, well-to-do people in this Middle Western city for three generations. The Carraways are something of a clan, and we have a tradition that we're descended from the Dukes of Buccleuch, but the actual founder of my line was my grandfather's brother, who came here in fifty-one, sent a substitute to the Civil War, and started the wholesale hardware business that my father carries on today.

I never saw this great-uncle, but I'm supposed to look like him—with special reference to the rather hard-boiled painting that hangs in father's office. I graduated from New Haven in 1915, just a quarter of a century after my father, and a little later I participated in that delayed Teutonic migration known as the Great War. I enjoyed the counter-raid so thoroughly that I came back restless. Instead of being the warm centre of the world, the Middle West now seemed like the ragged edge of the universe—so I decided to go East and learn the bond business. Everybody I knew was in the bond business, so I supposed it could support one more single man. All my aunts and uncles talked it over as if they were choosing a prep school for me, and finally said, "Why—ye-es," with very grave, hesitant faces. Father agreed to finance me for a year, and after various delays I came East, permanently, I thought, in the spring of twenty-two.

The practical thing was to find rooms in the city, but it was a warm season, and I had just left a country of wide lawns and friendly trees, so when a young man at the office suggested that we take a house together in a commuting town, it sounded like a great idea. He found the house, a weather-beaten cardboard bungalow at eighty a month, but at the last minute the firm ordered him to Washington, and I went out to the country alone. I had a dog—at least I had him for a few days until he ran away—and an old Dodge and a Finnish woman, who made my bed and cooked breakfast and muttered Finnish wisdom to herself over the electric stove.

It was lonely for a day or so until one morning some man, more recently arrived than I, stopped me on the road.

"How do you get to West Egg village?" he asked helplessly.

THE GREAT GATSBY

I told him. And as I walked on I was lonely no longer. I was a guide, a pathfinder, an original settler. He had casually conferred on me the freedom of the neighbourhood.

And so with the sunshine and the great bursts of leaves growing on the trees, just as things grow in fast movies, I had that familiar conviction that life was beginning over again with the summer.

There was so much to read, for one thing, and so much fine health to be pulled down out of the young breath-giving air. I bought a dozen volumes on banking and credit and investment securities, and they stood on my shelf in red and gold like new money from the mint, promising to unfold the shining secrets that only Midas and Morgan and Maecenas knew. And I had the high intention of reading many other books besides. I was rather literary in college—one year I wrote a series of very solemn and obvious editorials for the Yale News—and now I was going to bring back all such things into my life and become again that most limited of all specialists, the "well-rounded man." This isn't just an epigram—life is much more successfully looked at from a single window, after all.

It was a matter of chance that I should have rented a house in one of the strangest communities in North America. It was on that slender riotous island which extends itself due east of New York—and where there are, among other natural curiosities, two unusual formations of land. Twenty miles from the city a pair of enormous eggs, identical in contour and separated only by a courtesy bay, jut out into the most domesticated body of salt water in the Western hemisphere, the great wet barnyard of Long Island Sound. They are not perfect ovals—like the egg in the Columbus story, they are both crushed flat at the contact end—but their physical resemblance must be a source of perpetual wonder to the gulls that fly overhead. To the wingless a more interesting phenomenon is their dissimilarity in every particular except shape and size.

I lived at West Egg, the—well, the less fashionable of the two, though this is a most superficial tag to express the bizarre and not a little sinister contrast between them. My house was at the very tip of the egg, only fifty yards from the Sound, and squeezed between two huge places that rented for twelve or fifteen thousand a season. The one on my right was a colossal affair by any standard—it was a factual imitation of some Hôtel de Ville in Normandy, with a tower on one side, spanking new under a thin beard of raw ivy, and a marble swimming pool, and more than forty acres of lawn and garden. It was Gatsby's mansion. Or, rather, as I didn't know Mr. Gatsby, it was a mansion inhabited by a gentleman of that name. My own house was an eyesore, but it was a small eyesore, and it had been overlooked, so I had a view of the water, a partial view of my neighbour's lawn, and the consoling proximity of millionaires—all for eighty dollars a month.

Across the courtesy bay the white palaces of fashionable East Egg glittered along the water, and the history of the summer really begins on the evening I drove over there to have dinner with the Tom Buchanans. Daisy was my second cousin once removed, and I'd known Tom in college. And just after the war I spent two days with them in Chicago.

Her husband, among various physical accomplishments, had been one of the most powerful ends that ever played football at New Haven—a national figure in a way, one of those men who reach such an acute limited excellence at twenty-one that everything afterward savours of anticlimax. His family were enormously wealthy—even in college his freedom with money was a matter for reproach—but now he'd left Chicago and come

East in a fashion that rather took your breath away: for instance, he'd brought down a string of polo ponies from Lake Forest. It was hard to realize that a man in my own generation was wealthy enough to do that.

Why they came East I don't know. They had spent a year in France for no particular reason, and then drifted here and there unrestfully wherever people played polo and were rich together. This was a permanent move, said Daisy over the telephone, but I didn't believe it—I had no sight into Daisy's heart, but I felt that Tom would drift on forever seeking, a little wistfully, for the dramatic turbulence of some irrecoverable football game.

And so it happened that on a warm windy evening I drove over to East Egg to see two old friends whom I scarcely knew at all. Their house was even more elaborate than I expected, a cheerful red-and-white Georgian Colonial mansion, overlooking the bay. The lawn started at the beach and ran towards the front door for a quarter of a mile, jumping over sundials and brick walks and burning gardens—finally when it reached the house drifting up the side in bright vines as though from the momentum of its run. The front was broken by a line of French windows, glowing now with reflected gold and wide open to the warm windy afternoon, and Tom Buchanan in riding clothes was standing with his legs apart on the front porch.

He had changed since his New Haven years. Now he was a sturdy straw-haired man of thirty, with a rather hard mouth and a supercilious manner. Two shining arrogant eyes had established dominance over his face and gave him the appearance of always leaning aggressively forward. Not even the effeminate swank of his riding clothes could hide the enormous power of that body—he seemed to fill those glistening boots until he strained the top lacing, and you could see a great pack of muscle shifting when his shoulder moved under his thin coat. It was a body capable of enormous leverage—a cruel body.

His speaking voice, a gruff husky tenor, added to the impression of fractiousness he conveyed. There was a touch of paternal contempt in it, even toward people he liked—and there were men at New Haven who had hated his guts.

"Now, don't think my opinion on these matters is final," he seemed to say, "just because I'm stronger and more of a man than you are." We were in the same senior society, and while we were never intimate I always had the impression that he approved of me and wanted me to like him with some harsh, defiant wistfulness of his own.

We talked for a few minutes on the sunny porch.

"I've got a nice place here," he said, his eyes flashing about restlessly.

Turning me around by one arm, he moved a broad flat hand along the front vista, including in its sweep a sunken Italian garden, a half acre of deep, pungent roses, and a snub-nosed motorboat that bumped the tide offshore.

"It belonged to Demaine, the oil man." He turned me around again, politely and abruptly. "We'll go inside."

We walked through a high hallway into a bright rosy-coloured space, fragilely bound into the house by French windows at either end. The windows were ajar and gleaming white against the fresh grass outside that seemed to grow a little way into the house. A breeze blew through the room, blew curtains in at one end and out the other like pale flags, twisting them up toward the frosted wedding-cake of the ceiling, and then rippled over the wine-coloured rug, making a shadow on it as wind does on the sea.

THE GREAT GATSBY

The only completely stationary object in the room was an enormous couch on which two young women were buoyed up as though upon an anchored balloon. They were both in white, and their dresses were rippling and fluttering as if they had just been blown back in after a short flight around the house. I must have stood for a few moments listening to the whip and snap of the curtains and the groan of a picture on the wall. Then there was a boom as Tom Buchanan shut the rear windows and the caught wind died out about the room, and the curtains and the rugs and the two young women ballooned slowly to the floor.

The younger of the two was a stranger to me. She was extended full length at her end of the divan, completely motionless, and with her chin raised a little, as if she were balancing something on it which was quite likely to fall. If she saw me out of the corner of her eyes she gave no hint of it—indeed, I was almost surprised into murmuring an apology for having disturbed her by coming in.

The other girl, Daisy, made an attempt to rise—she leaned slightly forward with a conscientious expression—then she laughed, an absurd, charming little laugh, and I laughed too and came forward into the room.

"I'm p-paralysed with happiness."

She laughed again, as if she said something very witty, and held my hand for a moment, looking up into my face, promising that there was no one in the world she so much wanted to see. That was a way she had. She hinted in a murmur that the surname of the balancing girl was Baker. (I've heard it said that Daisy's murmur was only to make people lean toward her; an irrelevant criticism that made it no less charming.)

At any rate, Miss Baker's lips fluttered, she nodded at me almost imperceptibly, and then quickly tipped her head back again—the object she was balancing had obviously tottered a little and given her something of a fright. Again a sort of apology arose to my lips. Almost any exhibition of complete self-sufficiency draws a stunned tribute from me.

I looked back at my cousin, who began to ask me questions in her low, thrilling voice. It was the kind of voice that the ear follows up and down, as if each speech is an arrangement of notes that will never be played again. Her face was sad and lovely with bright things in it, bright eyes and a bright passionate mouth, but there was an excitement in her voice that men who had cared for her found difficult to forget: a singing compulsion, a whispered "Listen," a promise that she had done gay, exciting things just a while since and that there were gay, exciting things hovering in the next hour.

I told her how I had stopped off in Chicago for a day on my way East, and how a dozen people had sent their love through me.

"Do they miss me?" she cried ecstatically.

"The whole town is desolate. All the cars have the left rear wheel painted black as a mourning wreath, and there's a persistent wail all night along the north shore."

"How gorgeous! Let's go back, Tom. Tomorrow!" Then she added irrelevantly: "You ought to see the baby."

"I'd like to."

"She's asleep. She's three years old. Haven't you ever seen her?"

"Never."

"Well, you ought to see her. She's—"

Tom Buchanan, who had been hovering restlessly about the room, stopped and rested his hand on my shoulder.

"What you doing, Nick?"

THE GREAT GATSBY

"I'm a bond man."

"Who with?"

I told him.

"Never heard of them," he remarked decisively.

This annoyed me.

"You will," I answered shortly. "You will if you stay in the East."

"Oh, I'll stay in the East, don't you worry," he said, glancing at Daisy and then back at me, as if he were alert for something more. "I'd be a God damned fool to live anywhere else."

At this point Miss Baker said: "Absolutely!" with such suddenness that I started—it was the first word she had uttered since I came into the room. Evidently it surprised her as much as it did me, for she yawned and with a series of rapid, deft movements stood up into the room.

"I'm stiff," she complained, "I've been lying on that sofa for as long as I can remember."

"Don't look at me," Daisy retorted, "I've been trying to get you to New York all afternoon."

"No, thanks," said Miss Baker to the four cocktails just in from the pantry. "I'm absolutely in training."

Her host looked at her incredulously.

"You are!" He took down his drink as if it were a drop in the bottom of a glass. "How you ever get anything done is beyond me."

I looked at Miss Baker, wondering what it was she "got done." I enjoyed looking at her. She was a slender, small-breasted girl, with an erect carriage, which she accentuated by throwing her body backward at the shoulders like a young cadet. Her grey sun-strained eyes looked back at me with polite reciprocal curiosity out of a wan, charming, discontented face. It occurred to me now that I had seen her, or a picture of her, somewhere before.

"You live in West Egg," she remarked contemptuously. "I know somebody there."

"I don't know a single—"

"You must know Gatsby."

"Gatsby?" demanded Daisy. "What Gatsby?"

Before I could reply that he was my neighbour dinner was announced; wedging his tense arm imperatively under mine, Tom Buchanan compelled me from the room as though he were moving a checker to another square.

Slenderly, languidly, their hands set lightly on their hips, the two young women preceded us out on to a rosy-coloured porch, open toward the sunset, where four candles flickered on the table in the diminished wind.

"Why candles?" objected Daisy, frowning. She snapped them out with her fingers. "In two weeks it'll be the longest day in the year." She looked at us all radiantly. "Do you always watch for the longest day of the year and then miss it? I always watch for the longest day in the year and then miss it."

"We ought to plan something," yawned Miss Baker, sitting down at the table as if she were getting into bed.

"All right," said Daisy. "What'll we plan?" She turned to me helplessly: "What do people plan?"

Before I could answer her eyes fastened with an awed expression on her little finger.

"Look!" she complained; "I hurt it."

We all looked—the knuckle was black and blue.

"You did it, Tom," she said accusingly. "I know you didn't mean to, but you did do it. That's what I get for marrying a brute of a man, a great, big, hulking physical specimen of a—"

"I hate that word 'hulking,'" objected Tom crossly, "even in kidding."

"Hulking," insisted Daisy.

Sometimes she and Miss Baker talked at once, unobtrusively and with a bantering inconsequence that was never quite chatter, that was as cool as their white dresses and their impersonal eyes in the absence of all desire. They were here, and they accepted Tom and me, making only a polite pleasant effort to entertain or to be entertained. They knew that presently dinner would be over and a little later the evening too would be over and casually put away. It was sharply different from the West, where an evening was hurried from phase to phase towards its close, in a continually disappointed anticipation or else in sheer nervous dread of the moment itself.

"You make me feel uncivilized, Daisy," I confessed on my second glass of corky but rather impressive claret. "Can't you talk about crops or something?"

I meant nothing in particular by this remark, but it was taken up in an unexpected way.

"Civilization's going to pieces," broke out Tom violently. "I've gotten to be a terrible pessimist about things. Have you read The Rise of the Coloured Empires by this man Goddard?"

"Why, no," I answered, rather surprised by his tone.

"Well, it's a fine book, and everybody ought to read it. The idea is if we don't look out the white race will be—will be utterly submerged. It's all scientific stuff; it's been proved."

"Tom's getting very profound," said Daisy, with an expression of unthoughtful sadness. "He reads deep books with long words in them. What was that word we—"

"Well, these books are all scientific," insisted Tom, glancing at her impatiently. "This fellow has worked out the whole thing. It's up to us, who are the dominant race, to watch out or these other races will have control of things."

"We've got to beat them down," whispered Daisy, winking ferociously toward the fervent sun.

"You ought to live in California—" began Miss Baker, but Tom interrupted her by shifting heavily in his chair.

"This idea is that we're Nordics. I am, and you are, and you are, and—" After an infinitesimal hesitation he included Daisy with a slight nod, and she winked at me again. "—And we've produced all the things that go to make civilization—oh, science and art, and all that. Do you see?"

There was something pathetic in his concentration, as if his complacency, more acute than of old, was not enough to him any more. When, almost immediately, the telephone rang inside and the butler left the porch Daisy seized upon the momentary interruption and leaned towards me.

"I'll tell you a family secret," she whispered enthusiastically. "It's about the butler's nose. Do you want to hear about the butler's nose?"

"That's why I came over tonight."

"Well, he wasn't always a butler; he used to be the silver polisher for some people in New York that had a silver service for two hundred people. He had to polish it from morning till night, until finally it began to affect his nose—"

"Things went from bad to worse," suggested Miss Baker.

"Yes. Things went from bad to worse, until finally he had to give up his position."

For a moment the last sunshine fell with romantic affection upon her glowing face; her voice compelled me forward breathlessly as I listened—then the glow faded, each light deserting her with lingering regret, like children leaving a pleasant street at dusk.

The butler came back and murmured something close to Tom's ear, whereupon Tom frowned, pushed back his chair, and without a word went inside. As if his absence quickened something within her, Daisy leaned forward again, her voice glowing and singing.

"I love to see you at my table, Nick. You remind me of a—of a rose, an absolute rose. Doesn't he?" She turned to Miss Baker for confirmation: "An absolute rose?"

This was untrue. I am not even faintly like a rose. She was only extemporizing, but a stirring warmth flowed from her, as if her heart was trying to come out to you concealed in one of those breathless, thrilling words. Then suddenly she threw her napkin on the table and excused herself and went into the house.

Miss Baker and I exchanged a short glance consciously devoid of meaning. I was about to speak when she sat up alertly and said "Sh!" in a warning voice. A subdued impassioned murmur was audible in the room beyond, and Miss Baker leaned forward unashamed, trying to hear. The murmur trembled on the verge of coherence, sank down, mounted excitedly, and then ceased altogether.

"This Mr. Gatsby you spoke of is my neighbour—" I began.

"Don't talk. I want to hear what happens."

"Is something happening?" I inquired innocently.

"You mean to say you don't know?" said Miss Baker, honestly surprised. "I thought everybody knew."

"I don't."

"Why—" she said hesitantly. "Tom's got some woman in New York."

"Got some woman?" I repeated blankly.

Miss Baker nodded.

"She might have the decency not to telephone him at dinner time. Don't you think?"

Almost before I had grasped her meaning there was the flutter of a dress and the crunch of leather boots, and Tom and Daisy were back at the table.

"It couldn't be helped!" cried Daisy with tense gaiety.

She sat down, glanced searchingly at Miss Baker and then at me, and continued: "I looked outdoors for a minute, and it's very romantic outdoors. There's a bird on the lawn that I think must be a nightingale come over on the Cunard or White Star Line. He's singing away—" Her voice sang: "It's romantic, isn't it, Tom?"

"Very romantic," he said, and then miserably to me: "If it's light enough after dinner, I want to take you down to the stables."

The telephone rang inside, startlingly, and as Daisy shook her head decisively at Tom the subject of the stables, in fact all subjects, vanished into air. Among the broken fragments of the last five minutes at table I remember the candles being lit again, pointlessly, and I was conscious of wanting to look squarely at everyone, and yet to avoid all eyes. I couldn't guess what Daisy and Tom were thinking, but I doubt if even Miss Baker, who seemed to have mastered a certain hardy scepticism, was able utterly to put this fifth guest's shrill metallic urgency out of mind. To a certain temperament the situation might have seemed intriguing—my own instinct was to telephone immediately for the police.

The horses, needless to say, were not mentioned again. Tom and Miss Baker, with several feet of twilight between them, strolled back into the library, as if to a vigil beside a perfectly tangible body, while, trying to look pleasantly interested and a little deaf, I followed Daisy around a chain of connecting verandas to the porch in front. In its deep gloom we sat down side by side on a wicker settee.

Daisy took her face in her hands as if feeling its lovely shape, and her eyes moved gradually out into the velvet dusk. I saw that turbulent emotions possessed her, so I asked what I thought would be some sedative questions about her little girl.

"We don't know each other very well, Nick," she said suddenly. "Even if we are cousins. You didn't come to my wedding."

"I wasn't back from the war."

"That's true." She hesitated. "Well, I've had a very bad time, Nick, and I'm pretty cynical about everything."

Evidently she had reason to be. I waited but she didn't say any more, and after a moment I returned rather feebly to the subject of her daughter.

"I suppose she talks, and—eats, and everything."

"Oh, yes." She looked at me absently. "Listen, Nick; let me tell you what I said when she was born. Would you like to hear?"

"Very much."

"It'll show you how I've gotten to feel about—things. Well, she was less than an hour old and Tom was God knows where. I woke up out of the ether with an utterly abandoned feeling, and asked the nurse right away if it was a boy or a girl. She told me it was a girl, and so I turned my head away and wept. 'All right,' I said, 'I'm glad it's a girl. And I hope she'll be a fool—that's the best thing a girl can be in this world, a beautiful little fool.'

"You see I think everything's terrible anyhow," she went on in a convinced way. "Everybody thinks so—the most advanced people. And I know. I've been everywhere and seen everything and done everything." Her eyes flashed around her in a defiant way, rather like Tom's, and she laughed with thrilling scorn. "Sophisticated—God, I'm sophisticated!"

The instant her voice broke off, ceasing to compel my attention, my belief, I felt the basic insincerity of what she had said. It made me uneasy, as though the whole evening had been a trick of some sort to exact a contributory emotion from me. I waited, and sure enough, in a moment she looked at me with an absolute smirk on her lovely face, as if she had asserted her membership in a rather distinguished secret society to which she and Tom belonged.

Inside, the crimson room bloomed with light. Tom and Miss Baker sat at either end of the long couch and she read aloud to him from the Saturday Evening Post—the words, murmurous and uninflected, running together in a soothing tune. The lamplight, bright on his boots and dull on the autumn-leaf yellow of her hair, glinted along the paper as she turned a page with a flutter of slender muscles in her arms.

When we came in she held us silent for a moment with a lifted hand.

"To be continued," she said, tossing the magazine on the table, "in our very next issue."

Her body asserted itself with a restless movement of her knee, and she stood up.

"Ten o'clock," she remarked, apparently finding the time on the ceiling. "Time for this good girl to go to bed."

"Jordan's going to play in the tournament tomorrow," explained Daisy, "over at Westchester."

"Oh—you're Jordan Baker."

I knew now why her face was familiar—its pleasing contemptuous expression had looked out at me from many rotogravure pictures of the sporting life at Asheville and Hot Springs and Palm Beach. I had heard some story of her too, a critical, unpleasant story, but what it was I had forgotten long ago.

"Good night," she said softly. "Wake me at eight, won't you."

"If you'll get up."

"I will. Good night, Mr. Carraway. See you anon."

"Of course you will," confirmed Daisy. "In fact I think I'll arrange a marriage. Come over often, Nick, and I'll sort of—oh—fling you together. You know—lock you up accidentally in linen closets and push you out to sea in a boat, and all that sort of thing—"

"Good night," called Miss Baker from the stairs. "I haven't heard a word."

"She's a nice girl," said Tom after a moment. "They oughtn't to let her run around the country this way."

"Who oughtn't to?" inquired Daisy coldly.

"Her family."

"Her family is one aunt about a thousand years old. Besides, Nick's going to look after her, aren't you, Nick? She's going to spend lots of weekends out here this summer. I think the home influence will be very good for her."

Daisy and Tom looked at each other for a moment in silence.

"Is she from New York?" I asked quickly.

"From Louisville. Our white girlhood was passed together there. Our beautiful white—"

"Did you give Nick a little heart to heart talk on the veranda?" demanded Tom suddenly.

"Did I?" She looked at me. "I can't seem to remember, but I think we talked about the Nordic race. Yes, I'm sure we did. It sort of crept up on us and first thing you know—"

"Don't believe everything you hear, Nick," he advised me.

I said lightly that I had heard nothing at all, and a few minutes later I got up to go home. They came to the door with me and stood side by side in a cheerful square of light. As I started my motor Daisy peremptorily called: "Wait!

"I forgot to ask you something, and it's important. We heard you were engaged to a girl out West."

"That's right," corroborated Tom kindly. "We heard that you were engaged."

"It's a libel. I'm too poor."

"But we heard it," insisted Daisy, surprising me by opening up again in a flower-like way. "We heard it from three people, so it must be true."

Of course I knew what they were referring to, but I wasn't even vaguely engaged. The fact that gossip had published the banns was one of the reasons I had come East. You can't stop going with an old friend on account of rumours, and on the other hand I had no intention of being rumoured into marriage.

Their interest rather touched me and made them less remotely rich—nevertheless, I was confused and a little disgusted as I drove away. It seemed to me that the thing for Daisy to do was to rush out of the house, child in arms—but apparently there were no such intentions in her head. As for Tom, the fact that he "had some woman in New York" was really less surprising than that he had been depressed by a book. Something was making him nibble at the edge of stale ideas as if his sturdy physical egotism no longer nourished his peremptory heart.

Already it was deep summer on roadhouse roofs and in front of wayside garages, where new red petrol-pumps sat out in pools of light, and when I reached my estate at West Egg I ran the car under its shed and sat for a while on an abandoned grass roller in the yard. The wind had blown off, leaving a loud, bright night, with wings beating in the trees and a persistent organ sound as the full bellows of the earth blew the frogs full of life. The silhouette of a moving cat wavered across the moonlight, and, turning my head to watch it, I saw that I was not alone—fifty feet away a figure had emerged from the shadow of my neighbour's mansion and was standing with his hands in his pockets regarding the silver pepper of the stars. Something in his leisurely movements and the secure position of his feet upon the lawn suggested that it was Mr. Gatsby himself, come out to determine what share was his of our local heavens.

I decided to call to him. Miss Baker had mentioned him at dinner, and that would do for an introduction. But I didn't call to him, for he gave a sudden intimation that he was content to be alone—he stretched out his arms toward the dark water in a curious way, and, far as I was from him, I could have sworn he was trembling. Involuntarily I glanced seaward—and distinguished nothing except a single green light, minute and far away, that might have been the end of a dock. When I looked once more for Gatsby he had vanished, and I was alone again in the unquiet darkness.

II

About halfway between West Egg and New York the motor road hastily joins the railroad and runs beside it for a quarter of a mile, so as to shrink away from a certain desolate area of land. This is a valley of ashes—a fantastic farm where ashes grow like wheat into ridges and hills and grotesque gardens; where ashes take the forms of houses and chimneys and rising smoke and, finally, with a transcendent effort, of ash-grey men, who move dimly and already crumbling through the powdery air. Occasionally a line of grey cars crawls along an invisible track, gives out a ghastly creak, and comes to rest, and immediately the ash-grey men swarm up with leaden spades and stir up an impenetrable cloud, which screens their obscure operations from your sight.

But above the grey land and the spasms of bleak dust which drift endlessly over it, you perceive, after a moment, the eyes of Doctor T. J. Eckleburg. The eyes of Doctor T. J. Eckleburg are blue and gigantic—their retinas are one yard high. They look out of no face, but, instead, from a pair of enormous yellow spectacles which pass over a nonexistent nose. Evidently some wild wag of an oculist set them there to fatten his practice in the borough of Queens, and then sank down himself into eternal blindness, or forgot them and moved away. But his eyes, dimmed a little by many paintless days, under sun and rain, brood on over the solemn dumping ground.

The valley of ashes is bounded on one side by a small foul river, and, when the drawbridge is up to let barges through, the passengers on waiting trains can stare at the dismal scene for as long as half an hour. There is always a halt there of at least a minute, and it was because of this that I first met Tom Buchanan's mistress.

The fact that he had one was insisted upon wherever he was known. His acquaintances resented the fact that he turned up in popular cafés with her and, leaving her at a table, sauntered about, chatting with whomsoever he knew. Though I was curious to see her, I had no desire to meet her—but I did. I went up to New York with Tom on the train one afternoon, and when we stopped by the ash-heaps he jumped to his feet and, taking hold of my elbow, literally forced me from the car.

"We're getting off," he insisted. "I want you to meet my girl."

I think he'd tanked up a good deal at luncheon, and his determination to have my company bordered on violence. The supercilious assumption was that on Sunday afternoon I had nothing better to do.

I followed him over a low whitewashed railroad fence, and we walked back a hundred yards along the road under Doctor Eckleburg's persistent stare. The only building in sight was a small block of yellow brick sitting on the edge of the waste land, a sort of compact Main Street ministering to it, and contiguous to absolutely nothing. One of the three shops it contained was for rent and another was an all-night restaurant, approached by a trail of ashes; the third was a garage—Repairs. George B. Wilson. Cars bought and sold.—and I followed Tom inside.

The interior was unprosperous and bare; the only car visible was the dust-covered wreck of a Ford which crouched in a dim corner. It had occurred to me that this shadow of a garage must be a blind, and that sumptuous and romantic apartments were concealed overhead, when the proprietor himself appeared in the door of an office, wiping his hands on a piece of waste. He was a blond, spiritless man, anaemic, and faintly handsome. When he saw us a damp gleam of hope sprang into his light blue eyes.

"Hello, Wilson, old man," said Tom, slapping him jovially on the shoulder. "How's business?"

"I can't complain," answered Wilson unconvincingly. "When are you going to sell me that car?"

"Next week; I've got my man working on it now."

"Works pretty slow, don't he?"

"No, he doesn't," said Tom coldly. "And if you feel that way about it, maybe I'd better sell it somewhere else after all."

"I don't mean that," explained Wilson quickly. "I just meant—"

His voice faded off and Tom glanced impatiently around the garage. Then I heard footsteps on a stairs, and in a moment the thickish figure of a woman blocked out the light from the office door. She was in the middle thirties, and faintly stout, but she carried her flesh sensuously as some women can. Her face, above a spotted dress of dark blue crêpe-de-chine, contained no facet or gleam of beauty, but there was an immediately perceptible vitality about her as if the nerves of her body were continually smouldering. She smiled slowly and, walking through her husband as if he were a ghost, shook hands with Tom, looking him flush in the eye. Then she wet her lips, and without turning around spoke to her husband in a soft, coarse voice:

"Get some chairs, why don't you, so somebody can sit down."

"Oh, sure," agreed Wilson hurriedly, and went toward the little office, mingling immediately with the cement colour of the walls. A white ashen dust veiled his dark suit and his pale hair as it veiled everything in the vicinity—except his wife, who moved close to Tom.

"I want to see you," said Tom intently. "Get on the next train."

"All right."

"I'll meet you by the newsstand on the lower level."

She nodded and moved away from him just as George Wilson emerged with two chairs from his office door.

We waited for her down the road and out of sight. It was a few days before the Fourth of July, and a grey, scrawny Italian child was setting torpedoes in a row along the railroad track.

"Terrible place, isn't it," said Tom, exchanging a frown with Doctor Eckleburg.

"Awful."

"It does her good to get away."

"Doesn't her husband object?"

"Wilson? He thinks she goes to see her sister in New York. He's so dumb he doesn't know he's alive."

So Tom Buchanan and his girl and I went up together to New York—or not quite together, for Mrs. Wilson sat discreetly in another car. Tom deferred that much to the sensibilities of those East Eggers who might be on the train.

She had changed her dress to a brown figured muslin, which stretched tight over her rather wide hips as Tom helped her to the platform in New York. At the newsstand she bought a copy of Town Tattle and a moving-picture magazine, and in the station drugstore some cold cream and a small flask of perfume. Upstairs, in the solemn echoing drive she let four taxicabs drive away before she selected a new one, lavender-coloured with grey upholstery, and in this we slid out from the mass of the station into the glowing sunshine. But immediately she turned sharply from the window and, leaning forward, tapped on the front glass.

"I want to get one of those dogs," she said earnestly. "I want to get one for the apartment. They're nice to have—a dog."

We backed up to a grey old man who bore an absurd resemblance to John D. Rockefeller. In a basket swung from his neck cowered a dozen very recent puppies of an indeterminate breed.

"What kind are they?" asked Mrs. Wilson eagerly, as he came to the taxi-window.

"All kinds. What kind do you want, lady?"

"I'd like to get one of those police dogs; I don't suppose you got that kind?"

The man peered doubtfully into the basket, plunged in his hand and drew one up, wriggling, by the back of the neck.

"That's no police dog," said Tom.

"No, it's not exactly a police dog," said the man with disappointment in his voice. "It's more of an Airedale." He passed his hand over the brown washrag of a back. "Look at that coat. Some coat. That's a dog that'll never bother you with catching cold."

"I think it's cute," said Mrs. Wilson enthusiastically. "How much is it?"

"That dog?" He looked at it admiringly. "That dog will cost you ten dollars."

The Airedale—undoubtedly there was an Airedale concerned in it somewhere, though its feet were startlingly white—changed hands and settled down into Mrs. Wilson's lap, where she fondled the weatherproof coat with rapture.

"Is it a boy or a girl?" she asked delicately.

"That dog? That dog's a boy."

"It's a bitch," said Tom decisively. "Here's your money. Go and buy ten more dogs with it."

We drove over to Fifth Avenue, warm and soft, almost pastoral, on the summer Sunday afternoon. I wouldn't have been surprised to see a great flock of white sheep turn the corner.

"Hold on," I said, "I have to leave you here."

"No you don't," interposed Tom quickly. "Myrtle'll be hurt if you don't come up to the apartment. Won't you, Myrtle?"

"Come on," she urged. "I'll telephone my sister Catherine. She's said to be very beautiful by people who ought to know."

"Well, I'd like to, but—"

We went on, cutting back again over the Park toward the West Hundreds. At 158th Street the cab stopped at one slice in a long white cake of apartment-houses. Throwing a regal homecoming glance around the neighbourhood, Mrs. Wilson gathered up her dog and her other purchases, and went haughtily in.

"I'm going to have the McKees come up," she announced as we rose in the elevator. "And, of course, I got to call up my sister, too."

The apartment was on the top floor—a small living-room, a small dining-room, a small bedroom, and a bath. The living-room was crowded to the doors with a set of tapestried furniture entirely too large for it, so that to move about was to stumble continually over scenes of ladies swinging in the gardens of Versailles. The only picture was an over-enlarged photograph, apparently a hen sitting on a blurred rock. Looked at from a distance, however, the hen resolved itself into a bonnet, and the countenance of a stout old lady beamed down into the room. Several old copies of Town Tattle lay on the table together with a copy of Simon Called Peter, and some of the small scandal magazines of Broadway. Mrs. Wilson was first concerned with the dog. A reluctant elevator boy went for a box full of straw and some milk, to which he added on his own initiative a tin of large, hard dog biscuits—one of which decomposed apathetically in the saucer of milk all afternoon. Meanwhile Tom brought out a bottle of whisky from a locked bureau door.

I have been drunk just twice in my life, and the second time was that afternoon; so everything that happened has a dim, hazy cast over it, although until after eight o'clock the apartment was full of cheerful sun. Sitting on Tom's lap Mrs. Wilson called up several people on the telephone; then there were no cigarettes, and I went out to buy some at the drugstore on the corner. When I came back they had both disappeared, so I sat down discreetly in the living-room and read a chapter of Simon Called Peter—either it was terrible stuff or the whisky distorted things, because it didn't make any sense to me.

Just as Tom and Myrtle (after the first drink Mrs. Wilson and I called each other by our first names) reappeared, company commenced to arrive at the apartment door.

The sister, Catherine, was a slender, worldly girl of about thirty, with a solid, sticky bob of red hair, and a complexion powdered milky white. Her eyebrows had been plucked and then drawn on again at a more rakish angle, but the efforts of nature toward the restoration of the old alignment gave a blurred air to her face. When she moved about there was an incessant clicking as innumerable pottery bracelets jingled up and down upon her arms. She came in with such a proprietary haste, and looked around so possessively at the furniture that I wondered if she lived here. But when I asked her she laughed immoderately, repeated my question aloud, and told me she lived with a girl friend at a hotel.

Mr. McKee was a pale, feminine man from the flat below. He had just shaved, for there was a white spot of lather on his cheekbone, and he was most respectful in his greeting to everyone in the room. He informed me that he was in the "artistic game," and I gathered later that he was a photographer and had made the dim enlargement of Mrs. Wilson's mother which hovered like an ectoplasm on the wall. His wife was shrill, languid, handsome, and horrible. She told me with pride that her husband had photographed her a hundred and twenty-seven times since they had been married.

Mrs. Wilson had changed her costume some time before, and was now attired in an elaborate afternoon dress of cream-coloured chiffon, which gave out a continual rustle as she swept about the room. With the influence of the dress her personality had also undergone a change. The intense vitality that had been so remarkable in the garage was converted into impressive hauteur. Her laughter, her gestures, her assertions became more violently affected moment by moment, and as she expanded the room grew smaller around her, until she seemed to be revolving on a noisy, creaking pivot through the smoky air.

"My dear," she told her sister in a high, mincing shout, "most of these fellas will cheat you every time. All they think of is money. I had a woman up here last week to look at my feet, and when she gave me the bill you'd of thought she had my appendicitis out."

"What was the name of the woman?" asked Mrs. McKee.

"Mrs. Eberhardt. She goes around looking at people's feet in their own homes."

"I like your dress," remarked Mrs. McKee, "I think it's adorable."

Mrs. Wilson rejected the compliment by raising her eyebrow in disdain.

"It's just a crazy old thing," she said. "I just slip it on sometimes when I don't care what I look like."

"But it looks wonderful on you, if you know what I mean," pursued Mrs. McKee. "If Chester could only get you in that pose I think he could make something of it."

We all looked in silence at Mrs. Wilson, who removed a strand of hair from over her eyes and looked back at us with a brilliant smile. Mr. McKee regarded her intently with his head on one side, and then moved his hand back and forth slowly in front of his face.

"I should change the light," he said after a moment. "I'd like to bring out the modelling of the features. And I'd try to get hold of all the back hair."

"I wouldn't think of changing the light," cried Mrs. McKee. "I think it's—"

Her husband said "Sh!" and we all looked at the subject again, whereupon Tom Buchanan yawned audibly and got to his feet.

"You McKees have something to drink," he said. "Get some more ice and mineral water, Myrtle, before everybody goes to sleep."

"I told that boy about the ice." Myrtle raised her eyebrows in despair at the shiftlessness of the lower orders. "These people! You have to keep after them all the time."

She looked at me and laughed pointlessly. Then she flounced over to the dog, kissed it with ecstasy, and swept into the kitchen, implying that a dozen chefs awaited her orders there.

"I've done some nice things out on Long Island," asserted Mr. McKee.

Tom looked at him blankly.

"Two of them we have framed downstairs."

"Two what?" demanded Tom.

"Two studies. One of them I call Montauk Point—The Gulls, and the other I call Montauk Point—The Sea."

The sister Catherine sat down beside me on the couch.

"Do you live down on Long Island, too?" she inquired.

"I live at West Egg."

"Really? I was down there at a party about a month ago. At a man named Gatsby's. Do you know him?"

"I live next door to him."

"Well, they say he's a nephew or a cousin of Kaiser Wilhelm's. That's where all his money comes from."

"Really?"

She nodded.

"I'm scared of him. I'd hate to have him get anything on me."

This absorbing information about my neighbour was interrupted by Mrs. McKee's pointing suddenly at Catherine:

"Chester, I think you could do something with her," she broke out, but Mr. McKee only nodded in a bored way, and turned his attention to Tom.

"I'd like to do more work on Long Island, if I could get the entry. All I ask is that they should give me a start."

"Ask Myrtle," said Tom, breaking into a short shout of laughter as Mrs. Wilson entered with a tray. "She'll give you a letter of introduction, won't you, Myrtle?"

"Do what?" she asked, startled.

"You'll give McKee a letter of introduction to your husband, so he can do some studies of him." His lips moved silently for a moment as he invented, "'George B. Wilson at the Gasoline Pump,' or something like that."

Catherine leaned close to me and whispered in my ear:

"Neither of them can stand the person they're married to."

"Can't they?"

"Can't stand them." She looked at Myrtle and then at Tom. "What I say is, why go on living with them if they can't stand them? If I was them I'd get a divorce and get married to each other right away."

"Doesn't she like Wilson either?"

The answer to this was unexpected. It came from Myrtle, who had overheard the question, and it was violent and obscene.

"You see," cried Catherine triumphantly. She lowered her voice again. "It's really his wife that's keeping them apart. She's a Catholic, and they don't believe in divorce."

Daisy was not a Catholic, and I was a little shocked at the elaborateness of the lie.

"When they do get married," continued Catherine, "they're going West to live for a while until it blows over."

"It'd be more discreet to go to Europe."

"Oh, do you like Europe?" she exclaimed surprisingly. "I just got back from Monte Carlo."

"Really."

"Just last year. I went over there with another girl."

"Stay long?"

"No, we just went to Monte Carlo and back. We went by way of Marseilles. We had over twelve hundred dollars when we started, but we got gyped out of it all in two days in the private rooms. We had an awful time getting back, I can tell you. God, how I hated that town!"

The late afternoon sky bloomed in the window for a moment like the blue honey of the Mediterranean—then the shrill voice of Mrs. McKee called me back into the room.

"I almost made a mistake, too," she declared vigorously. "I almost married a little kike who'd been after me for years. I knew he was below me. Everybody kept saying to me: 'Lucille, that man's way below you!' But if I hadn't met Chester, he'd of got me sure."

"Yes, but listen," said Myrtle Wilson, nodding her head up and down, "at least you didn't marry him."

"I know I didn't."

"Well, I married him," said Myrtle, ambiguously. "And that's the difference between your case and mine."

"Why did you, Myrtle?" demanded Catherine. "Nobody forced you to."

Myrtle considered.

"I married him because I thought he was a gentleman," she said finally. "I thought he knew something about breeding, but he wasn't fit to lick my shoe."

"You were crazy about him for a while," said Catherine.

"Crazy about him!" cried Myrtle incredulously. "Who said I was crazy about him? I never was any more crazy about him than I was about that man there."

She pointed suddenly at me, and everyone looked at me accusingly. I tried to show by my expression that I expected no affection.

"The only crazy I was was when I married him. I knew right away I made a mistake. He borrowed somebody's best suit to get married in, and never even told me about it, and the man came after it one day when he was out: 'Oh, is that your suit?' I said. 'This is the first I ever heard about it.' But I gave it to him and then I lay down and cried to beat the band all afternoon."

"She really ought to get away from him," resumed Catherine to me. "They've been living over that garage for eleven years. And Tom's the first sweetie she ever had."

The bottle of whisky—a second one—was now in constant demand by all present, excepting Catherine, who "felt just as good on nothing at all." Tom rang for the janitor and sent him for some celebrated sandwiches, which were a complete supper in themselves. I wanted to get out and walk eastward toward the park through the soft twilight, but each time I tried to go I became entangled in some wild, strident argument which pulled me back, as if with ropes, into my chair. Yet high over the city our line of yellow windows must have contributed their share of human secrecy to the casual watcher in the darkening streets, and I saw him too, looking up and wondering. I was within and without, simultaneously enchanted and repelled by the inexhaustible variety of life.

Myrtle pulled her chair close to mine, and suddenly her warm breath poured over me the story of her first meeting with Tom.

"It was on the two little seats facing each other that are always the last ones left on the train. I was going up to New York to see my sister and spend the night. He had on a dress suit and patent leather shoes, and I couldn't keep my eyes off him, but every time he looked at me I had to pretend to be looking at the advertisement over his head. When we came into the station he was next to me, and his white shirtfront pressed against my arm, and so I told him I'd have to call a policeman, but he knew I lied. I was so excited that when I got into a taxi with him I didn't hardly know I wasn't getting into a subway train. All I kept thinking about, over and over, was 'You can't live forever; you can't live forever.'"

She turned to Mrs. McKee and the room rang full of her artificial laughter.

"My dear," she cried, "I'm going to give you this dress as soon as I'm through with it. I've got to get another one tomorrow. I'm going to make a list of all the things I've got to get. A massage and a wave, and a collar for the dog, and one of those cute little ashtrays where you touch a spring, and a wreath with a black silk bow for mother's grave that'll last all summer. I got to write down a list so I won't forget all the things I got to do."

It was nine o'clock—almost immediately afterward I looked at my watch and found it was ten. Mr. McKee was asleep on a chair with his fists clenched in his lap, like a photograph of a man of action. Taking out my handkerchief I wiped from his cheek the spot of dried lather that had worried me all the afternoon.

The little dog was sitting on the table looking with blind eyes through the smoke, and from time to time groaning faintly. People disappeared, reappeared, made plans to go somewhere, and then lost each other, searched for each other, found each other a few feet away. Some time toward midnight Tom Buchanan and Mrs. Wilson stood face to face discussing, in impassioned voices, whether Mrs. Wilson had any right to mention Daisy's name.

"Daisy! Daisy! Daisy!" shouted Mrs. Wilson. "I'll say it whenever I want to! Daisy! Dai—"

Making a short deft movement, Tom Buchanan broke her nose with his open hand.

Then there were bloody towels upon the bathroom floor, and women's voices scolding, and high over the confusion a long broken wail of pain. Mr. McKee awoke from his doze and started in a daze toward the door. When he had gone halfway he turned around and stared at the scene—his wife and Catherine scolding and consoling as they stumbled here and there among the crowded furniture with articles of aid, and the despairing figure on the couch, bleeding fluently, and trying to spread a copy of Town Tattle over the tapestry scenes of Versailles. Then Mr. McKee turned and continued on out the door. Taking my hat from the chandelier, I followed.

"Come to lunch some day," he suggested, as we groaned down in the elevator.

"Where?"

"Anywhere."

"Keep your hands off the lever," snapped the elevator boy.

"I beg your pardon," said Mr. McKee with dignity, "I didn't know I was touching it."

"All right," I agreed, "I'll be glad to."

… I was standing beside his bed and he was sitting up between the sheets, clad in his underwear, with a great portfolio in his hands.

"Beauty and the Beast … Loneliness … Old Grocery Horse … Brook'n Bridge …"

Then I was lying half asleep in the cold lower level of the Pennsylvania Station, staring at the morning Tribune, and waiting for the four o'clock train.

III

There was music from my neighbour's house through the summer nights. In his blue gardens men and girls came and went like moths among the whisperings and the champagne and the stars. At high tide in the afternoon I watched his guests diving from the tower of his raft, or taking the sun on the hot sand of his beach while his two motorboats slit the waters of the Sound, drawing aquaplanes over cataracts of foam. On weekends his Rolls-Royce became an omnibus, bearing parties to and from the city between nine in the morning and long past midnight, while his station wagon scampered like a brisk yellow bug to meet all trains. And on Mondays eight servants, including an extra gardener, toiled all day with mops and scrubbing-brushes and hammers and garden-shears, repairing the ravages of the night before.

Every Friday five crates of oranges and lemons arrived from a fruiterer in New York—every Monday these same oranges and lemons left his back door in a pyramid of pulpless halves. There was a machine in the kitchen which could extract the juice of two hundred oranges in half an hour if a little button was pressed two hundred times by a butler's thumb.

At least once a fortnight a corps of caterers came down with several hundred feet of canvas and enough coloured lights to make a Christmas tree of Gatsby's enormous garden. On buffet tables, garnished with glistening hors-d'oeuvre, spiced baked hams crowded against salads of harlequin designs and pastry pigs and turkeys bewitched to a dark gold. In the main hall a bar with a real brass rail was set up, and stocked with gins and liquors and with cordials so long forgotten that most of his female guests were too young to know one from another.

By seven o'clock the orchestra has arrived, no thin five-piece affair, but a whole pitful of oboes and trombones and saxophones and viols and cornets and piccolos, and low and high drums. The last swimmers have come in from the beach now and are dressing upstairs; the cars from New York are parked five deep in the drive, and already the halls and salons and verandas are gaudy with primary colours, and hair bobbed in strange new ways, and shawls beyond the dreams of Castile. The bar is in full swing, and floating rounds of cocktails permeate the garden outside, until the air is alive with chatter and laughter, and casual innuendo and introductions forgotten on the spot, and enthusiastic meetings between women who never knew each other's names.

The lights grow brighter as the earth lurches away from the sun, and now the orchestra is playing yellow cocktail music, and the opera of voices pitches a key higher. Laughter is easier minute by minute, spilled with prodigality, tipped out at a cheerful word. The groups change more swiftly, swell with new arrivals, dissolve and form in the same breath; already there are wanderers, confident girls who weave here and there among the stouter and more stable, become for a sharp, joyous moment the centre of a group, and then, excited with triumph, glide on through the sea-change of faces and voices and colour under the constantly changing light.

Suddenly one of these gypsies, in trembling opal, seizes a cocktail out of the air, dumps it down for courage and, moving her hands like Frisco, dances out alone on the canvas platform. A momentary hush; the orchestra leader varies his rhythm obligingly for her, and there is a burst of chatter as the erroneous news goes around that she is Gilda Gray's understudy from the Follies. The party has begun.

I believe that on the first night I went to Gatsby's house I was one of the few guests who had actually been invited. People were not invited—they went there. They got into automobiles which bore them out to Long Island, and somehow they ended up at Gatsby's door. Once there they were introduced by somebody who knew Gatsby, and after that they conducted themselves according to the rules of behaviour associated with an amusement park. Sometimes they came and went without having met Gatsby at all, came for the party with a simplicity of heart that was its own ticket of admission.

I had been actually invited. A chauffeur in a uniform of robin's-egg blue crossed my lawn early that Saturday morning with a surprisingly formal note from his employer: the honour would be entirely Gatsby's, it said, if I would attend his "little party" that night. He had seen me several times, and had intended to call on me long before, but a peculiar combination of circumstances had prevented it—signed Jay Gatsby, in a majestic hand.

Dressed up in white flannels I went over to his lawn a little after seven, and wandered around rather ill at ease among swirls and eddies of people I didn't know—though here and there was a face I had noticed on the commuting train. I was immediately struck by the number of young Englishmen dotted about; all well dressed, all looking a little hungry, and all talking in low, earnest voices to solid and prosperous Americans. I was sure that they were selling something: bonds or insurance or automobiles. They were at least agonizingly aware of the easy money in the vicinity and convinced that it was theirs for a few words in the right key.

THE GREAT GATSBY

As soon as I arrived I made an attempt to find my host, but the two or three people of whom I asked his whereabouts stared at me in such an amazed way, and denied so vehemently any knowledge of his movements, that I slunk off in the direction of the cocktail table—the only place in the garden where a single man could linger without looking purposeless and alone.

I was on my way to get roaring drunk from sheer embarrassment when Jordan Baker came out of the house and stood at the head of the marble steps, leaning a little backward and looking with contemptuous interest down into the garden.

Welcome or not, I found it necessary to attach myself to someone before I should begin to address cordial remarks to the passersby.

"Hello!" I roared, advancing toward her. My voice seemed unnaturally loud across the garden.

"I thought you might be here," she responded absently as I came up. "I remembered you lived next door to—"

She held my hand impersonally, as a promise that she'd take care of me in a minute, and gave ear to two girls in twin yellow dresses, who stopped at the foot of the steps.

"Hello!" they cried together. "Sorry you didn't win."

That was for the golf tournament. She had lost in the finals the week before.

"You don't know who we are," said one of the girls in yellow, "but we met you here about a month ago."

"You've dyed your hair since then," remarked Jordan, and I started, but the girls had moved casually on and her remark was addressed to the premature moon, produced like the supper, no doubt, out of a caterer's basket. With Jordan's slender golden arm resting in mine, we descended the steps and sauntered about the garden. A tray of cocktails floated at us through the twilight, and we sat down at a table with the two girls in yellow and three men, each one introduced to us as Mr. Mumble.

"Do you come to these parties often?" inquired Jordan of the girl beside her.

"The last one was the one I met you at," answered the girl, in an alert confident voice. She turned to her companion: "Wasn't it for you, Lucille?"

It was for Lucille, too.

"I like to come," Lucille said. "I never care what I do, so I always have a good time. When I was here last I tore my gown on a chair, and he asked me my name and address—inside of a week I got a package from Croirier's with a new evening gown in it."

"Did you keep it?" asked Jordan.

"Sure I did. I was going to wear it tonight, but it was too big in the bust and had to be altered. It was gas blue with lavender beads. Two hundred and sixty-five dollars."

"There's something funny about a fellow that'll do a thing like that," said the other girl eagerly. "He doesn't want any trouble with anybody."

"Who doesn't?" I inquired.

"Gatsby. Somebody told me—"

The two girls and Jordan leaned together confidentially.

"Somebody told me they thought he killed a man once."

A thrill passed over all of us. The three Mr. Mumbles bent forward and listened eagerly.

"I don't think it's so much that," argued Lucille sceptically; "It's more that he was a German spy during the war."

One of the men nodded in confirmation.

"I heard that from a man who knew all about him, grew up with him in Germany," he assured us positively.

"Oh, no," said the first girl, "it couldn't be that, because he was in the American army during the war." As our credulity switched back to her she leaned forward with enthusiasm. "You look at him sometimes when he thinks nobody's looking at him. I'll bet he killed a man."

She narrowed her eyes and shivered. Lucille shivered. We all turned and looked around for Gatsby. It was testimony to the romantic speculation he inspired that there were whispers about him from those who had found little that it was necessary to whisper about in this world.

The first supper—there would be another one after midnight—was now being served, and Jordan invited me to join her own party, who were spread around a table on the other side of the garden. There were three married couples and Jordan's escort, a persistent undergraduate given to violent innuendo, and obviously under the impression that sooner or later Jordan was going to yield him up her person to a greater or lesser degree. Instead of rambling, this party had preserved a dignified homogeneity, and assumed to itself the function of representing the staid nobility of the countryside—East Egg condescending to West Egg and carefully on guard against its spectroscopic gaiety.

"Let's get out," whispered Jordan, after a somehow wasteful and inappropriate half-hour; "this is much too polite for me."

We got up, and she explained that we were going to find the host: I had never met him, she said, and it was making me uneasy. The undergraduate nodded in a cynical, melancholy way.

The bar, where we glanced first, was crowded, but Gatsby was not there. She couldn't find him from the top of the steps, and he wasn't on the veranda. On a chance we tried an important-looking door, and walked into a high Gothic library, panelled with carved English oak, and probably transported complete from some ruin overseas.

A stout, middle-aged man, with enormous owl-eyed spectacles, was sitting somewhat drunk on the edge of a great table, staring with unsteady concentration at the shelves of books. As we entered he wheeled excitedly around and examined Jordan from head to foot.

"What do you think?" he demanded impetuously.

"About what?"

He waved his hand toward the bookshelves.

"About that. As a matter of fact you needn't bother to ascertain. I ascertained. They're real."

"The books?"

He nodded.

"Absolutely real—have pages and everything. I thought they'd be a nice durable cardboard. Matter of fact, they're absolutely real. Pages and—Here! Lemme show you."

Taking our scepticism for granted, he rushed to the bookcases and returned with Volume One of the Stoddard Lectures.

"See!" he cried triumphantly. "It's a bona-fide piece of printed matter. It fooled me. This fella's a regular Belasco. It's a triumph. What thoroughness! What realism! Knew when to stop, too—didn't cut the pages. But what do you want? What do you expect?"

He snatched the book from me and replaced it hastily on its shelf, muttering that if one brick was removed the whole library was liable to collapse.

"Who brought you?" he demanded. "Or did you just come? I was brought. Most people were brought."

Jordan looked at him alertly, cheerfully, without answering.

"I was brought by a woman named Roosevelt," he continued. "Mrs. Claud Roosevelt. Do you know her? I met her somewhere last night. I've been drunk for about a week now, and I thought it might sober me up to sit in a library."

"Has it?"

"A little bit, I think. I can't tell yet. I've only been here an hour. Did I tell you about the books? They're real. They're—"

"You told us."

We shook hands with him gravely and went back outdoors.

There was dancing now on the canvas in the garden; old men pushing young girls backward in eternal graceless circles, superior couples holding each other tortuously, fashionably, and keeping in the corners—and a great number of single girls dancing individually or relieving the orchestra for a moment of the burden of the banjo or the traps. By midnight the hilarity had increased. A celebrated tenor had sung in Italian, and a notorious contralto had sung in jazz, and between the numbers people were doing "stunts" all over the garden, while happy, vacuous bursts of laughter rose toward the summer sky. A pair of stage twins, who turned out to be the girls in yellow, did a baby act in costume, and champagne was served in glasses bigger than finger-bowls. The moon had risen higher, and floating in the Sound was a triangle of silver scales, trembling a little to the stiff, tinny drip of the banjoes on the lawn.

I was still with Jordan Baker. We were sitting at a table with a man of about my age and a rowdy little girl, who gave way upon the slightest provocation to uncontrollable laughter. I was enjoying myself now. I had taken two finger-bowls of champagne, and the scene had changed before my eyes into something significant, elemental, and profound.

At a lull in the entertainment the man looked at me and smiled.

"Your face is familiar," he said politely. "Weren't you in the First Division during the war?"

"Why yes. I was in the Twenty-eighth Infantry."

"I was in the Sixteenth until June nineteen-eighteen. I knew I'd seen you somewhere before."

We talked for a moment about some wet, grey little villages in France. Evidently he lived in this vicinity, for he told me that he had just bought a hydroplane, and was going to try it out in the morning.

"Want to go with me, old sport? Just near the shore along the Sound."

"What time?"

"Any time that suits you best."

It was on the tip of my tongue to ask his name when Jordan looked around and smiled.

"Having a gay time now?" she inquired.

"Much better." I turned again to my new acquaintance. "This is an unusual party for me. I haven't even seen the host. I live over there—" I waved my hand at the invisible hedge in the distance, "and this man Gatsby sent over his chauffeur with an invitation."

For a moment he looked at me as if he failed to understand.

"I'm Gatsby," he said suddenly.

"What!" I exclaimed. "Oh, I beg your pardon."

"I thought you knew, old sport. I'm afraid I'm not a very good host."

He smiled understandingly—much more than understandingly. It was one of those rare smiles with a quality of eternal reassurance in it, that you may come across four or five times in life. It faced—or seemed to face—the whole eternal world for an instant, and then concentrated on you with an irresistible prejudice in your favour. It understood you just so far as you wanted to be understood, believed in you as you would like to believe in yourself, and assured you that it had precisely the impression of you that, at your best, you hoped to convey. Precisely at that point it vanished—and I was looking at an elegant young roughneck, a year or two over thirty, whose elaborate formality of speech just missed being absurd. Some time before he introduced himself I'd got a strong impression that he was picking his words with care.

Almost at the moment when Mr. Gatsby identified himself a butler hurried toward him with the information that Chicago was calling him on the wire. He excused himself with a small bow that included each of us in turn.

"If you want anything just ask for it, old sport," he urged me. "Excuse me. I will rejoin you later."

When he was gone I turned immediately to Jordan—constrained to assure her of my surprise. I had expected that Mr. Gatsby would be a florid and corpulent person in his middle years.

"Who is he?" I demanded. "Do you know?"

"He's just a man named Gatsby."

"Where is he from, I mean? And what does he do?"

"Now you're started on the subject," she answered with a wan smile. "Well, he told me once he was an Oxford man."

A dim background started to take shape behind him, but at her next remark it faded away.

"However, I don't believe it."

"Why not?"

"I don't know," she insisted, "I just don't think he went there."

Something in her tone reminded me of the other girl's "I think he killed a man," and had the effect of stimulating my curiosity. I would have accepted without question the information that Gatsby sprang from the swamps of Louisiana or from the lower East Side of New York. That was comprehensible. But young men didn't—at least in my provincial inexperience I believed they didn't—drift coolly out of nowhere and buy a palace on Long Island Sound.

"Anyhow, he gives large parties," said Jordan, changing the subject with an urban distaste for the concrete. "And I like large parties. They're so intimate. At small parties there isn't any privacy."

There was the boom of a bass drum, and the voice of the orchestra leader rang out suddenly above the echolalia of the garden.

"Ladies and gentlemen," he cried. "At the request of Mr. Gatsby we are going to play for you Mr. Vladmir Tostoff's latest work, which attracted so much attention at Carnegie Hall last May. If you read the papers you know there was a big sensation." He smiled with jovial condescension, and added: "Some sensation!" Whereupon everybody laughed.

"The piece is known," he concluded lustily, "as 'Vladmir Tostoff's Jazz History of the World!'"

THE GREAT GATSBY

The nature of Mr. Tostoff's composition eluded me, because just as it began my eyes fell on Gatsby, standing alone on the marble steps and looking from one group to another with approving eyes. His tanned skin was drawn attractively tight on his face and his short hair looked as though it were trimmed every day. I could see nothing sinister about him. I wondered if the fact that he was not drinking helped to set him off from his guests, for it seemed to me that he grew more correct as the fraternal hilarity increased. When the "Jazz History of the World" was over, girls were putting their heads on men's shoulders in a puppyish, convivial way, girls were swooning backward playfully into men's arms, even into groups, knowing that someone would arrest their falls—but no one swooned backward on Gatsby, and no French bob touched Gatsby's shoulder, and no singing quartets were formed with Gatsby's head for one link.

"I beg your pardon."

Gatsby's butler was suddenly standing beside us.

"Miss Baker?" he inquired. "I beg your pardon, but Mr. Gatsby would like to speak to you alone."

"With me?" she exclaimed in surprise.

"Yes, madame."

She got up slowly, raising her eyebrows at me in astonishment, and followed the butler toward the house. I noticed that she wore her evening-dress, all her dresses, like sports clothes—there was a jauntiness about her movements as if she had first learned to walk upon golf courses on clean, crisp mornings.

I was alone and it was almost two. For some time confused and intriguing sounds had issued from a long, many-windowed room which overhung the terrace. Eluding Jordan's undergraduate, who was now engaged in an obstetrical conversation with two chorus girls, and who implored me to join him, I went inside.

The large room was full of people. One of the girls in yellow was playing the piano, and beside her stood a tall, red-haired young lady from a famous chorus, engaged in song. She had drunk a quantity of champagne, and during the course of her song she had decided, ineptly, that everything was very, very sad—she was not only singing, she was weeping too. Whenever there was a pause in the song she filled it with gasping, broken sobs, and then took up the lyric again in a quavering soprano. The tears coursed down her cheeks—not freely, however, for when they came into contact with her heavily beaded eyelashes they assumed an inky colour, and pursued the rest of their way in slow black rivulets. A humorous suggestion was made that she sing the notes on her face, whereupon she threw up her hands, sank into a chair, and went off into a deep vinous sleep.

"She had a fight with a man who says he's her husband," explained a girl at my elbow.

I looked around. Most of the remaining women were now having fights with men said to be their husbands. Even Jordan's party, the quartet from East Egg, were rent asunder by dissension. One of the men was talking with curious intensity to a young actress, and his wife, after attempting to laugh at the situation in a dignified and indifferent way, broke down entirely and resorted to flank attacks—at intervals she appeared suddenly at his side like an angry diamond, and hissed: "You promised!" into his ear.

The reluctance to go home was not confined to wayward men. The hall was at present occupied by two deplorably sober men and their highly indignant wives. The wives were sympathizing with each other in slightly raised voices.

"Whenever he sees I'm having a good time he wants to go home."

"Never heard anything so selfish in my life."

"We're always the first ones to leave."

"So are we."

"Well, we're almost the last tonight," said one of the men sheepishly. "The orchestra left half an hour ago."

In spite of the wives' agreement that such malevolence was beyond credibility, the dispute ended in a short struggle, and both wives were lifted, kicking, into the night.

As I waited for my hat in the hall the door of the library opened and Jordan Baker and Gatsby came out together. He was saying some last word to her, but the eagerness in his manner tightened abruptly into formality as several people approached him to say goodbye.

Jordan's party were calling impatiently to her from the porch, but she lingered for a moment to shake hands.

"I've just heard the most amazing thing," she whispered. "How long were we in there?"

"Why, about an hour."

"It was ... simply amazing," she repeated abstractedly. "But I swore I wouldn't tell it and here I am tantalizing you." She yawned gracefully in my face. "Please come and see me ... Phone book ... Under the name of Mrs. Sigourney Howard ... My aunt ..." She was hurrying off as she talked—her brown hand waved a jaunty salute as she melted into her party at the door.

Rather ashamed that on my first appearance I had stayed so late, I joined the last of Gatsby's guests, who were clustered around him. I wanted to explain that I'd hunted for him early in the evening and to apologize for not having known him in the garden.

"Don't mention it," he enjoined me eagerly. "Don't give it another thought, old sport." The familiar expression held no more familiarity than the hand which reassuringly brushed my shoulder. "And don't forget we're going up in the hydroplane tomorrow morning, at nine o'clock."

Then the butler, behind his shoulder:

"Philadelphia wants you on the phone, sir."

"All right, in a minute. Tell them I'll be right there … Good night."

"Good night."

"Good night." He smiled—and suddenly there seemed to be a pleasant significance in having been among the last to go, as if he had desired it all the time. "Good night, old sport … Good night."

But as I walked down the steps I saw that the evening was not quite over. Fifty feet from the door a dozen headlights illuminated a bizarre and tumultuous scene. In the ditch beside the road, right side up, but violently shorn of one wheel, rested a new coupé which had left Gatsby's drive not two minutes before. The sharp jut of a wall accounted for the detachment of the wheel, which was now getting considerable attention from half a dozen curious chauffeurs. However, as they had left their cars blocking the road, a harsh, discordant din from those in the rear had been audible for some time, and added to the already violent confusion of the scene.

A man in a long duster had dismounted from the wreck and now stood in the middle of the road, looking from the car to the tyre and from the tyre to the observers in a pleasant, puzzled way.

"See!" he explained. "It went in the ditch."

THE GREAT GATSBY

The fact was infinitely astonishing to him, and I recognized first the unusual quality of wonder, and then the man—it was the late patron of Gatsby's library.

"How'd it happen?"

He shrugged his shoulders.

"I know nothing whatever about mechanics," he said decisively.

"But how did it happen? Did you run into the wall?"

"Don't ask me," said Owl Eyes, washing his hands of the whole matter. "I know very little about driving—next to nothing. It happened, and that's all I know."

"Well, if you're a poor driver you oughtn't to try driving at night."

"But I wasn't even trying," he explained indignantly, "I wasn't even trying."

An awed hush fell upon the bystanders.

"Do you want to commit suicide?"

"You're lucky it was just a wheel! A bad driver and not even trying!"

"You don't understand," explained the criminal. "I wasn't driving. There's another man in the car."

The shock that followed this declaration found voice in a sustained "Ah-h-h!" as the door of the coupé swung slowly open. The crowd—it was now a crowd—stepped back involuntarily, and when the door had opened wide there was a ghostly pause. Then, very gradually, part by part, a pale, dangling individual stepped out of the wreck, pawing tentatively at the ground with a large uncertain dancing shoe.

Blinded by the glare of the headlights and confused by the incessant groaning of the horns, the apparition stood swaying for a moment before he perceived the man in the duster.

"Wha's matter?" he inquired calmly. "Did we run outa gas?"

"Look!"

Half a dozen fingers pointed at the amputated wheel—he stared at it for a moment, and then looked upward as though he suspected that it had dropped from the sky.

"It came off," someone explained.

He nodded.

"At first I din' notice we'd stopped."

A pause. Then, taking a long breath and straightening his shoulders, he remarked in a determined voice:

"Wonder'ff tell me where there's a gas'line station?"

At least a dozen men, some of them a little better off than he was, explained to him that wheel and car were no longer joined by any physical bond.

"Back out," he suggested after a moment. "Put her in reverse."

"But the wheel's off!"

He hesitated.

"No harm in trying," he said.

The caterwauling horns had reached a crescendo and I turned away and cut across the lawn toward home. I glanced back once. A wafer of a moon was shining over Gatsby's house, making the night fine as before, and surviving the laughter and the sound of his still glowing garden. A sudden emptiness seemed to flow now from the windows and the great doors, endowing with complete isolation the figure of the host, who stood on the porch, his hand up in a formal gesture of farewell.

THE GREAT GATSBY

Reading over what I have written so far, I see I have given the impression that the events of three nights several weeks apart were all that absorbed me. On the contrary, they were merely casual events in a crowded summer, and, until much later, they absorbed me infinitely less than my personal affairs.

Most of the time I worked. In the early morning the sun threw my shadow westward as I hurried down the white chasms of lower New York to the Probity Trust. I knew the other clerks and young bond-salesmen by their first names, and lunched with them in dark, crowded restaurants on little pig sausages and mashed potatoes and coffee. I even had a short affair with a girl who lived in Jersey City and worked in the accounting department, but her brother began throwing mean looks in my direction, so when she went on her vacation in July I let it blow quietly away.

I took dinner usually at the Yale Club—for some reason it was the gloomiest event of my day—and then I went upstairs to the library and studied investments and securities for a conscientious hour. There were generally a few rioters around, but they never came into the library, so it was a good place to work. After that, if the night was mellow, I strolled down Madison Avenue past the old Murray Hill Hotel, and over 33rd Street to the Pennsylvania Station.

I began to like New York, the racy, adventurous feel of it at night, and the satisfaction that the constant flicker of men and women and machines gives to the restless eye. I liked to walk up Fifth Avenue and pick out romantic women from the crowd and imagine that in a few minutes I was going to enter into their lives, and no one would ever know or disapprove.

Sometimes, in my mind, I followed them to their apartments on the corners of hidden streets, and they turned and smiled back at me before they faded through a door into warm darkness. At the enchanted metropolitan twilight I felt a haunting loneliness sometimes, and felt it in others—poor young clerks who loitered in front of windows waiting until it was time for a solitary restaurant dinner—young clerks in the dusk, wasting the most poignant moments of night and life.

Again at eight o'clock, when the dark lanes of the Forties were lined five deep with throbbing taxicabs, bound for the theatre district, I felt a sinking in my heart. Forms leaned together in the taxis as they waited, and voices sang, and there was laughter from unheard jokes, and lighted cigarettes made unintelligible circles inside. Imagining that I, too, was hurrying towards gaiety and sharing their intimate excitement, I wished them well.

For a while I lost sight of Jordan Baker, and then in midsummer I found her again. At first I was flattered to go places with her, because she was a golf champion, and everyone knew her name. Then it was something more. I wasn't actually in love, but I felt a sort of tender curiosity. The bored haughty face that she turned to the world concealed something—most affectations conceal something eventually, even though they don't in the beginning—and one day I found what it was. When we were on a house-party together up in Warwick, she left a borrowed car out in the rain with the top down, and then lied about it—and suddenly I remembered the story about her that had eluded me that night at Daisy's. At her first big golf tournament there was a row that nearly reached the newspapers—a suggestion that she had moved her ball from a bad lie in the semifinal round. The thing approached the proportions of a scandal—then died away.

THE GREAT GATSBY

A caddy retracted his statement, and the only other witness admitted that he might have been mistaken. The incident and the name had remained together in my mind.

Jordan Baker instinctively avoided clever, shrewd men, and now I saw that this was because she felt safer on a plane where any divergence from a code would be thought impossible. She was incurably dishonest. She wasn't able to endure being at a disadvantage and, given this unwillingness, I suppose she had begun dealing in subterfuges when she was very young in order to keep that cool, insolent smile turned to the world and yet satisfy the demands of her hard, jaunty body.

It made no difference to me. Dishonesty in a woman is a thing you never blame deeply—I was casually sorry, and then I forgot. It was on that same house-party that we had a curious conversation about driving a car. It started because she passed so close to some workmen that our fender flicked a button on one man's coat.

"You're a rotten driver," I protested. "Either you ought to be more careful, or you oughtn't to drive at all."

"I am careful."

"No, you're not."

"Well, other people are," she said lightly.

"What's that got to do with it?"

"They'll keep out of my way," she insisted. "It takes two to make an accident."

"Suppose you met somebody just as careless as yourself."

"I hope I never will," she answered. "I hate careless people. That's why I like you."

Her grey, sun-strained eyes stared straight ahead, but she had deliberately shifted our relations, and for a moment I thought I loved her. But I am slow-thinking and full of interior rules that act as brakes on my desires, and I knew that first I had to get myself definitely out of that tangle back home. I'd been writing letters once a week and signing them: "Love, Nick," and all I could think of was how, when that certain girl played tennis, a faint moustache of perspiration appeared on her upper lip. Nevertheless there was a vague understanding that had to be tactfully broken off before I was free.

Everyone suspects himself of at least one of the cardinal virtues, and this is mine: I am one of the few honest people that I have ever known.

IV

On Sunday morning while church bells rang in the villages alongshore, the world and its mistress returned to Gatsby's house and twinkled hilariously on his lawn.

"He's a bootlegger," said the young ladies, moving somewhere between his cocktails and his flowers. "One time he killed a man who had found out that he was nephew to Von Hindenburg and second cousin to the devil. Reach me a rose, honey, and pour me a last drop into that there crystal glass."

Once I wrote down on the empty spaces of a timetable the names of those who came to Gatsby's house that summer. It is an old timetable now, disintegrating at its folds, and headed "This schedule in effect July 5th, 1922." But I can still read the grey names, and they will give you a better impression than my generalities of those who accepted Gatsby's hospitality and paid him the subtle tribute of knowing nothing whatever about him.

From East Egg, then, came the Chester Beckers and the Leeches, and a man named Bunsen, whom I knew at Yale, and Doctor Webster Civet, who was drowned last summer up in Maine. And the Hornbeams and the Willie Voltaires, and a whole clan named Blackbuck, who always gathered in a corner and flipped up their noses like goats at whosoever came near. And the Ismays and the Chrysties (or rather Hubert Auerbach and Mr. Chrystie's wife), and Edgar Beaver, whose hair, they say, turned cotton-white one winter afternoon for no good reason at all.

THE GREAT GATSBY

Clarence Endive was from East Egg, as I remember. He came only once, in white knickerbockers, and had a fight with a bum named Etty in the garden. From farther out on the Island came the Cheadles and the O. R. P. Schraeders, and the Stonewall Jackson Abrams of Georgia, and the Fishguards and the Ripley Snells. Snell was there three days before he went to the penitentiary, so drunk out on the gravel drive that Mrs. Ulysses Swett's automobile ran over his right hand. The Dancies came, too, and S. B. Whitebait, who was well over sixty, and Maurice A. Flink, and the Hammerheads, and Beluga the tobacco importer, and Beluga's girls.

From West Egg came the Poles and the Mulreadys and Cecil Roebuck and Cecil Schoen and Gulick the State senator and Newton Orchid, who controlled Films Par Excellence, and Eckhaust and Clyde Cohen and Don S. Schwartz (the son) and Arthur McCarty, all connected with the movies in one way or another. And the Catlips and the Bembergs and G. Earl Muldoon, brother to that Muldoon who afterward strangled his wife. Da Fontano the promoter came there, and Ed Legros and James B. ("Rot-Gut") Ferret and the De Jongs and Ernest Lilly—they came to gamble, and when Ferret wandered into the garden it meant he was cleaned out and Associated Traction would have to fluctuate profitably next day.

A man named Klipspringer was there so often that he became known as "the boarder"—I doubt if he had any other home. Of theatrical people there were Gus Waize and Horace O'Donavan and Lester Myer and George Duckweed and Francis Bull. Also from New York were the Chromes and the Backhyssons and the Dennickers and Russel Betty and the Corrigans and the Kellehers and the Dewars and the Scullys and S. W. Belcher and the Smirkes and the young Quinns, divorced now, and Henry

L. Palmetto, who killed himself by jumping in front of a subway train in Times Square.

Benny McClenahan arrived always with four girls. They were never quite the same ones in physical person, but they were so identical one with another that it inevitably seemed they had been there before. I have forgotten their names—Jaqueline, I think, or else Consuela, or Gloria or Judy or June, and their last names were either the melodious names of flowers and months or the sterner ones of the great American capitalists whose cousins, if pressed, they would confess themselves to be.

In addition to all these I can remember that Faustina O'Brien came there at least once and the Baedeker girls and young Brewer, who had his nose shot off in the war, and Mr. Albrucksburger and Miss Haag, his fiancée, and Ardita Fitz-Peters and Mr. P. Jewett, once head of the American Legion, and Miss Claudia Hip, with a man reputed to be her chauffeur, and a prince of something, whom we called Duke, and whose name, if I ever knew it, I have forgotten.

All these people came to Gatsby's house in the summer.

At nine o'clock, one morning late in July, Gatsby's gorgeous car lurched up the rocky drive to my door and gave out a burst of melody from its three-noted horn.

It was the first time he had called on me, though I had gone to two of his parties, mounted in his hydroplane, and, at his urgent invitation, made frequent use of his beach.

"Good morning, old sport. You're having lunch with me today and I thought we'd ride up together."

He was balancing himself on the dashboard of his car with that resourcefulness of movement that is so peculiarly American—that comes, I suppose, with the absence of lifting work in youth and, even more, with the formless grace of our nervous, sporadic games. This quality was continually breaking through his punctilious manner in the shape of restlessness. He was never quite still; there was always a tapping foot somewhere or the impatient opening and closing of a hand.

He saw me looking with admiration at his car.

"It's pretty, isn't it, old sport?" He jumped off to give me a better view. "Haven't you ever seen it before?"

I'd seen it. Everybody had seen it. It was a rich cream colour, bright with nickel, swollen here and there in its monstrous length with triumphant hatboxes and supper-boxes and toolboxes, and terraced with a labyrinth of windshields that mirrored a dozen suns. Sitting down behind many layers of glass in a sort of green leather conservatory, we started to town.

I had talked with him perhaps half a dozen times in the past month and found, to my disappointment, that he had little to say. So my first impression, that he was a person of some undefined consequence, had gradually faded and he had become simply the proprietor of an elaborate roadhouse next door.

And then came that disconcerting ride. We hadn't reached West Egg village before Gatsby began leaving his elegant sentences unfinished and slapping himself indecisively on the knee of his caramel-coloured suit.

"Look here, old sport," he broke out surprisingly, "what's your opinion of me, anyhow?"

A little overwhelmed, I began the generalized evasions which that question deserves.

"Well, I'm going to tell you something about my life," he interrupted. "I don't want you to get a wrong idea of me from all these stories you hear."

So he was aware of the bizarre accusations that flavoured conversation in his halls.

"I'll tell you God's truth." His right hand suddenly ordered divine retribution to stand by. "I am the son of some wealthy people in the Middle West—all dead now. I was brought up in America but educated at Oxford, because all my ancestors have been educated there for many years. It is a family tradition."

He looked at me sideways—and I knew why Jordan Baker had believed he was lying. He hurried the phrase "educated at Oxford," or swallowed it, or choked on it, as though it had bothered him before. And with this doubt, his whole statement fell to pieces, and I wondered if there wasn't something a little sinister about him, after all.

"What part of the Middle West?" I inquired casually.

"San Francisco."

"I see."

"My family all died and I came into a good deal of money."

His voice was solemn, as if the memory of that sudden extinction of a clan still haunted him. For a moment I suspected that he was pulling my leg, but a glance at him convinced me otherwise.

"After that I lived like a young rajah in all the capitals of Europe—Paris, Venice, Rome—collecting jewels, chiefly rubies, hunting big game, painting a little, things for myself only, and trying to forget something very sad that had happened to me long ago."

THE GREAT GATSBY

With an effort I managed to restrain my incredulous laughter. The very phrases were worn so threadbare that they evoked no image except that of a turbaned "character" leaking sawdust at every pore as he pursued a tiger through the Bois de Boulogne.

"Then came the war, old sport. It was a great relief, and I tried very hard to die, but I seemed to bear an enchanted life. I accepted a commission as first lieutenant when it began. In the Argonne Forest I took the remains of my machine-gun battalion so far forward that there was a half mile gap on either side of us where the infantry couldn't advance. We stayed there two days and two nights, a hundred and thirty men with sixteen Lewis guns, and when the infantry came up at last they found the insignia of three German divisions among the piles of dead. I was promoted to be a major, and every Allied government gave me a decoration—even Montenegro, little Montenegro down on the Adriatic Sea!"

Little Montenegro! He lifted up the words and nodded at them—with his smile. The smile comprehended Montenegro's troubled history and sympathized with the brave struggles of the Montenegrin people. It appreciated fully the chain of national circumstances which had elicited this tribute from Montenegro's warm little heart. My incredulity was submerged in fascination now; it was like skimming hastily through a dozen magazines.

He reached in his pocket, and a piece of metal, slung on a ribbon, fell into my palm.

"That's the one from Montenegro."

To my astonishment, the thing had an authentic look. "Orderi di Danilo," ran the circular legend, "Montenegro, Nicolas Rex."

"Turn it."

"Major Jay Gatsby," I read, "For Valour Extraordinary."

"Here's another thing I always carry. A souvenir of Oxford days. It was taken in Trinity Quad—the man on my left is now the Earl of Doncaster."

It was a photograph of half a dozen young men in blazers loafing in an archway through which were visible a host of spires. There was Gatsby, looking a little, not much, younger—with a cricket bat in his hand.

Then it was all true. I saw the skins of tigers flaming in his palace on the Grand Canal; I saw him opening a chest of rubies to ease, with their crimson-lighted depths, the gnawings of his broken heart.

"I'm going to make a big request of you today," he said, pocketing his souvenirs with satisfaction, "so I thought you ought to know something about me. I didn't want you to think I was just some nobody. You see, I usually find myself among strangers because I drift here and there trying to forget the sad things that happened to me." He hesitated. "You'll hear about it this afternoon."

"At lunch?"

"No, this afternoon. I happened to find out that you're taking Miss Baker to tea."

"Do you mean you're in love with Miss Baker?"

"No, old sport, I'm not. But Miss Baker has kindly consented to speak to you about this matter."

I hadn't the faintest idea what "this matter" was, but I was more annoyed than interested. I hadn't asked Jordan to tea in order to discuss Mr. Jay Gatsby. I was sure the request would be something utterly fantastic, and for a moment I was sorry I'd ever set foot upon his overpopulated lawn.

He wouldn't say another word. His correctness grew on him as we neared the city. We passed Port Roosevelt, where there was a glimpse of red-belted oceangoing ships, and sped along a cobbled slum lined with the dark, undeserted saloons of the faded-gilt nineteen-hundreds. Then the valley of ashes opened out on both sides of us, and I had a glimpse of Mrs. Wilson straining at the garage pump with panting vitality as we went by.

With fenders spread like wings we scattered light through half Astoria—only half, for as we twisted among the pillars of the elevated I heard the familiar "jug-jug-spat!" of a motorcycle, and a frantic policeman rode alongside.

"All right, old sport," called Gatsby. We slowed down. Taking a white card from his wallet, he waved it before the man's eyes.

"Right you are," agreed the policeman, tipping his cap. "Know you next time, Mr. Gatsby. Excuse me!"

"What was that?" I inquired. "The picture of Oxford?"

"I was able to do the commissioner a favour once, and he sends me a Christmas card every year."

Over the great bridge, with the sunlight through the girders making a constant flicker upon the moving cars, with the city rising up across the river in white heaps and sugar lumps all built with a wish out of nonolfactory money. The city seen from the Queensboro Bridge is always the city seen for the first time, in its first wild promise of all the mystery and the beauty in the world.

A dead man passed us in a hearse heaped with blooms, followed by two carriages with drawn blinds, and by more cheerful carriages for friends. The friends looked out at us with the tragic eyes and short upper lips of southeastern Europe, and I was glad that the sight of Gatsby's splendid car was included in their sombre holiday. As we crossed Blackwell's Island a limousine passed us, driven by a white chauffeur, in which sat three modish negroes, two bucks and a girl. I laughed aloud as the yolks of their eyeballs rolled toward us in haughty rivalry.

"Anything can happen now that we've slid over this bridge," I thought; "anything at all …"

Even Gatsby could happen, without any particular wonder.

Roaring noon. In a well-fanned Forty-second Street cellar I met Gatsby for lunch. Blinking away the brightness of the street outside, my eyes picked him out obscurely in the anteroom, talking to another man.

"Mr. Carraway, this is my friend Mr. Wolfshiem."

A small, flat-nosed Jew raised his large head and regarded me with two fine growths of hair which luxuriated in either nostril. After a moment I discovered his tiny eyes in the half-darkness.

"—So I took one look at him," said Mr. Wolfshiem, shaking my hand earnestly, "and what do you think I did?"

"What?" I inquired politely.

But evidently he was not addressing me, for he dropped my hand and covered Gatsby with his expressive nose.

"I handed the money to Katspaugh and I said: 'All right, Katspaugh, don't pay him a penny till he shuts his mouth.' He shut it then and there."

Gatsby took an arm of each of us and moved forward into the restaurant, whereupon Mr. Wolfshiem swallowed a new sentence he was starting and lapsed into a somnambulatory abstraction.

"Highballs?" asked the head waiter.

"This is a nice restaurant here," said Mr. Wolfshiem, looking at the presbyterian nymphs on the ceiling. "But I like across the street better!"

"Yes, highballs," agreed Gatsby, and then to Mr. Wolfshiem: "It's too hot over there."

"Hot and small—yes," said Mr. Wolfshiem, "but full of memories."

"What place is that?" I asked.

"The old Metropole."

"The old Metropole," brooded Mr. Wolfshiem gloomily. "Filled with faces dead and gone. Filled with friends gone now forever. I can't forget so long as I live the night they shot Rosy Rosenthal there. It was six of us at the table, and Rosy had eat and drunk a lot all evening. When it was almost morning the waiter came up to him with a funny look and says somebody wants to speak to him outside. 'All right,' says Rosy, and begins to get up, and I pulled him down in his chair.

"'Let the bastards come in here if they want you, Rosy, but don't you, so help me, move outside this room.'

"It was four o'clock in the morning then, and if we'd of raised the blinds we'd of seen daylight."

"Did he go?" I asked innocently.

"Sure he went." Mr. Wolfshiem's nose flashed at me indignantly. "He turned around in the door and says: 'Don't let that waiter take away my coffee!' Then he went out on the sidewalk, and they shot him three times in his full belly and drove away."

"Four of them were electrocuted," I said, remembering.

"Five, with Becker." His nostrils turned to me in an interested way. "I understand you're looking for a business gonnegtion."

The juxtaposition of these two remarks was startling. Gatsby answered for me:

"Oh, no," he exclaimed, "this isn't the man."

"No?" Mr. Wolfshiem seemed disappointed.

"This is just a friend. I told you we'd talk about that some other time."

"I beg your pardon," said Mr. Wolfshiem, "I had a wrong man."

A succulent hash arrived, and Mr. Wolfshiem, forgetting the more sentimental atmosphere of the old Metropole, began to eat with ferocious delicacy. His eyes, meanwhile, roved very slowly all around the room—he completed the arc by turning to inspect the people directly behind. I think that, except for my presence, he would have taken one short glance beneath our own table.

"Look here, old sport," said Gatsby, leaning toward me, "I'm afraid I made you a little angry this morning in the car."

There was the smile again, but this time I held out against it.

"I don't like mysteries," I answered, "and I don't understand why you won't come out frankly and tell me what you want. Why has it all got to come through Miss Baker?"

"Oh, it's nothing underhand," he assured me. "Miss Baker's a great sportswoman, you know, and she'd never do anything that wasn't all right."

Suddenly he looked at his watch, jumped up, and hurried from the room, leaving me with Mr. Wolfshiem at the table.

"He has to telephone," said Mr. Wolfshiem, following him with his eyes. "Fine fellow, isn't he? Handsome to look at and a perfect gentleman."

"Yes."

"He's an Oggsford man."

"Oh!"

"He went to Oggsford College in England. You know Oggsford College?"

"I've heard of it."

"It's one of the most famous colleges in the world."

"Have you known Gatsby for a long time?" I inquired.

"Several years," he answered in a gratified way. "I made the pleasure of his acquaintance just after the war. But I knew I had discovered a man of fine breeding after I talked with him an hour. I said to myself: 'There's the kind of man you'd like to take home and introduce to your mother and sister.'" He paused. "I see you're looking at my cuff buttons."

I hadn't been looking at them, but I did now. They were composed of oddly familiar pieces of ivory.

"Finest specimens of human molars," he informed me.

"Well!" I inspected them. "That's a very interesting idea."

"Yeah." He flipped his sleeves up under his coat. "Yeah, Gatsby's very careful about women. He would never so much as look at a friend's wife."

When the subject of this instinctive trust returned to the table and sat down Mr. Wolfshiem drank his coffee with a jerk and got to his feet.

"I have enjoyed my lunch," he said, "and I'm going to run off from you two young men before I outstay my welcome."

"Don't hurry Meyer," said Gatsby, without enthusiasm. Mr. Wolfshiem raised his hand in a sort of benediction.

"You're very polite, but I belong to another generation," he announced solemnly. "You sit here and discuss your sports and your young ladies and your—" He supplied an imaginary noun with another wave of his hand. "As for me, I am fifty years old, and I won't impose myself on you any longer."

As he shook hands and turned away his tragic nose was trembling. I wondered if I had said anything to offend him.

"He becomes very sentimental sometimes," explained Gatsby. "This is one of his sentimental days. He's quite a character around New York—a denizen of Broadway."

"Who is he, anyhow, an actor?"

"No."

"A dentist?"

"Meyer Wolfshiem? No, he's a gambler." Gatsby hesitated, then added, coolly: "He's the man who fixed the World's Series back in 1919."

"Fixed the World's Series?" I repeated.

The idea staggered me. I remembered, of course, that the World's Series had been fixed in 1919, but if I had thought of it at all I would have thought of it as a thing that merely happened, the end of some inevitable chain. It never occurred to me that one man could start to play with the faith of fifty million people—with the single-mindedness of a burglar blowing a safe.

"How did he happen to do that?" I asked after a minute.

"He just saw the opportunity."

"Why isn't he in jail?"

"They can't get him, old sport. He's a smart man."

I insisted on paying the check. As the waiter brought my change I caught sight of Tom Buchanan across the crowded room.

"Come along with me for a minute," I said; "I've got to say hello to someone."

When he saw us Tom jumped up and took half a dozen steps in our direction.

"Where've you been?" he demanded eagerly. "Daisy's furious because you haven't called up."

THE GREAT GATSBY

"This is Mr. Gatsby, Mr. Buchanan."

They shook hands briefly, and a strained, unfamiliar look of embarrassment came over Gatsby's face.

"How've you been, anyhow?" demanded Tom of me. "How'd you happen to come up this far to eat?"

"I've been having lunch with Mr. Gatsby."

I turned toward Mr. Gatsby, but he was no longer there.

One October day in nineteen-seventeen—(said Jordan Baker that afternoon, sitting up very straight on a straight chair in the tea-garden at the Plaza Hotel)—I was walking along from one place to another, half on the sidewalks and half on the lawns. I was happier on the lawns because I had on shoes from England with rubber knobs on the soles that bit into the soft ground. I had on a new plaid skirt also that blew a little in the wind, and whenever this happened the red, white, and blue banners in front of all the houses stretched out stiff and said tut-tut-tut-tut, in a disapproving way.

The largest of the banners and the largest of the lawns belonged to Daisy Fay's house. She was just eighteen, two years older than me, and by far the most popular of all the young girls in Louisville. She dressed in white, and had a little white roadster, and all day long the telephone rang in her house and excited young officers from Camp Taylor demanded the privilege of monopolizing her that night. "Anyways, for an hour!"

When I came opposite her house that morning her white roadster was beside the kerb, and she was sitting in it with a lieutenant I had never seen before. They were so engrossed in each other that she didn't see me until I was five feet away.

"Hello, Jordan," she called unexpectedly. "Please come here."

I was flattered that she wanted to speak to me, because of all the older girls I admired her most. She asked me if I was going to the Red Cross to make bandages. I was. Well, then, would I tell them that she couldn't come that day? The officer looked at Daisy while she was speaking, in a way that every young girl wants to be looked at sometime, and because it seemed romantic to me I have remembered the incident ever since. His name was Jay Gatsby, and I didn't lay eyes on him again for over four years—even after I'd met him on Long Island I didn't realize it was the same man.

That was nineteen-seventeen. By the next year I had a few beaux myself, and I began to play in tournaments, so I didn't see Daisy very often. She went with a slightly older crowd—when she went with anyone at all. Wild rumours were circulating about her—how her mother had found her packing her bag one winter night to go to New York and say goodbye to a soldier who was going overseas. She was effectually prevented, but she wasn't on speaking terms with her family for several weeks. After that she didn't play around with the soldiers any more, but only with a few flat-footed, shortsighted young men in town, who couldn't get into the army at all.

By the next autumn she was gay again, gay as ever. She had a début after the armistice, and in February she was presumably engaged to a man from New Orleans. In June she married Tom Buchanan of Chicago, with more pomp and circumstance than Louisville ever knew before. He came down with a hundred people in four private cars, and hired a whole floor of the Muhlbach Hotel, and the day before the wedding he gave her a string of pearls valued at three hundred and fifty thousand dollars.

I was a bridesmaid. I came into her room half an hour before the bridal dinner, and found her lying on her bed as lovely as the June night in her flowered dress—and as drunk as a monkey. She had a bottle of Sauterne in one hand and a letter in the other.

"'Gratulate me," she muttered. "Never had a drink before, but oh how I do enjoy it."

"What's the matter, Daisy?"

I was scared, I can tell you; I'd never seen a girl like that before.

"Here, dearies." She groped around in a wastebasket she had with her on the bed and pulled out the string of pearls. "Take 'em downstairs and give 'em back to whoever they belong to. Tell 'em all Daisy's change' her mine. Say: 'Daisy's change' her mine!'"

She began to cry—she cried and cried. I rushed out and found her mother's maid, and we locked the door and got her into a cold bath. She wouldn't let go of the letter. She took it into the tub with her and squeezed it up in a wet ball, and only let me leave it in the soap-dish when she saw that it was coming to pieces like snow.

But she didn't say another word. We gave her spirits of ammonia and put ice on her forehead and hooked her back into her dress, and half an hour later, when we walked out of the room, the pearls were around her neck and the incident was over. Next day at five o'clock she married Tom Buchanan without so much as a shiver, and started off on a three months' trip to the South Seas.

I saw them in Santa Barbara when they came back, and I thought I'd never seen a girl so mad about her husband. If he left the room for a minute she'd look around uneasily, and say: "Where's Tom gone?" and wear the most abstracted expression until she saw him coming in the door. She used to sit on the sand with his head in her lap by the hour, rubbing her fingers over his eyes and looking at him with unfathomable delight. It was touching to see them together—it made you laugh in a hushed, fascinated way. That was in August. A week after I left Santa Barbara Tom ran into a wagon on the Ventura road one night, and ripped a front wheel off his car. The girl who was with him got into the papers, too, because her arm was broken—she was one of the chambermaids in the Santa Barbara Hotel.

The next April Daisy had her little girl, and they went to France for a year. I saw them one spring in Cannes, and later in Deauville, and then they came back to Chicago to settle down. Daisy was popular in Chicago, as you know. They moved with a fast crowd, all of them young and rich and wild, but she came out with an absolutely perfect reputation. Perhaps because she doesn't drink. It's a great advantage not to drink among hard-drinking people. You can hold your tongue and, moreover, you can time any little irregularity of your own so that everybody else is so blind that they don't see or care. Perhaps Daisy never went in for amour at all—and yet there's something in that voice of hers …

Well, about six weeks ago, she heard the name Gatsby for the first time in years. It was when I asked you—do you remember?—if you knew Gatsby in West Egg. After you had gone home she came into my room and woke me up, and said: "What Gatsby?" and when I described him—I was half asleep—she said in the strangest voice that it must be the man she used to know. It wasn't until then that I connected this Gatsby with the officer in her white car.

When Jordan Baker had finished telling all this we had left the Plaza for half an hour and were driving in a victoria through Central Park. The sun had gone down behind the tall apartments of the movie stars in the West Fifties, and the clear voices of children, already gathered like crickets on the grass, rose through the hot twilight:

"I'm the Sheik of Araby. Your love belongs to me. At night when you're asleep Into your tent I'll creep—"

"It was a strange coincidence," I said.

"But it wasn't a coincidence at all."

"Why not?"

"Gatsby bought that house so that Daisy would be just across the bay."

Then it had not been merely the stars to which he had aspired on that June night. He came alive to me, delivered suddenly from the womb of his purposeless splendour.

"He wants to know," continued Jordan, "if you'll invite Daisy to your house some afternoon and then let him come over."

The modesty of the demand shook me. He had waited five years and bought a mansion where he dispensed starlight to casual moths—so that he could "come over" some afternoon to a stranger's garden.

"Did I have to know all this before he could ask such a little thing?"

"He's afraid, he's waited so long. He thought you might be offended. You see, he's regular tough underneath it all."

Something worried me.

"Why didn't he ask you to arrange a meeting?"

"He wants her to see his house," she explained. "And your house is right next door."

"Oh!"

"I think he half expected her to wander into one of his parties, some night," went on Jordan, "but she never did. Then he began asking people casually if they knew her, and I was the first one he found. It was that night he sent for me at his dance, and you should have heard the elaborate way he worked up to it. Of course, I immediately suggested a luncheon in New York—and I thought he'd go mad:

"'I don't want to do anything out of the way!' he kept saying. 'I want to see her right next door.'

"When I said you were a particular friend of Tom's, he started to abandon the whole idea. He doesn't know very much about Tom, though he says he's read a Chicago paper for years just on the chance of catching a glimpse of Daisy's name."

It was dark now, and as we dipped under a little bridge I put my arm around Jordan's golden shoulder and drew her toward me and asked her to dinner. Suddenly I wasn't thinking of Daisy and Gatsby any more, but of this clean, hard, limited person, who dealt in universal scepticism, and who leaned back jauntily just within the circle of my arm. A phrase began to beat in my ears with a sort of heady excitement: "There are only the pursued, the pursuing, the busy, and the tired."

"And Daisy ought to have something in her life," murmured Jordan to me.

"Does she want to see Gatsby?"

"She's not to know about it. Gatsby doesn't want her to know. You're just supposed to invite her to tea."

We passed a barrier of dark trees, and then the façade of Fifty-Ninth Street, a block of delicate pale light, beamed down into the park. Unlike Gatsby and Tom Buchanan, I had no girl whose disembodied face floated along the dark cornices and blinding signs, and so I drew up the girl beside me, tightening my arms. Her wan, scornful mouth smiled, and so I drew her up again closer, this time to my face.

V

When I came home to West Egg that night I was afraid for a moment that my house was on fire. Two o'clock and the whole corner of the peninsula was blazing with light, which fell unreal on the shrubbery and made thin elongating glints upon the roadside wires. Turning a corner, I saw that it was Gatsby's house, lit from tower to cellar.

At first I thought it was another party, a wild rout that had resolved itself into "hide-and-go-seek" or "sardines-in-the-box" with all the house thrown open to the game. But there wasn't a sound. Only wind in the trees, which blew the wires and made the lights go off and on again as if the house had winked into the darkness. As my taxi groaned away I saw Gatsby walking toward me across his lawn.

"Your place looks like the World's Fair," I said.

"Does it?" He turned his eyes toward it absently. "I have been glancing into some of the rooms. Let's go to Coney Island, old sport. In my car."

"It's too late."

"Well, suppose we take a plunge in the swimming pool? I haven't made use of it all summer."

"I've got to go to bed."

"All right."

He waited, looking at me with suppressed eagerness.

"I talked with Miss Baker," I said after a moment. "I'm going to call up Daisy tomorrow and invite her over here to tea."

"Oh, that's all right," he said carelessly. "I don't want to put you to any trouble."

"What day would suit you?"

"What day would suit you?" he corrected me quickly. "I don't want to put you to any trouble, you see."

"How about the day after tomorrow?"

He considered for a moment. Then, with reluctance: "I want to get the grass cut," he said.

We both looked down at the grass—there was a sharp line where my ragged lawn ended and the darker, well-kept expanse of his began. I suspected that he meant my grass.

"There's another little thing," he said uncertainly, and hesitated.

"Would you rather put it off for a few days?" I asked.

"Oh, it isn't about that. At least—" He fumbled with a series of beginnings. "Why, I thought—why, look here, old sport, you don't make much money, do you?"

"Not very much."

This seemed to reassure him and he continued more confidently.

"I thought you didn't, if you'll pardon my—you see, I carry on a little business on the side, a sort of side line, you understand. And I thought that if you don't make very much—You're selling bonds, aren't you, old sport?"

"Trying to."

"Well, this would interest you. It wouldn't take up much of your time and you might pick up a nice bit of money. It happens to be a rather confidential sort of thing."

I realize now that under different circumstances that conversation might have been one of the crises of my life. But, because the offer was obviously and tactlessly for a service to be rendered, I had no choice except to cut him off there.

"I've got my hands full," I said. "I'm much obliged but I couldn't take on any more work."

"You wouldn't have to do any business with Wolfshiem." Evidently he thought that I was shying away from the "gonnegtion" mentioned at lunch, but I assured him he was wrong. He waited a moment longer, hoping I'd begin a conversation, but I was too absorbed to be responsive, so he went unwillingly home.

The evening had made me lightheaded and happy; I think I walked into a deep sleep as I entered my front door. So I don't know whether or not Gatsby went to Coney Island, or for how many hours he "glanced into rooms" while his house blazed gaudily on. I called up Daisy from the office next morning, and invited her to come to tea.

"Don't bring Tom," I warned her.

"What?"

"Don't bring Tom."

"Who is 'Tom'?" she asked innocently.

The day agreed upon was pouring rain. At eleven o'clock a man in a raincoat, dragging a lawn-mower, tapped at my front door and said that Mr. Gatsby had sent him over to cut my grass. This reminded me that I had forgotten to tell my Finn to come back, so I drove into West Egg Village to search for her among soggy whitewashed alleys and to buy some cups and lemons and flowers.

The flowers were unnecessary, for at two o'clock a greenhouse arrived from Gatsby's, with innumerable receptacles to contain it. An hour later the front door opened nervously, and Gatsby in a white flannel suit, silver shirt, and gold-coloured tie, hurried in. He was pale, and there were dark signs of sleeplessness beneath his eyes.

"Is everything all right?" he asked immediately.

"The grass looks fine, if that's what you mean."

"What grass?" he inquired blankly. "Oh, the grass in the yard." He looked out the window at it, but, judging from his expression, I don't believe he saw a thing.

"Looks very good," he remarked vaguely. "One of the papers said they thought the rain would stop about four. I think it was The Journal. Have you got everything you need in the shape of—of tea?"

I took him into the pantry, where he looked a little reproachfully at the Finn. Together we scrutinized the twelve lemon cakes from the delicatessen shop.

"Will they do?" I asked.

"Of course, of course! They're fine!" and he added hollowly, "… old sport."

The rain cooled about half-past three to a damp mist, through which occasional thin drops swam like dew. Gatsby looked with vacant eyes through a copy of Clay's Economics, starting at the Finnish tread that shook the kitchen floor, and peering towards the bleared windows from time to time as if a series of invisible but alarming happenings were taking place outside. Finally he got up and informed me, in an uncertain voice, that he was going home.

"Why's that?"

"Nobody's coming to tea. It's too late!" He looked at his watch as if there was some pressing demand on his time elsewhere. "I can't wait all day."

"Don't be silly; it's just two minutes to four."

He sat down miserably, as if I had pushed him, and simultaneously there was the sound of a motor turning into my lane. We both jumped up, and, a little harrowed myself, I went out into the yard.

Under the dripping bare lilac-trees a large open car was coming up the drive. It stopped. Daisy's face, tipped sideways beneath a three-cornered lavender hat, looked out at me with a bright ecstatic smile.

"Is this absolutely where you live, my dearest one?"

The exhilarating ripple of her voice was a wild tonic in the rain. I had to follow the sound of it for a moment, up and down, with my ear alone, before any words came through. A damp streak of hair lay like a dash of blue paint across her cheek, and her hand was wet with glistening drops as I took it to help her from the car.

"Are you in love with me," she said low in my ear, "or why did I have to come alone?"

"That's the secret of Castle Rackrent. Tell your chauffeur to go far away and spend an hour."

"Come back in an hour, Ferdie." Then in a grave murmur: "His name is Ferdie."

"Does the gasoline affect his nose?"

"I don't think so," she said innocently. "Why?"

We went in. To my overwhelming surprise the living-room was deserted.

"Well, that's funny," I exclaimed.

"What's funny?"

She turned her head as there was a light dignified knocking at the front door. I went out and opened it. Gatsby, pale as death, with his hands plunged like weights in his coat pockets, was standing in a puddle of water glaring tragically into my eyes.

With his hands still in his coat pockets he stalked by me into the hall, turned sharply as if he were on a wire, and disappeared into the living-room. It wasn't a bit funny. Aware of the loud beating of my own heart I pulled the door to against the increasing rain.

For half a minute there wasn't a sound. Then from the living-room I heard a sort of choking murmur and part of a laugh, followed by Daisy's voice on a clear artificial note:

"I certainly am awfully glad to see you again."

A pause; it endured horribly. I had nothing to do in the hall, so I went into the room.

Gatsby, his hands still in his pockets, was reclining against the mantelpiece in a strained counterfeit of perfect ease, even of boredom. His head leaned back so far that it rested against the face of a defunct mantelpiece clock, and from this position his distraught eyes stared down at Daisy, who was sitting, frightened but graceful, on the edge of a stiff chair.

"We've met before," muttered Gatsby. His eyes glanced momentarily at me, and his lips parted with an abortive attempt at a laugh. Luckily the clock took this moment to tilt dangerously at the pressure of his head, whereupon he turned and caught it with trembling fingers, and set it back in place. Then he sat down, rigidly, his elbow on the arm of the sofa and his chin in his hand.

"I'm sorry about the clock," he said.

My own face had now assumed a deep tropical burn. I couldn't muster up a single commonplace out of the thousand in my head.

"It's an old clock," I told them idiotically.

I think we all believed for a moment that it had smashed in pieces on the floor.

"We haven't met for many years," said Daisy, her voice as matter-of-fact as it could ever be.

"Five years next November."

The automatic quality of Gatsby's answer set us all back at least another minute. I had them both on their feet with the desperate suggestion that they help me make tea in the kitchen when the demoniac Finn brought it in on a tray.

Amid the welcome confusion of cups and cakes a certain physical decency established itself. Gatsby got himself into a shadow and, while Daisy and I talked, looked conscientiously from one to the other of us with tense, unhappy eyes. However, as calmness wasn't an end in itself, I made an excuse at the first possible moment, and got to my feet.

"Where are you going?" demanded Gatsby in immediate alarm.

"I'll be back."

"I've got to speak to you about something before you go."

He followed me wildly into the kitchen, closed the door, and whispered: "Oh, God!" in a miserable way.

"What's the matter?"

"This is a terrible mistake," he said, shaking his head from side to side, "a terrible, terrible mistake."

"You're just embarrassed, that's all," and luckily I added: "Daisy's embarrassed too."

"She's embarrassed?" he repeated incredulously.

"Just as much as you are."

"Don't talk so loud."

THE GREAT GATSBY

"You're acting like a little boy," I broke out impatiently. "Not only that, but you're rude. Daisy's sitting in there all alone."

He raised his hand to stop my words, looked at me with unforgettable reproach, and, opening the door cautiously, went back into the other room.

I walked out the back way—just as Gatsby had when he had made his nervous circuit of the house half an hour before—and ran for a huge black knotted tree, whose massed leaves made a fabric against the rain. Once more it was pouring, and my irregular lawn, well-shaved by Gatsby's gardener, abounded in small muddy swamps and prehistoric marshes. There was nothing to look at from under the tree except Gatsby's enormous house, so I stared at it, like Kant at his church steeple, for half an hour. A brewer had built it early in the "period" craze, a decade before, and there was a story that he'd agreed to pay five years' taxes on all the neighbouring cottages if the owners would have their roofs thatched with straw. Perhaps their refusal took the heart out of his plan to Found a Family—he went into an immediate decline. His children sold his house with the black wreath still on the door. Americans, while willing, even eager, to be serfs, have always been obstinate about being peasantry.

After half an hour, the sun shone again, and the grocer's automobile rounded Gatsby's drive with the raw material for his servants' dinner—I felt sure he wouldn't eat a spoonful. A maid began opening the upper windows of his house, appeared momentarily in each, and, leaning from the large central bay, spat meditatively into the garden. It was time I went back. While the rain continued it had seemed like the murmur of their voices, rising and swelling a little now and then with gusts of emotion. But in the new silence I felt that silence had fallen within the house too.

I went in—after making every possible noise in the kitchen, short of pushing over the stove—but I don't believe they heard a sound. They were sitting at either end of the couch, looking at each other as if some question had been asked, or was in the air, and every vestige of embarrassment was gone. Daisy's face was smeared with tears, and when I came in she jumped up and began wiping at it with her handkerchief before a mirror. But there was a change in Gatsby that was simply confounding. He literally glowed; without a word or a gesture of exultation a new well-being radiated from him and filled the little room.

"Oh, hello, old sport," he said, as if he hadn't seen me for years. I thought for a moment he was going to shake hands.

"It's stopped raining."

"Has it?" When he realized what I was talking about, that there were twinkle-bells of sunshine in the room, he smiled like a weather man, like an ecstatic patron of recurrent light, and repeated the news to Daisy. "What do you think of that? It's stopped raining."

"I'm glad, Jay." Her throat, full of aching, grieving beauty, told only of her unexpected joy.

"I want you and Daisy to come over to my house," he said, "I'd like to show her around."

"You're sure you want me to come?"

"Absolutely, old sport."

Daisy went upstairs to wash her face—too late I thought with humiliation of my towels—while Gatsby and I waited on the lawn.

"My house looks well, doesn't it?" he demanded. "See how the whole front of it catches the light."

I agreed that it was splendid.

"Yes." His eyes went over it, every arched door and square tower. "It took me just three years to earn the money that bought it."

"I thought you inherited your money."

"I did, old sport," he said automatically, "but I lost most of it in the big panic—the panic of the war."

I think he hardly knew what he was saying, for when I asked him what business he was in he answered: "That's my affair," before he realized that it wasn't an appropriate reply.

"Oh, I've been in several things," he corrected himself. "I was in the drug business and then I was in the oil business. But I'm not in either one now." He looked at me with more attention. "Do you mean you've been thinking over what I proposed the other night?"

Before I could answer, Daisy came out of the house and two rows of brass buttons on her dress gleamed in the sunlight.

"That huge place there?" she cried pointing.

"Do you like it?"

"I love it, but I don't see how you live there all alone."

"I keep it always full of interesting people, night and day. People who do interesting things. Celebrated people."

Instead of taking the shortcut along the Sound we went down to the road and entered by the big postern. With enchanting murmurs Daisy admired this aspect or that of the feudal silhouette against the sky, admired the gardens, the sparkling odour of jonquils and the frothy odour of hawthorn and plum blossoms and the pale gold odour of kiss-me-at-the-gate. It was strange to reach the marble steps and find no stir of bright dresses in and out the door, and hear no sound but bird voices in the trees.

And inside, as we wandered through Marie Antoinette music-rooms and Restoration Salons, I felt that there were guests concealed behind every couch and table, under orders to be breathlessly silent until we had passed through. As Gatsby closed the door of "the Merton College Library" I could have sworn I heard the owl-eyed man break into ghostly laughter.

We went upstairs, through period bedrooms swathed in rose and lavender silk and vivid with new flowers, through dressing-rooms and poolrooms, and bathrooms with sunken baths—intruding into one chamber where a dishevelled man in pyjamas was doing liver exercises on the floor. It was Mr. Klipspringer, the "boarder." I had seen him wandering hungrily about the beach that morning. Finally we came to Gatsby's own apartment, a bedroom and a bath, and an Adam's study, where we sat down and drank a glass of some Chartreuse he took from a cupboard in the wall.

He hadn't once ceased looking at Daisy, and I think he revalued everything in his house according to the measure of response it drew from her well-loved eyes. Sometimes too, he stared around at his possessions in a dazed way, as though in her actual and astounding presence none of it was any longer real. Once he nearly toppled down a flight of stairs.

His bedroom was the simplest room of all—except where the dresser was garnished with a toilet set of pure dull gold. Daisy took the brush with delight, and smoothed her hair, whereupon Gatsby sat down and shaded his eyes and began to laugh.

"It's the funniest thing, old sport," he said hilariously. "I can't—When I try to—"

He had passed visibly through two states and was entering upon a third. After his embarrassment and his unreasoning joy he was consumed with wonder at her presence. He had been full of the idea so long, dreamed it right through to the end, waited with his teeth set, so to speak, at an inconceivable pitch of intensity. Now, in the reaction, he was running down like an over-wound clock.

Recovering himself in a minute he opened for us two hulking patent cabinets which held his massed suits and dressing-gowns and ties, and his shirts, piled like bricks in stacks a dozen high.

"I've got a man in England who buys me clothes. He sends over a selection of things at the beginning of each season, spring and fall."

He took out a pile of shirts and began throwing them, one by one, before us, shirts of sheer linen and thick silk and fine flannel, which lost their folds as they fell and covered the table in many-coloured disarray. While we admired he brought more and the soft rich heap mounted higher—shirts with stripes and scrolls and plaids in coral and apple-green and lavender and faint orange, with monograms of indian blue. Suddenly, with a strained sound, Daisy bent her head into the shirts and began to cry stormily.

"They're such beautiful shirts," she sobbed, her voice muffled in the thick folds. "It makes me sad because I've never seen such—such beautiful shirts before."

After the house, we were to see the grounds and the swimming pool, and the hydroplane, and the midsummer flowers—but outside Gatsby's window it began to rain again, so we stood in a row looking at the corrugated surface of the Sound.

"If it wasn't for the mist we could see your home across the bay," said Gatsby. "You always have a green light that burns all night at the end of your dock."

Daisy put her arm through his abruptly, but he seemed absorbed in what he had just said. Possibly it had occurred to him that the colossal significance of that light had now vanished forever. Compared to the great distance that had separated him from Daisy it had seemed very near to her, almost touching her. It had seemed as close as a star to the moon. Now it was again a green light on a dock. His count of enchanted objects had diminished by one.

I began to walk about the room, examining various indefinite objects in the half darkness. A large photograph of an elderly man in yachting costume attracted me, hung on the wall over his desk.

"Who's this?"

"That? That's Mr. Dan Cody, old sport."

The name sounded faintly familiar.

"He's dead now. He used to be my best friend years ago."

There was a small picture of Gatsby, also in yachting costume, on the bureau—Gatsby with his head thrown back defiantly—taken apparently when he was about eighteen.

"I adore it," exclaimed Daisy. "The pompadour! You never told me you had a pompadour—or a yacht."

"Look at this," said Gatsby quickly. "Here's a lot of clippings—about you."

They stood side by side examining it. I was going to ask to see the rubies when the phone rang, and Gatsby took up the receiver.

"Yes ... Well, I can't talk now ... I can't talk now, old sport ... I said a small town ... He must know what a small town is ... Well, he's no use to us if Detroit is his idea of a small town ..."

He rang off.

"Come here quick!" cried Daisy at the window.

The rain was still falling, but the darkness had parted in the west, and there was a pink and golden billow of foamy clouds above the sea.

"Look at that," she whispered, and then after a moment: "I'd like to just get one of those pink clouds and put you in it and push you around."

I tried to go then, but they wouldn't hear of it; perhaps my presence made them feel more satisfactorily alone.

"I know what we'll do," said Gatsby, "we'll have Klipspringer play the piano."

He went out of the room calling "Ewing!" and returned in a few minutes accompanied by an embarrassed, slightly worn young man, with shell-rimmed glasses and scanty blond hair. He was now decently clothed in a "sport shirt," open at the neck, sneakers, and duck trousers of a nebulous hue.

"Did we interrupt your exercise?" inquired Daisy politely.

"I was asleep," cried Mr. Klipspringer, in a spasm of embarrassment. "That is, I'd been asleep. Then I got up ..."

"Klipspringer plays the piano," said Gatsby, cutting him off. "Don't you, Ewing, old sport?"

"I don't play well. I don't—hardly play at all. I'm all out of prac—"

"We'll go downstairs," interrupted Gatsby. He flipped a switch. The grey windows disappeared as the house glowed full of light.

In the music-room Gatsby turned on a solitary lamp beside the piano. He lit Daisy's cigarette from a trembling match, and sat down with her on a couch far across the room, where there was no light save what the gleaming floor bounced in from the hall.

When Klipspringer had played "The Love Nest" he turned around on the bench and searched unhappily for Gatsby in the gloom.

"I'm all out of practice, you see. I told you I couldn't play. I'm all out of prac—"

"Don't talk so much, old sport," commanded Gatsby. "Play!"

"In the morning, In the evening, Ain't we got fun—"

Outside the wind was loud and there was a faint flow of thunder along the Sound. All the lights were going on in West Egg now; the electric trains, men-carrying, were plunging home through the rain from New York. It was the hour of a profound human change, and excitement was generating on the air.

"One thing's sure and nothing's surer The rich get richer and the poor get—children. In the meantime, In between time—"

As I went over to say goodbye I saw that the expression of bewilderment had come back into Gatsby's face, as though a faint doubt had occurred to him as to the quality of his present happiness. Almost five years! There must have been moments even that afternoon when Daisy tumbled short of his dreams—not through her own fault, but because of the colossal vitality of his illusion. It had gone beyond her, beyond everything. He had thrown himself into it with a creative passion, adding to it all the time, decking it out with every bright feather that drifted his way. No amount of fire or freshness can challenge what a man can store up in his ghostly heart.

THE GREAT GATSBY

As I watched him he adjusted himself a little, visibly. His hand took hold of hers, and as she said something low in his ear he turned toward her with a rush of emotion. I think that voice held him most, with its fluctuating, feverish warmth, because it couldn't be over-dreamed—that voice was a deathless song.

They had forgotten me, but Daisy glanced up and held out her hand; Gatsby didn't know me now at all. I looked once more at them and they looked back at me, remotely, possessed by intense life. Then I went out of the room and down the marble steps into the rain, leaving them there together.

VI

About this time an ambitious young reporter from New York arrived one morning at Gatsby's door and asked him if he had anything to say.

"Anything to say about what?" inquired Gatsby politely.

"Why—any statement to give out."

It transpired after a confused five minutes that the man had heard Gatsby's name around his office in a connection which he either wouldn't reveal or didn't fully understand. This was his day off and with laudable initiative he had hurried out "to see."

It was a random shot, and yet the reporter's instinct was right. Gatsby's notoriety, spread about by the hundreds who had accepted his hospitality and so become authorities upon his past, had increased all summer until he fell just short of being news. Contemporary legends such as the "underground pipeline to Canada" attached themselves to him, and there was one persistent story that he didn't live in a house at all, but in a boat that looked like a house and was moved secretly up and down the Long Island shore. Just why these inventions were a source of satisfaction to James Gatz of North Dakota, isn't easy to say.

James Gatz—that was really, or at least legally, his name. He had changed it at the age of seventeen and at the specific moment that witnessed the beginning of his career—when he saw Dan Cody's yacht drop anchor over the most insidious flat on Lake Superior. It was James Gatz who had been loafing along the beach that afternoon in a torn green jersey and a pair of canvas pants, but it was already Jay Gatsby who borrowed a rowboat, pulled out to the Tuolomee, and informed Cody that a wind might catch him and break him up in half an hour.

I suppose he'd had the name ready for a long time, even then. His parents were shiftless and unsuccessful farm people—his imagination had never really accepted them as his parents at all. The truth was that Jay Gatsby of West Egg, Long Island, sprang from his Platonic conception of himself. He was a son of God—a phrase which, if it means anything, means just that—and he must be about His Father's business, the service of a vast, vulgar, and meretricious beauty. So he invented just the sort of Jay Gatsby that a seventeen-year-old boy would be likely to invent, and to this conception he was faithful to the end.

For over a year he had been beating his way along the south shore of Lake Superior as a clam-digger and a salmon-fisher or in any other capacity that brought him food and bed. His brown, hardening body lived naturally through the half-fierce, half-lazy work of the bracing days. He knew women early, and since they spoiled him he became contemptuous of them, of young virgins because they were ignorant, of the others because they were hysterical about things which in his overwhelming self-absorption he took for granted.

But his heart was in a constant, turbulent riot. The most grotesque and fantastic conceits haunted him in his bed at night. A universe of ineffable gaudiness spun itself out in his brain while the clock ticked on the washstand and the moon soaked with wet light his tangled clothes upon the floor. Each night he added to the pattern of his fancies until drowsiness closed down upon some vivid scene with an oblivious embrace. For a while these reveries provided an outlet for his imagination; they were a satisfactory hint of the unreality of reality, a promise that the rock of the world was founded securely on a fairy's wing.

An instinct toward his future glory had led him, some months before, to the small Lutheran College of St. Olaf's in southern Minnesota. He stayed there two weeks, dismayed at its ferocious indifference to the drums of his destiny, to destiny itself, and despising the janitor's work with which he was to pay his way through. Then he drifted back to Lake Superior, and he was still searching for something to do on the day that Dan Cody's yacht dropped anchor in the shallows alongshore.

Cody was fifty years old then, a product of the Nevada silver fields, of the Yukon, of every rush for metal since seventy-five. The transactions in Montana copper that made him many times a millionaire found him physically robust but on the verge of soft-mindedness, and, suspecting this, an infinite number of women tried to separate him from his money. The none too savoury ramifications by which Ella Kaye, the newspaper woman, played Madame de Maintenon to his weakness and sent him to sea in a yacht, were common property of the turgid journalism in 1902. He had been coasting along all too hospitable shores for five years when he turned up as James Gatz's destiny in Little Girl Bay.

To young Gatz, resting on his oars and looking up at the railed deck, that yacht represented all the beauty and glamour in the world. I suppose he smiled at Cody—he had probably discovered that people liked him when he smiled. At any rate Cody asked him a few questions (one of them elicited the brand new name) and found that he was quick and extravagantly ambitious. A few days later he took him to Duluth and bought him a blue coat, six pairs of white duck trousers, and a yachting cap. And when the Tuolomee left for the West Indies and the Barbary Coast, Gatsby left too.

He was employed in a vague personal capacity—while he remained with Cody he was in turn steward, mate, skipper, secretary, and even jailor, for Dan Cody sober knew what lavish doings Dan Cody drunk might soon be about, and he provided for such contingencies by reposing more and more trust in Gatsby. The arrangement lasted five years, during which the boat went three times around the Continent. It might have lasted indefinitely except for the fact that Ella Kaye came on board one night in Boston and a week later Dan Cody inhospitably died.

I remember the portrait of him up in Gatsby's bedroom, a grey, florid man with a hard, empty face—the pioneer debauchee, who during one phase of American life brought back to the Eastern seaboard the savage violence of the frontier brothel and saloon. It was indirectly due to Cody that Gatsby drank so little. Sometimes in the course of gay parties women used to rub champagne into his hair; for himself he formed the habit of letting liquor alone.

And it was from Cody that he inherited money—a legacy of twenty-five thousand dollars. He didn't get it. He never understood the legal device that was used against him, but what remained of the millions went intact to Ella Kaye. He was left with his singularly appropriate education; the vague contour of Jay Gatsby had filled out to the substantiality of a man.

He told me all this very much later, but I've put it down here with the idea of exploding those first wild rumours about his antecedents, which weren't even faintly true. Moreover he told it to me at a time of confusion, when I had reached the point of believing everything and nothing about him. So I take advantage of this short halt, while Gatsby, so to speak, caught his breath, to clear this set of misconceptions away.

It was a halt, too, in my association with his affairs. For several weeks I didn't see him or hear his voice on the phone—mostly I was in New York, trotting around with Jordan and trying to ingratiate myself with her senile aunt—but finally I went over to his house one Sunday afternoon. I hadn't been there two minutes when somebody brought Tom Buchanan in for a drink. I was startled, naturally, but the really surprising thing was that it hadn't happened before.

They were a party of three on horseback—Tom and a man named Sloane and a pretty woman in a brown riding-habit, who had been there previously.

"I'm delighted to see you," said Gatsby, standing on his porch. "I'm delighted that you dropped in."

As though they cared!

"Sit right down. Have a cigarette or a cigar." He walked around the room quickly, ringing bells. "I'll have something to drink for you in just a minute."

He was profoundly affected by the fact that Tom was there. But he would be uneasy anyhow until he had given them something, realizing in a vague way that that was all they came for. Mr. Sloane wanted nothing. A lemonade? No, thanks. A little champagne? Nothing at all, thanks ... I'm sorry—

"Did you have a nice ride?"

"Very good roads around here."

"I suppose the automobiles—"

"Yeah."

Moved by an irresistible impulse, Gatsby turned to Tom, who had accepted the introduction as a stranger.

"I believe we've met somewhere before, Mr. Buchanan."

"Oh, yes," said Tom, gruffly polite, but obviously not remembering. "So we did. I remember very well."

"About two weeks ago."

"That's right. You were with Nick here."

"I know your wife," continued Gatsby, almost aggressively.

"That so?"

Tom turned to me.

"You live near here, Nick?"

"Next door."

"That so?"

Mr. Sloane didn't enter into the conversation, but lounged back haughtily in his chair; the woman said nothing either—until unexpectedly, after two highballs, she became cordial.

"We'll all come over to your next party, Mr. Gatsby," she suggested. "What do you say?"

"Certainly; I'd be delighted to have you."

"Be ver' nice," said Mr. Sloane, without gratitude. "Well—think ought to be starting home."

"Please don't hurry," Gatsby urged them. He had control of himself now, and he wanted to see more of Tom. "Why don't you—why don't you stay for supper? I wouldn't be surprised if some other people dropped in from New York."

"You come to supper with me," said the lady enthusiastically. "Both of you."

This included me. Mr. Sloane got to his feet.

"Come along," he said—but to her only.

"I mean it," she insisted. "I'd love to have you. Lots of room."

Gatsby looked at me questioningly. He wanted to go and he didn't see that Mr. Sloane had determined he shouldn't.

"I'm afraid I won't be able to," I said.

"Well, you come," she urged, concentrating on Gatsby.

Mr. Sloane murmured something close to her ear.

"We won't be late if we start now," she insisted aloud.

"I haven't got a horse," said Gatsby. "I used to ride in the army, but I've never bought a horse. I'll have to follow you in my car. Excuse me for just a minute."

The rest of us walked out on the porch, where Sloane and the lady began an impassioned conversation aside.

"My God, I believe the man's coming," said Tom. "Doesn't he know she doesn't want him?"

"She says she does want him."

"She has a big dinner party and he won't know a soul there." He frowned. "I wonder where in the devil he met Daisy. By God, I may be old-fashioned in my ideas, but women run around too much these days to suit me. They meet all kinds of crazy fish."

Suddenly Mr. Sloane and the lady walked down the steps and mounted their horses.

THE GREAT GATSBY

"Come on," said Mr. Sloane to Tom, "we're late. We've got to go."

And then to me: "Tell him we couldn't wait, will you?"

Tom and I shook hands, the rest of us exchanged a cool nod, and they trotted quickly down the drive, disappearing under the August foliage just as Gatsby, with hat and light overcoat in hand, came out the front door.

Tom was evidently perturbed at Daisy's running around alone, for on the following Saturday night he came with her to Gatsby's party. Perhaps his presence gave the evening its peculiar quality of oppressiveness—it stands out in my memory from Gatsby's other parties that summer. There were the same people, or at least the same sort of people, the same profusion of champagne, the same many-coloured, many-keyed commotion, but I felt an unpleasantness in the air, a pervading harshness that hadn't been there before. Or perhaps I had merely grown used to it, grown to accept West Egg as a world complete in itself, with its own standards and its own great figures, second to nothing because it had no consciousness of being so, and now I was looking at it again, through Daisy's eyes. It is invariably saddening to look through new eyes at things upon which you have expended your own powers of adjustment.

They arrived at twilight, and, as we strolled out among the sparkling hundreds, Daisy's voice was playing murmurous tricks in her throat.

"These things excite me so," she whispered. "If you want to kiss me any time during the evening, Nick, just let me know and I'll be glad to arrange it for you. Just mention my name. Or present a green card. I'm giving out green—"

"Look around," suggested Gatsby.

"I'm looking around. I'm having a marvellous—"

"You must see the faces of many people you've heard about."

Tom's arrogant eyes roamed the crowd.

"We don't go around very much," he said; "in fact, I was just thinking I don't know a soul here."

"Perhaps you know that lady." Gatsby indicated a gorgeous, scarcely human orchid of a woman who sat in state under a white-plum tree. Tom and Daisy stared, with that peculiarly unreal feeling that accompanies the recognition of a hitherto ghostly celebrity of the movies.

"She's lovely," said Daisy.

"The man bending over her is her director."

He took them ceremoniously from group to group:

"Mrs. Buchanan … and Mr. Buchanan—" After an instant's hesitation he added: "the polo player."

"Oh no," objected Tom quickly, "not me."

But evidently the sound of it pleased Gatsby for Tom remained "the polo player" for the rest of the evening.

"I've never met so many celebrities," Daisy exclaimed. "I liked that man—what was his name?—with the sort of blue nose."

Gatsby identified him, adding that he was a small producer.

"Well, I liked him anyhow."

"I'd a little rather not be the polo player," said Tom pleasantly, "I'd rather look at all these famous people in—in oblivion."

Daisy and Gatsby danced. I remember being surprised by his graceful, conservative foxtrot—I had never seen him dance before. Then they sauntered over to my house and sat on the steps for half an hour, while at her request I remained watchfully in the garden. "In case there's a fire or a flood," she explained, "or any act of God."

Tom appeared from his oblivion as we were sitting down to supper together. "Do you mind if I eat with some people over here?" he said. "A fellow's getting off some funny stuff."

"Go ahead," answered Daisy genially, "and if you want to take down any addresses here's my little gold pencil." ... She looked around after a moment and told me the girl was "common but pretty," and I knew that except for the half-hour she'd been alone with Gatsby she wasn't having a good time.

We were at a particularly tipsy table. That was my fault—Gatsby had been called to the phone, and I'd enjoyed these same people only two weeks before. But what had amused me then turned septic on the air now.

"How do you feel, Miss Baedeker?"

The girl addressed was trying, unsuccessfully, to slump against my shoulder. At this inquiry she sat up and opened her eyes.

"Wha'?"

A massive and lethargic woman, who had been urging Daisy to play golf with her at the local club tomorrow, spoke in Miss Baedeker's defence:

"Oh, she's all right now. When she's had five or six cocktails she always starts screaming like that. I tell her she ought to leave it alone."

"I do leave it alone," affirmed the accused hollowly.

"We heard you yelling, so I said to Doc Civet here: 'There's somebody that needs your help, Doc.'"

"She's much obliged, I'm sure," said another friend, without gratitude, "but you got her dress all wet when you stuck her head in the pool."

"Anything I hate is to get my head stuck in a pool," mumbled Miss Baedeker. "They almost drowned me once over in New Jersey."

"Then you ought to leave it alone," countered Doctor Civet.

"Speak for yourself!" cried Miss Baedeker violently. "Your hand shakes. I wouldn't let you operate on me!"

It was like that. Almost the last thing I remember was standing with Daisy and watching the moving-picture director and his Star. They were still under the white-plum tree and their faces were touching except for a pale, thin ray of moonlight between. It occurred to me that he had been very slowly bending toward her all evening to attain this proximity, and even while I watched I saw him stoop one ultimate degree and kiss at her cheek.

"I like her," said Daisy, "I think she's lovely."

But the rest offended her—and inarguably because it wasn't a gesture but an emotion. She was appalled by West Egg, this unprecedented "place" that Broadway had begotten upon a Long Island fishing village—appalled by its raw vigour that chafed under the old euphemisms and by the too obtrusive fate that herded its inhabitants along a shortcut from nothing to nothing. She saw something awful in the very simplicity she failed to understand.

I sat on the front steps with them while they waited for their car. It was dark here in front; only the bright door sent ten square feet of light volleying out into the soft black morning. Sometimes a shadow moved against a dressing-room blind above, gave way to another shadow, an indefinite procession of shadows, who rouged and powdered in an invisible glass.

"Who is this Gatsby anyhow?" demanded Tom suddenly. "Some big bootlegger?"

"Where'd you hear that?" I inquired.

"I didn't hear it. I imagined it. A lot of these newly rich people are just big bootleggers, you know."

"Not Gatsby," I said shortly.

He was silent for a moment. The pebbles of the drive crunched under his feet.

"Well, he certainly must have strained himself to get this menagerie together."

A breeze stirred the grey haze of Daisy's fur collar.

"At least they are more interesting than the people we know," she said with an effort.

"You didn't look so interested."

"Well, I was."

Tom laughed and turned to me.

"Did you notice Daisy's face when that girl asked her to put her under a cold shower?"

Daisy began to sing with the music in a husky, rhythmic whisper, bringing out a meaning in each word that it had never had before and would never have again. When the melody rose her voice broke up sweetly, following it, in a way contralto voices have, and each change tipped out a little of her warm human magic upon the air.

"Lots of people come who haven't been invited," she said suddenly. "That girl hadn't been invited. They simply force their way in and he's too polite to object."

"I'd like to know who he is and what he does," insisted Tom. "And I think I'll make a point of finding out."

"I can tell you right now," she answered. "He owned some drugstores, a lot of drugstores. He built them up himself."

The dilatory limousine came rolling up the drive.

"Good night, Nick," said Daisy.

Her glance left me and sought the lighted top of the steps, where "Three O'Clock in the Morning," a neat, sad little waltz of that year, was drifting out the open door. After all, in the very casualness of Gatsby's party there were romantic possibilities totally absent from her world. What was it up there in the song that seemed to be calling her back inside? What would happen now in the dim, incalculable hours? Perhaps some unbelievable guest would arrive, a person infinitely rare and to be marvelled at, some authentically radiant young girl who with one fresh glance at Gatsby, one moment of magical encounter, would blot out those five years of unwavering devotion.

I stayed late that night. Gatsby asked me to wait until he was free, and I lingered in the garden until the inevitable swimming party had run up, chilled and exalted, from the black beach, until the lights were extinguished in the guestrooms overhead. When he came down the steps at last the tanned skin was drawn unusually tight on his face, and his eyes were bright and tired.

"She didn't like it," he said immediately.

"Of course she did."

"She didn't like it," he insisted. "She didn't have a good time."

He was silent, and I guessed at his unutterable depression.

"I feel far away from her," he said. "It's hard to make her understand."

"You mean about the dance?"

"The dance?" He dismissed all the dances he had given with a snap of his fingers. "Old sport, the dance is unimportant."

He wanted nothing less of Daisy than that she should go to Tom and say: "I never loved you." After she had obliterated four years with that sentence they could decide upon the more practical measures to be taken.

One of them was that, after she was free, they were to go back to Louisville and be married from her house—just as if it were five years ago.

"And she doesn't understand," he said. "She used to be able to understand. We'd sit for hours—"

He broke off and began to walk up and down a desolate path of fruit rinds and discarded favours and crushed flowers.

"I wouldn't ask too much of her," I ventured. "You can't repeat the past."

"Can't repeat the past?" he cried incredulously. "Why of course you can!"

He looked around him wildly, as if the past were lurking here in the shadow of his house, just out of reach of his hand.

"I'm going to fix everything just the way it was before," he said, nodding determinedly. "She'll see."

He talked a lot about the past, and I gathered that he wanted to recover something, some idea of himself perhaps, that had gone into loving Daisy. His life had been confused and disordered since then, but if he could once return to a certain starting place and go over it all slowly, he could find out what that thing was …

… One autumn night, five years before, they had been walking down the street when the leaves were falling, and they came to a place where there were no trees and the sidewalk was white with moonlight. They stopped here and turned toward each other. Now it was a cool night with that mysterious excitement in it which comes at the two changes of the year. The quiet lights in the houses were humming out into the darkness and there was a stir and bustle among the stars. Out of the corner of his eye Gatsby saw that the blocks of the sidewalks really formed a ladder and mounted to a secret place above the trees—he could climb to it, if he climbed alone, and once there he could suck on the pap of life, gulp down the incomparable milk of wonder.

His heart beat faster as Daisy's white face came up to his own. He knew that when he kissed this girl, and forever wed his unutterable visions to her perishable breath, his mind would never romp again like the mind of God. So he waited, listening for a moment longer to the tuning-fork that had been struck upon a star. Then he kissed her. At his lips' touch she blossomed for him like a flower and the incarnation was complete.

Through all he said, even through his appalling sentimentality, I was reminded of something—an elusive rhythm, a fragment of lost words, that I had heard somewhere a long time ago. For a moment a phrase tried to take shape in my mouth and my lips parted like a dumb man's, as though there was more struggling upon them than a wisp of startled air. But they made no sound, and what I had almost remembered was uncommunicable forever.

VII

It was when curiosity about Gatsby was at its highest that the lights in his house failed to go on one Saturday night—and, as obscurely as it had begun, his career as Trimalchio was over. Only gradually did I become aware that the automobiles which turned expectantly into his drive stayed for just a minute and then drove sulkily away. Wondering if he were sick I went over to find out—an unfamiliar butler with a villainous face squinted at me suspiciously from the door.

"Is Mr. Gatsby sick?"

"Nope." After a pause he added "sir" in a dilatory, grudging way.

"I hadn't seen him around, and I was rather worried. Tell him Mr. Carraway came over."

"Who?" he demanded rudely.

"Carraway."

"Carraway. All right, I'll tell him."

Abruptly he slammed the door.

My Finn informed me that Gatsby had dismissed every servant in his house a week ago and replaced them with half a dozen others, who never went into West Egg village to be bribed by the tradesmen, but ordered moderate supplies over the telephone. The grocery boy reported that the kitchen looked like a pigsty, and the general opinion in the village was that the new people weren't servants at all.

Next day Gatsby called me on the phone.

"Going away?" I inquired.

"No, old sport."

"I hear you fired all your servants."

"I wanted somebody who wouldn't gossip. Daisy comes over quite often—in the afternoons."

So the whole caravansary had fallen in like a card house at the disapproval in her eyes.

"They're some people Wolfshiem wanted to do something for. They're all brothers and sisters. They used to run a small hotel."

"I see."

He was calling up at Daisy's request—would I come to lunch at her house tomorrow? Miss Baker would be there. Half an hour later Daisy herself telephoned and seemed relieved to find that I was coming. Something was up. And yet I couldn't believe that they would choose this occasion for a scene—especially for the rather harrowing scene that Gatsby had outlined in the garden.

The next day was broiling, almost the last, certainly the warmest, of the summer. As my train emerged from the tunnel into sunlight, only the hot whistles of the National Biscuit Company broke the simmering hush at noon. The straw seats of the car hovered on the edge of combustion; the woman next to me perspired delicately for a while into her white shirtwaist, and then, as her newspaper dampened under her fingers, lapsed despairingly into deep heat with a desolate cry. Her pocketbook slapped to the floor.

"Oh, my!" she gasped.

I picked it up with a weary bend and handed it back to her, holding it at arm's length and by the extreme tip of the corners to indicate that I had no designs upon it—but everyone near by, including the woman, suspected me just the same.

"Hot!" said the conductor to familiar faces. "Some weather! ... Hot! ... Hot! ... Hot! ... Is it hot enough for you? Is it hot? Is it ...?"

My commutation ticket came back to me with a dark stain from his hand. That anyone should care in this heat whose flushed lips he kissed, whose head made damp the pyjama pocket over his heart!

... Through the hall of the Buchanans' house blew a faint wind, carrying the sound of the telephone bell out to Gatsby and me as we waited at the door.

"The master's body?" roared the butler into the mouthpiece. "I'm sorry, madame, but we can't furnish it—it's far too hot to touch this noon!"

What he really said was: "Yes ... Yes ... I'll see."

He set down the receiver and came toward us, glistening slightly, to take our stiff straw hats.

"Madame expects you in the salon!" he cried, needlessly indicating the direction. In this heat every extra gesture was an affront to the common store of life.

The room, shadowed well with awnings, was dark and cool. Daisy and Jordan lay upon an enormous couch, like silver idols weighing down their own white dresses against the singing breeze of the fans.

"We can't move," they said together.

Jordan's fingers, powdered white over their tan, rested for a moment in mine.

"And Mr. Thomas Buchanan, the athlete?" I inquired.

Simultaneously I heard his voice, gruff, muffled, husky, at the hall telephone.

THE GREAT GATSBY

Gatsby stood in the centre of the crimson carpet and gazed around with fascinated eyes. Daisy watched him and laughed, her sweet, exciting laugh; a tiny gust of powder rose from her bosom into the air.

"The rumour is," whispered Jordan, "that that's Tom's girl on the telephone."

We were silent. The voice in the hall rose high with annoyance: "Very well, then, I won't sell you the car at all … I'm under no obligations to you at all … and as for your bothering me about it at lunch time, I won't stand that at all!"

"Holding down the receiver," said Daisy cynically.

"No, he's not," I assured her. "It's a bona-fide deal. I happen to know about it."

Tom flung open the door, blocked out its space for a moment with his thick body, and hurried into the room.

"Mr. Gatsby!" He put out his broad, flat hand with well-concealed dislike. "I'm glad to see you, sir … Nick …"

"Make us a cold drink," cried Daisy.

As he left the room again she got up and went over to Gatsby and pulled his face down, kissing him on the mouth.

"You know I love you," she murmured.

"You forget there's a lady present," said Jordan.

Daisy looked around doubtfully.

"You kiss Nick too."

"What a low, vulgar girl!"

"I don't care!" cried Daisy, and began to clog on the brick fireplace. Then she remembered the heat and sat down guiltily on the couch just as a freshly laundered nurse leading a little girl came into the room.

"Bles-sed pre-cious," she crooned, holding out her arms. "Come to your own mother that loves you."

The child, relinquished by the nurse, rushed across the room and rooted shyly into her mother's dress.

"The bles-sed pre-cious! Did mother get powder on your old yellowy hair? Stand up now, and say—How-de-do."

Gatsby and I in turn leaned down and took the small reluctant hand. Afterward he kept looking at the child with surprise. I don't think he had ever really believed in its existence before.

"I got dressed before luncheon," said the child, turning eagerly to Daisy.

"That's because your mother wanted to show you off." Her face bent into the single wrinkle of the small white neck. "You dream, you. You absolute little dream."

"Yes," admitted the child calmly. "Aunt Jordan's got on a white dress too."

"How do you like mother's friends?" Daisy turned her around so that she faced Gatsby. "Do you think they're pretty?"

"Where's Daddy?"

"She doesn't look like her father," explained Daisy. "She looks like me. She's got my hair and shape of the face."

Daisy sat back upon the couch. The nurse took a step forward and held out her hand.

"Come, Pammy."

"Goodbye, sweetheart!"

With a reluctant backward glance the well-disciplined child held to her nurse's hand and was pulled out the door, just as Tom came back, preceding four gin rickeys that clicked full of ice.

Gatsby took up his drink.

"They certainly look cool," he said, with visible tension.

We drank in long, greedy swallows.

"I read somewhere that the sun's getting hotter every year," said Tom genially. "It seems that pretty soon the earth's going to fall into the sun—or wait a minute—it's just the opposite—the sun's getting colder every year.

"Come outside," he suggested to Gatsby, "I'd like you to have a look at the place."

I went with them out to the veranda. On the green Sound, stagnant in the heat, one small sail crawled slowly toward the fresher sea. Gatsby's eyes followed it momentarily; he raised his hand and pointed across the bay.

"I'm right across from you."

"So you are."

Our eyes lifted over the rose-beds and the hot lawn and the weedy refuse of the dog-days alongshore. Slowly the white wings of the boat moved against the blue cool limit of the sky. Ahead lay the scalloped ocean and the abounding blessed isles.

"There's sport for you," said Tom, nodding. "I'd like to be out there with him for about an hour."

We had luncheon in the dining-room, darkened too against the heat, and drank down nervous gaiety with the cold ale.

"What'll we do with ourselves this afternoon?" cried Daisy, "and the day after that, and the next thirty years?"

"Don't be morbid," Jordan said. "Life starts all over again when it gets crisp in the fall."

"But it's so hot," insisted Daisy, on the verge of tears, "and everything's so confused. Let's all go to town!"

Her voice struggled on through the heat, beating against it, moulding its senselessness into forms.

"I've heard of making a garage out of a stable," Tom was saying to Gatsby, "but I'm the first man who ever made a stable out of a garage."

"Who wants to go to town?" demanded Daisy insistently. Gatsby's eyes floated toward her. "Ah," she cried, "you look so cool."

Their eyes met, and they stared together at each other, alone in space. With an effort she glanced down at the table.

"You always look so cool," she repeated.

She had told him that she loved him, and Tom Buchanan saw. He was astounded. His mouth opened a little, and he looked at Gatsby, and then back at Daisy as if he had just recognized her as someone he knew a long time ago.

"You resemble the advertisement of the man," she went on innocently. "You know the advertisement of the man—"

"All right," broke in Tom quickly, "I'm perfectly willing to go to town. Come on—we're all going to town."

He got up, his eyes still flashing between Gatsby and his wife. No one moved.

"Come on!" His temper cracked a little. "What's the matter, anyhow? If we're going to town, let's start."

His hand, trembling with his effort at self-control, bore to his lips the last of his glass of ale. Daisy's voice got us to our feet and out on to the blazing gravel drive.

"Are we just going to go?" she objected. "Like this? Aren't we going to let anyone smoke a cigarette first?"

"Everybody smoked all through lunch."

"Oh, let's have fun," she begged him. "It's too hot to fuss."

He didn't answer.

"Have it your own way," she said. "Come on, Jordan."

They went upstairs to get ready while we three men stood there shuffling the hot pebbles with our feet. A silver curve of the moon hovered already in the western sky. Gatsby started to speak, changed his mind, but not before Tom wheeled and faced him expectantly.

"Have you got your stables here?" asked Gatsby with an effort.

"About a quarter of a mile down the road."

"Oh."

A pause.

"I don't see the idea of going to town," broke out Tom savagely. "Women get these notions in their heads—"

"Shall we take anything to drink?" called Daisy from an upper window.

"I'll get some whisky," answered Tom. He went inside.

Gatsby turned to me rigidly:

"I can't say anything in his house, old sport."

"She's got an indiscreet voice," I remarked. "It's full of—" I hesitated.

"Her voice is full of money," he said suddenly.

That was it. I'd never understood before. It was full of money—that was the inexhaustible charm that rose and fell in it, the jingle of it, the cymbals' song of it ... High in a white palace the king's daughter, the golden girl ...

Tom came out of the house wrapping a quart bottle in a towel, followed by Daisy and Jordan wearing small tight hats of metallic cloth and carrying light capes over their arms.

"Shall we all go in my car?" suggested Gatsby. He felt the hot, green leather of the seat. "I ought to have left it in the shade."

"Is it standard shift?" demanded Tom.

"Yes."

"Well, you take my coupé and let me drive your car to town."

The suggestion was distasteful to Gatsby.

"I don't think there's much gas," he objected.

"Plenty of gas," said Tom boisterously. He looked at the gauge. "And if it runs out I can stop at a drugstore. You can buy anything at a drugstore nowadays."

A pause followed this apparently pointless remark. Daisy looked at Tom frowning, and an indefinable expression, at once definitely unfamiliar and vaguely recognizable, as if I had only heard it described in words, passed over Gatsby's face.

"Come on, Daisy," said Tom, pressing her with his hand toward Gatsby's car. "I'll take you in this circus wagon."

He opened the door, but she moved out from the circle of his arm.

"You take Nick and Jordan. We'll follow you in the coupé."

She walked close to Gatsby, touching his coat with her hand. Jordan and Tom and I got into the front seat of Gatsby's car, Tom pushed the unfamiliar gears tentatively, and we shot off into the oppressive heat, leaving them out of sight behind.

"Did you see that?" demanded Tom.

"See what?"

He looked at me keenly, realizing that Jordan and I must have known all along.

"You think I'm pretty dumb, don't you?" he suggested. "Perhaps I am, but I have a—almost a second sight, sometimes, that tells me what to do. Maybe you don't believe that, but science—"

He paused. The immediate contingency overtook him, pulled him back from the edge of theoretical abyss.

"I've made a small investigation of this fellow," he continued. "I could have gone deeper if I'd known—"

"Do you mean you've been to a medium?" inquired Jordan humorously.

"What?" Confused, he stared at us as we laughed. "A medium?"

"About Gatsby."

"About Gatsby! No, I haven't. I said I'd been making a small investigation of his past."

"And you found he was an Oxford man," said Jordan helpfully.

"An Oxford man!" He was incredulous. "Like hell he is! He wears a pink suit."

"Nevertheless he's an Oxford man."

"Oxford, New Mexico," snorted Tom contemptuously, "or something like that."

"Listen, Tom. If you're such a snob, why did you invite him to lunch?" demanded Jordan crossly.

"Daisy invited him; she knew him before we were married—God knows where!"

We were all irritable now with the fading ale, and aware of it we drove for a while in silence. Then as Doctor T. J. Eckleburg's faded eyes came into sight down the road, I remembered Gatsby's caution about gasoline.

"We've got enough to get us to town," said Tom.

"But there's a garage right here," objected Jordan. "I don't want to get stalled in this baking heat."

Tom threw on both brakes impatiently, and we slid to an abrupt dusty stop under Wilson's sign. After a moment the proprietor emerged from the interior of his establishment and gazed hollow-eyed at the car.

"Let's have some gas!" cried Tom roughly. "What do you think we stopped for—to admire the view?"

"I'm sick," said Wilson without moving. "Been sick all day."

"What's the matter?"

"I'm all run down."

"Well, shall I help myself?" Tom demanded. "You sounded well enough on the phone."

With an effort Wilson left the shade and support of the doorway and, breathing hard, unscrewed the cap of the tank. In the sunlight his face was green.

"I didn't mean to interrupt your lunch," he said. "But I need money pretty bad, and I was wondering what you were going to do with your old car."

"How do you like this one?" inquired Tom. "I bought it last week."

"It's a nice yellow one," said Wilson, as he strained at the handle.

"Like to buy it?"

"Big chance," Wilson smiled faintly. "No, but I could make some money on the other."

"What do you want money for, all of a sudden?"

"I've been here too long. I want to get away. My wife and I want to go West."

"Your wife does," exclaimed Tom, startled.

"She's been talking about it for ten years." He rested for a moment against the pump, shading his eyes. "And now she's going whether she wants to or not. I'm going to get her away."

The coupé flashed by us with a flurry of dust and the flash of a waving hand.

"What do I owe you?" demanded Tom harshly.

"I just got wised up to something funny the last two days," remarked Wilson. "That's why I want to get away. That's why I been bothering you about the car."

"What do I owe you?"

"Dollar twenty."

The relentless beating heat was beginning to confuse me and I had a bad moment there before I realized that so far his suspicions hadn't alighted on Tom. He had discovered that Myrtle had some sort of life apart from him in another world, and the shock had made him physically sick. I stared at him and then at Tom, who had made a parallel discovery less than an hour before—and it occurred to me that there was no difference between men, in intelligence or race, so profound as the difference between the sick and the well. Wilson was so sick that he looked guilty, unforgivably guilty—as if he had just got some poor girl with child.

"I'll let you have that car," said Tom. "I'll send it over tomorrow afternoon."

That locality was always vaguely disquieting, even in the broad glare of afternoon, and now I turned my head as though I had been warned of something behind. Over the ash-heaps the giant eyes of Doctor T. J. Eckleburg kept their vigil, but I perceived, after a moment, that other eyes were regarding us with peculiar intensity from less than twenty feet away.

In one of the windows over the garage the curtains had been moved aside a little, and Myrtle Wilson was peering down at the car. So engrossed was she that she had no consciousness of being observed, and one emotion after another crept into her face like objects into a slowly developing picture. Her expression was curiously familiar—it was an expression I had often seen on women's faces, but on Myrtle Wilson's face it seemed purposeless and inexplicable until I realized that her eyes, wide with jealous terror, were fixed not on Tom, but on Jordan Baker, whom she took to be his wife.

There is no confusion like the confusion of a simple mind, and as we drove away Tom was feeling the hot whips of panic. His wife and his mistress, until an hour ago secure and inviolate, were slipping precipitately from his control. Instinct made him step on the accelerator with the double purpose of overtaking Daisy and leaving Wilson behind, and we sped along toward Astoria at fifty miles an hour, until, among the spidery girders of the elevated, we came in sight of the easygoing blue coupé.

"Those big movies around Fiftieth Street are cool," suggested Jordan. "I love New York on summer afternoons when everyone's away. There's something very sensuous about it—overripe, as if all sorts of funny fruits were going to fall into your hands."

The word "sensuous" had the effect of further disquieting Tom, but before he could invent a protest the coupé came to a stop, and Daisy signalled us to draw up alongside.

"Where are we going?" she cried.

"How about the movies?"

"It's so hot," she complained. "You go. We'll ride around and meet you after." With an effort her wit rose faintly. "We'll meet you on some corner. I'll be the man smoking two cigarettes."

"We can't argue about it here," Tom said impatiently, as a truck gave out a cursing whistle behind us. "You follow me to the south side of Central Park, in front of the Plaza."

Several times he turned his head and looked back for their car, and if the traffic delayed them he slowed up until they came into sight. I think he was afraid they would dart down a side-street and out of his life forever.

But they didn't. And we all took the less explicable step of engaging the parlour of a suite in the Plaza Hotel.

The prolonged and tumultuous argument that ended by herding us into that room eludes me, though I have a sharp physical memory that, in the course of it, my underwear kept climbing like a damp snake around my legs and intermittent beads of sweat raced cool across my back. The notion originated with Daisy's suggestion that we hire five bathrooms and take cold baths, and then assumed more tangible form as "a place to have a mint julep." Each of us said over and over that it was a "crazy idea"—we all talked at once to a baffled clerk and thought, or pretended to think, that we were being very funny …

The room was large and stifling, and, though it was already four o'clock, opening the windows admitted only a gust of hot shrubbery from the Park. Daisy went to the mirror and stood with her back to us, fixing her hair.

"It's a swell suite," whispered Jordan respectfully, and everyone laughed.

"Open another window," commanded Daisy, without turning around.

"There aren't any more."

"Well, we'd better telephone for an axe—"

"The thing to do is to forget about the heat," said Tom impatiently. "You make it ten times worse by crabbing about it."

He unrolled the bottle of whisky from the towel and put it on the table.

"Why not let her alone, old sport?" remarked Gatsby. "You're the one that wanted to come to town."

There was a moment of silence. The telephone book slipped from its nail and splashed to the floor, whereupon Jordan whispered, "Excuse me"—but this time no one laughed.

"I'll pick it up," I offered.

"I've got it." Gatsby examined the parted string, muttered "Hum!" in an interested way, and tossed the book on a chair.

"That's a great expression of yours, isn't it?" said Tom sharply.

"What is?"

"All this 'old sport' business. Where'd you pick that up?"

"Now see here, Tom," said Daisy, turning around from the mirror, "if you're going to make personal remarks I won't stay here a minute. Call up and order some ice for the mint julep."

As Tom took up the receiver the compressed heat exploded into sound and we were listening to the portentous chords of Mendelssohn's Wedding March from the ballroom below.

"Imagine marrying anybody in this heat!" cried Jordan dismally.

"Still—I was married in the middle of June," Daisy remembered. "Louisville in June! Somebody fainted. Who was it fainted, Tom?"

"Biloxi," he answered shortly.

"A man named Biloxi. 'Blocks' Biloxi, and he made boxes—that's a fact—and he was from Biloxi, Tennessee."

"They carried him into my house," appended Jordan, "because we lived just two doors from the church. And he stayed three weeks, until Daddy told him he had to get out. The day after he left Daddy died."

After a moment she added as if she might have sounded irreverent, "There wasn't any connection."

"I used to know a Bill Biloxi from Memphis," I remarked.

"That was his cousin. I knew his whole family history before he left. He gave me an aluminium putter that I use today."

The music had died down as the ceremony began and now a long cheer floated in at the window, followed by intermittent cries of "Yea—ea—ea!" and finally by a burst of jazz as the dancing began.

"We're getting old," said Daisy. "If we were young we'd rise and dance."

"Remember Biloxi," Jordan warned her. "Where'd you know him, Tom?"

"Biloxi?" He concentrated with an effort. "I didn't know him. He was a friend of Daisy's."

"He was not," she denied. "I'd never seen him before. He came down in the private car."

"Well, he said he knew you. He said he was raised in Louisville. Asa Bird brought him around at the last minute and asked if we had room for him."

Jordan smiled.

"He was probably bumming his way home. He told me he was president of your class at Yale."

Tom and I looked at each other blankly.

"Biloxi?"

"First place, we didn't have any president—"

Gatsby's foot beat a short, restless tattoo and Tom eyed him suddenly.

"By the way, Mr. Gatsby, I understand you're an Oxford man."

"Not exactly."

"Oh, yes, I understand you went to Oxford."

"Yes—I went there."

A pause. Then Tom's voice, incredulous and insulting:

"You must have gone there about the time Biloxi went to New Haven."

Another pause. A waiter knocked and came in with crushed mint and ice but the silence was unbroken by his "thank you" and the soft closing of the door. This tremendous detail was to be cleared up at last.

"I told you I went there," said Gatsby.

"I heard you, but I'd like to know when."

"It was in nineteen-nineteen, I only stayed five months. That's why I can't really call myself an Oxford man."

Tom glanced around to see if we mirrored his unbelief. But we were all looking at Gatsby.

"It was an opportunity they gave to some of the officers after the armistice," he continued. "We could go to any of the universities in England or France."

I wanted to get up and slap him on the back. I had one of those renewals of complete faith in him that I'd experienced before.

Daisy rose, smiling faintly, and went to the table.

"Open the whisky, Tom," she ordered, "and I'll make you a mint julep. Then you won't seem so stupid to yourself … Look at the mint!"

"Wait a minute," snapped Tom, "I want to ask Mr. Gatsby one more question."

"Go on," Gatsby said politely.

"What kind of a row are you trying to cause in my house anyhow?"

They were out in the open at last and Gatsby was content.

"He isn't causing a row," Daisy looked desperately from one to the other. "You're causing a row. Please have a little self-control."

"Self-control!" repeated Tom incredulously. "I suppose the latest thing is to sit back and let Mr. Nobody from Nowhere make love to your wife. Well, if that's the idea you can count me out … Nowadays people begin by sneering at family life and family institutions, and next they'll throw everything overboard and have intermarriage between black and white."

Flushed with his impassioned gibberish, he saw himself standing alone on the last barrier of civilization.

"We're all white here," murmured Jordan.

"I know I'm not very popular. I don't give big parties. I suppose you've got to make your house into a pigsty in order to have any friends—in the modern world."

Angry as I was, as we all were, I was tempted to laugh whenever he opened his mouth. The transition from libertine to prig was so complete.

"I've got something to tell you, old sport—" began Gatsby. But Daisy guessed at his intention.

"Please don't!" she interrupted helplessly. "Please let's all go home. Why don't we all go home?"

"That's a good idea," I got up. "Come on, Tom. Nobody wants a drink."

"I want to know what Mr. Gatsby has to tell me."

"Your wife doesn't love you," said Gatsby. "She's never loved you. She loves me."

"You must be crazy!" exclaimed Tom automatically.

Gatsby sprang to his feet, vivid with excitement.

"She never loved you, do you hear?" he cried. "She only married you because I was poor and she was tired of waiting for me. It was a terrible mistake, but in her heart she never loved anyone except me!"

At this point Jordan and I tried to go, but Tom and Gatsby insisted with competitive firmness that we remain—as though neither of them had anything to conceal and it would be a privilege to partake vicariously of their emotions.

"Sit down, Daisy," Tom's voice groped unsuccessfully for the paternal note. "What's been going on? I want to hear all about it."

"I told you what's been going on," said Gatsby. "Going on for five years—and you didn't know."

Tom turned to Daisy sharply.

"You've been seeing this fellow for five years?"

"Not seeing," said Gatsby. "No, we couldn't meet. But both of us loved each other all that time, old sport, and you didn't know. I used to laugh sometimes"—but there was no laughter in his eyes—"to think that you didn't know."

"Oh—that's all." Tom tapped his thick fingers together like a clergyman and leaned back in his chair.

"You're crazy!" he exploded. "I can't speak about what happened five years ago, because I didn't know Daisy then—and I'll be damned if I see how you got within a mile of her unless you brought the groceries to the back door. But all the rest of that's a God damned lie. Daisy loved me when she married me and she loves me now."

"No," said Gatsby, shaking his head.

THE GREAT GATSBY

"She does, though. The trouble is that sometimes she gets foolish ideas in her head and doesn't know what she's doing." He nodded sagely. "And what's more, I love Daisy too. Once in a while I go off on a spree and make a fool of myself, but I always come back, and in my heart I love her all the time."

"You're revolting," said Daisy. She turned to me, and her voice, dropping an octave lower, filled the room with thrilling scorn: "Do you know why we left Chicago? I'm surprised that they didn't treat you to the story of that little spree."

Gatsby walked over and stood beside her.

"Daisy, that's all over now," he said earnestly. "It doesn't matter any more. Just tell him the truth—that you never loved him—and it's all wiped out forever."

She looked at him blindly. "Why—how could I love him—possibly?"

"You never loved him."

She hesitated. Her eyes fell on Jordan and me with a sort of appeal, as though she realized at last what she was doing—and as though she had never, all along, intended doing anything at all. But it was done now. It was too late.

"I never loved him," she said, with perceptible reluctance.

"Not at Kapiolani?" demanded Tom suddenly.

"No."

From the ballroom beneath, muffled and suffocating chords were drifting up on hot waves of air.

"Not that day I carried you down from the Punch Bowl to keep your shoes dry?" There was a husky tenderness in his tone … "Daisy?"

"Please don't." Her voice was cold, but the rancour was gone from it. She looked at Gatsby. "There, Jay," she said—but her hand as she tried to light a cigarette was trembling. Suddenly she threw the cigarette and the burning match on the carpet.

"Oh, you want too much!" she cried to Gatsby. "I love you now—isn't that enough? I can't help what's past." She began to sob helplessly. "I did love him once—but I loved you too."

Gatsby's eyes opened and closed.

"You loved me too?" he repeated.

"Even that's a lie," said Tom savagely. "She didn't know you were alive. Why—there's things between Daisy and me that you'll never know, things that neither of us can ever forget."

The words seemed to bite physically into Gatsby.

"I want to speak to Daisy alone," he insisted. "She's all excited now—"

"Even alone I can't say I never loved Tom," she admitted in a pitiful voice. "It wouldn't be true."

"Of course it wouldn't," agreed Tom.

She turned to her husband.

"As if it mattered to you," she said.

"Of course it matters. I'm going to take better care of you from now on."

"You don't understand," said Gatsby, with a touch of panic. "You're not going to take care of her any more."

"I'm not?" Tom opened his eyes wide and laughed. He could afford to control himself now. "Why's that?"

"Daisy's leaving you."

"Nonsense."

"I am, though," she said with a visible effort.

THE GREAT GATSBY

"She's not leaving me!" Tom's words suddenly leaned down over Gatsby. "Certainly not for a common swindler who'd have to steal the ring he put on her finger."

"I won't stand this!" cried Daisy. "Oh, please let's get out."

"Who are you, anyhow?" broke out Tom. "You're one of that bunch that hangs around with Meyer Wolfshiem—that much I happen to know. I've made a little investigation into your affairs—and I'll carry it further tomorrow."

"You can suit yourself about that, old sport," said Gatsby steadily.

"I found out what your 'drugstores' were." He turned to us and spoke rapidly. "He and this Wolfshiem bought up a lot of side-street drugstores here and in Chicago and sold grain alcohol over the counter. That's one of his little stunts. I picked him for a bootlegger the first time I saw him, and I wasn't far wrong."

"What about it?" said Gatsby politely. "I guess your friend Walter Chase wasn't too proud to come in on it."

"And you left him in the lurch, didn't you? You let him go to jail for a month over in New Jersey. God! You ought to hear Walter on the subject of you."

"He came to us dead broke. He was very glad to pick up some money, old sport."

"Don't you call me 'old sport'!" cried Tom. Gatsby said nothing. "Walter could have you up on the betting laws too, but Wolfshiem scared him into shutting his mouth."

That unfamiliar yet recognizable look was back again in Gatsby's face.

"That drugstore business was just small change," continued Tom slowly, "but you've got something on now that Walter's afraid to tell me about."

I glanced at Daisy, who was staring terrified between Gatsby and her husband, and at Jordan, who had begun to balance an invisible but absorbing object on the tip of her chin. Then I turned back to Gatsby—and was startled at his expression. He looked—and this is said in all contempt for the babbled slander of his garden—as if he had "killed a man." For a moment the set of his face could be described in just that fantastic way.

It passed, and he began to talk excitedly to Daisy, denying everything, defending his name against accusations that had not been made. But with every word she was drawing further and further into herself, so he gave that up, and only the dead dream fought on as the afternoon slipped away, trying to touch what was no longer tangible, struggling unhappily, undespairingly, toward that lost voice across the room.

The voice begged again to go.

"Please, Tom! I can't stand this any more."

Her frightened eyes told that whatever intentions, whatever courage she had had, were definitely gone.

"You two start on home, Daisy," said Tom. "In Mr. Gatsby's car."

She looked at Tom, alarmed now, but he insisted with magnanimous scorn.

"Go on. He won't annoy you. I think he realizes that his presumptuous little flirtation is over."

They were gone, without a word, snapped out, made accidental, isolated, like ghosts, even from our pity.

After a moment Tom got up and began wrapping the unopened bottle of whisky in the towel.

"Want any of this stuff? Jordan? ... Nick?"

I didn't answer.

"Nick?" He asked again.

"What?"

"Want any?"

"No ... I just remembered that today's my birthday."

I was thirty. Before me stretched the portentous, menacing road of a new decade.

It was seven o'clock when we got into the coupé with him and started for Long Island. Tom talked incessantly, exulting and laughing, but his voice was as remote from Jordan and me as the foreign clamour on the sidewalk or the tumult of the elevated overhead. Human sympathy has its limits, and we were content to let all their tragic arguments fade with the city lights behind. Thirty—the promise of a decade of loneliness, a thinning list of single men to know, a thinning briefcase of enthusiasm, thinning hair. But there was Jordan beside me, who, unlike Daisy, was too wise ever to carry well-forgotten dreams from age to age. As we passed over the dark bridge her wan face fell lazily against my coat's shoulder and the formidable stroke of thirty died away with the reassuring pressure of her hand.

So we drove on toward death through the cooling twilight.

The young Greek, Michaelis, who ran the coffee joint beside the ashheaps was the principal witness at the inquest. He had slept through the heat until after five, when he strolled over to the garage, and found George Wilson sick in his office—really sick, pale as his own pale hair and shaking all over. Michaelis advised him to go to bed, but Wilson refused, saying that he'd miss a lot of business if he did. While his neighbour was trying to persuade him a violent racket broke out overhead.

"I've got my wife locked in up there," explained Wilson calmly. "She's going to stay there till the day after tomorrow, and then we're going to move away."

Michaelis was astonished; they had been neighbours for four years, and Wilson had never seemed faintly capable of such a statement. Generally he was one of these worn-out men: when he wasn't working, he sat on a chair in the doorway and stared at the people and the cars that passed along the road. When anyone spoke to him he invariably laughed in an agreeable, colourless way. He was his wife's man and not his own.

So naturally Michaelis tried to find out what had happened, but Wilson wouldn't say a word—instead he began to throw curious, suspicious glances at his visitor and ask him what he'd been doing at certain times on certain days. Just as the latter was getting uneasy, some workmen came past the door bound for his restaurant, and Michaelis took the opportunity to get away, intending to come back later. But he didn't. He supposed he forgot to, that's all. When he came outside again, a little after seven, he was reminded of the conversation because he heard Mrs. Wilson's voice, loud and scolding, downstairs in the garage.

"Beat me!" he heard her cry. "Throw me down and beat me, you dirty little coward!"

A moment later she rushed out into the dusk, waving her hands and shouting—before he could move from his door the business was over.

The "death car" as the newspapers called it, didn't stop; it came out of the gathering darkness, wavered tragically for a moment, and then disappeared around the next bend. Mavro Michaelis wasn't even sure of its colour—he told the first policeman that it was light green. The other car, the one going toward New York, came to rest a hundred yards beyond, and its driver hurried back to where Myrtle Wilson, her life violently extinguished, knelt in the road and mingled her thick dark blood with the dust.

Michaelis and this man reached her first, but when they had torn open her shirtwaist, still damp with perspiration, they saw that her left breast was swinging loose like a flap, and there was no need to listen for the heart beneath. The mouth was wide open and ripped a little at the corners, as though she had choked a little in giving up the tremendous vitality she had stored so long.

We saw the three or four automobiles and the crowd when we were still some distance away.

"Wreck!" said Tom. "That's good. Wilson'll have a little business at last."

He slowed down, but still without any intention of stopping, until, as we came nearer, the hushed, intent faces of the people at the garage door made him automatically put on the brakes.

"We'll take a look," he said doubtfully, "just a look."

I became aware now of a hollow, wailing sound which issued incessantly from the garage, a sound which as we got out of the coupé and walked toward the door resolved itself into the words "Oh, my God!" uttered over and over in a gasping moan.

"There's some bad trouble here," said Tom excitedly.

He reached up on tiptoes and peered over a circle of heads into the garage, which was lit only by a yellow light in a swinging metal basket overhead. Then he made a harsh sound in his throat, and with a violent thrusting movement of his powerful arms pushed his way through.

The circle closed up again with a running murmur of expostulation; it was a minute before I could see anything at all. Then new arrivals deranged the line, and Jordan and I were pushed suddenly inside.

Myrtle Wilson's body, wrapped in a blanket, and then in another blanket, as though she suffered from a chill in the hot night, lay on a worktable by the wall, and Tom, with his back to us, was bending over it, motionless. Next to him stood a motorcycle policeman taking down names with much sweat and correction in a little book. At first I couldn't find the source of the high, groaning words that echoed clamorously through the bare garage—then I saw Wilson standing on the raised threshold of his office, swaying back and forth and holding to the doorposts with both hands. Some man was talking to him in a low voice and attempting, from time to time, to lay a hand on his shoulder, but Wilson neither heard nor saw. His eyes would drop slowly from the swinging light to the laden table by the wall, and then jerk back to the light again, and he gave out incessantly his high, horrible call:

"Oh, my Ga-od! Oh, my Ga-od! Oh, Ga-od! Oh, my Ga-od!"

Presently Tom lifted his head with a jerk and, after staring around the garage with glazed eyes, addressed a mumbled incoherent remark to the policeman.

"M-a-v—" the policeman was saying, "—o—"

"No, r—" corrected the man, "M-a-v-r-o—"

"Listen to me!" muttered Tom fiercely.

"r—" said the policeman, "o—"

"g—"

"g—" He looked up as Tom's broad hand fell sharply on his shoulder. "What you want, fella?"

"What happened?—that's what I want to know."

"Auto hit her. Ins'antly killed."

"Instantly killed," repeated Tom, staring.

"She ran out ina road. Son-of-a-bitch didn't even stopus car."

"There was two cars," said Michaelis, "one comin', one goin', see?"

"Going where?" asked the policeman keenly.

"One goin' each way. Well, she"—his hand rose toward the blankets but stopped halfway and fell to his side—"she ran out there an' the one comin' from N'York knock right into her, goin' thirty or forty miles an hour."

"What's the name of this place here?" demanded the officer.

"Hasn't got any name."

A pale well-dressed negro stepped near.

"It was a yellow car," he said, "big yellow car. New."

"See the accident?" asked the policeman.

"No, but the car passed me down the road, going faster'n forty. Going fifty, sixty."

"Come here and let's have your name. Look out now. I want to get his name."

Some words of this conversation must have reached Wilson, swaying in the office door, for suddenly a new theme found voice among his grasping cries:

"You don't have to tell me what kind of car it was! I know what kind of car it was!"

Watching Tom, I saw the wad of muscle back of his shoulder tighten under his coat. He walked quickly over to Wilson and, standing in front of him, seized him firmly by the upper arms.

"You've got to pull yourself together," he said with soothing gruffness.

Wilson's eyes fell upon Tom; he started up on his tiptoes and then would have collapsed to his knees had not Tom held him upright.

"Listen," said Tom, shaking him a little. "I just got here a minute ago, from New York. I was bringing you that coupé we've been talking about. That yellow car I was driving this afternoon wasn't mine—do you hear? I haven't seen it all afternoon."

Only the negro and I were near enough to hear what he said, but the policeman caught something in the tone and looked over with truculent eyes.

"What's all that?" he demanded.

"I'm a friend of his." Tom turned his head but kept his hands firm on Wilson's body. "He says he knows the car that did it … It was a yellow car."

Some dim impulse moved the policeman to look suspiciously at Tom.

"And what colour's your car?"

"It's a blue car, a coupé."

"We've come straight from New York," I said.

Someone who had been driving a little behind us confirmed this, and the policeman turned away.

"Now, if you'll let me have that name again correct—"

Picking up Wilson like a doll, Tom carried him into the office, set him down in a chair, and came back.

"If somebody'll come here and sit with him," he snapped authoritatively. He watched while the two men standing closest glanced at each other and went unwillingly into the room. Then Tom shut the door on them and came down the single step, his eyes avoiding the table. As he passed close to me he whispered: "Let's get out."

Self-consciously, with his authoritative arms breaking the way, we pushed through the still gathering crowd, passing a hurried doctor, case in hand, who had been sent for in wild hope half an hour ago.

Tom drove slowly until we were beyond the bend—then his foot came down hard, and the coupé raced along through the night. In a little while I heard a low husky sob, and saw that the tears were overflowing down his face.

"The God damned coward!" he whimpered. "He didn't even stop his car."

The Buchanans' house floated suddenly toward us through the dark rustling trees. Tom stopped beside the porch and looked up at the second floor, where two windows bloomed with light among the vines.

"Daisy's home," he said. As we got out of the car he glanced at me and frowned slightly.

"I ought to have dropped you in West Egg, Nick. There's nothing we can do tonight."

A change had come over him, and he spoke gravely, and with decision. As we walked across the moonlight gravel to the porch he disposed of the situation in a few brisk phrases.

"I'll telephone for a taxi to take you home, and while you're waiting you and Jordan better go in the kitchen and have them get you some supper—if you want any." He opened the door. "Come in."

"No, thanks. But I'd be glad if you'd order me the taxi. I'll wait outside."

Jordan put her hand on my arm.

"Won't you come in, Nick?"

"No, thanks."

I was feeling a little sick and I wanted to be alone. But Jordan lingered for a moment more.

"It's only half-past nine," she said.

I'd be damned if I'd go in; I'd had enough of all of them for one day, and suddenly that included Jordan too. She must have seen something of this in my expression, for she turned abruptly away and ran up the porch steps into the house. I sat down for a few minutes with my head in my hands, until I heard the phone taken up inside and the butler's voice calling a taxi. Then I walked slowly down the drive away from the house, intending to wait by the gate.

I hadn't gone twenty yards when I heard my name and Gatsby stepped from between two bushes into the path. I must have felt pretty weird by that time, because I could think of nothing except the luminosity of his pink suit under the moon.

"What are you doing?" I inquired.

"Just standing here, old sport."

Somehow, that seemed a despicable occupation. For all I knew he was going to rob the house in a moment; I wouldn't have been surprised to see sinister faces, the faces of "Wolfshiem's people," behind him in the dark shrubbery.

"Did you see any trouble on the road?" he asked after a minute.

"Yes."

He hesitated.

"Was she killed?"

"Yes."

"I thought so; I told Daisy I thought so. It's better that the shock should all come at once. She stood it pretty well."

He spoke as if Daisy's reaction was the only thing that mattered.

"I got to West Egg by a side road," he went on, "and left the car in my garage. I don't think anybody saw us, but of course I can't be sure."

I disliked him so much by this time that I didn't find it necessary to tell him he was wrong.

"Who was the woman?" he inquired.

"Her name was Wilson. Her husband owns the garage. How the devil did it happen?"

"Well, I tried to swing the wheel—" He broke off, and suddenly I guessed at the truth.

"Was Daisy driving?"

"Yes," he said after a moment, "but of course I'll say I was. You see, when we left New York she was very nervous and she thought it would steady her to drive—and this woman rushed out at us just as we were passing a car coming the other way. It all happened in a minute, but it seemed to me that she wanted to speak to us, thought we were somebody she knew. Well, first Daisy turned away from the woman toward the other car, and then she lost her nerve and turned back. The second my hand reached the wheel I felt the shock—it must have killed her instantly."

"It ripped her open—"

"Don't tell me, old sport." He winced. "Anyhow—Daisy stepped on it. I tried to make her stop, but she couldn't, so I pulled on the emergency brake. Then she fell over into my lap and I drove on.

"She'll be all right tomorrow," he said presently. "I'm just going to wait here and see if he tries to bother her about that unpleasantness this afternoon. She's locked herself into her room, and if he tries any brutality she's going to turn the light out and on again."

"He won't touch her," I said. "He's not thinking about her."

"I don't trust him, old sport."

"How long are you going to wait?"

"All night, if necessary. Anyhow, till they all go to bed."

A new point of view occurred to me. Suppose Tom found out that Daisy had been driving. He might think he saw a connection in it—he might think anything. I looked at the house; there were two or three bright windows downstairs and the pink glow from Daisy's room on the ground floor.

"You wait here," I said. "I'll see if there's any sign of a commotion."

I walked back along the border of the lawn, traversed the gravel softly, and tiptoed up the veranda steps. The drawing-room curtains were open, and I saw that the room was empty. Crossing the porch where we had dined that June night three months before, I came to a small rectangle of light which I guessed was the pantry window. The blind was drawn, but I found a rift at the sill.

Daisy and Tom were sitting opposite each other at the kitchen table, with a plate of cold fried chicken between them, and two bottles of ale. He was talking intently across the table at her, and in his earnestness his hand

THE GREAT GATSBY

had fallen upon and covered her own. Once in a while she looked up at him and nodded in agreement.

They weren't happy, and neither of them had touched the chicken or the ale—and yet they weren't unhappy either. There was an unmistakable air of natural intimacy about the picture, and anybody would have said that they were conspiring together.

As I tiptoed from the porch I heard my taxi feeling its way along the dark road toward the house. Gatsby was waiting where I had left him in the drive.

"Is it all quiet up there?" he asked anxiously.

"Yes, it's all quiet." I hesitated. "You'd better come home and get some sleep."

He shook his head.

"I want to wait here till Daisy goes to bed. Good night, old sport."

He put his hands in his coat pockets and turned back eagerly to his scrutiny of the house, as though my presence marred the sacredness of the vigil. So I walked away and left him standing there in the moonlight—watching over nothing.

VIII

I couldn't sleep all night; a foghorn was groaning incessantly on the Sound, and I tossed half-sick between grotesque reality and savage, frightening dreams. Toward dawn I heard a taxi go up Gatsby's drive, and immediately I jumped out of bed and began to dress—I felt that I had something to tell him, something to warn him about, and morning would be too late.

Crossing his lawn, I saw that his front door was still open and he was leaning against a table in the hall, heavy with dejection or sleep.

"Nothing happened," he said wanly. "I waited, and about four o'clock she came to the window and stood there for a minute and then turned out the light."

His house had never seemed so enormous to me as it did that night when we hunted through the great rooms for cigarettes. We pushed aside curtains that were like pavilions, and felt over innumerable feet of dark wall for electric light switches—once I tumbled with a sort of splash upon the keys of a ghostly piano. There was an inexplicable amount of dust everywhere, and the rooms were musty, as though they hadn't been aired for many days. I found the humidor on an unfamiliar table, with two stale, dry cigarettes inside. Throwing open the French windows of the drawing-room, we sat smoking out into the darkness.

"You ought to go away," I said. "It's pretty certain they'll trace your car."

"Go away now, old sport?"

"Go to Atlantic City for a week, or up to Montreal."

He wouldn't consider it. He couldn't possibly leave Daisy until he knew what she was going to do. He was clutching at some last hope and I couldn't bear to shake him free.

It was this night that he told me the strange story of his youth with Dan Cody—told it to me because "Jay Gatsby" had broken up like glass against Tom's hard malice, and the long secret extravaganza was played out. I think that he would have acknowledged anything now, without reserve, but he wanted to talk about Daisy.

She was the first "nice" girl he had ever known. In various unrevealed capacities he had come in contact with such people, but always with indiscernible barbed wire between. He found her excitingly desirable. He went to her house, at first with other officers from Camp Taylor, then alone. It amazed him—he had never been in such a beautiful house before. But what gave it an air of breathless intensity, was that Daisy lived there—it was as casual a thing to her as his tent out at camp was to him. There was a ripe mystery about it, a hint of bedrooms upstairs more beautiful and cool than other bedrooms, of gay and radiant activities taking place through its corridors, and of romances that were not musty and laid away already in lavender but fresh and breathing and redolent of this year's shining motorcars and of dances whose flowers were scarcely withered. It excited him, too, that many men had already loved Daisy—it increased her value in his eyes. He felt their presence all about the house, pervading the air with the shades and echoes of still vibrant emotions.

But he knew that he was in Daisy's house by a colossal accident. However glorious might be his future as Jay Gatsby, he was at present a penniless young man without a past, and at any moment the invisible cloak of his uniform might slip from his shoulders. So he made the most of his time. He took what he could get, ravenously and unscrupulously—eventually he took Daisy one still October night, took her because he had no real right to touch her hand.

He might have despised himself, for he had certainly taken her under false pretences. I don't mean that he had traded on his phantom millions, but he had deliberately given Daisy a sense of security; he let her believe that he was a person from much the same strata as herself—that he was fully able to take care of her. As a matter of fact, he had no such facilities—he had no comfortable family standing behind him, and he was liable at the whim of an impersonal government to be blown anywhere about the world.

But he didn't despise himself and it didn't turn out as he had imagined. He had intended, probably, to take what he could and go—but now he found that he had committed himself to the following of a grail. He knew that Daisy was extraordinary, but he didn't realize just how extraordinary a "nice" girl could be. She vanished into her rich house, into her rich, full life, leaving Gatsby—nothing. He felt married to her, that was all.

When they met again, two days later, it was Gatsby who was breathless, who was, somehow, betrayed. Her porch was bright with the bought luxury of star-shine; the wicker of the settee squeaked fashionably as she turned toward him and he kissed her curious and lovely mouth. She had caught a cold, and it made her voice huskier and more charming than ever, and Gatsby was overwhelmingly aware of the youth and mystery that wealth imprisons and preserves, of the freshness of many clothes, and of Daisy, gleaming like silver, safe and proud above the hot struggles of the poor.

"I can't describe to you how surprised I was to find out I loved her, old sport. I even hoped for a while that she'd throw me over, but she didn't, because she was in love with me too. She thought I knew a lot because I knew different things from her ... Well, there I was, way off my ambitions, getting deeper in love every minute, and all of a sudden I didn't care. What was the use of doing great things if I could have a better time telling her what I was going to do?"

On the last afternoon before he went abroad, he sat with Daisy in his arms for a long, silent time. It was a cold fall day, with fire in the room and her cheeks flushed. Now and then she moved and he changed his arm a little, and once he kissed her dark shining hair. The afternoon had made them tranquil for a while, as if to give them a deep memory for the long parting the next day promised. They had never been closer in their month of love, nor communicated more profoundly one with another, than when she brushed silent lips against his coat's shoulder or when he touched the end of her fingers, gently, as though she were asleep.

He did extraordinarily well in the war. He was a captain before he went to the front, and following the Argonne battles he got his majority and the command of the divisional machine-guns. After the armistice he tried frantically to get home, but some complication or misunderstanding sent him to Oxford instead. He was worried now—there was a quality of nervous despair in Daisy's letters. She didn't see why he couldn't come. She was feeling the pressure of the world outside, and she wanted to see him and feel his presence beside her and be reassured that she was doing the right thing after all.

For Daisy was young and her artificial world was redolent of orchids and pleasant, cheerful snobbery and orchestras which set the rhythm of the year, summing up the sadness and suggestiveness of life in new tunes. All night the saxophones wailed the hopeless comment of the "Beale Street Blues" while a hundred pairs of golden and silver slippers shuffled the shining dust. At the grey tea hour there were always rooms that throbbed incessantly with this low, sweet fever, while fresh faces drifted here and there like rose petals blown by the sad horns around the floor.

Through this twilight universe Daisy began to move again with the season; suddenly she was again keeping half a dozen dates a day with half a dozen men, and drowsing asleep at dawn with the beads and chiffon of an evening-dress tangled among dying orchids on the floor beside her bed. And all the time something within her was crying for a decision. She wanted her life shaped now, immediately—and the decision must be made by some force—of love, of money, of unquestionable practicality—that was close at hand.

That force took shape in the middle of spring with the arrival of Tom Buchanan. There was a wholesome bulkiness about his person and his position, and Daisy was flattered. Doubtless there was a certain struggle and a certain relief. The letter reached Gatsby while he was still at Oxford.

THE GREAT GATSBY

It was dawn now on Long Island and we went about opening the rest of the windows downstairs, filling the house with grey-turning, gold-turning light. The shadow of a tree fell abruptly across the dew and ghostly birds began to sing among the blue leaves. There was a slow, pleasant movement in the air, scarcely a wind, promising a cool, lovely day.

"I don't think she ever loved him." Gatsby turned around from a window and looked at me challengingly. "You must remember, old sport, she was very excited this afternoon. He told her those things in a way that frightened her—that made it look as if I was some kind of cheap sharper. And the result was she hardly knew what she was saying."

He sat down gloomily.

"Of course she might have loved him just for a minute, when they were first married—and loved me more even then, do you see?"

Suddenly he came out with a curious remark.

"In any case," he said, "it was just personal."

What could you make of that, except to suspect some intensity in his conception of the affair that couldn't be measured?

He came back from France when Tom and Daisy were still on their wedding trip, and made a miserable but irresistible journey to Louisville on the last of his army pay. He stayed there a week, walking the streets where their footsteps had clicked together through the November night and revisiting the out-of-the-way places to which they had driven in her white car. Just as Daisy's house had always seemed to him more mysterious and gay than other houses, so his idea of the city itself, even though she was gone from it, was pervaded with a melancholy beauty.

He left feeling that if he had searched harder, he might have found her—that he was leaving her behind. The day-coach—he was penniless now—was hot. He went out to the open vestibule and sat down on a folding-chair, and the station slid away and the backs of unfamiliar buildings moved by. Then out into the spring fields, where a yellow trolley raced them for a minute with people in it who might once have seen the pale magic of her face along the casual street.

The track curved and now it was going away from the sun, which, as it sank lower, seemed to spread itself in benediction over the vanishing city where she had drawn her breath. He stretched out his hand desperately as if to snatch only a wisp of air, to save a fragment of the spot that she had made lovely for him. But it was all going by too fast now for his blurred eyes and he knew that he had lost that part of it, the freshest and the best, forever.

It was nine o'clock when we finished breakfast and went out on the porch. The night had made a sharp difference in the weather and there was an autumn flavour in the air. The gardener, the last one of Gatsby's former servants, came to the foot of the steps.

"I'm going to drain the pool today, Mr. Gatsby. Leaves'll start falling pretty soon, and then there's always trouble with the pipes."

"Don't do it today," Gatsby answered. He turned to me apologetically. "You know, old sport, I've never used that pool all summer?"

I looked at my watch and stood up.

"Twelve minutes to my train."

I didn't want to go to the city. I wasn't worth a decent stroke of work, but it was more than that—I didn't want to leave Gatsby. I missed that train, and then another, before I could get myself away.

"I'll call you up," I said finally.

"Do, old sport."

"I'll call you about noon."

We walked slowly down the steps.

"I suppose Daisy'll call too." He looked at me anxiously, as if he hoped I'd corroborate this.

"I suppose so."

"Well, goodbye."

We shook hands and I started away. Just before I reached the hedge I remembered something and turned around.

"They're a rotten crowd," I shouted across the lawn. "You're worth the whole damn bunch put together."

I've always been glad I said that. It was the only compliment I ever gave him, because I disapproved of him from beginning to end. First he nodded politely, and then his face broke into that radiant and understanding smile, as if we'd been in ecstatic cahoots on that fact all the time. His gorgeous pink rag of a suit made a bright spot of colour against the white steps, and I thought of the night when I first came to his ancestral home, three months before. The lawn and drive had been crowded with the faces of those who guessed at his corruption—and he had stood on those steps, concealing his incorruptible dream, as he waved them goodbye.

I thanked him for his hospitality. We were always thanking him for that—I and the others.

"Goodbye," I called. "I enjoyed breakfast, Gatsby."

Up in the city, I tried for a while to list the quotations on an interminable amount of stock, then I fell asleep in my swivel-chair. Just before noon the phone woke me, and I started up with sweat breaking out on my forehead. It was Jordan Baker; she often called me up at this hour because the uncertainty of her own movements between hotels and clubs and private houses made her hard to find in any other way. Usually her voice came over the wire as something fresh and cool, as if a divot from a green golf-links had come sailing in at the office window, but this morning it seemed harsh and dry.

"I've left Daisy's house," she said. "I'm at Hempstead, and I'm going down to Southampton this afternoon."

Probably it had been tactful to leave Daisy's house, but the act annoyed me, and her next remark made me rigid.

"You weren't so nice to me last night."

"How could it have mattered then?"

Silence for a moment. Then:

"However—I want to see you."

"I want to see you, too."

"Suppose I don't go to Southampton, and come into town this afternoon?"

"No—I don't think this afternoon."

"Very well."

"It's impossible this afternoon. Various—"

We talked like that for a while, and then abruptly we weren't talking any longer. I don't know which of us hung up with a sharp click, but I know I didn't care. I couldn't have talked to her across a tea-table that day if I never talked to her again in this world.

I called Gatsby's house a few minutes later, but the line was busy. I tried four times; finally an exasperated central told me the wire was being kept open for long distance from Detroit. Taking out my timetable, I drew a small circle around the three-fifty train. Then I leaned back in my chair and tried to think. It was just noon.

When I passed the ash-heaps on the train that morning I had crossed deliberately to the other side of the car. I supposed there'd be a curious crowd around there all day with little boys searching for dark spots in the dust, and some garrulous man telling over and over what had happened, until it became less and less real even to him and he could tell it no longer, and Myrtle Wilson's tragic achievement was forgotten. Now I want to go back a little and tell what happened at the garage after we left there the night before.

They had difficulty in locating the sister, Catherine. She must have broken her rule against drinking that night, for when she arrived she was stupid with liquor and unable to understand that the ambulance had already gone to Flushing. When they convinced her of this, she immediately fainted, as if that was the intolerable part of the affair. Someone, kind or curious, took her in his car and drove her in the wake of her sister's body.

Until long after midnight a changing crowd lapped up against the front of the garage, while George Wilson rocked himself back and forth on the couch inside. For a while the door of the office was open, and everyone who came into the garage glanced irresistibly through it. Finally someone said it was a shame, and closed the door. Michaelis and several other men were with him; first, four or five men, later two or three men. Still later Michaelis had to ask the last stranger to wait there fifteen minutes longer, while he went back to his own place and made a pot of coffee. After that, he stayed there alone with Wilson until dawn.

About three o'clock the quality of Wilson's incoherent muttering changed—he grew quieter and began to talk about the yellow car. He announced that he had a way of finding out whom the yellow car belonged to, and then he blurted out that a couple of months ago his wife had come from the city with her face bruised and her nose swollen.

But when he heard himself say this, he flinched and began to cry "Oh, my God!" again in his groaning voice. Michaelis made a clumsy attempt to distract him.

"How long have you been married, George? Come on there, try and sit still a minute, and answer my question. How long have you been married?"

"Twelve years."

"Ever had any children? Come on, George, sit still—I asked you a question. Did you ever have any children?"

The hard brown beetles kept thudding against the dull light, and whenever Michaelis heard a car go tearing along the road outside it sounded to him like the car that hadn't stopped a few hours before. He didn't like to go into the garage, because the work bench was stained where the body had been lying, so he moved uncomfortably around the office—he knew every object in it before morning—and from time to time sat down beside Wilson trying to keep him more quiet.

"Have you got a church you go to sometimes, George? Maybe even if you haven't been there for a long time? Maybe I could call up the church and get a priest to come over and he could talk to you, see?"

"Don't belong to any."

"You ought to have a church, George, for times like this. You must have gone to church once. Didn't you get married in a church? Listen, George, listen to me. Didn't you get married in a church?"

"That was a long time ago."

The effort of answering broke the rhythm of his rocking—for a moment he was silent. Then the same half-knowing, half-bewildered look came back into his faded eyes.

"Look in the drawer there," he said, pointing at the desk.

"Which drawer?"

"That drawer—that one."

Michaelis opened the drawer nearest his hand. There was nothing in it but a small, expensive dog-leash, made of leather and braided silver. It was apparently new.

"This?" he inquired, holding it up.

Wilson stared and nodded.

"I found it yesterday afternoon. She tried to tell me about it, but I knew it was something funny."

"You mean your wife bought it?"

"She had it wrapped in tissue paper on her bureau."

Michaelis didn't see anything odd in that, and he gave Wilson a dozen reasons why his wife might have bought the dog-leash. But conceivably Wilson had heard some of these same explanations before, from Myrtle, because he began saying "Oh, my God!" again in a whisper—his comforter left several explanations in the air.

"Then he killed her," said Wilson. His mouth dropped open suddenly.

"Who did?"

"I have a way of finding out."

"You're morbid, George," said his friend. "This has been a strain to you and you don't know what you're saying. You'd better try and sit quiet till morning."

"He murdered her."

"It was an accident, George."

Wilson shook his head. His eyes narrowed and his mouth widened slightly with the ghost of a superior "Hm!"

"I know," he said definitely. "I'm one of these trusting fellas and I don't think any harm to nobody, but when I get to know a thing I know it. It was the man in that car. She ran out to speak to him and he wouldn't stop."

Michaelis had seen this too, but it hadn't occurred to him that there was any special significance in it. He believed that Mrs. Wilson had been running away from her husband, rather than trying to stop any particular car.

"How could she of been like that?"

"She's a deep one," said Wilson, as if that answered the question. "Ah-h-h—"

He began to rock again, and Michaelis stood twisting the leash in his hand.

"Maybe you got some friend that I could telephone for, George?"

This was a forlorn hope—he was almost sure that Wilson had no friend: there was not enough of him for his wife. He was glad a little later when he noticed a change in the room, a blue quickening by the window, and realized that dawn wasn't far off. About five o'clock it was blue enough outside to snap off the light.

Wilson's glazed eyes turned out to the ash-heaps, where small grey clouds took on fantastic shapes and scurried here and there in the faint dawn wind.

"I spoke to her," he muttered, after a long silence. "I told her she might fool me but she couldn't fool God. I took her to the window"—with an effort he got up and walked to the rear window and leaned with his face pressed against it—"and I said 'God knows what you've been doing, everything you've been doing. You may fool me, but you can't fool God!'"

Standing behind him, Michaelis saw with a shock that he was looking at the eyes of Doctor T. J. Eckleburg, which had just emerged, pale and enormous, from the dissolving night.

"God sees everything," repeated Wilson.

"That's an advertisement," Michaelis assured him. Something made him turn away from the window and look back into the room. But Wilson stood there a long time, his face close to the window pane, nodding into the twilight.

By six o'clock Michaelis was worn out, and grateful for the sound of a car stopping outside. It was one of the watchers of the night before who had promised to come back, so he cooked breakfast for three, which he and the other man ate together. Wilson was quieter now, and Michaelis went home to sleep; when he awoke four hours later and hurried back to the garage, Wilson was gone.

His movements—he was on foot all the time—were afterward traced to Port Roosevelt and then to Gad's Hill, where he bought a sandwich that he didn't eat, and a cup of coffee. He must have been tired and walking slowly, for he didn't reach Gad's Hill until noon. Thus far there was no difficulty in accounting for his time—there were boys who had seen a man "acting sort of crazy," and motorists at whom he stared oddly from the side of the road. Then for three hours he disappeared from view. The police, on the strength of what he said to Michaelis, that he "had a way of finding out," supposed that he spent that time going from garage to garage thereabout, inquiring for a yellow car. On the other hand, no garage man who had seen him ever came forward, and perhaps he had an easier, surer way of finding out what he wanted to know. By half-past two he was in West Egg, where he asked someone the way to Gatsby's house. So by that time he knew Gatsby's name.

At two o'clock Gatsby put on his bathing-suit and left word with the butler that if anyone phoned word was to be brought to him at the pool. He stopped at the garage for a pneumatic mattress that had amused his guests during the summer, and the chauffeur helped him to pump it up. Then he gave instructions that the open car wasn't to be taken out under any circumstances—and this was strange, because the front right fender needed repair.

THE GREAT GATSBY

Gatsby shouldered the mattress and started for the pool. Once he stopped and shifted it a little, and the chauffeur asked him if he needed help, but he shook his head and in a moment disappeared among the yellowing trees.

No telephone message arrived, but the butler went without his sleep and waited for it until four o'clock—until long after there was anyone to give it to if it came. I have an idea that Gatsby himself didn't believe it would come, and perhaps he no longer cared. If that was true he must have felt that he had lost the old warm world, paid a high price for living too long with a single dream. He must have looked up at an unfamiliar sky through frightening leaves and shivered as he found what a grotesque thing a rose is and how raw the sunlight was upon the scarcely created grass. A new world, material without being real, where poor ghosts, breathing dreams like air, drifted fortuitously about ... like that ashen, fantastic figure gliding toward him through the amorphous trees.

The chauffeur—he was one of Wolfshiem's protégés—heard the shots—afterwards he could only say that he hadn't thought anything much about them. I drove from the station directly to Gatsby's house and my rushing anxiously up the front steps was the first thing that alarmed anyone. But they knew then, I firmly believe. With scarcely a word said, four of us, the chauffeur, butler, gardener, and I hurried down to the pool.

There was a faint, barely perceptible movement of the water as the fresh flow from one end urged its way toward the drain at the other. With little ripples that were hardly the shadows of waves, the laden mattress moved irregularly down the pool. A small gust of wind that scarcely corrugated the surface was enough to disturb its accidental course with its accidental burden. The touch of a cluster of leaves revolved it slowly, tracing, like the leg of transit, a thin red circle in the water.

It was after we started with Gatsby toward the house that the gardener saw Wilson's body a little way off in the grass, and the holocaust was complete.

IX

After two years I remember the rest of that day, and that night and the next day, only as an endless drill of police and photographers and newspaper men in and out of Gatsby's front door. A rope stretched across the main gate and a policeman by it kept out the curious, but little boys soon discovered that they could enter through my yard, and there were always a few of them clustered open-mouthed about the pool. Someone with a positive manner, perhaps a detective, used the expression "madman" as he bent over Wilson's body that afternoon, and the adventitious authority of his voice set the key for the newspaper reports next morning.

Most of those reports were a nightmare—grotesque, circumstantial, eager, and untrue. When Michaelis's testimony at the inquest brought to light Wilson's suspicions of his wife I thought the whole tale would shortly be served up in racy pasquinade—but Catherine, who might have said anything, didn't say a word. She showed a surprising amount of character about it too—looked at the coroner with determined eyes under that corrected brow of hers, and swore that her sister had never seen Gatsby, that her sister was completely happy with her husband, that her sister had been into no mischief whatever. She convinced herself of it, and cried into her handkerchief, as if the very suggestion was more than she could endure. So Wilson was reduced to a man "deranged by grief" in order that the case might remain in its simplest form. And it rested there.

THE GREAT GATSBY

But all this part of it seemed remote and unessential. I found myself on Gatsby's side, and alone. From the moment I telephoned news of the catastrophe to West Egg village, every surmise about him, and every practical question, was referred to me. At first I was surprised and confused; then, as he lay in his house and didn't move or breathe or speak, hour upon hour, it grew upon me that I was responsible, because no one else was interested—interested, I mean, with that intense personal interest to which everyone has some vague right at the end.

I called up Daisy half an hour after we found him, called her instinctively and without hesitation. But she and Tom had gone away early that afternoon, and taken baggage with them.

"Left no address?"

"No."

"Say when they'd be back?"

"No."

"Any idea where they are? How I could reach them?"

"I don't know. Can't say."

I wanted to get somebody for him. I wanted to go into the room where he lay and reassure him: "I'll get somebody for you, Gatsby. Don't worry. Just trust me and I'll get somebody for you—"

Meyer Wolfshiem's name wasn't in the phone book. The butler gave me his office address on Broadway, and I called Information, but by the time I had the number it was long after five, and no one answered the phone.

"Will you ring again?"

"I've rung three times."

"It's very important."

"Sorry. I'm afraid no one's there."

I went back to the drawing-room and thought for an instant that they were chance visitors, all these official people who suddenly filled it. But, though they drew back the sheet and looked at Gatsby with shocked eyes, his protest continued in my brain:

"Look here, old sport, you've got to get somebody for me. You've got to try hard. I can't go through this alone."

Someone started to ask me questions, but I broke away and going upstairs looked hastily through the unlocked parts of his desk—he'd never told me definitely that his parents were dead. But there was nothing—only the picture of Dan Cody, a token of forgotten violence, staring down from the wall.

Next morning I sent the butler to New York with a letter to Wolfshiem, which asked for information and urged him to come out on the next train. That request seemed superfluous when I wrote it. I was sure he'd start when he saw the newspapers, just as I was sure there'd be a wire from Daisy before noon—but neither a wire nor Mr. Wolfshiem arrived; no one arrived except more police and photographers and newspaper men. When the butler brought back Wolfshiem's answer I began to have a feeling of defiance, of scornful solidarity between Gatsby and me against them all.

Dear Mr. Carraway. This has been one of the most terrible shocks of my life to me I hardly can believe it that it is true at all. Such a mad act as that man did should make us all think. I cannot come down now as I am tied up in some very important business and cannot get mixed up in this thing now. If there is anything I can do a little later let me know in a letter by Edgar. I hardly know where I am when I hear about a thing like this and am completely knocked down and out.

THE GREAT GATSBY

Yours truly

Meyer Wolfshiem

and then hasty addenda beneath:

Let me know about the funeral etc do not know his family at all.

When the phone rang that afternoon and Long Distance said Chicago was calling I thought this would be Daisy at last. But the connection came through as a man's voice, very thin and far away.

"This is Slagle speaking …"

"Yes?" The name was unfamiliar.

"Hell of a note, isn't it? Get my wire?"

"There haven't been any wires."

"Young Parke's in trouble," he said rapidly. "They picked him up when he handed the bonds over the counter. They got a circular from New York giving 'em the numbers just five minutes before. What d'you know about that, hey? You never can tell in these hick towns—"

"Hello!" I interrupted breathlessly. "Look here—this isn't Mr. Gatsby. Mr. Gatsby's dead."

There was a long silence on the other end of the wire, followed by an exclamation … then a quick squawk as the connection was broken.

I think it was on the third day that a telegram signed Henry C. Gatz arrived from a town in Minnesota. It said only that the sender was leaving immediately and to postpone the funeral until he came.

It was Gatsby's father, a solemn old man, very helpless and dismayed, bundled up in a long cheap ulster against the warm September day. His eyes leaked continuously with excitement, and when I took the bag and umbrella from his hands he began to pull so incessantly at his sparse grey beard that I had difficulty in getting off his coat. He was on the point of collapse, so I took him into the music-room and made him sit down while I sent for something to eat. But he wouldn't eat, and the glass of milk spilled from his trembling hand.

"I saw it in the Chicago newspaper," he said. "It was all in the Chicago newspaper. I started right away."

"I didn't know how to reach you."

His eyes, seeing nothing, moved ceaselessly about the room.

"It was a madman," he said. "He must have been mad."

"Wouldn't you like some coffee?" I urged him.

"I don't want anything. I'm all right now, Mr.—"

"Carraway."

"Well, I'm all right now. Where have they got Jimmy?"

I took him into the drawing-room, where his son lay, and left him there. Some little boys had come up on the steps and were looking into the hall; when I told them who had arrived, they went reluctantly away.

After a little while Mr. Gatz opened the door and came out, his mouth ajar, his face flushed slightly, his eyes leaking isolated and unpunctual tears. He had reached an age where death no longer has the quality of ghastly surprise, and when he looked around him now for the first time and saw the height and splendour of the hall and the great rooms opening out from it into other rooms, his grief began to be mixed with an awed pride.

I helped him to a bedroom upstairs; while he took off his coat and vest I told him that all arrangements had been deferred until he came.

"I didn't know what you'd want, Mr. Gatsby—"

"Gatz is my name."

"—Mr. Gatz. I thought you might want to take the body West."

He shook his head.

"Jimmy always liked it better down East. He rose up to his position in the East. Were you a friend of my boy's, Mr.—?"

"We were close friends."

"He had a big future before him, you know. He was only a young man, but he had a lot of brain power here."

He touched his head impressively, and I nodded.

"If he'd of lived, he'd of been a great man. A man like James J. Hill. He'd of helped build up the country."

"That's true," I said, uncomfortably.

He fumbled at the embroidered coverlet, trying to take it from the bed, and lay down stiffly—was instantly asleep.

That night an obviously frightened person called up, and demanded to know who I was before he would give his name.

"This is Mr. Carraway," I said.

"Oh!" He sounded relieved. "This is Klipspringer."

I was relieved too, for that seemed to promise another friend at Gatsby's grave. I didn't want it to be in the papers and draw a sightseeing crowd, so I'd been calling up a few people myself. They were hard to find.

"The funeral's tomorrow," I said. "Three o'clock, here at the house. I wish you'd tell anybody who'd be interested."

"Oh, I will," he broke out hastily. "Of course I'm not likely to see anybody, but if I do."

His tone made me suspicious.

"Of course you'll be there yourself."

"Well, I'll certainly try. What I called up about is—"

"Wait a minute," I interrupted. "How about saying you'll come?"

"Well, the fact is—the truth of the matter is that I'm staying with some people up here in Greenwich, and they rather expect me to be with them tomorrow. In fact, there's a sort of picnic or something. Of course I'll do my best to get away."

I ejaculated an unrestrained "Huh!" and he must have heard me, for he went on nervously:

"What I called up about was a pair of shoes I left there. I wonder if it'd be too much trouble to have the butler send them on. You see, they're tennis shoes, and I'm sort of helpless without them. My address is care of B. F.—"

I didn't hear the rest of the name, because I hung up the receiver.

After that I felt a certain shame for Gatsby—one gentleman to whom I telephoned implied that he had got what he deserved. However, that was my fault, for he was one of those who used to sneer most bitterly at Gatsby on the courage of Gatsby's liquor, and I should have known better than to call him.

The morning of the funeral I went up to New York to see Meyer Wolfshiem; I couldn't seem to reach him any other way. The door that I pushed open, on the advice of an elevator boy, was marked "The Swastika Holding Company," and at first there didn't seem to be anyone inside. But when I'd shouted "hello" several times in vain, an argument broke out behind a partition, and presently a lovely Jewess appeared at an interior door and scrutinized me with black hostile eyes.

"Nobody's in," she said. "Mr. Wolfshiem's gone to Chicago."

The first part of this was obviously untrue, for someone had begun to whistle "The Rosary," tunelessly, inside.

"Please say that Mr. Carraway wants to see him."

"I can't get him back from Chicago, can I?"

At this moment a voice, unmistakably Wolfshiem's, called "Stella!" from the other side of the door.

"Leave your name on the desk," she said quickly. "I'll give it to him when he gets back."

"But I know he's there."

She took a step toward me and began to slide her hands indignantly up and down her hips.

"You young men think you can force your way in here any time," she scolded. "We're getting sickantired of it. When I say he's in Chicago, he's in Chicago."

I mentioned Gatsby.

"Oh-h!" She looked at me over again. "Will you just—What was your name?"

She vanished. In a moment Meyer Wolfshiem stood solemnly in the doorway, holding out both hands. He drew me into his office, remarking in a reverent voice that it was a sad time for all of us, and offered me a cigar.

"My memory goes back to when first I met him," he said. "A young major just out of the army and covered over with medals he got in the war. He was so hard up he had to keep on wearing his uniform because he couldn't buy some regular clothes. First time I saw him was when he came into Winebrenner's poolroom at Forty-third Street and asked for a job. He hadn't eat anything for a couple of days. 'Come on have some lunch with me,' I said. He ate more than four dollars' worth of food in half an hour."

"Did you start him in business?" I inquired.

"Start him! I made him."

"Oh."

"I raised him up out of nothing, right out of the gutter. I saw right away he was a fine-appearing, gentlemanly young man, and when he told me he was at Oggsford I knew I could use him good. I got him to join the American Legion and he used to stand high there. Right off he did some work for a client of mine up to Albany. We were so thick like that in everything"—he held up two bulbous fingers—"always together."

I wondered if this partnership had included the World's Series transaction in 1919.

"Now he's dead," I said after a moment. "You were his closest friend, so I know you'll want to come to his funeral this afternoon."

"I'd like to come."

"Well, come then."

The hair in his nostrils quivered slightly, and as he shook his head his eyes filled with tears.

"I can't do it—I can't get mixed up in it," he said.

"There's nothing to get mixed up in. It's all over now."

"When a man gets killed I never like to get mixed up in it in any way. I keep out. When I was a young man it was different—if a friend of mine died, no matter how, I stuck with them to the end. You may think that's sentimental, but I mean it—to the bitter end."

I saw that for some reason of his own he was determined not to come, so I stood up.

"Are you a college man?" he inquired suddenly.

For a moment I thought he was going to suggest a "gonnegtion," but he only nodded and shook my hand.

"Let us learn to show our friendship for a man when he is alive and not after he is dead," he suggested. "After that my own rule is to let everything alone."

When I left his office the sky had turned dark and I got back to West Egg in a drizzle. After changing my clothes I went next door and found Mr. Gatz walking up and down excitedly in the hall. His pride in his son and in his son's possessions was continually increasing and now he had something to show me.

"Jimmy sent me this picture." He took out his wallet with trembling fingers. "Look there."

It was a photograph of the house, cracked in the corners and dirty with many hands. He pointed out every detail to me eagerly. "Look there!" and then sought admiration from my eyes. He had shown it so often that I think it was more real to him now than the house itself.

"Jimmy sent it to me. I think it's a very pretty picture. It shows up well."

"Very well. Had you seen him lately?"

"He come out to see me two years ago and bought me the house I live in now. Of course we was broke up when he run off from home, but I see now there was a reason for it. He knew he had a big future in front of him. And ever since he made a success he was very generous with me."

He seemed reluctant to put away the picture, held it for another minute, lingeringly, before my eyes. Then he returned the wallet and pulled from his pocket a ragged old copy of a book called Hopalong Cassidy.

"Look here, this is a book he had when he was a boy. It just shows you."

He opened it at the back cover and turned it around for me to see. On the last flyleaf was printed the word schedule, and the date September 12, 1906. And underneath:

Rise from bed 6:00 a.m.

Dumbell exercise and wall-scaling 6:15-6:30 "

Study electricity, etc. 7:15-8:15 "

Work 8:30-4:30 p.m.

Baseball and sports 4:30-5:00 "

Practise elocution, poise and how to attain it 5:00-6:00 "

Study needed inventions 7:00-9:00 "

General Resolves

* No wasting time at Shafters or [a name, indecipherable]
* No more smoking or chewing.
* Bath every other day
* Read one improving book or magazine per week
* Save $5.00 [crossed out] $3.00 per week
* Be better to parents

"I came across this book by accident," said the old man. "It just shows you, don't it?"

"It just shows you."

"Jimmy was bound to get ahead. He always had some resolves like this or something. Do you notice what he's got about improving his mind? He was always great for that. He told me I et like a hog once, and I beat him for it."

He was reluctant to close the book, reading each item aloud and then looking eagerly at me. I think he rather expected me to copy down the list for my own use.

A little before three the Lutheran minister arrived from Flushing, and I began to look involuntarily out the windows for other cars. So did Gatsby's father. And as the time passed and the servants came in and stood waiting in the hall, his eyes began to blink anxiously, and he spoke of the rain in a worried, uncertain way. The minister glanced several times at his watch, so I took him aside and asked him to wait for half an hour. But it wasn't any use. Nobody came.

About five o'clock our procession of three cars reached the cemetery and stopped in a thick drizzle beside the gate—first a motor hearse, horribly black and wet, then Mr. Gatz and the minister and me in the limousine, and a little later four or five servants and the postman from West Egg, in Gatsby's station wagon, all wet to the skin. As we started through the gate into the cemetery I heard a car stop and then the sound of someone splashing after us over the soggy ground. I looked around. It was the man with owl-eyed glasses whom I had found marvelling over Gatsby's books in the library one night three months before.

I'd never seen him since then. I don't know how he knew about the funeral, or even his name. The rain poured down his thick glasses, and he took them off and wiped them to see the protecting canvas unrolled from Gatsby's grave.

I tried to think about Gatsby then for a moment, but he was already too far away, and I could only remember, without resentment, that Daisy hadn't sent a message or a flower. Dimly I heard someone murmur "Blessed are the dead that the rain falls on," and then the owl-eyed man said "Amen to that," in a brave voice.

We straggled down quickly through the rain to the cars. Owl-eyes spoke to me by the gate.

"I couldn't get to the house," he remarked.

"Neither could anybody else."

"Go on!" He started. "Why, my God! they used to go there by the hundreds."

He took off his glasses and wiped them again, outside and in.

"The poor son-of-a-bitch," he said.

One of my most vivid memories is of coming back West from prep school and later from college at Christmas time. Those who went farther than Chicago would gather in the old dim Union Station at six o'clock of a December evening, with a few Chicago friends, already caught up into their own holiday gaieties, to bid them a hasty goodbye. I remember the fur coats of the girls returning from Miss This-or-That's and the chatter of frozen breath and the hands waving overhead as we caught sight of old acquaintances, and the matchings of invitations: "Are you going to the Ordways'? the Herseys'? the Schultzes'?" and the long green tickets clasped tight in our gloved hands. And last the murky yellow cars of the Chicago, Milwaukee and St. Paul railroad looking cheerful as Christmas itself on the tracks beside the gate.

When we pulled out into the winter night and the real snow, our snow, began to stretch out beside us and twinkle against the windows, and the dim lights of small Wisconsin stations moved by, a sharp wild brace came suddenly into the air. We drew in deep breaths of it as we walked back from dinner through the cold vestibules, unutterably aware of our identity with this country for one strange hour, before we melted indistinguishably into it again.

That's my Middle West—not the wheat or the prairies or the lost Swede towns, but the thrilling returning trains of my youth, and the street lamps and sleigh bells in the frosty dark and the shadows of holly wreaths thrown by lighted windows on the snow. I am part of that, a little solemn with the feel of those long winters, a little complacent from growing up in the Carraway house in a city where dwellings are still called through decades by a family's name. I see now that this has been a story of the West, after all—Tom and Gatsby, Daisy and Jordan and I, were all Westerners, and perhaps we possessed some deficiency in common which made us subtly unadaptable to Eastern life.

Even when the East excited me most, even when I was most keenly aware of its superiority to the bored, sprawling, swollen towns beyond the Ohio, with their interminable inquisitions which spared only the children and the very old—even then it had always for me a quality of distortion.

West Egg, especially, still figures in my more fantastic dreams. I see it as a night scene by El Greco: a hundred houses, at once conventional and grotesque, crouching under a sullen, overhanging sky and a lustreless moon. In the foreground four solemn men in dress suits are walking along the sidewalk with a stretcher on which lies a drunken woman in a white evening dress. Her hand, which dangles over the side, sparkles cold with jewels. Gravely the men turn in at a house—the wrong house. But no one knows the woman's name, and no one cares.

After Gatsby's death the East was haunted for me like that, distorted beyond my eyes' power of correction. So when the blue smoke of brittle leaves was in the air and the wind blew the wet laundry stiff on the line I decided to come back home.

There was one thing to be done before I left, an awkward, unpleasant thing that perhaps had better have been let alone. But I wanted to leave things in order and not just trust that obliging and indifferent sea to sweep my refuse away. I saw Jordan Baker and talked over and around what had happened to us together, and what had happened afterward to me, and she lay perfectly still, listening, in a big chair.

She was dressed to play golf, and I remember thinking she looked like a good illustration, her chin raised a little jauntily, her hair the colour of an autumn leaf, her face the same brown tint as the fingerless glove on her knee. When I had finished she told me without comment that she was engaged to another man. I doubted that, though there were several she could have married at a nod of her head, but I pretended to be surprised. For just a minute I wondered if I wasn't making a mistake, then I thought it all over again quickly and got up to say goodbye.

"Nevertheless you did throw me over," said Jordan suddenly. "You threw me over on the telephone. I don't give a damn about you now, but it was a new experience for me, and I felt a little dizzy for a while."

We shook hands.

"Oh, and do you remember"—she added—"a conversation we had once about driving a car?"

"Why—not exactly."

"You said a bad driver was only safe until she met another bad driver? Well, I met another bad driver, didn't I? I mean it was careless of me to make such a wrong guess. I thought you were rather an honest, straightforward person. I thought it was your secret pride."

"I'm thirty," I said. "I'm five years too old to lie to myself and call it honour."

She didn't answer. Angry, and half in love with her, and tremendously sorry, I turned away.

One afternoon late in October I saw Tom Buchanan. He was walking ahead of me along Fifth Avenue in his alert, aggressive way, his hands out a little from his body as if to fight off interference, his head moving sharply here and there, adapting itself to his restless eyes. Just as I slowed up to avoid overtaking him he stopped and began frowning into the windows of a jewellery store. Suddenly he saw me and walked back, holding out his hand.

"What's the matter, Nick? Do you object to shaking hands with me?"

"Yes. You know what I think of you."

"You're crazy, Nick," he said quickly. "Crazy as hell. I don't know what's the matter with you."

"Tom," I inquired, "what did you say to Wilson that afternoon?"

He stared at me without a word, and I knew I had guessed right about those missing hours. I started to turn away, but he took a step after me and grabbed my arm.

"I told him the truth," he said. "He came to the door while we were getting ready to leave, and when I sent down word that we weren't in he tried to force his way upstairs. He was crazy enough to kill me if I hadn't told him who owned the car. His hand was on a revolver in his pocket every minute he was in the house—" He broke off defiantly. "What if I did tell him? That fellow had it coming to him. He threw dust into your eyes just like he did in Daisy's, but he was a tough one. He ran over Myrtle like you'd run over a dog and never even stopped his car."

There was nothing I could say, except the one unutterable fact that it wasn't true.

"And if you think I didn't have my share of suffering—look here, when I went to give up that flat and saw that damn box of dog biscuits sitting there on the sideboard, I sat down and cried like a baby. By God it was awful—"

I couldn't forgive him or like him, but I saw that what he had done was, to him, entirely justified. It was all very careless and confused. They were careless people, Tom and Daisy—they smashed up things and creatures and then retreated back into their money or their vast carelessness, or whatever it was that kept them together, and let other people clean up the mess they had made …

THE GREAT GATSBY

I shook hands with him; it seemed silly not to, for I felt suddenly as though I were talking to a child. Then he went into the jewellery store to buy a pearl necklace—or perhaps only a pair of cuff buttons—rid of my provincial squeamishness forever.

Gatsby's house was still empty when I left—the grass on his lawn had grown as long as mine. One of the taxi drivers in the village never took a fare past the entrance gate without stopping for a minute and pointing inside; perhaps it was he who drove Daisy and Gatsby over to East Egg the night of the accident, and perhaps he had made a story about it all his own. I didn't want to hear it and I avoided him when I got off the train.

I spent my Saturday nights in New York because those gleaming, dazzling parties of his were with me so vividly that I could still hear the music and the laughter, faint and incessant, from his garden, and the cars going up and down his drive. One night I did hear a material car there, and saw its lights stop at his front steps. But I didn't investigate. Probably it was some final guest who had been away at the ends of the earth and didn't know that the party was over.

On the last night, with my trunk packed and my car sold to the grocer, I went over and looked at that huge incoherent failure of a house once more. On the white steps an obscene word, scrawled by some boy with a piece of brick, stood out clearly in the moonlight, and I erased it, drawing my shoe raspingly along the stone. Then I wandered down to the beach and sprawled out on the sand.

Most of the big shore places were closed now and there were hardly any lights except the shadowy, moving glow of a ferryboat across the Sound. And as the moon rose higher the inessential houses began to melt away until gradually I became aware of the old island here that flowered once for Dutch sailors' eyes—a fresh, green breast of the new world. Its vanished trees, the trees that had made way for Gatsby's house, had once pandered in whispers to the last and greatest of all human dreams; for a transitory enchanted moment man must have held his breath in the presence of this continent, compelled into an aesthetic contemplation he neither understood nor desired, face to face for the last time in history with something commensurate to his capacity for wonder.

And as I sat there brooding on the old, unknown world, I thought of Gatsby's wonder when he first picked out the green light at the end of Daisy's dock. He had come a long way to this blue lawn, and his dream must have seemed so close that he could hardly fail to grasp it. He did not know that it was already behind him, somewhere back in that vast obscurity beyond the city, where the dark fields of the republic rolled on under the night.

Gatsby believed in the green light, the orgastic future that year by year recedes before us. It eluded us then, but that's no matter—tomorrow we will run faster, stretch out our arms further … And one fine morning—

So we beat on, boats against the current, borne back ceaselessly into the past.

ABOUT THE AUTHOR

F. Scott Fitzgerald was born in 1896 in St. Paul, Minnesota, and attended Princeton University, which he left in 1917 to join the Army.

He has been called the epitome of the "Jazz Age," a term he himself coined to describe his generation as "grown up to find all Gods dead, all wars fought, all faiths in man shaken."

In 1920, he married Zelda Sayre.

Fitzgerald is the author of the best-selling novels *This Side of Paradise* (1920) and *The Beautiful and Damned* (1922), as well as two volumes of short stories, *Flappers and Philosophers* (1920) and *Tales of the Jazz Age* (1922).

The Great Gatsby is his third novel, marking the full maturity of his talent.